The Comedown

A. MARIE

Editing: My Notes in the Margin
Proofreading: Judy Zweifel, Judy's Proofreading
Cover Design: Murphy Rae
Formatting: Champagne Book Design

Playlist

You can find the full playlist link as well as bonus material and inspiration boards on my website amarieauthor.com.

Not 20 Anymore—Bebe Rexha
Put The Gun Down—Andy Black
Runaway—Lil Peep
Black Widow—Fame on Fire, Twiggy
Stay—iamjakehill
This Mess—Tyler Posey
Broken Girls—Gabbie Hanna
Switchblade—neverwaves
Royals—Otep
Good Girls Bad Guys—Falling In Reverse
Spotlight—Letdown.
Cover Me In Sunshine—P!nk, Willow Sage Hart
fleabag—YUNGBLUD
I Hate Everything About You—Halocene, Violet Orlandi
Disgust Me—New Years Day
FUCK IT UP—Hearts & Colors
Deity—Valeree
You Should See Me in a Crown—Clio Cadence
Or Nah—Ty Dolla $ign, The Weeknd, Wiz Khalifa, Mustard
Goddess—Xana
All the Good Girls Go to Hell—Halocene
Sorry For Writing All The Songs About You—Clara Mae
I Think I'm OKAY—Machine Gun Kelly, YUNGBLUD, Travis Barker
Last Resort (Reloaded)—Papa Roach, Jeris Johnson
Movie Star—The Veronicas, FR33SOL, Lavva
Bad Romance—Thirty Seconds To Mars
Cover Me In Sunshine (Piano Version)—Will Adagio
Stay—Rihanna, Mikky Ekko

Take Me to Church—Hozier
Let's Get Lost—G-Eazy, Devon Baldwin
Falling Skies—YUNGBLUD, Charlotte Lawrence
I GUESS I'M IN LOVE—Clinton Kane
Every Time You Leave—I Prevail, Delaney Jane
Shallow—Lady Gaga, Bradley Cooper
@ my worst—blackbear
Dancing Without Music—BRDGS
Bad Love—Lilith Czar
Kills Me Just the Same—Cimorelli
Call Me When You're Sober—Evanescence
The Drug In Me Is You—Falling In Reverse
Afterlife—Hailee Steinfeld
Lose You to Love Me—Travis Atreo

Any lyrics written in this book are original to the author.
Lyrics from other artists' songs that go along
with the storyline are only described, not quoted,
as to avoid copyright infringement.
Those lyrics can be found on several streaming
services or lyric library websites for reference.

This book is a 150k-word rockstar romance standalone.
It contains foul language, consensual sexual situations, violence,
and drug and alcohol use intended for audiences 18+.
Subjects pertaining to sexual assault, self-harm,
eating disorders, suicide, and addiction are present as well.
The word rape is used. It is not graphic and is not shown,
only referenced as a past memory.

For the lost.

Chapter 1

Collette

This is it. The Family Julez Tour.

Keep your head up, smile on, and don't show weakness.

This is the big leagues. In the entertainment industry, you cannot show weakness on the first day. You cannot show weakness ever. A lesson I learned the hard way…a long time ago. I've been at this for seventeen years now—more than half my life—and with the exception of the short stint I took off to give birth to my son, Holter, I've been on just as many, if not more, tour buses.

I consider the last decade. Averaging around two hundred shows a year…most of them while on one tour or another…yeah, definitely more buses. I'm in and out of buses and airplanes more than I am my own home.

If I had my own home, I think to myself as we head toward the bigger of the two garnet-red and gold tour buses.

From the outside, they look just like all the others. At least this time, one of them is meant only for me and my team. It's considerably smaller than the headliner's, but it's mine.

I glance over at Holter beside me, slowing so I can stretch this moment alone with him out a little longer.

Having my own bus allows me to keep my son with me. I've been away from him for the last two tours, and I've missed him. God, have I missed him. I tried to fly back to him on my days off, but at thirteen years old, he's becoming his own person with his own interests and his own life, so my off days now have to match up with his. Luckily, this tour's largely during the summer—thirty dates over the next two months—otherwise he'd still be at the casita we're renting, with his full-time nanny, Mary, looking after him. I'm not sure I'll even be able to bring him on tour with me after this one. This fall, after The Family Julez Tour wraps, Holter plans on trying out for his school's basketball team, possibly giving him commitments that can't be fulfilled over a computer screen. Remote schooling can only encompass so much.

"I'm so happy you're here," I tell him, smiling when he pretends to roll his eyes. He's already taller than I am, making most people assume he's sixteen or seventeen, but to me, I'll only ever see him as the little boy that used to pick dandelion bouquets for me and make me kiss his boo-boos.

"Me, too," he mutters, and I smile even wider, tugging on the crook of his elbow to walk arm in arm with him.

"So…what do we think?" I ask as we approach the headliner's bus. "Smooth sailing or—"

The door slides open, and a roll of thick smoke unfolds like a red carpet.

"Or," Holter says instantly.

Artists doing drugs on tour is about as standard as celebrities wearing stilettos to award shows. It's inevitable, and I knew what I was getting myself into, but I do have my son with me this time. He's older now. He notices stuff like this and actually knows what it is. *Kind of.* This sort of thing would've gone completely over his head two years ago.

I release Holter's arm, placing myself in front of him.

Head up, smile on, and for Christ's sake, don't show weakness.

I know why I was hired as the opening act for the game's newest rapper, Julez—image. His is shit and mine is not. I've spent the last fourteen years ensuring it's not, and now Julez's record label thinks I can help their client's reputation, too.

Image fades eventually, but impact lasts forever, and more than image, I want my impact to transcend all obstacles, even time. *Especially* time. Which is why I signed on to The Family Julez Tour anyway. Not for any other excuse than the one I use to sign on to all the other tours I go on—I just want my songs to reach the right people, the people that need the words I sing as much as I did when writing them. Image is an important part of your impact, but it's not all of it, and Julez has a whole other fanbase than what I'm used to, listeners my art can hopefully impact. He strictly raps, while I dabble in several different subgenres that all fall under the much bigger, much broader genre of pop. Pop and rap don't typically collide, particularly for entire tours. Thanks to this new digital age we're in, collaborations between the two genres are happening more and more, but it's still not mainstream yet.

It'll be interesting to see if that changes after this.

The tour's manager, Bruce, comes from around the front of Julez's bus, sticking a large hand out, and I take it in mine, meeting his eyes even though they want to drop to the ground and burrow until all of me is hidden. Bruce managed the last tour my ex-husband, Bodee Keys, and I did together, and that one… Well, a lot's changed since then. *A lot.*

We both fell out with my ex, otherwise he wouldn't have agreed to work with me again.

"Ms. Keys, we meet again."

"It's Abrams." Bodee and I weren't married long enough for me to take his last name. "And I go by Collette," I say, keeping ahold of his hand despite him trying to pull it away already. Some artists that use stage names prefer to be called their given names in private, but my given name is my stage name, and while it may not ring as strongly as it once did, it still fucking rings, even at thirty-three years old. I wouldn't be here, trying to help revive someone else's career, if it didn't.

"It's been a long time."

"That it has," I agree, then with bated breath, I wait for him to elaborate, sending a sideways glance as a reminder of our audience. A young audience that doesn't need to know what happened on the last tour we did together. Holter knows parts, the parts I allow him to know, but he doesn't know the whole truth. I'm not even sure Bruce does. Luckily, Holter's all too aware that entertainment news is just that—entertainment—because the story that circulates about the fallout between me and his father isn't even close to what really went down.

Bruce keeps his grin in place.

So, he's not going to bring anything up? I release my breath, filling my lungs. This is good. Professional.

"I gotta say, I didn't think we'd be here again. What's it been…?"

Maybe not.

I narrow my eyes, filling in the blank for him with, "A little over fourteen years."

Now, would Bruce be saying this to a man? Perhaps. But would he be saying it *like this* to a man, like he can't believe I'm still going, performing into my thirties? Definitely not. My ex is ten years older than me and tours frequently as well, but I can guarantee the only reaction he gets is awed respect.

"Especially as a mother now, too." He sends a pointed look past my shoulder at Holter.

There it is. Not only am I an aging woman—thirty's the new fifty-five in show business, for women only, of course—but I'm also a mother. A double whammy in this biased world that's absolutely steeped in double-standard expectations. Unfortunately, this has become a common occurrence talking to basically anyone anymore. I get asked questions men my age, or fathers of any age, would never get asked, and I'm expected to answer them all in a pleasant, politically correct way. Otherwise, I run the risk of being labeled aggressive. Aggression in powerful men is applauded, expected even, and usually results in them gaining *more* power. But aggression in powerful women negates our power altogether because ours stems from "emotions" and emotions aren't valid.

Just valid enough to be terrifying for men to encounter, but not valid enough to be taken seriously.

Misogynistic logic…an oxymoron if I've ever heard one. Much like entertainment news.

After giving Bruce's hand a firm squeeze up near his wrist, I finally let it go, making sure I don't break eye contact to say, "Hope you'll be able to keep up, Bruce."

I'm well aware of my age and what I'm up against. Popstars half my age crop up every day, and if I wasn't touring constantly, keeping my impact up as much as my image, my name wouldn't still ring like it does today. I've fought like hell to keep my career from fizzling out, and I've sacrificed a lot along the way, too.

Behind me, I hear Holter shuffle his feet, so I turn to give him an apologetic look. It doesn't scratch the surface for everything I'm sorry for though. Not even close.

I really am happy he's here.

Bruce clears his throat. "I'll try my best."

I face him again, saying simply, "Be sure that you do," before bringing Holter forward for an introduction.

"Pleased to meet you, sir," Bruce says to Holter, making my heart squeeze. *Sir.* How is my son old enough to be called sir already?

"So, are you two ready to meet Julez?"

Julez, huh? Not his given name? Microaggressions. They sound exactly how they taste—revolting.

I wave a hand at Bruce to go ahead of me but instruct Holter to wait over on our bus. Some tours are family-friendly, but the skunky sweet smell of weed threatening to knock me off my feet as I approach Julez's bus tells me everything I need to know. This one isn't.

Yet another reason to be grateful for having my own bus.

Inside, all I can make out are heads. And smoke. Smoke so dense I have to wave a hand in front of my face just to see…and breathe. Big entourages are a telltale sign of overcompensating, and the way Julez's bus is practically bursting at the seams right now has me wondering what exactly the rapper's overcompensating for.

"Where's Julez?" Bruce asks the person closest to him, only getting a sluggish headshake in return.

It's eleven o'clock in the morning—in the fucking morning—and these people are already fried out of their minds. On day one.

"Whassup?" a deep voice calls from somewhere further back in the bus before breaking into obnoxious laughter.

Bruce looks back, grinning at me like I should be so lucky, then does a double take, obviously expecting Holter to still be with me. Did he really think I'd be okay with my son being hot-boxed?

"I got someone that wants to meet you," he tells…Julez, I'm assuming.

There's a long pause with no response whatsoever, and I spin on my heel, not wanting to waste another second of my time. I'm the fucking opener of his tour, if he can't pull his head out of his ass long enough to meet me, then that's on him. We can keep this impersonal. I've dealt with every kind of personality imaginable over the years, even a singer that refused to use his voice for anything other than performances. He literally typed all conversations on his phone, then used an app that read it aloud for him. It was one of the quieter tours I've been on, but not the worst by far.

Someone coughs on my waist as I pass and I push my middle finger into their forehead to get them out of my way, watching as they slink back into their seat like a popped balloon fluttering to earth.

"What's she wearing?" I hear at my back, and against my better judgement, I cast a look over my shoulder. *Is he serious?* Julez should know what I look like and what I'm usually dressed in considering he follows me on social media. He even commented the fire emoji on one of my bikini pictures. The comment was made last year—at two in the morning—after our tour was announced publicly, but the post was from two years before that. So not only was Julez scrolling my feed, he went *deep* while doing it because I post a lot.

Aside from that, I'm wearing what the tour's stylist sent me to wear. This meeting was supposed to be photographed even though I haven't seen a single camera since I boarded this bus. Which is weird now that I think about it. I thought there'd be more press today. Or just press in general. Sometimes this moment is recorded for a news outlet or even just social media.

A slimy-looking man appears from the smoke, clutching two phones in his fists as he flicks his gaze over me, letting it linger on my ass before saying, "I'm Slade," unimpressed.

Julez's agent. I could've guessed. Even though we've had dozens of conversations in the last twelve months, we have yet to meet in person, but once you know one Slade, you learn to recognize all Slades. They're...slimy. There's no other way to describe them honestly.

"How's the bus?" he sneers.

I smile broadly, telling him, "Mine." He did not want to give me my own bus, but in the end, I won. Thank God, too, because there's no way I'd be able to keep Holter with me this go-around if I hadn't.

I don't even think *I'd* survive in this environment on a daily basis, not to mention when the sun goes down along with people's inhibitions.

He scoffs, then focusing back on one of the lit-up screens in his hands, he says, "Julez will be up here in a minute if you want to take a seat."

A seat? To wait? For an introduction? Like I'm a groupie? I was performing in sold-out stadiums while Julez was still in school, popping pimples and chasing girls that probably stuffed their bras.

First impressions are just that, impressions of what people want you to think of them, but after a while, everybody's true colors come out. Some are full-on artists while others are the equivalent of cavemen using twigs to smear their own excrement. It just depends on what your tastes are and how much you're willing to tolerate.

I no longer accept shit paintings. Life's too short, too beautiful, and I demand kaleidoscopes now.

I don't need to meet Julez face-to-face to get an impression of him—it's pretty damn clear—so I curb a laugh, saying to no one in particular, "I don't think so. He knows where to find me." Before I can turn around though, the smoke parts to reveal another man.

Looking like he just rolled out of bed and grabbed the same pants he wore last night, Julez stumbles forward, holding a cup of red Jell-O in one hand. He's shirtless, revealing more tattoos than skin, and his jeans are clinging to his slim hips like a sinner hanging on to their last shred of hope at being redeemed. As he leans down to take a wobbly bite, strands of longish blond hair flop over his forehead, showing the newly dyed cobalt-blue tips that are meant to match the jewel-tone aesthetic of the entire tour. His hair's only long on the top though and it's got a wave that gives him an almost innocent look as he peers at me from underneath it.

He's colorful. Extremely colorful. Black, red, and green tattoos with purple, orange, and blue hues cover his entire torso like a vibrant mosaic of visible tokens. I can make out words, faces, sketches, even a wing. It's broken and has drops of blood dripping from the split in a way that has my heart aching without even knowing the meaning behind it—assuming there is one.

He's also got a double piercing below his bottom lip that I have to tear my gaze away from to meet his blue eyes. They're red in every way, but still blue around the pupils. A hypnotizing blue, bordering on teal.

With a long lick off his spoon, Julez shrugs, saying, "She'll do," and I finally release my chuckle, but it's nothing like the others now filling the bus. Theirs are amused *with* him. Mine's amused *at* him.

This is ridiculous.

"Name's Collette. And you're right, I do a lot." A whistle rings out that I ignore. "You'll see for yourself soon enough." *If he actually makes it on a stage.*

I give him an ironic wink and leave, descending the few stairs off the bus slowly so I can school my features before I hit the bottom in case there are any photogs lurking nearby. One must never tip off the press that anything's amiss. *Image, image, image.*

"I know who you are," that same deep voice rasps behind me, stopping me again.

When I turn around, Julez is taking up the stairs I just stepped away from, the cup of Jell-O still in his hand while the other's above his head, holding on to the doorframe.

I stare at him, making sure I've got a grin in place that could pass as friendly, but then he says, "A has-been," and I drop the act along with the smile.

In all the chatter regarding my age, nobody's actually had the balls to call me a has-been. At least not to my face.

"I'd rather be a has-been than a never-was," I tell him. "Blink and all this can be gone." Like little lambs to the slaughter, they all fall in line in the beginning, happy to watch everything around them instead of where they're going. Then, one day, it's too late. The career they never really tried for is over before it even got a start.

If Julez keeps going like this, that's exactly what could happen. I've seen it enough times myself to know.

How many one-hit wonders have jumped directly into the revolving door that is the music industry only to be spit back out just as quickly? More than those of us still standing, that's for sure. Droves more.

The hand above his head drops by his side, revealing a tattoo of an auxiliary cable plugged into his veins in the crook of his elbow. Julez

blinks, swaying a little when he does, and I frown even harder, studying his face.

Is he okay?

"Boss man," Slade says, poking his head around the corner, but
when Julez attempts to swing his attention over his shoulder, his body
ends up falling forward, resulting in him landing face-first on the ground
with the plastic cup crinkling beneath his weight.

All I can do is stare down at his limp body in the grass, my heart
jumping into my throat.

What the hell?

I wait for Julez to laugh, or talk, or even just move, but he doesn't.
My gaze snaps to Slade, but he only shakes his head, sighing in
annoyance.

Annoyance? Is he annoyed right now?

That can't be right.

But then, nobody from the big bus rushes out to help and I think
maybe it can be because nothing else happens. *Nothing.*

"Oh my God," I croak, dropping down next to Julez, immediately
placing my fingers on his throat.

Please don't be dead, I mentally beg on repeat as I feel around,
searching out a pulse, any pulse, even a faint one.

Slade pounds down the steps loudly—slowly, but loudly—to stand
over us with as much concern as someone would give a pile of dirty
laundry sitting in the corner of a room.

A tiny flicker of a pulse flutters against my middle fingertip, and I
exhale shakily. He's alive. *Barely.*

"He's fine. He just passed out. He hasn't slept in three days."

Fine? Someone that hasn't slept in three days isn't fucking fine.

"I need to get him back on board before somebody gets a shot of
this." Over his shoulder, he barks an order, and not a moment later a
bulky guy comes lumbering outside to scoop Julez's body off the grass.

My hand's still on his neck and the bald man gives me a look that
says *let the hell go,* so I do, rubbing my middle finger under his jawline
one last time just to make sure he's still got a pulse.

I watch them disappear back on to the bus, wishing I could…I
don't know. Help Julez somehow. Does he need help?

Of course he does. He just passed out cold after staying up for three days straight.

But I didn't sign up for that kind of help. *Image.* I'm here to make Julez look better, not necessarily be better.

"You're gonna need to rein in your reactions going forward," Slade says, reminding me of his presence. Why is he still here? Shouldn't he be taking care of his client?

"Reactions to what? A man almost dying in front of me? Is that going to be a regular occurrence?"

"Look, everyone here's aware he goes hard and knows to act accordingly. You were warned."

I was warned ahead of time what this tour might look like, but that doesn't mean I was prepared for what I just saw. It's not even that I thought Julez died, it's that nobody else seemed to notice. Nobody seemed to care. And *that* I wasn't expecting at all, or how the revelation would make me feel.

"I like your outfit."

What?

I slide my eyes over to Slade in time to see him taking in my exposed thighs. Never have I wished for sweatpants more than I do right now. Unfortunately, I'm in a skirt the size of a washcloth.

Do not show weakness, not even in a miniskirt.

Especially not in a miniskirt.

I lift my head higher, popping my hip out to the side as I regard him coolly.

"Not as much as the red bikini you wore in Barbados though."

Red bikini. Barbados. The post from three years ago that "Julez" commented on.

So it wasn't Julez after all. It was his slimeball agent.

Warning bells ring through my head, ricocheting off old memories I like to keep hidden far, far out of sight.

I wait until he's gone to pull my phone out, dialing my assistant with shaky fingers.

"Irelynn, get my lawyers."

Chapter 2

Julian

I blink my eyes open, my fingers already awake and scratching the side of my neck, so I let my hand fall down my chest, then my abs and…

What in the filthy fucklord is this?

On my stomach there's some sort of…goo? Is this fucking goo?

It's too thick to be blood.

I think.

I sniff a piece just in case, recognizing the familiar strawberry scent instantly, then stick the chunk in my mouth, swallowing it whole.

But wait, how did it get on my stomach? Did I *American Pie* my Jell-O? I do love Jell-O.

I tug the waist of my boxers off my abdomen, taking stock down below.

Clear.

No clue how it got on my stomach. I don't even remember…

Sticking my fingers in my hairline, I push my palms into my eyes and shake my head at myself. *When do I ever fucking remember?*

I swing my legs off the side of the bed, already over the lack of noise, except my feet don't touch the floor. They land on a person.

I squint through the dark.

Two people.

A quick glance around the room reveals even more lumps that are most likely bodies, too. Groans go off like landmines on a battlefield as I push my way through what's supposed to be my private bedroom. My bus comes with one private room in the back with twelve bunks in the hall leading up to it. Bunks that are fucking packed when I pass by, heading to the bathroom.

That's fucking taken too though, and I eye the windows, wondering if my aim is good enough to try it. We're already on the road or else I'd use the other bus. Even though it's a smaller bus, it's got a similar layout to mine. I figured someone as big time as Collette wouldn't accept anything less than her own room, so I made sure hers had one, too.

Whatever. No sweat off my sac. It's not like I was expecting a little thing called gratitude or, I don't know, an introduction. This is my fucking tour and I hand-picked her to join me on it. My label wanted someone more…viral, some brand-new influencer looking to test their musical "skills" by piggybacking off an actual artist, but I wasn't having it. The number of likes you get holds more weight than the amount of hours of hard work you put in anymore, and since I seem to be the only motherfucker who doesn't live and breathe social media, I went for real talent, choosing to tour with Collette instead. Even though she's been on my collab bucket list for-fucking-ever, I never expected my label to go for it. They gotta be close to pulling the plug on this whole thing any fucking day now, but somehow, some way, they delivered. They got me Collette, and once the tour was a done deal, we jumped right into working on a track together.

It wasn't enough to satisfy me though. Not like I thought it would. Not like I *hoped* it would. Probably because we didn't even meet then either.

Why haven't we met yet?

"Ayo," I call up to the driver, blanking on his name. "Pull over."

If one bus stops, the other has to stop, too. It's one of like seven rules for tour life. Number one being no shitting on the bus. Obviously.

"Sir? It's close to midnight. It's not safe."

Muttering under my breath, I rip a couple bunk curtains back, finally finding my bodyguard on the third occupied bed, and jab him until he grunts, rolling over to peer sleepy-eyed at me.

"Safety," I say, jerking a thumb over my shoulder at Bare as he drags himself out of the bunk he was just snoozin' in. "Now pull over. I gotta take a leak."

After a brief hesitation, the driver does what he's told, calling over the radio to the other bus to do the same.

Fuck yeah. I'm 'bout to meet Collette. Finally.

I look down, gathering the rest of the Jell-O on me before flinging it into the kitchen sink.

"Boss man, I can empty the bathroom for you. Just say the word."

The moans and banging coming from inside the bathroom kick up a notch, and I grin, shaking my head at my bodyguard.

"It won't take long." I just want to…make sure Collette's bus is in order. Fluffed pillows, fresh towels. Hospitality shit. I'm nothing if not an accommodating host. Ask the motherfuckers currently sleeping in my bed. In it, around it, probably even under it, too.

Fuck. Not even a full day in and I'm already suffocating.

I need fresh air.

The second we're stopped on the side of the highway, Bare trails me outside so we both can piss, then I tell him to stay put, heading straight for the bus behind mine.

The door's already open for me, so I take the stairs two at a time, clapping my man, Antonio, on the back in a hug. He was my driver last tour and he's a good guy actually. Really good. Naturally good.

Last Thanksgiving, he invited me to his house to eat dinner with his entire family. I didn't even have to sign a single autograph or fight for my own seat or give out a loan. I was just a regular person again, and for like a fucking millisecond, I felt like part of a family.

Not that I know what an actual family feels like, but…

Anyway, of course I gave him to Collette.

"What's up, boss man? Miss me already?" Antonio asks, and I give him a real smile, wishing I could tell him the truth. That I do miss him. Him and that feeling I've only ever felt at his house, around his family.

Instead, I say, "Just wanted to meet *The* Collette."

I swear his eyebrows crinkle but those things are like furry caterpillars, so it's hard to tell. He doesn't say anything, and I don't bother asking as I make my way past, immediately noticing how different everything feels over here. While similar in style, Collette's bus is the opposite of mine in damn near every other way. For starters, it's silent, like graveyard-at-dusk silent. Not in a creepy way though, in a peaceful, hopeful way that I didn't even think existed.

And it smells good, too. Homey.

Or whatever. I don't know. It smells like what I bet a real home smells like.

With flowers. Maybe.

Is that flowers?

I slow my steps by a table, eyeing the humidifier humming peacefully and the wide candle beside it. It's not lit but the lid's off, so I inhale, reading the label at the same time. Peonies.

Thankfully, Collette's bus is free of passed-out passengers littering the fucking floor, making it a clear shot to the back bedroom.

The curtains to all eight bunks are drawn when I pass, but I'm not even sure they're all full.

Where are all her friends? Does she even have any?

I reach the wood door sooner than anticipated, then stare at it. And stare at it.

And…stare at it.

Should I knock? Burst in and bounce on the bed?

What if someone's in her bed with her though? And what if he's making her bed bounce right now?

If it were anyone else—literally anyone else—I'd have already broken this fucker down and gone inside to raise absolute hell. My last opening act got sandwiches to the face on their first night. Crazy assholes ate them after they woke up, too.

That might've been the only good memory from that whole tour.

But I can't do that to Collette. I mean I could. Hell, I've done worse. I just…don't want to, I guess.

Standing here, questioning myself, I'm starting to feel something I don't typically feel—embarrassment—only because I do whatever I have to just to outrun the accompanying shame it brings. Any time I even sense embarrassment creeping up, I down another shot or snort another line in hopes of fending it off that much longer.

Every one of my bones rattles inside my body with it now, and I mash my lips together, calling out my best ally to join me instead—anger. Shit, anger serves me so well I can't believe it's not on my payroll. *Everyone else is.*

I gave this woman the bus, the room, the driver, the entire fucking tour, and what? I'm not allowed to have a little fun? Because she used to be a big deal a decade ago?

She was a big deal before that.

And after, too. Not even I can lie about that. Collette has that thing people in show business spend years and millions of dollars trying to replicate but can't because it's that fucking rare. *She's fucking rare.*

All at once the anger leaves my body, making my chin drop. This was stupid. Leave rare-fucking-Collette to her beauty sleep so she can keep being—

"Touch that handle and I'll carve out your fucking pancreas," a soft voice threatens behind me.

My mind screams at me to pull away, but the door half an inch from my face prevents any movement. Oh, and the knife tip pressing into my back just under my rib cage.

The fuck?

I figured Collette would have her own security detail, but I didn't know they'd be…female.

I'm actually kinda into it. Not the knife though.

Well…maybe.

"I'll leave it as my parting gift," the woman says, then chuckles a sinister laugh.

Confused even more, I frown, resting my forehead against the door. Collette's security guard isn't sticking around?

"Where are you going?" I ask so quietly I'm not even sure she hears me, but she's quick to whisper back, "Far from here."

Take me with, sits on the tip of my tongue but I swallow it down. Embarrassment can kiss my ass.

"Is everything all right?" I hear Antonio ask hesitantly, and I tell him, "Uh, no."

Nice of you to join us, dude. Wanna, like, seize the weapon and the woman holding it?

Where's Bare, by the fucking way?

"This sicko was trying to get into my son's room."

"What?" I shove off the door, feeling the metallic point of the knife nick my skin.

"How'd he even make it on the bus?" the woman ignores my puncture to ask, and I answer smugly, "I walked on."

"You walked on to the wrong bus, asshole."

The knife cuts, full-on cuts, into my back, and I hiss, surprisingly finding myself welcoming the sting instead of resisting it.

"Hold on, okay?" Jesus fuck. "This is my tour. I was trying to find Collette. I don't know anything about your son, or whatever the fuck." I didn't know there were kids on here. I would've…knocked first or something.

There's a brief pause, then that sinister laugh of hers echoes off the tight area, wrapping around me like a bandage to my new wound.

"You found me, little lamb."

Little lamb? Who's that? Me?

The second the pressure finally disappears, I spin around to find *The* Collette standing directly in front of me. It's dark as shit back here, but it doesn't matter. She stands out like a ray of sunshine breaking through the sky of the thick-ass mammatus clouds I have tattooed on my left shoulder. I let her warmth settle over me and into me, completely forgetting the fact that she just stuck my ass and my blood's probably running on to the carpet.

She can add it to my tab; as usual there's already a running tally.

A light near the front flicks on and I can see enough of Collette now to make out that pretty face of hers. No, not pretty. Earth-shattering.

Or maybe the earth really is splintering right now. I don't know, but I feel unstable as fuck coming face-to-face with her.

Is this what it's like to be starstruck? Or is this something else?

I've never seen her this close, only on a screen or from across the room at the occasional award show. Fuck. She's so different, yet exactly the same. Her hair's definitely different though. Collette's known for wearing wigs all the time. Wigs of different colors, lengths, shapes—she rocks 'em all. And fucking slays in them, too.

Right now though, she's not wearing one, and I'm having a hard time looking away. Short blonde hair ending just below her jaw doesn't have a hint of color to it and I can't help but think if she had blue tips too, she'd look like my queen. It's somewhat wavy in a just-fucked kind of way, so I send my gaze over her shoulder, checking to see if maybe she was.

Luckily, no one's there. Bastard's probably still in the bunk.

Why was she in a bunk to begin with?

She said her son was in the bedroom. I remember seeing him with her during the award circuits over the past couple years—that's the only date she's ever taken to any—but I didn't know she brought him along on tour with us. That'll make this…interesting.

Or not.

Probably not. Kids are the worst.

I don't know that for sure, but I think it's safe to assume. They don't seem like very much fun at all.

"And here I thought our first meeting was as bad as it could get," she sneers, throwing me for a fucking loop.

First meeting?

When did we—

"I always did have a knack for epic departures." Her lips and cheeks move like her tongue's licking her teeth, but she doesn't say anything more.

First, talk of a parting gift, and now, she's saying this is a departure? Goddamn it.

What did I do?

That motherfucker embarrassment peeks its thick head out, catching me by the balls for the second time tonight.

If I admit I don't remember meeting her, it'll only make the embarrassment spread, taking hold and possibly dragging me back to the pits of hell my mind really is and I ain't about to risk that. Not even for *The* Collette.

Anger I don't even have to call on comes back to me in a snap. Anger so strong my lips form into a grin as I stare Collette down.

"I got word you were trying to back out," I lie, stepping into her space. "And thought I'd come deliver the good news myself." When she doesn't retreat one single bit, all the blood left in my body rushes straight to my cock, my tight-ass jeans thankfully keeping it from reaching full mast. "You're locked in. You ain't goin' anywhere." And that part's no lie. We signed contracts for this tour, so if she does try to get out of it...

I don't want her to get out of it. Soon as I'm off this bus, I'm calling my legal team to make sure she can't. I'll go for broke. I don't give a fuck.

Collette stares back at me, the frown on her face doing nothing to change how beautiful she is.

"Good news? I thought you'd be happy to see this *has-been* off." She doesn't use those self-righteous finger quotes, but only because she's still got the knife in her grip as her other hand starts fingering the blade.

Did I really call her that? A has-been? This shit's worse than I thought.

She must've started it. Her and that sharp tongue and even sharper knife. That's the only explanation.

"What can I say? I'm a charitable guy like that." I give her one of my crowd-pleasing smiles that only makes her frown harder.

Fuck her. I do charity.

Once.

Collette shifts from one foot to the other, like she's bored with me already, and I consider laughing just to piss her off even more. That or throw her over my shoulder and show her just how not-boring I can be.

Would she let me though? Would she even let me touch her?

My hands by my sides tremble with the urge to do just that, but the weapon in hers keeps me from following through.

Eh. I'd still chance it. For Collette, I'd chance a hell of a lot more than a tangle with a knife.

I let my eyes fall down the rest of her body, coming to a full stop on her stomach—her exposed stomach. She's in a red crop top and baggy sleep shorts that dip *way* down, revealing a fuckton of that toned stomach I already knew she had. I don't think I've ever seen anything sexier. Fuck that. I know I haven't. Not even that one music video she did on a motorcycle in the desert.

Actually no, it's a toss-up. That video gave me jerk-off material for weeks.

"You think you have something to teach me?" she asks, bringing me back to the moment, and a grin automatically splits my face. *Why yes, I do.* "You think I'd want anything from you?"

"Who fucking doesn't?" I scoff, then eye her for a full minute, wondering how the fuck nothing on her moves in a reaction to that. Even though I said it as a joke, it's true, and I thought she'd be able to relate. At least enough to fucking thaw a bit, damn.

Why isn't she reacting?

I smile even wider, finally making something on her move—her eyes. They fall to my neck—the same part I woke up rubbing randomly—before bouncing back up to my eyes, narrowed to slits.

Ugh, she's still pissy. Women are so difficult. This would've already been forgotten about if Collette was a dude.

Although, it definitely wouldn't have been as entertaining. Or sexy.

The urge to touch her wins out and I flatten a palm to her middle, guiding her to the side so I can get by, but as soon as my skin meets hers, it's like an introduction for the fucking ages, and I'm the one fighting my body's natural reaction by going as still as she just was. I swear there are fireworks filling the sky with a harpist in the corner and everything. I try to block it out though because all I want to focus on is the feel of Collette right now.

The fucking *feel* of her.

She's soft and smooth and warm. So fucking warm.

Goddamn, I never want to let go.

But I do.

Technically, she does it for me by shoving my hand off first, but the point is I was planning on letting go…eventually.

"Stay the fuck off my bus," she threatens to my back, and I lick my bottom lip with the underside of my tongue. *Called it.* She ain't goin' anywhere.

"Boss man, you're bleeding," Antonio reminds me on my way out, and I give him an obligatory nod.

I wake up to red, I bleed red, and now the next time I close my eyes, that's all I'll be picturing—Collette in a red crop top that cut right through *my* middle.

Red coats my vision, hemorrhaging out like this indecision.
All that ambition finally led me here, carved up by my own incisions.
Reaching for the top, had me bracing the fall.
Never seen it coming, now I'm caught in her palm.
Bleed me out quick 'cause I've been dyin' to meet my inglorious end.

More lyrics fill my head, so I quicken my steps off Collette's bus, then back to mine, going in search of something to write on.

I can already tell I won't be getting any sleep tonight because I *will* be seeing more of Collette tomorrow, making me look forward to another day…for once.

Chapter 3

Collette

Joint interviews are one of my least favorite parts of this job, mainly because they're with people I barely know but have to pretend I go way back with and actually like. The only thing I hate more are the joint photo shoots that typically accompany them. Photo shoots by myself aren't as bad, but the ones with other people…I'd rather bleach my asshole again.

Lucky me, I have both today. Not the anal bleaching—*thank God that trend faded quicker than the area between my cheeks*—but press as well as a shoot with none other than Julez, the man that boarded my bus in the middle of the night after calling me a has-been and passing out in front of me.

I talked to my lawyers for three hours yesterday, trying to find a way off this tour, with Julez and his…Slade, and I was going to do it. Come hell or high water, first thing today I was planning on quitting—something I *never* do anymore—but when I went to bed last night, instead of dreaming about walking away, my sleep was plagued with visions of Julez's lifeless body lying facedown in the grass. Then, as if my nightmares weren't satisfied with only being subliminal, Julez himself materialized next to my bunk, in peril yet again as my own knife dug into his back. And it felt almost…symbolic.

It sounds crazy. It probably is crazy.

I need more sleep.

But even I can't deny that he was different than our first meeting. He was just as arrogant, but in a trying-too-hard way that was evident even in the dark. He was quieter, more methodical, and I found myself wanting to know what was going through his head.

So, now, here I am, getting ready to do an entire day of press with him in San Diego with bags under my eyes so big if I were flying, they'd charge me the extra baggage fee just to set foot on the plane.

Dressed in an oversized men's white button-down and a pair of royal-blue five-inch heels, my assistant, Irelynn, helps me get the belt around my waist in place, tightening it enough to cinch but not cut off circulation. It's a very thin line. With the top three buttons undone, I press a hand to my chest to bend down and kiss Holter's dark brown hair. He's quick to turn his phone screen away though, making me instantly suspicious.

"Who are you talking to?" I stop to ask.

"Nobody."

Mary and I exchange looks as I stuff a snack in my clutch.

"The full page of text messages I just glimpsed says otherwise, but okay. Enjoy talking to nobody," I say to Holter before telling him and Mary what time to expect me back.

Mary's been with us since Holter and I were discharged from the hospital and she goes with him everywhere. On the tours I go on alone, she stays home with my son, taking care of him full-time, and the tours I get to bring Holter along on, she comes, too, watching him when I can't. I would've preferred to be one of those moms that brings her child everywhere with her, but Mary really is the second-best option. She's a certified teacher, speaks two languages, and earned a bachelor's degree in childhood development. In all actuality, she's probably a better mom than I am.

She's probably a better mom than I am.

Honestly this was never my plan, to be apart from my own child this much. I always thought if I put in enough work, eventually I'd get to a point where I could be with him every day, but I've yet to reach it, and with Holter already being thirteen years old, I'm not sure I will.

We say our goodbyes, then when my heels clack against the pavement as I'm stepping off the bus, a deep voice beside me asks, "Where's your security?" pulling me from the melancholic thoughts I lose myself in more than I'd like to admit.

I crank my head to find Julez leaning against the side of my bus with a hand up to his mouth. I can't tell if he's smoking because of the big, fat rings adorning his fingers, but when he suddenly drops his hand, I see he's not.

"You felt it last night," I tell him, pulling a few blue strands off my glossed lips. It's not my favorite shade, but the stylist wanted our hair to match for today's junket.

"Thanks for that, by the way. It's been a while since I've been fucking shanked."

"What can I say?" I tip a shoulder, throwing his words back at him. "I'm charitable like that."

He scoffs before changing the subject swiftly with, "Blue looks good on you."

Our eyes hold for a beat, then I tell him honestly, "You, too." I've been aware of Julez since he blew up a couple years ago, but only from afar as we've never crossed paths before this. Seeing him this close though, I kind of wish we had. He's extremely easy on the eyes.

"My bodyguard will keep an eye on your boy while we're gone."

"Um, thanks?" He goes to wave me off, and I quickly add in, "But that's okay. He's taken care of."

I'm not only confident in Mary looking after Holter academically and emotionally, but also physically. We both take yearly self-defense classes, and while my weapon of choice is a knife, hers is mace. She knows who's allowed around Holter, but more importantly, who's not. I've used a bodyguard over the years, especially when Holter was little and reached for any stranger who'd bat an eye in his direction, but I've found the smaller and more trustworthy my circle gets, the tighter we all band together as a family to keep him safe. Nowadays, I can typically get by without a bodyguard at all.

We're staying in a hotel the next couple nights, so while I'm busy doing interviews today, Holter and Mary, along with the rest of my team, will head over without me to get everything situated. Since this is a US-only tour, we'll have a good mix of nights on the road and nights spent in hotels. Some shows are back-to-back while others have two or three days in between, and with us driving to all of them, my team will be there every step of the way. Unlike a lot of other artists who are always searching for the hottest, newest dancers, I strive for consistency and dependability, so once I find a backup dancer I trust, truly trust, I don't replace them. The four I have now, I've been touring with for at least a decade. I have no doubt each and every one would give their life to protect Holter's. It's never come to that thankfully, but I can see why that'd be a foreign concept to Julez. Yesterday's events proved that.

"Will someone be guarding him?" he asks, coming to stand directly in front of me, forcing me to tilt my chin to meet his eye. He's tall. Well over six feet. At only five and a half feet myself, the heels I'm wearing do a good job hiding our vast height difference, but last night I was barefoot and had to stand on my tiptoes just to reach his shoulder blades, so I know exactly how tall he really is.

"Why do you care all of a sudden? Last night you let yourself on to my bus while everybody was asleep, then you tried to break into—"

"Are you fucking kidding me with that? You're making me out to be some kind of pedo. How was I supposed to know your kid was in that room?"

Holter and I used to be able to share a bed on tour, but now that he's older, I just let him have the whole room to himself. My team, I trust. But other artists' teams… There are a lot of different kinds of people hanging around on tours—a lot—which can create opportunities for the more predatory ones to be able to seek out prey unnoticed. So, just like last night, if the bus has a private room, and Holter's in it alone, I make sure I sleep in one of the bunks closest to the door and I do it armed.

"You still stood outside a closed door like you were about to open it without permission," I point out, letting myself look over the rest of him. Thankfully, he cleaned up for our interviews today. He's wearing a white sleeveless hoodie with the hood pulled up just enough to cover the crown of his head while still showing off his blue tips sticking out the front. The armpits are low-cut, revealing a fair amount of his colorful tattoos on his arms and chest, and his pants are different from the ones I saw him in yesterday. They're black skinny jeans with ragged slices all down the fronts. He's not just easy on the eyes, he's fucking hot.

Julez seems to have the same idea as he takes me in as well, his chest rising and falling steadily until his gaze reaches the bottom of my shirtdress. The hands by his sides flex and I cock my head, studying him.

"Do you have any restraint? At all?"

He sticks those hands behind his back so abruptly, I grin. *I didn't think so.*

His gaze jumps to something over my shoulder, and he murmurs, "I just wanted to see you while I still could," before saying louder, "Collette, this is Bare."

Um, what? I turn around, trying to keep up. He's the one that told me I was locked into the contract I signed, so what does he mean "while I still could"? And who is—

"Bear? Like the animal?" I ask, giving the man that carted Julez off just yesterday a hesitant look.

"No." He chuckles. "Bare, like he could kill someone with his bare hands."

I shake the big guy's hand, regarding it with even more hesitancy. "He'll be with…Holden?"

"Holter. And no, he won't." I just told him that.

"Holter. Shit, sorry," Julez says before telling Bare, "Kid's inside. Call me if you need anything."

"Excuse me?" *Am I not speaking clearly? Is that the issue?*

"What?" Julez asks like he's genuinely confused.

"That's my son. I decide who's around him, and if anything, Bare would be calling me. Not you."

"But you'll be with me all day."

"Have you ever taken care of another human being? Or been responsible for one? Do you even understand what that entails?"

"I trust Bare with my life."

"Is that supposed to impress me? Yesterday I watched you pass out from exhaustion and…who knows what else. You clearly don't give a shit about your own life."

Something that looks an awful lot like shame colors his face a split second before he wipes away all emotion to relax back into an unbothered slouch.

"So, then, give him your number 'cause he ain't leaving this bus unless your boy does."

Since we don't have time to conduct an actual interview, I advise Bare to stay far away from my son while he's on my bus, giving him the typical instructions I'd give any guard. Basically, don't get too close unless absolutely necessary. Keep eyes on Holter and Mary, but not hands. Hands, the ones that can kill apparently, are to be used on serious threats only, but never, ever my family.

We exchange numbers, making Julez laugh.

"What?"

"This isn't gonna work." He gestures at me

"*This* is what I was told to wear," I say before he bends forward, lining his shoulder up with my stomach and lifting, taking me with him as he stands again.

"Put. Me. Down," I grit, keeping one hand on my head and one on my ass because I honestly don't know what's worse—my wig falling off or my ass hanging out.

"Nah, I don't think so, Poohbear. You're too uptight and we're about to be together the whole day. If there's no chemistry, nobody's gonna wanna see our show."

"We don't have any chemistry because we don't know each other." *Literally.* "And tonight's show sold out twenty minutes after the tickets went live." That's why they added a second night here.

Also, Poohbear? *What?*

His hand covers the one at my ass and I snarl, squirming in his hold, but he just chuckles, telling me, "Don't worry. I won't let anybody else see."

The fact that he used the word "else" does not escape my notice, and even as his hand remains, I don't remove mine, so we go into the building exactly like this, with Julez growling, "Eyes down, motherfucker," to every person we pass, even women.

Once we're on the seventeenth floor, Julez sets me back on my feet, and with the hand on my head already balled into a fist, I swing at his face. He jerks back though, missing my punch with another laugh.

"You seem to struggle with the concept of permission, so let me spell it out for you, you do not get to touch me again unless *I permit you to.*"

Julez holds his hands up in innocence while his face shows straight sin.

We spend the next thirty minutes with our separate teams, getting camera-ready, then we meet up again in the hallway. The interviews are being held in a hotel, a different one than where we're staying, and we walk into the first room with smiles in place but no more "chemistry" than we had downstairs.

Julez shoots ahead of me, angling one of the chairs so it's not straight at the camera or the interviewer next to it. When I don't immediately move to sit, he waves me forward, telling me to take a seat in the chair he just repositioned.

Okay…

As I attempt to drop into the seat as gingerly as possible, Julez continues to stand in front of me, and only when my legs are tightly crossed and I'm fully situated, does he finally sit in his own chair.

Four interviews later—four cramped rooms full of people, lighting, cameras, and mics later—Julez is still doing the exact same routine every time we enter. He makes sure my chair is angled away from anyone's view, then blocks me while I fix myself. It's like he thinks he's protecting my virtue or something, which is wholly unnecessary thanks to me having lots and lots of practice at this sort of thing, but I can't bring myself to stop him since I actually find the gesture…cute, maybe? A tad domineering, but in a sweet sort of way. No other man has ever made the effort, so maybe I'm just not used to it.

It's sad how the bare minimum still manages to impress me somehow.

Julez hasn't touched me again and he appears to be just as engrossed in my responses as the person interviewing us, if not more so. Whenever a question is directed at me, I can feel his heavy stare aimed my way the entire time I'm answering. Then when it's his turn, I find myself doing the same—watching him with genuine interest, hanging off his every word.

I was right, there's a lot going on in Julez's mind. He just keeps it all in for some reason.

We're in the middle of our sixth interview when my stomach growls so loud the noise cuts through the uneasy silence from Julez refusing to answer a question about why he thinks he didn't get nominated for a Mousai Award this year. The nominees were just announced and neither of us made our respective categories.

Julez looks at me to ask, "You hungry?" and I fight a frown. Everybody in this room now knows I'm hungry. If he'd been speaking, nobody would though. It was a crappy question with no right way to answer, but him not even trying made the situation more awkward than it needed to be.

"Just answer the question," I say from the side of my mouth, then smile brightly for the interviewer, explaining, "I had a small breakfast. Life on the road, you know?"

I try to laugh if off but Julez cuts through it with, "Then you should eat."

"I'll eat later," I lie just to get him to drop it.

He pushes to standing, saying, "You'll eat now," then turns to me, bending like he's about to pick me up again, and I give him my best *don't even think about it* look.

"Can I touch you yet?"

Mindful of his body in front of mine, I'm able to stand without flashing anyone, and I tell him flatly, "No," before apologizing to the room, informing them we'll be right back.

Julez follows me into the hallway, saying over his shoulder, "No, we won't," making me shake my head as I accept my clutch from Irelynn.

"Yes, we will. I just need a snack."

"A snack?" he parrots, his thumbs flying across his phone screen. "Your stomach growled so loud I thought you were gonna set off the San Andreas Fault."

I roll my eyes, pulling out the pouch I packed earlier.

"What the fuck is that?" he asks, and I glance up at him, only to follow his gaze locked on the pouch of baby food in my hands. "Who's got the baby?"

"Nobody. It just makes an easy snack to eat in a pinch."

After unscrewing the cap, I fit the tube portion in my mouth, careful to get the inside of my lips around it without smudging my lip gloss, then suck as fast as I can.

"It's full of vitamins and nutrients," Irelynn tells him in complete monotone, probably from hearing me say it so many times.

"And it's easy to pack," I say when I've finished most of the blueberry-sweet potato mash. Julez is still staring at me like I have three heads, so I shrug, asking him, "Weren't you the one eating Jell-O?"

"So what? Jell-O's for everybody."

"It's the same thing."

"No the fuck it's not. Jell-O's fucking delicious. Babies only like that shit…" He points at the flattened pouch. "…because they don't know what delicious is yet."

"Nipples are supposed to be for babies, too, but I'm sure that doesn't stop you from enjoying them for yourself."

A smile splits his smooth face. "Facts."

I can't help but smile too before glancing at the thin skin under his jaw where I felt his heartbeat yesterday. I can just make out the slightest thrumming.

Irelynn pulls me from my reverie, reminding us of the photo shoot coming up, and I nod, agreeing, "We should get back in there."

"I already told them we weren't coming back. They pissed me off."

"Why? Because they asked about the—"

"Come on," he says, spinning on his heel and heading for the elevator.

"We have work to do."

"That's not work. That's bullshit. And you're hungry, so…"

"So?"

Punching the call button, Julez drops his head back between his shoulders, and says to the ceiling, "So, follow me," except it doesn't sound like follow me. It sounds almost like fall with me.

I look at Irelynn, but she's focused on Julez.

Smiling, she finally twists to meet my eyes.

"Oh, no. Irelynn…"

"I'll just shuffle things around, so instead of having a break before the shoot, you can take one now."

"I just ate."

Neither of us expands on that statement, at least not audibly. Irelynn does give me a look though, a look that I ignore to return my attention down the hall where Julez is now studying me, awaiting my decision.

"A quick bite," I tell Julez, walking toward him after taking one of the two stainless steel water bottles with solid twist caps from Irelynn. We're very careful to keep two on hand at all times. One is full of water while the other is kept empty for occasions like this.

Julez doesn't bother with a reply, only holds the elevator doors for me to pass through, then he's back to staring at his phone during the ride down to ground level. I pull my own cell out to check on Holter, immediately finding a new photo sitting in our thread. It's the back of Bare's bald head as he stands guard outside the bus. *Good.* At least someone from Julez's team understands boundaries.

Just as the elevator doors slide open, Julez reaches a hand out behind him, and I alternate between studying it and the side of his face as he scans the lobby. *Does he really expect me to hold his hand?* He catches my eye, then his fist clenches suddenly, a frown settling on his face as he exits, strolling toward the main entrance.

"Where are you—"

A metallic-blue McLaren Spider comes to a screeching halt just outside the front doors of the hotel itself and Slade gets out, coming directly inside to hand Julez the key.

What's going on? Is the car his?

"Gimme a minute," Julez tells me, then to his agent, "Stay with her."

He proceeds to go outside and stand in front of the supercar, holding his signature pose of his chin propped between his thumb and his index finger alongside his middle finger fashioned into a gun, all while wearing a vacant expression on his face as a couple guys holding different kinds of cameras snap photo after photo. One's even operating a drone circling Julez and the McLaren.

Everybody around the scene is in a stupefied state, gawking at the rapper and the car behind him that's worth just under half a million dollars. Can't say I blame them. The futuristic design is sexy.

So is the man posing in front of it, but the car…it's definitely the star here. Not even I could compete next to it.

Beside me, Slade is careful to keep his voice low for my ears only, saying, "Whatever he's about to do, I need you to go along with. Within reason."

My lips twitch. "Within reason? What does that even mean?"

Slade finally breaks his stare from his client, swinging it to me, and I turn to face him fully, crossing my arms over my chest while letting my smirk take shape.

"It means do your fucking job and make sure he looks good for the cameras."

There are always, *always*, cameras trained on us, but I don't have any control over that. Some celebrities do. Some even call the paps on themselves for ideal photo ops. But…

Wait, is that what this is? I figured I was here to improve Julez's public image, but I never agreed to setup scenarios. Technically I never agreed to help his image at all. My job, as far as I'm concerned, is to perform—onstage, not off. That's what I was hired to do. That's *all* I was hired to do.

"Looks like he's doing a fine job making himself look good for the cameras all on his own," I tell Slade, dropping my arms by my sides to turn away. "If you'll excuse me, I have actual work to do." I don't know what Julez is doing right now, or exactly what Slade is inferring, and I honestly don't care. I can't believe I'm even entertaining this shit.

Slade's hand grips my arm, pulling me to a stop. I look down at his fingers clenched around my elbow, then up at him.

My smile long gone, I threaten, "Remove your hand or I'll remove the meat off each and every one of your finger bones."

Slade makes sure to get a squeeze in before dropping his hand entirely, and says, "They're called phalanges," with the sort of false superiority I could probably squish with the toe of my stiletto.

"They'll be called fish food if you ever touch me again because I'll be throwing the pieces off the fucking pier after I'm done carving them from your hand. Got it?"

We hold each other's stare, nothing else around us registering until Julez calls out, "Ayo, Collette, let's go!" from across the lobby.

I break the connection to glance at my tour mate standing in the open doorway. "Where?"

"Far from here," he echoes my words from last night.

Far from here sounds good right about now. And in a McLaren Spider? Even better.

Ignoring all the stares and flashes around us, I approach him, asking, "Is that yours?" while gesturing out the floor-to-ceiling windows.

He holds out his hand for me again, saying, "I just bought a couple days with it," but I sidestep both him and the doorman to go outside.

So that's what he was doing—trading, essentially. Whatever company loaned it to him did so in exchange for the photos he just provided them with.

Julez catches up to me easily, opening the passenger door by lifting the scissor-style door not only up but also outward, and I climb inside the low-to-the-ground car, trying to keep a hand in front of my crotch. Once again Julez takes matters into his own hands by perching down in front of me, blocking my lap with his body.

"Good?" he asks, and I roll my eyes even though I do find it cute. Annoying, but cute.

Alone inside, I admire the sleek, minimalistic interior, rubbing my hands over the smooth surfaces. *Sexy, sexy.*

Finally seated in the driver's side, Julez asks, "What was that in there?" and using my most practiced voice, I question, "What was what?"

"With Slade."

I tear my eyes from the leather dashboard to look between his.

"I took care of it myself, so why do you care?"

"Stop asking me that," he snaps.

If he cares?

"I just…fucking do."

If that were true, he wouldn't have the kind of man he feels the need to question around, now would he?

Sadly, I already know the answer.

"What'd he say to you?"

I sigh, relaxing into the seat that could fit a racecar.

"Nothing worth repeating." It's not like I can anyway.

"Want the top down?" he asks, and I grin so hard my cheeks hurt.

"Absolutely not." I can only imagine what would happen to my hair.

With a push of a button on the center console, the McLaren

rumbles to life beneath us, making it hard to make out Julez saying, "I shouldn't have left you with him."

"Slade?"

"Yeah. Don't go near him anymore."

"You're the one that told him to stay with me."

"It won't happen again."

As much as I'd love to believe that… I don't believe it. Not for a second. We're on a tour together for the next two months and I seriously doubt Julez will be coherent for all of it. He doesn't seem to have an assistant and Slade is…

"Slade's your agent, right?"

On a nod, he pushes down on one of the levers between us, shifting into Drive, then punches the gas, peeling away from the hotel, out of the lot, and into traffic.

"And my manager."

"*And* your manager? You pay him for both?"

He shoots me a flat look that has me sighing all over again as I shake my head. Managers don't work for agencies like agents do, so they don't have a cap in what they can earn from their clients. Slade could, and most likely does, charge Julez *anything* he wants. Yes, Slade's doing two jobs—supposedly—but he shouldn't be. Some of the responsibilities agents and managers have overlap, so you could technically, if you really wanted to, get away with only hiring one, but no professional should be claiming to be both. If they are, they sure as hell shouldn't be charging for it, especially if one of those job titles doesn't have a cap on how much income they can demand.

"You need a separate manager. And an assistant." *And a new agent,* I want to say, but don't. I know better than anyone how useless it is barking up that particular tree.

Julez scoffs. "And put more hands in my pocket?"

"As opposed to the grab-hands you've got in there now?" I reply sarcastically, and when he cuts me a hard look, all I do is arch an eyebrow. *I said what I said.*

"Whose grab-hands you talking about?"

"Yours," I say, choosing to redirect him instead, but he doesn't bite. Men in power are all the same—no accountability whatsoever. Because if they did manage to take responsibility for their bad behavior, they'd risk their power being revoked altogether.

"I ask first."

"Yeah, now." I scowl. "Where are we going really?" While I'd love to get as far from here as possible, we can't.

Although, with how fast this car's rumored to be, maybe.

"That depends."

"On?"

His head turns my way while his eyes stay fixed on the road. "What are you in the mood for?"

"Money." Which we'll be out of if we're gone for too long.

Julez's knuckles turn white, then he shifts to grab something from his back pocket before dropping a small pile of cash on my lap.

"What's this?" I ask when he doesn't even acknowledge the odd act.

"Money. Fill up." His tone is downright scathing.

I didn't mean I wanted money from him. *Why would he even assume that?*

Fucking male egos.

I roll down the window and toss the bills out, watching in the side mirror as they scatter through the air like pollen during spring. Horns blaring all around us make me grin as the glass slides back up soundlessly.

Julez does a double take over his shoulder. "The fuck did you do that for?"

"I have my own money because I *make* my own money. I don't need shit from you or anyone else."

"But you said—"

"We walked out halfway through our obligations, and if we don't go back and finish them, we'll be on the hook for that."

"We don't get paid for that shit."

"Not directly, but in the long run, we most certainly do. It's like what you said about our chemistry and people wanting to see it in person. How will they know what they're missing if the media doesn't show them?"

"So you're all about being seen?"

Me being seen? Isn't that what *he's* all about? I thought that's why I was here.

"I know a place crawling with paps. We can grab you something to eat and the pictures will be everywhere by the time the check comes. Boom. Publicity. And we don't have to finish those whack fucking interviews."

A publicity date? This is all starting to bring up memories I prefer to leave in the past.

"Just…take me back."

"What do you mean? I thought you were hungry."

"Not that hungry," I mumble but he must hear me because he side-eyes me, his attention completely off the road and missing the line of cars quickly building up.

"Watch out!" I yell, pointing at the windshield.

He cuts lanes, dipping around a delivery truck smoothly, but backed-up traffic greets us in the other lane as well causing him to slam on the brake to avoid collision. His right arm shoots out to the side at the same time, blocking my chest from flying forward before the seat belt can even engage, and we come to a stop inches away from the car's bumper in front of us.

"Shit. Are you okay?" he asks, scanning me from head to toe.

Gently, I guide his arm back to his side, nodding.

"I think I should drive."

"What? Why? That was nothing."

Because I don't trust that you're not under some sort of influence. Because I don't trust you to get us back safely. Because I don't trust you, period.

Opening my door, I quickly get out and hurry around the vented hood, hearing Julez yell from inside about us being on a highway. *Oh, now he notices.*

"Scoot over," I tell him when I reach the driver's side, opening his door until it's high in the air.

Someone in another car screams my name, and I say, "Hurry," practically shoving his long body over the center console.

"Can you even drive in those heels?" he asks when I'm seated again, and I give him an unimpressed look, putting the car back into Drive.

"I do *everything* in these heels." I even add a wink so there's no confusion.

His eyebrows scrape the roof but I turn my focus out the windshield, mashing the throttle to the carpet and instantly swerving us on to the shoulder to pass all the traffic. There's bound to be an exit up here somewhere…

"Tacos."

"What?"

"Tacos," Julez repeats. "Don't take us back yet. Let's get tacos instead."

"Tacos?"

"What? You don't like tacos?"

"I do. But there's only one way to eat tacos in San Diego and it's not somewhere crawling with paps."

"Perfect," he says.

"Perfect."

Several minutes later we're creeping our way into the uneven parking lot of a taco truck, an authentic taco truck, too, not the artisanal, hipster-ran kind.

After killing the engine, I glance over at Julez.

"Still doubting my abilities in heels?"

"You got multiple personalities."

I let out a laugh, unbuckling my seat belt to grab my clutch and water bottle.

"Me? I have multiple personalities? You're one to talk." He's a completely different person today from who he was yesterday, even last night.

When he doesn't unbuckle, I ask, "Are you coming?" and he nods his head once, pushing out his bottom lip to thumb it.

"I was gonna wait 'til you got out but fuck it." Sticking that same hand down the front of his jeans, he adjusts what looks like a solid erection, and I get out of the car, more laughter spilling from my lips.

The heels under me twist in a pothole full of tiny pebbles as soon as I attempt to stand, and my knees sway to one side, causing me to sag back against the car.

Julez is in front of me in a flash, saying, "Give me permission."

"For what?" I attempt to stand on my own again, refusing to admit

I actually did find something I can't do in heels—navigate gravel-filled potholes.

"You know what." He gives me his back, squatting down. "Give me permission."

"A piggyback ride? Have you not seen what I'm wearing?" I all but shriek. It's not even a full dress, it's a fucking shirt for Christ's sake.

"All I see is what you're wearing," he says under his breath. "Get on, but don't wrap your legs around my waist."

I'm already shaking my head. "You can't hold me like that. I'll choke you."

Julez only chuckles like that scenario's not as bad as I'm making it sound.

"Seriously, I'll just go barefoot."

Chapter 4

Collette

As luck would have it, going barefoot on gravel is just as bad as trying to walk on it with heels, so keeping my legs straight down his backside, I let Julez carry me over to the taco truck to place our orders at the window, and it's as humiliating as it sounds. But also, kind of, and I do mean *kind of*, fun. I can't remember the last time I got a piggyback ride from someone—and never from someone who smells so good. Even after lugging me around twice now and sitting through multiple interviews, Julez somehow still smells delicious. His scent is sweet, citrusy, and spicy all at once.

After depositing me at a picnic table, he goes to get our food, and I start with, "So, Julez," when he returns.

"Julian."

I eye him over the mound of cilantro decorating his torta as he sits across from me.

"That's your real name?"

He nods, taking a massive bite.

"Okay, Julian, you're from Pittsburgh, right?" He lit up when he spoke about it to an interviewer earlier.

"Born and raised."

"I should've known from your accent."

"I don't have an accent."

I tilt my head, grinning. "You have a slight accent." Not as noticeable as some Pittsburghers I've met, but paying such close attention to him all morning, I could definitely hear one when he spoke. "You draw some words out more than others and you used a weird word."

"Which one?"

"During one of our interviews you said 'slippy.'"

"That's a word."

I try not to laugh, telling him, "It's *part* of a word. It's pronounced slippery, with an r in there."

He points at me using his torta. "Have your jokes carry your ass back to the car 'cause I ain't doing it." Pausing for a second, he adds, "But be careful. Shit's slippy," and I lose the battle, cracking up.

"We were just starting to bond, too."

"And my back's paying the fucking price for it."

"Consider us even for making me carry that last interview we did."

His eyes roll, but the side of his lips pull into a smirk.

"What about you? You're a Cali girl?"

"Not originally, no. I'm from Oregon."

"I thought I read you were from California?"

Julian reading? A book gripped in those tattooed hands of his as he slowly turns the pages? That's something I'd like to see.

I take a tiny sip from my pineapple-flavored Jarritos. "We moved to California when I was fifteen."

"Wasn't that right before you were discovered?"

"Discovered…" I trail off. "Yeah." That's how it seemed at the time, but now that I'm older, I use another term to describe how my ex-husband, Bodee Keys, swept me up into his extravagant lifestyle…just not out loud.

"By Bodee."

It's not a question but I answer with, "Mmhmm," anyway.

"You started touring with him…the next year?"

I nod. "When I was sixteen." I was way too young to make a decision like that. I was way too young to even be in that position at all.

"And he was…"

I know he knows, so all I say is, "He was Bodee Keys." All I need to say is his name. Bodee Keys gets anything he wants. *Anything.* He's the biggest music star this world has ever seen.

"Your parents were okay with it?"

"My parents were okay with the money I was suddenly bringing in."

"But you two didn't start dating until you were eighteen?"

The fact that I was underage and Bodee was ten years older than me didn't matter to my parents, only to the general public, which is why we kept our romantic relationship under wraps until I was legal.

"That's what was reported."

"Reporters get it wrong all the time."

I shrug noncommittally. Julian seems smart enough to read between the lines. Of course Bodee and I were together during those first few years I opened for him. That's the main reason I was "discovered."

"Did you even graduate high school?"

I smile, happy to be talking about something I'm actually proud of. "Yes. And college."

"How'd you swing that? I can barely get dressed on the road."

Julian being shirtless for our first encounter springs to mind. Something tells me his lack of clothing has more to do with choice than time though.

"Online courses mostly. I graduated with my associate's degree right before I had Holter."

"With Bodee." Back to another statement. A statement that's not entirely accurate though. Bodee is Holter's father, but I didn't have Holter with him. Not exactly. I had Holter on my own. But Bodee's more famous than both Julian and I put together, and unfortunately, so was our relationship, so everybody thinks they know all about it, down to every last detail—the details Bodee wants them to have.

"Hey, I thought you were gonna eat."

"I am."

"You haven't taken a single bite."

Julian waits, his half-eaten torta sitting idle on his plate, so I lift my taco to my mouth, taking a small bite. I give him a tight smile, pretending to chew as I let the food weigh down my tongue. The flavors are just how I remember—amazing—and I contemplate swallowing, but don't. As soon as Julian takes his own bite, I quickly unscrew the cap to my water bottle, and spit the bite out completely, acting like I'm getting a drink.

"Anyway, what'd Bodee do?" Julian asks, and I wipe at my lips, covering the bottle with the cap again.

"What do you mean?"

"What'd he do to make you leave him?"

"He filed for the annulment, not me," I say carefully.

"So? I know he did something to fuck that up. What was it?"

I study him, asking, "Why would you think that? Nobody else does."

Rumors regarding the instantaneous collapse of my and Bodee's marriage swirled faster than an F5 tornado. So fast they almost uprooted my entire career. Almost because I didn't let them. I held my head high and kept working, booking gigs wherever I could, right up until the night my water broke. I wasn't guilty, so I had no reason to act like it. That doesn't mean I wasn't treated like it though. Bodee knew what he was doing when he filed for that annulment first. Bodee always knows what he's doing.

"Because that guy's a fucking bum."

Buying myself time, I repeat the same process of spitting out my next bite after savoring the flavor of the greasy corn tortilla holding the expertly seasoned, chewy carne. I didn't bother with onions, radishes, or cilantro. They're harder to get rid of without making a mess.

When I'm finished getting the meat and tortilla mixture into the empty water bottle, my tone comes out as smooth as room-temp butter. "Are we talking about the same person? Bodee Keys?"

Julian pins me with a hard stare, saying, "Bodee fucking Keys, the punk-ass that almost bit my ear off last year when we got into it in the bathroom at The Americana's. Yeah, that Bodee Keys."

What?

That's…unbelievable actually. I can't even imagine it. I try though as I lift a tortilla chip to my mouth, licking the salt off every surface. *Julian's glowering face as he pushes into Bodee's. His lean muscles tensed.*

I drop the now-damp chip to my plate before taking another drink from my Jarritos, letting the liquid soothe my raw tongue.

Bodee being challenged for once, probably all red-faced and stunned.

"The fuck? Did you just suck off that chip?"

I blink, reality coming back into focus.

"What? No." I try to laugh it off. "I just wanted a taste without actually filling up."

That *is* the truth, just not to the extent I'm making it seem, but Julian's frown doesn't soften a bit.

"Taste…" His eyes shift from mine to the metal bottle on the table.

We both reach for it at the same time, but he gets a better hold of the cylinder first, wrestling it from my grip.

"Don't," I warn.

He only shakes it next to his ear, saying, "Doesn't sound like any liquid in here to me, so why were you pretending to sip off it?"

I narrow my eyes on him. "Do you even realize the pressure I'm under? What's expected of every woman in the public eye? Every fucking day, no matter what I do, I get comments, fucking headlines, entire articles, about my looks, about my weight. And they don't stop there, they attack my character, my whole existence. I go to the gym regularly and I've got an exercise addiction. I skip a week and I'm letting myself go. A rib sticks out and I'm on the verge of hospitalization. One dimple of cellulite and I'm plus-size. I can never just be 'healthy' because the definition for it shifts faster than the wind."

After a long pause, he says, "This definitely ain't healthy," then puts the water bottle on the bench he's sitting on, out of my view, and I purse my lips. *I need that.*

It's easy for him to buck a system that isn't rigged against him. It's so much easier for the men. Their bodies don't do the talking for them like women's do. That's the first thing we're judged on—our appearance—and it doesn't stop there. It only gets worse. So much worse. Nobody's keeping track of Julian's diet, or his workout schedule, but mine? Mine is ridiculed on a regular basis.

"I… I only do it when I'm on tour."

"Yeah? And how often are you on tour?"

My eyes fall to the table between us. I'm always on tour, but I don't have to tell Julian that. He's obviously done his homework on me.

I taste food, tricking my brain into thinking I'm eating it, then I spit it out before it can actually affect my body in any way. It's exhausting and I wish I didn't have to, but sacrifices must be made to keep a certain appearance. A certain image. Julian should be able to understand that if he was willing to tour with me, a pop singer, just to improve his.

"Personally, I think it'd be sexy as fuck if you finished that taco."

"What?"

"You heard me. I wanna watch you eat that taco."

"I don't care what you want."

He shrugs. "But you do care about getting back to those interviews…"

"And?"

"And eat up and we'll leave. I'll even carry you, how 'bout that?"

My chest expands on an inhale as I pick up the rest of the taco, taking my first real bite today, then chew, actually chew. The flavors burst not only on my tongue but around it, making my mouth salivate for more. My eyes close as I swallow, my stomach calming significantly from the food making its way down my throat. *Damn, that's good.*

I finish the taco in only three more bites, then the Jarritos is next as I drain the rest of the yellow soft drink. It's not much, probably nothing to a lot of people, but this is the fullest I've felt in a while. And as much as I keep expecting the guilt to come from eating one stupid taco and soda, it never does.

Julian's watchful gaze pierces mine as he leans forward to say, "You're fucking perfect, Collette. Exactly as you are."

I search his eyes. They don't have an ounce of red right now, revealing amber flecks among the teal. Flecks like stepping-stones into a forbidden garden. The kind I could lose myself following. *One, two, three, four…*

Just below his jawline, I find the spot where I can make out his heartbeat. I wonder what his pulse feels like right now. Fast and frenzied? Or slow and stable? My hand is raised and moving for the nearly visible vein before I realize what I'm doing.

Right as I'm about to make contact, Julian says, "What? Do I got food on me or something?"

I pull my hand back and tuck it under my thigh, shaking my head.

"Perfection is a myth."

"I used to think the same thing."

"Until?"

"Until..."

When he doesn't elaborate, I say, "Now you," and his eyebrows plummet.

"You should eat, too."

"I'll fucking destroy this thing. I'm not the one with an eating disorder."

My gaze flits around us. Christ's sake, did he have to say that out loud? Julian may not have...an issue with food, but it's clear he doesn't take care of himself properly.

I remove the key to the McLaren from my clutch, holding it up for him to see. I don't need Julian in order to leave. I ate the taco, not because he bribed me, but because I wanted to. I can be like him—I can buck the same system—I just haven't had to for a while. Being finely tuned to how I'm perceived, and molding myself to fit a better narrative, has been my second profession since my ex beat me to filing that annulment first. I wanted out, not him. But he knew how it would look, he knew how *I* would look, if he filed it first, so he did.

"Eat up and I'll let you watch me drive your sweet ride out of here."

"You like the car, huh?"

"My panties didn't soak themselves on the drive here."

Julian chokes and I laugh.

"Goddamn. I didn't know you'd be so scrappy."

"Like I said this morning, you don't know me."

He busies himself eating, then once his plate's empty, I ask, "What made you get into it with Bodee?"

"I fucking hate that guy." He looks away. "Always have."

"Did he do something to you?"

Julian's eyes meet mine again and hold, but he doesn't answer, only continues looking at me like I should already know somehow. But I don't. I don't have a clue what they'd be fighting about aside from their egos. Both men clearly have one, and egos flare like fireworks on the Fourth of July at award ceremonies—that's a given—but people don't typically risk getting physical. Also because of egos. And possibly losing future work.

Does Julian share those same reservations though?

I close an eye, squinting the other, and ask quietly, "Did you win?"

"Would you be pissed if I did?"

Even though I know what he's asking, I still shake my head. I don't know why I'm being honest with him. Perhaps we really are bonding.

Julian's eyes thin. "Would you be pissed if I didn't?"

This time I'm not quite sure what he means and he doesn't bother explaining himself.

"You did win." I smile and Julian licks his bottom lip, brushing the piercings underneath with his tongue.

"Fuck yeah, I won."

I'm not surprised I didn't hear about it. Bodee would never let something like that get out.

"I didn't know you'd be so brave…"

He holds his hands out. "You don't know—"

"…but stupid." I interlock my fingers, resting my chin on my knuckles. "Nobody goes after Bodee Keys and lives to tell the tale."

"You did."

"I didn't go after him." Not really. I ran and I have yet to look back. Only forward. Always forward, because I can't go back to the night I ran away from him. I refuse to.

"You're trying to tell me you're not a scrapper?"

"When I need to be, yes, but I wasn't always."

A tween girl with her phone aimed at us catches my attention, and I force a laugh, changing the subject by asking, "You said he bit you?"

This isn't the time or place. There will never be a time or place where I speak freely about what Bodee did to end our marriage quicker than it started.

"Yeah, right here." He points to a faint crescent scar on his earlobe. "I figured that's why you keep a knife on you." His laugh sounds just as fake as mine but with an added dark undercurrent to it. Dark and dangerous.

"Hmm…" I consider my next words. Bodee himself was not the reason for me carrying a knife for protection, but that doesn't mean my time with him wasn't. "Now that I think about it, he was a bit of a biter," I joke, trying to break up the tension now blanketing us, but if anything, it only hugs tighter, practically choking the conversation dry.

"I, um, I meant in bed," I clarify.

"I know what you meant. It wasn't funny."

Oh. It's jealousy closing in around us, not…never mind. I've toured enough times to know this happens, more often than most people realize, too. When you spend months on end with someone going through the same rigorous lifestyle as you, there's bound to be certain feelings, emotions, connections, but in my experience, it's better to nip them in the bud before they even get a chance to develop, otherwise things can get messy. Really, really messy.

"Do you have a girlfriend, Julian? Fiancée? Wife?"

"No. You got a man?"

"Besides Bodee, have you ever seen me with one? Actually *with* a man, not just in the same photograph as them?"

He thinks for a minute, then gives a headshake.

"And you never will. That's because I'm very careful to keep my business out of the public eye. I do that by not dating anybody in this industry." I widen my eyes at him, trying to convey what I'm not voicing. I will not be hooking up with anyone from this tour, hot, protective rappers included. That part of my life is private and I plan on keeping it that way.

"So, you're sayin' you only fuck nobodies?"

"Yes."

"At hotels or what?"

"Basically." Where else am I going to bring a one-night stand? Around my son?

My focus shifts to the girl behind him still taking pictures, but his harsh laughter brings my attention back quicker than the snap of a rubber band.

"What's the alias you use at the hotels?"

"I'm not telling you. You'll probably steal it and try to use it for yourself."

"I won't use it. I don't need to. I fuck on my bus with witnesses and my shit still doesn't end up in the news."

"It shouldn't." With the amount of non-disclosure agreements his agent makes everybody sign, Julian could fuck like a pornstar every day with nobody outside his circle the wiser.

Not that I'd want to see him try.

"What's that supposed to mean?"

"Nothing," I say quickly. I shouldn't have said anything. "You just have a lot to learn, little lamb." I don't make everybody I come into contact with sign an NDA, but I can trust the few people I keep close. I wouldn't trust the people I saw on Julian's bus with my lipstick.

"You gotta stop calling me that. Nothing about me is little."

My eyes go wide remembering the situation in his pants when we arrived, and I bite on my lips to keep from smiling. Julian notices though and lets his smile loose.

"Excuse me? Can I get your autograph?" the tween asks me shyly.

Right as I finish signing her phone case, a group of guys comes over, loud and boisterous, bordering on obnoxious. They're wearing muscle shirts with what looks like baby oil slathered all over their torsos beneath the fabric, and they all have the same haircut of long curly hair on top of their heads that falls into their eyes every few seconds so they can strategically shake it back off. They look like clones of each other... and every other twentysomething I see whenever I get on social media. They don't even bother with pleasantries, just jump right into demands of Julian, like reciting their favorite lines from some of his songs.

Julian wasn't far off about having multiple personalities. A lot of us in the entertainment business have dual personas, but Julian's public personality is...unique. Most performers become more energetic when dealing with fans, dialing up their enthusiasm for appearance's sake. Julian though, he's much less animated. Who he was just a moment ago is not who he is now dealing with the group. He's bordering on lethargic. It's hard to describe and even harder to watch.

The guys give their opinion of Julian's latest album in comparison to his last one, asking him why it hasn't earned any awards yet—as if Julian has any control over that—and just like earlier when he was asked a similar question, Julian starts shutting down completely, refusing to engage any further.

Slowly and carefully, I climb up on the bench seat, locking my knees to keep my legs as straight as arrows as I bend at the waist to gather our trash. Thankfully, the group goes silent, zeroed in on my movements just like I hoped they would.

One bare foot in front of the other, I walk to the seat's edge to toss it all in the metal garbage bin.

"You guys know who that is?" I hear Julian ask, feeling his gaze on me, too.

They all say, "Yeah," with the amount of excitement people use when seeing a clown at a rodeo. Like I'm just *here*.

Fame's such a double-edged sword. You want to have your time separate from the outside world to live a "normal" life, but at the same time you crave recognition, too.

They know who I am but didn't want my autograph or a photo with me. I should be grateful, seriously, but the sting of rejection still lands and makes my lips flatten.

"We're performing together tonight."

The awe in Julian's voice has me whipping around to see if his facial expression matches, and oddly, it does.

"No shit? Will you play that hot song you two made?"

I answer, "No," the same time Julian says, "Yes," confusing me further. Call me jaded, but the "has-been" talk really had me convinced this was a pairing he wasn't fully on board with. It'd make sense for us to perform together, but when I didn't see our song on tonight's set list, I assumed it was his way of giving his label the middle finger for trying to put us together in the first place.

I offer to take some pictures for the guys and they each hand me their phones. Julian does his usual pose throughout every one, never once breaking character, and when I look down at the final image, I notice his expression onscreen looks just as forced as it does in real life.

The group leaves us alone and Julian comes over to my side of the table, putting his back to me.

"Can I touch you yet?" he asks over his shoulder, and I wrap my arms around his neck, telling him, "No," before letting him carry me back to the McLaren. He gives his head a subtle shake, but I can tell he's smiling by the way his cheek expands.

"Our song isn't on the set list for tonight."

"When did you see it last?"

"This morning." I went over it while my nails were drying.

"Check again, Poohbear."

"What's with the nickname?"

When we make it to the driver's side, Julian bends back, helping me down, then he turns around to face me, leaning in like he's going to tell me a secret.

"Back up."

"Why? I ain't—"

"Because it looks bad." We had a few minutes of privacy, but now every phone here is pointed our way. A piggyback ride is bad enough. Him looking like he's about to kiss me, even if he isn't, is even harder to explain away.

Straightening, he pops a shoulder, saying, "Poohbear suits you," and I frown.

"It does not," I say, pushing him away from me, making him clutch his chest with laughter.

"Yeah. It does, Poohbear."

Chapter 5

Collette

Thanks to the McLaren's 710 horsepower, I manage to get us back in time to squeeze in one last interview before we're whisked over to the photo shoot. Unfortunately, the interview went pretty much the same as the one we walked out on did, and Julian's mood hasn't improved since returning to work. He's like one of those traditional balance scales—one wrong move and he tips all the way to one side.

Julian and I both did our own individual promo shots for the tour announcement last year, so now they want to get updated ones with the two of us together. His sour attitude is making what already feels like a chore even more difficult.

"Put your hand on him," the photographer tells me, and I wrap my right hand over Julian's shoulder, arching my fingers so it looks like my nails are digging into his skin, then smize into the camera.

Every few clicks, I angle my head and body differently, alternating between my top go-to poses. Even if Julian wasn't in the middle of a tantrum, or whatever this is, it's clear he's not as experienced in this part of the job, and every so often I give him my own instructions on how to pose to try and complement what I'm doing. He barely acknowledges me though as he moves his body in the most robotic ways possible.

Forget lethargic, he's downright catatonic right now.

I just want to shake him and scream, "Wake up!" Where is he? Better yet, *who* is he?

"All right, time to lose the clothes," the photographer says, then yells out behind him, "Where's the sock?"

The infamous cock sock. It's basically fabric in the shape of a sock that goes over a man's bare penis to give him…modesty, I guess. I mean, we can all make out the size and shape even through the fabric, but if it makes them feel more comfortable, I'm all for it. It's essentially the male form of nipple pasties.

"I can use my hands," Julian slurs, his eyes glossed over.

Did he take something? He was not like this at lunch.

"Are you sure?" I ask.

For answer, he drops his distressed moto-style jeans.

I turn away quickly, going off to the side to get my blonde wig with blue tips smoothed and sprayed again in an attempt to give him some privacy. Along with the wig, I'm also wearing one of the outfits from the show—a wraparound crop top with high-waisted jeans—while Julian's in…nothing. With the tour titled Family Julez I get the reference, but couldn't they have shot him in the buff during his solo shoot?

"Okay, Collette, on your knees in front of him."

Julian's head snaps up from trying to pull his jeans over his stark-white high-tops while keeping his junk in one hand. *Why isn't he taking off his shoes first?* He miraculously catches himself before falling, then says, "What?" in a slow and exaggerated tone.

Christ. This is definitely not the Julian I just spent the afternoon getting to know. No matter. I fight my own battles.

Slade goes over to tug Julian's pants the rest of the way off, one leg at a time, not even checking on his client to see if he's okay while doing it.

"Why?" I ask the photographer. He usually puts out good content, but this is just cheap. He might as well have me deep throat my mic while we're at it.

"So I can get the shot," he says like I'm a moron.

"I'm not doing that," I tell him just as point-blank, making the entire room go silent—funeral silent.

Out of the corner of my eye, I see my assistant pulling out her phone, ready to make some calls should this escalate.

The photographer finally looks up from his camera, glaring at me like I'm a bug on his lens. "The man's naked. What else am I supposed to do with you?"

"Not make me kneel before him?" I hazard. Us women are good for other things. Lots of other things. Thousands of other things. Millions.

With steam rolling off his shoulders, he sneers, "Got any better ideas?"

I look at Julian, telling him, "Don't move your hands," then walk over to place one of mine just over top of his knuckles, making it look like I'm holding his package, too. With my jaw directly over my shoulder and on the verge of touching Julian's, I look back at the camera, ignoring his stare on my face.

"Hold that," the photographer says before clicking goes off in rapid-fire succession.

"Stop looking at me," I whisper to Julian when dozens of clicks in he still hasn't taken his eyes off me.

"I can't help it."

"Try," I grit, dropping my chin to look through my lashes.

"There's nothing else worth looking at."

Despite telling myself not to, I meet his eyes, already grinning. What I find isn't what I was expecting though, causing my lips to relax just as quickly. Julian's serious. Or at least he's trying to be through the brain fog he's trapped in. He's on something, that much is obvious, I just don't know what. He didn't take anything while he was with me, so it had to have been after we returned.

His knuckles start to swell against my palm, and his lips finally spread as he rasps, "You keep doing this to me."

I don't have to look to know what he's talking about. His growing erection says it all.

But if he was telling the truth about his size, then we won't be able to keep his cock hidden much longer.

Without breaking eye contact with him, I ask Irelynn to get one of the guitars I saw by the clothing racks, and when she brings it to us,

I stand in front of Julian, blocking him like he did for me all day, then help to place the body of the guitar over his crotch.

I catch a glimpse during the transition, and he was not exaggerating. Not. At. All.

"No, no, no. Take that out. He doesn't play guitar," someone that sounds like Slade says.

Julian surprises me by saying, "Yes, I do."

I can only raise my eyebrows in response.

"I can play, I just—"

"He's a rapper," Slade snaps. "He doesn't fucking play guitar."

A gloomy cloud crosses Julian's face and it's like watching him settle under it, using the cold dark coverage it provides to his advantage as he reverts back to the expressionless Julez.

"Maybe you can play for me sometime," I say, trying to pull him out of it.

"I'm a rapper. I rap."

Okay, then.

"Can we get back to work here? It's not like we're in the middle of a fucking shoot or anything," the photographer bitches, and I press the tip of my tongue into my cheek to keep from lashing out. *I hate these so much.*

Turning toward the camera, I drape my left arm across the back of Julian's neck to hang off one of his shoulders, then bite a pick between my teeth. After several clicks, I take it out using my right hand, and hold it up for Julian. He wastes no time biting it, too, brushing my fingers with his lips in what shouldn't be a sexual way but because it's Julian, it's *overly* sexual.

Before I can let go, he rips the pick from my grasp and spits it out, sinking his teeth into my thumb instead.

My pussy clenches from the contact and I jerk back automatically. With my arm still around him, the movement pulls Julian closer, then he's turning himself to step into me, his hands going straight to my hips after letting go of the guitar. The feral look in his gaze has me clearing my suddenly dry throat.

What is happening right now?

Improvising during a photo shoot is one thing, but this is not improvisation. Julian's not a good model. Looks-wise he's a beautiful subject, but he hasn't shown enough skill to be able to pass this off as improv. This is something else entirely.

With the guitar between us, Julian crushes my hips against it, but with the clicks still going, I try to stifle any outward reactions. Inside though, I'm burning the hell up.

Julian's sole focus on my lips makes me feel that much hotter, so I lick them, hoping the moisture will cool me down.

It doesn't. I'm inflamed.

"Lick them lips, bet they taste like sweet honey."

Is he singing one of his songs right now?

"Gimme a minute with you, baby,
and I'll stretch it to last forever,
tucked right between those hips."

"Julian," I warn. He has to stop this. I have to stop this. I shouldn't be reacting like this to his touch. I should be pissed he's manhandling me…again.

Much quieter, he starts over.

"Roll my name off them lips,
keep it flowing like Pooh's sweet honey.
Gimme a minute with you, baby,
and I promise I'll last forever,
tucked right between *your* hips."

His grip on my hips contracts, emphasizing the last word of…whatever this is supposed to be. He's high. He doesn't know what he's doing.

But I do.

Or at least I should.

When his head starts to lower, I grab his jaw and crank his face away from mine so he's looking at the camera.

"Got it?" I ask, and the photographer says, "Not yet."

"Too bad," I say, releasing Julian's face. "We're done." Julian was done before he even walked in here, but I did my part.

A huffy Slade storms over to the photographer, snarling about not being able to even use any of the pictures with the guitar, and amongst all the chaos, I lift my foot up behind me, reaching down to pull my Shuffle knife out of my stiletto bootie. Julian's still got ahold of me, so I bring my arm back up to join the other one with the pocketknife concealed in my palm, then flick the blade open behind his head.

Catching his gaze, I ask, "Julian, remember earlier?"

"When your panties were drenched?"

"No, not that part." Figures that's what he'd remember though.

"Which part?"

I cut the strap of the guitar in one swift motion, saying, "The part when I told you not to touch me without permission," then step back, causing the guitar to fall to the floor. My eyes don't stray from his at first, but when they do, I let them fall *slowly* down the rest of him, lingering on his stiff, naked cock. The rest of the room starts to fade away until I bring myself back from the illusion.

Not happening.

Spinning on my heel, I take the bottle full of water from Irelynn's frozen hand. Just before I make it to the door, I hear Julian say, "Send those pictures to me. I want 'em," and I shake my head on my way out.

Look who decided to join us.

Chapter 6

Julian

Collette's fucking insane.

Most people think I'm insane, but that stunt she just pulled…god*damn*. Every person in that fucking room saw my cock. At least it was rock hard and didn't have that pathetic sock hanging off it like a droopy elephant trunk. Now *that* would've been embarrassing.

I've never been around someone so impulsive and impulse is practically my middle name. Julian Impulse Zimmerman. Fucking JIZ. Jesus, talk about a stage name.

"What time are they opening the doors?" I ask Bruce, dragging my ass up the steps of my bus. Fed up with rude interviewers and even ruder fans and just…everything, I asked Slade for something to take the edge off as soon as Collette and I got back, but whatever he gave me took all the edges off and now things are blurred to absolute shit.

The dozens of different faces staring back at me when I reach the top aren't blurry though—or not blurry enough—and I have to unfocus my eyes until they kinda fade into the background as they all go back to the party that's already in full swing.

Bruce yells, "Five!" for me to hear.

I scowl back at him, pushing my way through bodies. "Why the fuck so early? The show doesn't start 'til eight." That doesn't leave a lot of time for anything.

"If you head over now, we can get you both in before fans show up."

A guy I met a couple nights ago, and who has been sleeping here ever since, passes me a bong with a bowl loaded with green. I take it from him, pulling a lighter from my pocket. I don't know his name, only that he's along for the ride now. *Just like the rest of them.*

"Let Collette do her thing first, and I'll catch her when I get there." I wave him off, but he doesn't leave right away, so I gotta look over at him while bringing the bong up to my mouth. *What the fuck does he want now?*

Probably what everybody wants—more.

"When will that be?"

A handful of women I've never seen before board the bus, making me blank on whatever the fuck Bruce just asked. When is what?

Why is he still here? Doesn't he have something to do?

He snaps his fingers in front of my face, and I groan, telling him, "I don't know, man. When do you need me?"

"Now. Right now."

One of the new chicks catches my eye, revealing piercings in her dimples when she smiles. Dimple piercings? How the fuck am I supposed to concentrate now?

"Julez?"

"Yeah. I'll be there," I tell him, nodding dimple-piercing girl over. We both know I didn't give a specific time, but oh well. He'll see me when he sees me. And if he doesn't…then he should probably just look for a new job.

Shit, whatever. Collette's a pro. I'm sure she can handle whatever I throw at her during our performance together. As for my team, we got this shit down. I trust everyone from my lighting, sound, and pyro guys to Axel, my drummer, so if I'm a little late to sound check, it's not the end of the world.

"Hey," says a feminine voice I wouldn't mind hearing a little louder. And closer.

"Hey," I say back, feeling just as shy and awkward as I used to be before all this. Before money and fame did the talking for me. Before people stopped listening to me at all and started asking what I could do for them.

I didn't feel shy and awkward today with Collette though. I felt good. Better than good. Then our lunch together was over and it was right back to the same purgatory I've been held prisoner in for the last two years.

I yell for someone to crank the music, then light the bowl, letting the vibe circle me like a hungry shark until I start to finally sink. Just for a while. Just until…

Someone's yelling at me. *I think.* Honestly, I can't really tell. Their lips are moving—that I can tell—but I can't make out anything they're saying. I can't hear anything actually. Except for my heartbeat fucking pounding in my ears. Is it supposed to be that loud?

Why is it so loud?

I glance to the side, finding a heavy curtain staring back at me. *What's his problem?*

Looking at the person in my face again, I nod because it seems like the response they want, but when their face turns redder, I bark out a laugh, stumbling over my own feet and wishing the water would take me back under already. Why did I resurface again? I don't want to be here. I don't want to be anywhere, not even in my own mind.

Especially not in my own mind.

I catch sight of an angel—a sweaty, gorgeous angel—and think maybe I made it out. I'm finally out of purgatory.

Until she turns to face me, reminding me I found one place I do wanna be—wherever Collette is.

Wanting to follow her, I lurch forward and into the person currently stiff-arming the fuck outta me, keeping me from taking a single step.

"Fuck. Off," I tell them. I'm going to her and nobody can stop me. Except this person. This fucking "Statue motherfucker!" I yell the last part out loud in their face. Fucking nebby piece of shit. I should get Collette over here, see if she thinks nebby's a real word or not. It is, at least where I come from, but I bet she wouldn't think so. She'll tell me it's actually "nosey" and probably tease me about it like she did earlier, but I won't mind because she's fun when she's wound up about something. Even when she's raking my ass over the coals for shortening a word, I like having her attention on me.

The asshole holding me back freezes, then we're both held captive as Collette pushes her hair out of her face, screaming into the mic held above her as she bends backward. Even though I can't hear it, I know exactly which song she's singing. It's about a breakup, the kind that leaves you fucking wrecked. Near the end, she lets out a scream that's so raw, swear to God I choked up the first time I heard it, all too aware of what it takes to be broken like that by someone you love.

I figured the song was about her ex, Bodee Keys, so when I finally laid eyes on the motherfucker, I made sure to return the favor. Even if it wasn't about Bodee, I still would've beat that guy's ass. He gave up *The* Collette. The dickhead had it coming. Ten years older than Collette, had her tour with him for years—her *teen* years—before finally putting a ring on it, and then he filed for an annulment right out the gate? That shit don't add up. I don't care what the news says, I know he's the reason they're not together anymore. He did something…something bad.

Collette's eyes snag on mine, and instead of returning the smile I'm trying like hell to give her, there's straight disgust across her features—all of them, even her nose. That shit is fucking *scrunched* in irritation right now.

Not wanting to see that ever again, I attempt to scrub the memory from my eyes myself, but my hands don't actually work when I try to lift them.

What the fuck?

Bruce—*is it Bruce?*—is still holding me in place, and I swear I'm about to lose my shit if he doesn't let go. As soon as I get feeling back in my body, it's fucking on. I don't give a fuck if he's the tour manager or not, I'm fucking swinging for the fences.

Suddenly Collette's right in front of me, then something crashes into my stomach, and I double over to puke. I don't want to, it just kind of happens.

"What the fuck was that?" I ask, glancing around for what could've hit me.

I see Collette's fist a moment before my stomach caves in again with enough force to make me puke so loud—

Oh, shit. I can hear again.

"Ready?" I ask her after standing and wiping my mouth with the sleeve of my shirt. If she's done with her set, then that means our song's up next. That's the order I put everything in anyway. They better not have changed it around on me. I wasn't here to rehearse, but I still run shit.

"You got puke on my shoes, asshole." Her headshake gives me vertigo it's so fucking violent. "I need to change, then I'll meet you up there."

I'm the asshole? She was the one that made me puke. Twice.

But wait…

"*Up* there? What does that mean?"

Without another word, Collette shoves past me, and I'm held hostage by her ass swaying forcefully from all that attitude she's working to contain. Remind me to piss her off more often 'cause *fuck.*

"Can you do this?" Bruce asks, and I scoff, not taking my eyes off Collette.

Slade appears, tossing a cup of cold water at my face, making me finally look away. No questions, no underestimating. He knows what's up. I can turn it on when needed.

"Let's go, boys," I tell them both, pushing past and on to the stage. Axel's already getting situated at the drums when he stops to throw me a glare.

I flip him off, grinning from ear to ear. "What? I'm here, motherfucker."

How *did* I get here?

The crowd erupts in absolute mayhem, and without even needing to see her performance for myself, I can tell Collette fucking killed it. The energy in the stadium helps clear my head, and I shake the last drops of water from my face, grabbing my mic stand to drag it downstage.

Spread out around the place are lit-up ten-foot tall plastic jewels. Some are around the pit and some are hanging over the stands. They all cycle through different shades of jewel tones though, blinking in harmony with each other. It all looks so much better than they made it sound when the concept was explained to me.

I should've came earlier to enjoy it when no one was here. Damn it.

"What the fuck is up, San Diego?" I yell, smiling when everybody rocks the building on its foundation. "Give it up one more time for the one and only Collette!"

The roar surges so high, I wince, remembering my earpieces too late. I need to be able to hear, but not this damn much.

I gesture to someone offstage, and not a moment later, they're brought out to me.

"I don't know if you've heard, but Collette and I actually made a song together."

Together? Ha! She wrote her lyrics and had her people send it to mine, then I filled in the rest with my pieces and sent it back, except I sent it to Collette directly. She never responded though. Instead, she had her own producer record her parts without any heads up beforehand. I ended up having to record mine afterward, but with a different producer—the one my label wanted me to use. The whole experience was…disappointing. I wanted to be in the studio myself to watch her as she sang in the booth. I wanted her to watch me spit my bars. I've made plenty of other tracks the same way, but with Collette, I wanted it to be…I don't know…more personal.

Now I'm finally getting my wish, and I can only feel one of my legs and half of my fingers.

Fuck. I never should've taken that pill Slade gave me. I don't even know what the pill was, just that it made me feel like a fucking zombie. A super horny zombie. And judging by Collette's reaction to the grope sesh I didn't bother getting permission for—fucking oops—I took it too far.

The crowd finally calms, so I take my cue, telling them, "Since this is our first time performing it together, I thought yinz could help start us off." This always buys me time. Whenever I can't remember lyrics, I just have the fans sing them to me. They pay me, but then *they* sing to *me*. Unfortunately, I still gotta stand up here and act like I give a shit. Like I love hearing twelve thousand people butchering the fuck out of lyrics I originally butchered the fuck out of in hopes my label would actually approve them. *What a fucking world.*

The crowd breaks into the intro at all different times, so I make a joke of it, having them start over again. By the third time, we're all laughing and I've got both legs and most of my fingers in working order again. I swear my eyelids aren't even attached to my face because my eyes are so dry it's like blinking through a wasteland.

We finally get the intro right, but with no sign of Collette, I start to think she's blowing me off out of spite for missing rehearsal.

The first verse approaches, then her voice comes through loud and clear. I scan the stage, searching for her, but don't spot her anywhere.

Where is she?

A commotion in the crowd pulls my attention away to see the blue hair she's wearing again in the middle of a group of people. A group… of fans. *Fuuuck.* She's not supposed to be down there, especially without a bodyguard within reach, and no, those Rent-A-Cops the stadium hires for the night don't fucking count. They're about as helpful as one-ply toilet paper.

Every nerve ending in my body fires to life, burning off any last bit of haziness, and I jump straight off the stage, landing on both feet. Multiple shouts go off behind me, but I'm already walking for her. I don't give a fuck. Follow me or don't, but I'm going to Collette.

I fight to keep my steps slow and calculated even though all I want to do is run. Fans are like flies at the first whiff of shit, they can smell slip-ups a mile away. If I had attended rehearsal, this shit wouldn't be happening right now, I can guarantee that. Not unless I had Bare here to personally escort Collette off and back on the stage to me.

I stage-dive all the time, sometimes without Bare nearby, but that's me and I don't care if I get hurt. I don't even consider it a good show if I'm not bleeding afterward, but Collette getting hurt…

I'll have someone's head if she so much as gets a scratch on her.

Just as we're about to jump into our first shared chorus, I take off, jogging up to her to take her hand in mine. With a yank, she's against me, between my arms, and I can breathe again. She can punish me all she wants for touching her without asking later, but for now, she couldn't pry my hands off her if she tried. Nobody could.

We lose ourselves to the lyrics, the crowd around us simultaneously singing along and screaming at our proximity—both to each other and them.

Looking into my eyes, she fucking belts her own chorus, and I forget my plan to get her back onstage. I forget what I'm supposed to be doing, period. I even forget the thousands of people watching our every move until all that remains is Collette with her silvery eyes that had a greenish tint to them earlier, but now are a blueish gray with a dark blue ring around the irises.

During the break before her next verse, she drops the mic by her side to smile and it's one of the best fucking smiles I've ever seen. All I can do is smile back, then she's leaving me to face everyone else as she spins in my arms, singing her part to the crowd with me glued to her back. I'm fully aware how fucking bad this looks for me to be embracing her like this, I just don't give a shit.

Her back relaxes into me as she angles her head up to gaze into my eyes, and we do our shared chorus again, neither of us blinking now.

Blink and all this can be gone.

Who said that to me? Whoever it was, they were right because I never want this moment to end. Must be why my eyelids are making blinking impossible right now.

Our part ends, then out of nowhere Collette's body drops through my arms. Frozen, I watch as her ass glides back up my legs, coming to a full stop against my cock. Legs straight as fuck while she's still bent in half, the rest of her body rises slowly, and I trace her spine as she rolls up to standing, taking the back of her neck into my palm to tug her even closer.

The song's about finding the right person, not for forever, just for one night. It was an easy song to write because I've written twenty others exactly like it, but now that I've met Collette, I want to rewrite the entire fucking thing, word by word.

With her sweet, flowery scent filling my nose, I almost miss my verse until her ass slams into me, making me groan. I use the voice change to slip into my solo, then halfway through, Collette gets it in her head she can spin away from me. I manage to catch her fingers in one hand just before she's out of reach though, keeping hold of her. She hypes the people closest to us by mouthing my lyrics while dancing to the beat, and I pull her back to me, loving the way her lips mirror mine as we face each other like we're battling. She keeps time flawlessly, not once getting tripped up, and I can imagine her rapping her own words one day.

We finish with one more chorus together, and just as the final notes of the song fill the stadium, Collette drags me after her, sneaking between two rows to enter through a door in the concrete wall.

Already anticipating us, the employee standing there shuts the door with an airtight *whoosh*, then Collette takes off in a sprint, keeping me with her.

"Come on. You don't have a lot of time," she calls over her shoulder. "Your drummer's covering for your dumb ass right now."

Sure enough, Axel's notorious drum work penetrates the thick walls, echoing down the corridor.

"How am I the dumbass? You were the one in the crowd without any protection."

"Because I was going to walk up and join you, but you ruined everything when you didn't wait. Didn't you see the set of stairs on the side of the stage?"

I pull up short, making Collette stop, too. Of course, I didn't see any fucking stairs. Unlike Collette who obviously knows secret passages around this place, I've never even been in this venue.

"Who the fuck authorized that?"

"You."

"The fuck I did."

"Slade said you okayed it earlier. He even held his phone up while on speaker."

"Was my face on the fucking screen?"

When she doesn't say anything, I have my answer. Motherfucker lied, which isn't surprising, but he put Collette at risk doing it, and that pisses me off.

"Why were you even talking to Slade? I told you not to go near him."

"I don't take orders from you." She laughs that threatening laugh of hers, the one I've decided I don't really like directed at me. "And neither does your agent, apparently." Her sneer is laced with something I can't pinpoint, it's like disgust but a thousand times worse.

"He will." I didn't relay the same message to Slade yet, but I will.

"Sure. Look, I gotta get back to Holter. Can you make it back yourself, or do you need—"

"I need your help."

Neither of us makes a sound.

"I need your help finding the stage. I don't know this fucking place."

She leads me all the way to backstage, and the whole time, the only thing I can think about is the feel of her hand in mine. Not what song is next, not what's happening after the show, just her skin touching my skin. So. Fucking. Simple. Why couldn't she hold my hand earlier? Whenever I tried, she looked at my hand like it was as dangerous as her knife.

"Collette?"

Her hands find my chest and I prepare to beg, to bribe, hell, I don't care what she asks for, I just don't want this to be over yet, but she says, "The bass sounds like shit on the floor monitors because the bigger ones haven't shown up yet. You'd know that if you were here for sound check. Good luck," then pushes, sending my ass sprawling back on to the stage. When I turn around, she's gone and I'm right back where I started—purgatory, but now with low-quality speakers.

What an asshole.

Chapter 7

Collette

"Thanks again, Antonio. I appreciate it."

"No worries. I'm happy to help. I forgot my heartburn medication last night, so I needed to make a stop here anyway," the driver says, rubbing his chest with a grimace.

The hotel everyone stayed in last night is only a mile from the ocean, so Holter and I woke up early to jog along the shoreline while having the beach to ourselves. We were surprised to stumble across Antonio, who was sitting by himself in the sand, staring out at the waves. He looked so contemplative, I didn't want to bother him, but when we returned and he still hadn't moved from his spot, I asked if he could let me on the bus to grab a few things for the day. After dropping Holter back off in the hotel suite to shower, we walk down the street to where both buses were parked overnight. The hood of my oversized hoodie is pulled down to my eyebrows and I'm wearing the biggest pair of sunglasses I own. Neither prevent me from being able to make out the telltale sign of a rager on Julian's bus as we approach. Probably because it's still going on…at eight thirty in the morning.

"Is it always like this?" I ask Antonio, and he gives an entirely different grimace, nodding. "Even without Julian there?" I know he had his own suite last night.

"Julian?" Antonio gives me a long look before saying, "Julian's never there."

"What do you mean? Where is he?"

A series of several thumps has us both twisting our heads in time to see Julian sliding down the steps of his bus, catching himself on the railing before his ass hits the last one.

"Maybe there," Antonio says, and I cock my head.

"Only maybe?"

His lips purse. "Only maybe."

"Good afternoon," Julian greets when he stands, bowing dramatically.

"It's morning," I tell him.

He drops the act to examine his surroundings. "Which morning?"

"I'll unlock the door, then leave you with the keys," Antonio tells me.

"That's not necessary. I'll only be a minute."

The older man eyes Julian who's studying us through red, puffy eyes.

"You can give them to Bruce later and I'll just get them from—"

"I'm not giving them to Bruce." I don't want another man having access to my belongings.

"I'll hold on to them," Julian offers, but neither of us acknowledges him because Julian having access to my sleeping quarters is a *hard* no, even if I'm not sleeping here tonight.

Why did he?

"I promise I'll be quick," I tell Antonio, gesturing for him to go ahead and unlock the door to the smaller of the two buses. "I don't want to be around here any longer than I have to."

With the door now open, Antonio turns to face me, lowering his voice to say, "He's in a lot of pain."

"What kind of pain?"

"The kind nobody can see."

I look over at Julian. He's trying to light a cigarette but can't get the flint wheel to roll correctly and ends up throwing it across the pavement of the abandoned parking lot we're in, flipping the inanimate object off when it skitters to a stop a good distance away.

"Because he doesn't want anybody to see or because nobody bothers to look?"

"Both."

"Hey!" I call over to Julian. "Have you eaten?"

Julian holds up the unlit cigarette. "Does it look like it?"

A cigarette for breakfast? And he thinks he doesn't have an eating disorder…

"Leave that out here and I'll make you breakfast."

"Need me to run to the store?" Antonio asks, ushering me inside.

"No, thanks. We should have enough."

He gets his medication, then lingers near the kitchen, watching Julian climb—literally on his hands and knees—up the few steps on to the bus.

"Do you want me to stick around? I've got a brand-new crossword puzzle I wouldn't mind spending an hour or two on."

"I'll be okay," I assure him. "Go stretch your legs while you can. Seriously, enjoy your time off this thing."

He hands me the keys with plans to meet up later so I can give them back to him directly, then steps over a laid-out Julian.

I watch the rapper lying motionless in the middle of the aisle for a minute before going to stand over him.

"Are you alive?"

"No."

"Why not? What happened to you?"

"Same thing that happened to you."

"You have no idea what happened to me." Nobody does.

"I don't have to know to know," he replies, and I give up, shaking my head at both myself and him. I have to stop engaging with him when he's completely out of it. The problem with that is, it seems like he's out of it a lot.

Antonio's words echo through my head. *Julian's never there.*

"What's on your forehead? It looks like some kind of indent."

One of his tatted hands reaches up, feeling the wrong side of his forehead, and I bend over, guiding him to the correct spot. It's a red misshapen oval, about three inches long and one inch wide.

"The table."

The table…on his forehead?

"Did you fall asleep on it?"

"Uh-huh."

"Couldn't find your bed?" I try to laugh but he says, "They were all taken," cutting it off at the start. *What?*

The fingers with the word MAMAS go limp on his face and his breath begins flowing through them audibly as he passes out. In this moment he doesn't look like the tough guy that raps about "killing his enemies" and poses with his hand in the shape of a gun. He looks... helpless. *I need your help*, he said to me last night, confirming my original suspicions.

I push my hood back and remove my sunglasses, tossing them aside and wondering how I'm supposed to move him. I'm not waking him, but he can't just sleep on the floor, can he? It's better than being hunched over a fucking table.

I could go over to his bus and get Bare, except the idea of leaving him alone on here makes me uneasy.

I don't want him to...steal anything.

Sighing, I grab a pillow from my bunk, and get it under his head as gently as I can without disturbing him. I drape a blanket over his body next, and when I pull it up to his chest, I depress my middle finger against the side of his throat, waiting until his pulse pushes back. The tiny flickers do nothing to appease my racing mind though.

"What am I going to do with you, little lamb? You're a mess."

The saddest part is while everyone knows it, nobody seems to care.

"Ugh," comes from the front of the bus, so I tear my eyes from the travel itinerary Irelynn forwarded me to watch Julian sit up, frowning at the blanket in his grip.

"What is this?"

"A blanket," I say, putting my phone down next to my paperback on the table. "Hungry?"

"For the blanket?"

I laugh, saying, "I did promise to feed you..."

He drops his head in his hands, asking a muffled, "What time is it?"

"Noon."

His head lifts and he finally turns to face me. "Jesus. How long have I been out?"

"A while."

"Did you find me here or something?"

"No," I answer, picking at the corners of my book.

"Then what am I doing here?"

"That's a good question."

"What are you doing here? I thought you stayed in the hotel last night."

"I did. I just…" I glance at the kitchen I cleaned twice before I sat down to read. Only a few chapters in though, the constant email notifications coming from my phone pulled me away from the fictional world I was quickly falling in love with. Facing fire-breathing dragons sounds so much easier than the monsters this world breeds. "Want some lunch?"

"You gonna actually eat it?"

I get to my feet, rolling my eyes. "Since *somebody* misplaced my water bottle yesterday, I guess I have to."

"You're welcome." He groans as he hefts himself off the floor, making me smile. I do eat, just not as many meals as I make it look like.

"So," I say, grabbing all the ingredients for deli-sliced-ham sandwiches. "What happened? Looks like you had a rough night."

He drops down into the booth-style table, spinning my book around to read the title. "Fuck if I know."

"You don't remember?"

"I try not to," he mutters before lifting the novel and asking, "You read?"

"When I can, yeah. Do you?"

Sadly, Julian only laughs, setting the book back down. *So much for that fantasy.*

"The new monitor speakers are supposed to be here this afternoon. They didn't show up yet, did they?"

At the sink, I shrug. "I don't know. I've been in here."

"For how long?"

I wash my hands longer than necessary.

"A while."

"Collette?"

My hands holding the dish towel freeze.

"Was that blanket… Did you do that?"

Slowly, I turn around, leaning back against the counter to consider Julian.

"And the pillow? That was you, too?"

"I'm sorry. I couldn't lift you by myself," I explain.

"You're sorry?"

I nod. If I woke up on the floor, I wouldn't be happy either. My back would be even less happy, but I'm older than Julian. Also, my back hates me, has ever since I birthed an eight-pound, ten-ounce baby. My dance routines help keep me limber, but my spine still gives me pushback every now and then, especially after a rough night's sleep.

"I don't know how I ended up in here." His head jerks back. "But, uh…"

"I should've called Bare," I admit. I had the bodyguard's number all along and I didn't use it. It's just that…I was never worried about Julian stealing. I was worried he wouldn't wake up, and I didn't want him out of my sight until I was sure he would.

"Bare? No, Collette, I'm trying to thank you."

"Thank me?"

"Yeah. I can't remember the last time I woke up with a blanket *and* a pillow."

That doesn't sound right. Is he high still?

"What about when you stay in a hotel?"

Julian and I regard one another for a long time, then he scoots forward, his hand up to his mouth. Behind it, he asks, "Do you want anything?" It sounds like the ring on his thumb is between his lips when he says it.

"Do I *want* anything?"

"Yeah. Like reimbursement or whatever."

"For?"

"Crashing here. You probably had better things to do than—"

"Julian?"

His hand drops to his lap, and I see him hastily spinning the thumb ring with the tip of his pointer finger.

"Yeah?"

"What do you want on your sandwich?"

He glances behind me, swallowing.

"Whatever you're havin.'"

"Okay."

I turn back around, my eyes on everything in front of me without really seeing any of it. He wants to *pay* me? He thinks I deserve compensation for loaning him a spot on a floor to sleep, along with a pillow and a blanket for a few hours?

What kind of reality is he living in?

The same one I do, where everything that comes free isn't actually free.

"I'm gonna get cleaned up," he says before I hear footsteps shuffling toward the bathroom.

"Okay," I repeat, then thinking better of it, I add, "Don't smoke in there."

Julian's laugh is husky and full of sleep. *Is he still high?*

Chapter 8

Julian

Mother of cunt.

I don't know how I made my way over here, or why the fuck I was sleeping on Collette's floor, or why she was letting me…

She was letting me, right? She wouldn't have given me a pillow and blanket otherwise. She would've given my ass the boot. She didn't though, and now I don't know what my next move is because I…

I offered her…

Fuck. Why did I do that?

Because as fucking humiliating as it was to ask Collette if she wanted payment for letting me sleep on her floor, it would've been a thousand times worse if she asked me first. I'd rather lose my hearing than listen to her ask me for something like that. Not because I wouldn't give her anything she asked me for, but because then she'd be just like everybody else in my life.

I'm splashing water on my face, contemplating sticking my entire head under the faucet, when I hear a man's voice.

When I come out of the bathroom, Collette's building a third sandwich with four other slices of bread out on plates, and a teen boy—not a man—is standing next to her, snagging one of the finished sandwiches before she can stop him.

"Hey, that was Julian's," Collette scolds, and I bring my hand up, already sliding my thumb ring over so I can chew on the skin underneath.

"Ooh, Julian, huh? Is that why you never came back to the hotel?"

"I did go back to the hotel actually, but you took so long in the shower, I got bored and left again."

"You did?" the boy asks around a mouthful, his eyebrows almost touching.

Collette laughs. "No, I've been here the whole time. But your showers do last forever."

The kid's face turns red, and I bite the cracked, sore skin that never gets a chance to heal even harder to keep from laughing. I don't want to interrupt this moment. I never had this. *I never had a mom.*

I did, just not for long. And she wasn't like this. She wasn't even coherent enough to be like this.

An older woman, followed by Irelynn, boards the bus, and I slink further back into the shadows, still not ready to interrupt because as soon as they're all together, I get that same feeling, the one I got when I spent Thanksgiving at Antonio's, like I'm around an actual family. It doesn't matter that they're not my family, I just want to watch how one operates, what they sound like, what they *feel* like.

The three women chat about the day ahead, finishing each other's sentences, and stopping every once in a while to smile genuinely at one another. There's plenty of banter, too, but in an entertaining way that has me wishing I could be a part of it. I'd happily take some licks, if only just to be included.

Sometimes, during press, I get asked about the people I keep around me, and I usually give some cheesy answer about them being like family, but I never mean it. I thought it was because I just didn't know what family was supposed to be like, but now that I've finally seen two for myself, to try and use that word to describe my entourage would be like putting a finger condom over my cock—it doesn't fucking fit.

Collette's eyes seek mine out and it's like our first night on her bus all over again, her sunshine breaking through my forever darkness. She gives me a secretive grin that pulls me from out of the shadows.

I should leave. I'm not part of any family, not even my own.

"Oh, man, sorry," Collette's kid says as soon as he spots me, motioning to the sandwich that was meant for me. "I didn't know you were still here."

"Don't worry about it," I tell him. "I was just taking off anyway."

Sticking his free hand out, he asks, "Julez, right?" and I shake it, telling him, "Call me Julian. You're Holter?"

He nods, stuffing another bite in his mouth.

"Holter, manners," Collette warns as the older woman behind him flicks one of his ears.

With his mouth half-full, he complains, "It's not fair when you two gang up on me."

"Think about kids that live with both parents, they get it all the time," Irelynn says, and Collette curses, dropping the knife in her hold.

"Are you okay?" I reach out a hand, wanting to touch her, but hold myself back.

With a tight smile, she says, "I'm fine. Here. Just take mine."

"You said you would eat."

"I will. I'll have…" She rolls on to her tiptoes to reach into a high cupboard, pulling out another one of those packets of baby food, but it's out of her hand and tossed back into the cupboard before she can settle back on to her heels.

She glares at me, and I smirk, closing the cupboard to emphasize my point.

"You said you were leaving."

"I lied." Just because I know I should leave doesn't mean I actually want to. Besides, everybody knows I never do what I'm supposed to.

Without taking her eyes from mine, she brings the sandwich up to take a bite. It's weak compared to her son's, but teenage boys are like cows grazing in a field. Those motherfuckers never stop eating.

"Go sit with your boy and I'll make my own," I tell her, hoping like hell she won't kick me off the bus for ordering her around. It's not exactly an order, I just feel bad she missed time with Holter to take care of me. If I can make it up to them, even in this tiny stupid way that probably doesn't mean anything to anyone else, I will.

Collette hands sandwiches off to Irelynn and the other woman, introducing her to me as Mary, Holter's nanny. Nobody's allowed to actually call her his nanny since he's a teen now, so she's just…Mary.

I introduce myself to her, too, before piling one slice of bread with a handful of ham, then squirting mustard all over it. I'm not using mayonnaise. I didn't know that's all Collette had or I would've said something sooner. I'll choke it down dry with no sandwich lube at all before I use mayonnaise.

Finished, I sit next to Collette at the table, telling Holter, "You got tall, dude. I think it was at last year's Mousai Awards when I saw you last, and I swear you weren't half this size."

"Yeah, I get it from my dad." His eyes touch on his mom, then drop.

"Bodee is very tall," Collette chirps, and the other women agree like well-trained robots. "We should have you two stand next to each other to measure when he gets here. See who's taller."

Gets here?

"When I went with him last month, we did that, and he was still taller than me by two inches."

"That was last month and I'm pretty sure you grow half an inch a day, so…" Collette laughs, but I'm still stuck on that whole "when he gets here" part. The "last month" part isn't sitting right either. Holter hasn't seen his dad, his richer-than-shit dad, for a month? Bodee's got his own private jet. I've seen it. It's got his ugly fucking mug on the sides.

"Are you tired of being on tour yet?" I ask Holter, trying to get off the topic of Bodee Keys.

Holter chuckles. "It just started."

"Yeah, this one did, but I mean tour life in general. How do you handle school when you're always traveling? Friends? When do you see them?"

"Sometimes I do remote schooling, but I haven't had to for…what? Has it been a full year?"

Collette's head rocks side to side like she's doing the math. "This past year, you did it almost all in person."

"And my best friend lives," he makes a face at Collette that makes her snort, "up the driveway from me, so I see him every day. His dad takes us to school, and Mary and I eat dinner there a couple times a week."

Mary adds, "More since they built that pizza oven."

Collette nods, saying, "Oh, yeah, I still need to try that."

I turn to her. "I thought you just came off another tour on to this one."

"And one before that," Irelynn says, then winces, looking at Collette, too.

"Unfortunately, it isn't always…suitable for Holter to come along, so Mary stays with him when I can't, and I fly back to see him whenever I get the chance."

"What? Like on your days off?"

"Days off?" she questions, tilting her head to the side, and I laugh. It's a strained laugh because I'm confused. Is she being serious right now? She never gets a day off?

Out of the corner of my eye, I see Holter wince and I think I have my answer.

I want to ask more, I want to ask so fucking much, but the sudden color on Collette's face keeps me from pressing her on it. Why does she tour so much still? It sounds like she's touring all year long, which is typical for new artists just starting out and trying to get their name out there, not superstars that have been around for over fifteen years.

"We make it work, right?"

Holter, Mary, and Irelynn all respond with, "Right," except it's not mechanical this time. They mean it. They really are a family. An unconventional one according to society's outdated definition, but there's no denying that together, the three women and Holter, pull it off somehow.

What about Bodee though? What role does he play in all this? It doesn't sound like he even has one.

"Well, I'm glad you could make it this time," I tell Holter honestly. I wasn't really sure what it'd be like having a kid hanging around on tour, but I can tell how happy Collette is having her son here. "Let me know if you need anything and I'll make sure you get it, okay?"

"Can you get—"

"Holter," both Collette and Mary scold at the same time.

"You know the rule, anything you need, *I* get for you," Collette tells her boy, and he rolls his eyes, looking exactly like his mom when she does the same move.

I have to bite into my sandwich to hide my smile.

Conversation picks up and I try to catch every bit of it while also making sure Collette eats all of her meal. Her knee keeps brushing mine under the table, but neither of us apologizes. I know I'm not sorry. I want to touch more of her. She just won't let me. Even when I ask, she shuts me down.

I spread my legs wider, making sure my knee's closer to hers.

This scene isn't that different from the shit that happens on my bus, yet it is. People are always talking around me, and there's usually at least one body part or another touching me, but that…is nothing like this.

"Dad?"

Everything in my body locks up except my eyes as they swing to Holter, but he's looking over my shoulder, and when I follow his gaze, I find Bodee motherfucking Keys standing there.

"Julez," he greets calmly. "Good to see you again."

"Can't say the same, Bodee." *Motherfucker.*

"You two know each other already?" Holter asks, but before I can answer, Collette practically forces my ass off the seat, climbing out behind me to stand in front of Bodee.

Bodee shifts his gaze to smile down at her. "Good God, blondie, you just keep getting better with age, don't you?"

I hate him. I hate him calling Collette blondie. I hate him saying she gets better with age like he knows. He doesn't know.

Does he know?

On second thought, I hate him saying anything to Collette. If I could throw down with him right now, I would. I fucking *hate* him.

"You don't even look sick," he says, and Collette must be just as confused as I am because she cocks one eyebrow at her ex-husband, waiting until he explains with, "I caught a clip from last night's performance…you sounded nasally."

"No, she didn't," I say before anyone else even gets the chance. Technically I only heard Collette do one song, but that was enough. She wasn't fucking nasally.

Collette looks at me, then Bodee, only saying, "I thought you didn't get in until later."

He clucks his tongue. "You know I love the element of surprise."

Holter coughs, drawing everybody's attention. It's a fake cough, too, so it really makes us all stop and study him.

For a kid that just got surprised by the dad he hasn't seen in a month, he don't look too excited. I'm no genius, but I'm thinking it might have something to do with that same dad not even bothering to greet him. Bodee went out of his way to acknowledge both me and Collette, but not his own son…who I'm guessing is the reason he's here now.

Unless he's here to see Collette…

Is he here to see Collette? I don't like the idea of that. In fact, I fucking hate it, almost as much as I hate Bodee.

Bodee finally looks at Holter, and grins. "Hi, son. Want to get out of here?" He makes this face that basically says "here" is the last place he wants to be.

Would it be weird if I brought up the whole kicking-Bodee's-ass thing? I kinda wanna bring it up—now. Like right fucking now. Just a little reminder that while he may have more money than me, I can still beat the shit out of him.

"And go where?" Holter asks, so I decide not to say anything.

"Wherever you want."

"Umm. Not wherever." Collette places herself in Bodee's line of vision again, raising her eyebrows. "That's not what we agreed to and you know it. Not to mention we have some business to take care of first."

"Like what?"

"Like is Jack enjoying his vacation?"

"Collette, I assure you *John* is savoring every moment of his time away on O'ahu."

Who the fuck are they talking about and why are they talking about him like that? Like it's some kind of code. And is it Jack or John? Or are they two different people?

Collette holds Bodee's eyes for a beat longer, then nods. "Okay, you guys can go. But stay local. I'll see you tomorrow morning," she tells Holter, giving his forehead a kiss. "Be safe. I love you."

The boy passes, and I say, "See ya, dude," gaining Bodee's attention.

Bodee stares at me, but says to Collette, "Have dinner with us."

Yeah, Imma bring it up. That or just fight him again. Whatever shuts him up faster.

Luckily, Collette turns her ex down, telling him, "I have a show."

"We all do."

Now what does *that* mean? Because I know for a fucking fact Bodee's not performing in town tonight. I would've heard about it.

Bodee's eyes crinkle as he takes in my tattoos, so I cross my arms over my chest, making sure the worst of them are easier for him to make out.

"Meet us after."

I'm already grinning, waiting for Collette to tell him off for trying to give her an order, but she doesn't. She only sighs, peering past him to remind Holter to keep his phone charged and on.

Bodee takes one last look around in the smuggest way possible before turning to follow Holter off the bus.

Nobody makes a move, so when Mary starts to get up from the couch, it echoes throughout the whole bus.

"Mary." Mary freezes, and quieter, Collette adds, "Stay close."

"Always."

"You don't give her the night off when Holter's with his dad?" I ask when the nanny we can't call a nanny is gone.

"No," is all Collette says, then she disappears into the bathroom.

Irelynn leans forward to whisper, "Just so you know, Mary would never let Collette give her the night off when Holter goes with Bodee."

"Why?"

"Because the *only* person Bodee looks out for is Bodee."

"But he just—"

"If there's an opportunity to look like an involved father, he'll take it. Bodee was already coming to San Diego, he didn't come for Holter."

"And Collette? What was that shit about them having dinner?"

Irelynn shakes her head. "It'd be a heavily photographed spectacle. It's *always* a heavily photographed spectacle. Bodee likes to put in a high-profile appearance with Collette every so often."

"And Collette goes along with it?"

"Same objective, just for different audiences."

"What does that mean?"

"Collette doesn't want Holter to know, and Bodee doesn't want everyone else to know."

"Know what?"

Irelynn doesn't even blink when she says, "That Collette hates Bodee's guts."

I fucking knew it.

Tonight's show blasts last night's out of the water and it's not even done yet. Our speakers showed up in time and aren't exploding into static every time a beat drops.

I stuck around all day to make sure shit was exactly the way it was supposed to be. I even stayed just offstage after rehearsals to watch Collette's set.

And as soon as our performance together wraps, I don't even hesitate to follow her backstage, pulling her to a stop.

Her eyes are wide when she turns around to face me. "What are you doing? You should be—"

"Come back out there with me."

"What? We don't have any more songs together."

"I'll think of some."

"On the spot?" She laughs, doubting my ability.

I grin at her, the hook I wrote earlier already spinning in my head. I gave Collette some time alone after Bodee took off, but the impression she and her family made on me during my time with them had me scribbling lyrics anywhere I could once I left her bus. I couldn't fucking stop the words once they hit. I would've recorded them on my phone's voice recording app, but my bus is way too fucking loud for that.

"Yeah, on the spot," I tell her.

Doesn't she know all the freestyle battles I've been in? And fucking murdered?

"I can't," she admits gently. So gentle suspicion needles its way into my brain. Collette may be a lot of things, but gentle ain't one of them. Not from what I've seen so far.

"You're not really going to meet Bodee, are you?" When she doesn't answer, I repeat, "Are you?"

She finally shakes her head. "You don't understand."

"You could make me."

"No, I couldn't." Instead of being condescending, her voice sounds tired. Or sad. But then, out of nowhere, she changes her entire tune, saying, "I need to go get ready."

"Ready? You look perfect." She opens her mouth, so I quickly add, "Exactly how you are."

"For the stage, sure, but not for a date."

Not for a *what?* Did she really just use the word date? Because she told me the thing she most definitely did not have was a fucking man, but that's not how she's acting right now, throwing that word around like she actually meant to.

"You mean the thing with Bodee, right? Or do you mean you actually have a…" Fuck that. I'm not saying it.

"I mean I have a date tonight, Julian. *After* the thing with Bodee."

I press my palms into my eyelids, pushing 'til I see spots behind them. She said it. She fucking said it. *Date.*

When I drop my hands, Collette's already walking away, telling me to "Break a leg" but why would I need to do that when she just took out both my legs for me? One word, said two too many times, causing double the motherfucking damage.

Fuck.

Chants of "Julez" come into sharp focus, assaulting my ears in a way they weren't just a few minutes ago, and I wish I was back on Collette's bus again. Back to the only quiet I've ever found comfort in. The only *place* I've ever felt comfort in.

Maybe even the only person I've ever felt comfort in. But she just fucking left me…for a *date.*

Chapter 9

Collette

"I'm sorry, ma'am, but there aren't any rooms available at this time."

I look up from my phone, finally meeting the receptionist's stare. We're the only two people in the entire lobby, and luckily, her expression doesn't hold an ounce of recognition. Since it's so late, I figured I could get away with booking a room in the same hotel my team's using. Even with Holter staying with Bodee tonight, I wouldn't use my own suite. That's way too personal.

I should've just gone to another hotel, damn it.

"Not even one?" I try again. "It's just for the night." Not even a whole night. We'll be in and out in an hour. *If that.*

The receptionist shakes her head apologetically, and I blow out a breath, adjusting the beanie on my head. With it pulled low and covering my blonde hair, it's no wonder she doesn't recognize me. I don't go anywhere with my natural hair anymore. That's why I don't wear wigs on dates.

"What's goin' on, Poohbear?" Julian asks suddenly as he lifts himself to plant his ass on the front desk counter before picking a flower from the hotel's impressive floral arrangement.

Shit.

There goes my cover. At least I didn't give her my alias yet.

"Shouldn't you be on stage?"

"Just got done."

He does have a suite reserved here, too, but he didn't even use it last night, so why is he—

He didn't even use it.

"Hey, is anyone in your room right now?"

Something fiery flashes in his eyes, but he only shrugs, saying, "Probably. Why?"

"I'm trying to book a room, but there's—"

"No availability?" he guesses correctly, making my eyes narrow on him.

"Yeah."

"Hmm. Guess that ruins your *plans*."

"It's a date."

"It's a fucking joke," he sneers.

"Whatever he paid you to say this, I'll double," I tell the reception- ist, no longer concerned with anonymity.

"Ma'am, he's not—"

Julian whistles, plucking the petals off the flower one by one before grabbing another from the vase. "*Double?* This bozo better be worth it."

"One room. One night. I'll take whatever you have," I tell her, pull- ing out my wallet and lifting my eyebrows. "And you can charge me whatever you want."

"I apologize, but there's nothing I can do. Truly. All the rooms have been reserved for tonight already."

"By who? Is there a convention in—"

Her eyes skate over to Julian, and I cut myself off, hanging my head to shake it. This can't be happening.

A noise like a shoe scuff pulls my head up like a puppeteer holding its string, and I find Julian towering over me as he stands on the shiny marble counter between me and the receptionist.

"Aw, little lamb, you've severely underestimated me."

He sticks his hands in his pockets and rocks on the balls of his feet, asking, "How so?"

"By assuming I need a bed at all."

I push off from the counter, heading back to Victor, who I left in the parking lot. I don't think Victor's his real name just like the name I gave him isn't mine, but that's the beauty of the dating app I use. We're all incognito and looking for the same thing—anonymous sex. After the past few days I've had, not to mention the ludicrous "dinner" with my ex I just endured, I need this. I *need* this.

Shoes landing on the freshly mopped floor go off like a grenade, startling the silence, and I pick up the pace.

"I gotta see this guy," Julian says behind me.

"No. You don't," I say without turning around, but he catches up to me in the parking lot in a matter of seconds, so I stop, folding my arms over my chest. "What are you doing?"

"I just wanna meet the guy you blew me off for."

"I didn't blow you off. I did my job and now I'm enjoying the fruits of that labor."

"With a fuck," he snarls.

I grin. "I knew you'd understand."

"I don't."

"What part don't you understand?"

"The part where you sneak off to go fuck a rando in his Porsche."

"How do you know what kind of car he drives?"

He waves a hand out to his side, gesturing to a gunmetal-gray Porsche…with Victor sitting inside…waving back.

Stop waving, Victor.

"We'll use my bus," I say, unlocking my phone.

"Antonio's not around, if that's who you're about to call." Julian's lips are curved into a smug smile when I look up at him.

If only I hadn't given Antonio the keys back this afternoon.

"Maybe I'll use your bus. You said it yourself, you can fuck all you want on there and nobody says anything."

Julian pushes into my space, not quite touching me, but only just. "Don't go near my bus."

"I don't take orders from you."

"Don't. Go. Near. My. Bus."

"Why?"

"Because it's not a good place for you."

"But it's a good place for you?"

Julian doesn't answer, only continues gazing down at me, and if Victor didn't know who I was before, there's a good chance he's figured it out now.

"What is this even about? What do you want?" Surely he can find something more interesting to do with his time than prevent me from getting laid.

"I wanna take you somewhere."

I sigh. "Can you wait twenty minutes?"

"Twenty minutes? Fuck, Collette, you'll be lucky if that guy lasts longer than twenty *seconds*. I almost blew my load just watching you handle the Spider yesterday."

"Then you might want to look away for this next part," I say on my way past, but with a few of his long-legged strides, Julian overtakes me, reaching Victor's Porsche first. He opens the driver's door, speaking in low tones to Victor, and when I try to open the passenger door, the locks click into place, keeping me out.

Julian shoots me a glare over the top of the car that I let myself envision slapping right off, until the Porsche speeds away, abruptly ending the fantasy.

Julian just smirks at me, jiggling the McLaren's key.

"I hate you," I breathe, making his lips sink into a frown.

"Words hurt, Poohbear."

I ignore his disapproving headshake, stretching a hand out for the key. Keeping it out of reach as he walks backward to the car, he mansplains that because he knows where we're going, he should be the one to drive. The image of him crawling up my bus steps this morning only to promptly pass out runs through my head, so as soon as we're inside the rented supercar, I ask if his seat goes back any further.

Julian finds the button, demonstrating that it does, and I climb over the center console, sitting on his lap and pushing the same button until the seat's as far back as it'll go.

"The fuck are you doing?" Julian asks as I push his legs out to the side to give mine more room under the steering wheel. It helps that the bottom of it isn't a complete circle.

"Driving. There's no way you're sober."

"I'm sober."

His strong thighs flex beneath me when I give him a look through the rearview mirror.

"Yeah, right."

Starting the engine, I close my eyes to appreciate the vibration.

"I'm…" He swallows hard, the sound louder than the car's purr. "Fucked."

Of course he is.

I open my eyes, finding his studying mine.

"You're allowed to touch me whenever you want, but I still can't touch you. How do you even know I want you on my cock?"

That's fair.

"Sorry," I mutter, starting to lift myself. "But you still can't drive." He can get out and go around.

His forearm locks over my lap, keeping me in place.

"Don't *fucking* move."

"I don't take—"

"You'll take this order," he says arrogantly.

"What makes you so sure?"

For answer, his foot depresses the gas pedal, revving the engine. "Because you like this too much to pass up."

Another good point.

"Okay…so, you do want me on your cock?"

"I've wanted you on my cock since I was a teenager with your poster hanging above my bed."

"Color me flattered," I deadpan. It astounds me the amount of people who say the same exact thing as if I actually like hearing it. I don't, especially now that I have my own teenager. I really don't need to think about what he does with the posters he has up in his room.

"You asked."

"I was trying to be respectful."

"Well, don't. You have my full permission to degrade the fuck outta me any time you want."

My chuckle fills the car. He's so ridiculous. A walking contradiction.

"So, I don't need to apologize for leaving you naked at the photo shoot?"

"You can… With your lips around my—"

"Offer rescinded. I will not be apologizing."

Now he's the one laughing. "Yeah, I figured. I had it comin' anyway."

Hesitantly, like he thinks I'll actually leave, he removes his arm, and I settle myself lower between his thighs, saying, "Yes, you did."

His voice deepens to ask, "How are your panties now, Collette?"

"You really want to know?"

"Fuck yeah."

"Close your eyes."

"Wh—"

"Close your eyes."

His eyelids flutter closed, so I grip the tops of his hands on his thighs, exhaling until my back expands against his chest, his rapidly beating heart knocking my shoulder blade.

With my head cocked to the side and watching the spot below his jawline to see the beats myself, I whisper, "Inhale through your nose."

The chest at my back stretches until Julian's lungs are so full I swear they can't expand any further, but somehow they do.

His breath whooshes out.

"I'm gonna fucking—"

"The only thing you're going to do is smell my want. The want you wouldn't let me satisfy by chasing off—"

His thumbs swoop over to catch the tops of my hands, holding me hostage as he brings our hands in, simultaneously rubbing the insides of his thighs and the outsides of mine. A moan almost slips out, but I manage to swallow it in time to hear Julian growl, "I swear to fuck, you better not say another motherfucker's name right now."

"Why? Why go through all this trouble, Julian?"

His eyes open, lowering to meet mine as he twists his head my way.

"You really wanna know?"

I follow his lead by repeating his words back to him. "Fuck yeah." But I'm not sure they're as true as when he said them. I'm not sure about any of this. My panties are in worse shape now than they were yesterday, and it's not just the car.

Julian releases his hold on my hands, telling me, "Drive."

It wasn't just the car yesterday either.

Chapter 10

Collette

Fluorescent lighting gyrates through the windshield directly on our faces.

"I can't go in there."

"Why not? You too good for a strip club?"

I roll my eyes. "I can't go inside because I'm not dressed for appearances."

I have no makeup on, my hair isn't done, and I'm in leather joggers, a loose sweatshirt, and a beanie for Christ's sake. What I'm not wearing is a bra, and my sweatshirt has holes in it—everywhere.

"You look fuckable to me."

That was the idea. I'm dressed to get undressed, very, very quickly. Like I said though, not for public appearances.

"And yet you stopped me from actually getting fucked."

"Pull down your pants. I'll make sure you get fucked."

Julian's hard cock presses into my lower back as his breathing quickens.

"How kind of you," I drawl as sarcastically as I can through my own breath change. It would be so easy to sit up and slide down his cock, right here, right now. It would be *too* easy. "But I already told you, I don't fuck the talent." Not when I have my own to look out for.

I lift the McLaren's door, but Julian's quick to fist the key before I can.

Standing outside and eyeing the building, I ask, "How do you know this place is discreet?"

"Because I'll make it fucking discreet."

I can only imagine what that'll look like.

"You have the subtlety of a nuclear bomb, you know that?"

Julian follows me out albeit slower to adjust the erection in his jeans. "What do you mean?"

I gesture at the car.

"This is too much? Your ex has his own PJ."

"Don't bring Bodee into this."

"You're the one that went to dinner with the guy."

Don't remind me, I want to say, but don't. Can't. I can, it's just… better if I don't. It's easier.

Julian eyes me for a beat, then softly, he says, "I got it for you."

"What?"

"The car. I thought you'd like it."

I scoff, dropping my stare to the dark asphalt. "Because I'm easily impressed by expensive items." What a load of horseshit.

"It wasn't about the price tag. I thought… Fuck."

Our eyes meet just as he's lifting a hand to his mouth, and he freezes, tucking it into a pocket instead.

"You like races, don't you? You never miss the one in Indy."

"They invite me to sing the National Anthem," I say slowly, watching him.

He clears his throat. "Not every time."

I crack a small smile, shaking my head. "No, not every time. You're right, whether I'm singing there or not, I never miss a race. If I get in early enough, they even let me do a couple laps around the empty track." And I love it. I more than love it. It's like no other feeling in the world driving that fast, that unrestrained. *Being* that unrestrained.

He gestures at the car, repeating, "I got it for you."

Julian pays attention. More than he lets on.

Fixing my shirt so one shoulder shows, I say, "Fine, I'll go in, but you owe me a lap dance."

"I'll do my best."

"Not from you." I snort, although I wouldn't mind watching him try. "From one of the male dancers inside."

A laugh smothered by a cough has me side-eyeing Julian as we approach the door.

"This one has both men and women performers, right?"

His answer is a shit-eating grin.

Julian hands a large stack of cash to the security guard just inside, and I wait until we're alone to voice my thoughts, telling him, "I seriously hate you." The only dancers onstage are all female. *What could he possibly want to show me here?*

"Still want that lap dance, Poohbear?"

Without looking away from him, I say, "Absolutely." I've been with women before. Not necessarily one-on-one, but I wouldn't be opposed to it.

Julian chuckles, guiding me over to a table in the back corner. At first it appears empty, but as we get closer, I make out his drummer along with a bunch of other men.

Julian gives introductions, saying, "Boys, you know Collette," while accepting a glass of amber liquid. As he's busy tossing it back, I sneak my hand into his pocket, stealing the key back.

As much as I enjoyed driving on Julian's lap, it was distracting. Julian himself is incredibly distracting.

I tuck the key away, then take a seat next to the drummer that I only got the chance to speak with in passing.

"What's your poison?" Axel asks me, indicating to the bottles of alcohol littering the table.

I answer honestly, saying, "Damaged men."

"It's like that, huh?" He laughs.

I eye Julian watching me over his glass. "Unfortunately."

"Lucky for you, that's on tap tonight," Axel jokes.

"This one's as damaged as they *come*," another guy leans over to say, jerking a thumb at the drummer, then proceeds to shake up a bottle of champagne before spraying it all over the table, making everybody laugh.

After I wipe the cold liquid from my face, I ask, "It's like that, huh?"

Shrugging, he repeats my answer of, "Unfortunately," with an easy smile.

He's got a grungy, almost emo look to him, with monochrome tattoos and dark, smudged eyeliner. His hair's a dark brown and similarly cut to Julian's, where it's longer on the top than the back and sides. His energy is calm, but in an assessing sort of way, and I wouldn't be surprised if he's just as observant as his friend.

"I'm Axel," he says.

I take his hand, asking, "Is that your real name or stage name?"

Axel keeps my hand, drawing me closer to him so he can speak against the shell of my ear. "Both. I started out going by a different stage name, but everyone kept calling me Axel, and it just kinda stuck. Last year, I had my name changed to Axel legally. Like you, right?"

"I didn't change mine. Collette's always been my real name. What was your original stage name?"

"XL."

I rear back, giving him a more thorough once-over. He's about the same size as Julian except a tad more muscular. He has nice biceps, the kind you could easily sink your nails into.

"Wanna see why?" Axel taunts with an arched eyebrow that I can't help but snicker at. He's sexy, too, but nothing like the way Julian is. My panties are wholly unaffected by him, and I don't really care to see what he's packing. Of course, I'm interested in finding out if he lives up to the namesake, but not *that* interested.

With my hand still in his, he stands, pulling me up, too.

Just as I lean in to give him the same talk I gave Julian, he drops back into his chair from a vicious shove, releasing my hand to put both of his up innocently.

"Sit the fuck down," Julian warns him in a tone I haven't heard before.

"Just having a little bit of fun," Axel says with that relaxed smile of his.

"Not with her."

"What's your deal tonight?" I ask Julian. "First, you scared off my date—"

"Damn right I did. Now you get to see why." Julian drains the rest of his drink, his eyes glazing over when they find mine. He drags two chairs over with zero tact whatsoever, just knocking into people left and right, then tells me to take a seat in one of them.

After sitting down, I make a show of getting my lap ready.

"Oh, shit," one of the guys at the table says. "This should be good."

A couple names are thrown around as recommendations, but Julian doesn't seem to hear any as he motions a dancer over, his face severe, like he's…

What is he right now? He was somewhat playful before when I said he owed me a lap dance, but now that's all gone, and in its place is what looks and feels like anger. Why is he so damn angry? What happened?

Otep's metal rendition of "Royals" starts up and every stage suddenly has a dancer on it, spinning rapidly around the poles. The synchronicity is breathtaking and it's all I can do to sit here, watching in awe.

Julian sits next to me, draping an arm over the back of my chair, and when the tall blonde in a bandage dress saunters over, he nods at his own lap. Not mine.

What the—

She immediately pulls her dress over her head and gets to work dancing on top of Julian's thighs. Julian doesn't take his eyes off the woman on his lap, but now, I can't take my eyes off him. What the hell is this?

The dancer lifts a platform-heeled foot over Julian's shoulder and proceeds to bounce directly over his cock with ass cheeks that shake like maracas.

My face grows unbearably warm and my holey sweatshirt feels restricting. *Stifling.*

Finally, finally, Julian's gaze swings over to mine. "What do you think?"

"About?"

He leans back, his hips lifting off the chair so the dancer hits his cock even harder with each bounce.

Christ.

"I think…" I think this is what *he* would've done. This is exactly what Bodee did do. This and so much more. And I used to go along with it, not just because I thought I had to, but because I actually wanted to.

But things have changed. *I've* changed. And I no longer want to.

"I think you made a good choice." The woman on his lap could melt ice and can clearly out-dance me on my best day. "Enjoy."

I try to stand, but Julian's hand latches on to my shoulder, keeping me seated.

"You ain't goin' anywhere."

"Keep underestimating me," I threaten. "I get off on proving people wrong."

"That'll be the only way you're getting off tonight."

Excuse me? Does he really think he has a say in when and where I get off? And by who?

I shake off his hand, then catching the eye of another gorgeous dancer, I give her a small nod with a slant to my lips that Julian must see because he asks what I'm doing.

I don't answer though. In a second, I won't need to.

The dancer wastes no time making her way over to me, then she's leaning down, dropping her arms to my shoulders so her face is only inches from mine.

"Hi, baby, I'm Krystall. I've had my eye on you since you walked in."

"Oh, yeah?" I ask instead of giving my name. I don't know if she knows who I am, but I'm not about to make it public knowledge.

"Yeah," she says, licking her top lip and almost touching mine with her tongue.

"Collette!" Julian barks, and I'm really hoping that mound of bills he gave the security is enough to keep this from getting out. He's like a bull in a goddamn china shop when it comes to discretion.

Ignoring Julian as well, she asks, "You good?" with a click of her tongue ring against her teeth, and I nod. "You good with *whatever?*" Her eyes spark with meaning as her ass behind her starts swaying side to side.

"I'm good," I promise her. "Just make sure to put this on his tab."

I jerk my head at Julian, making sure I don't actually look his way, but Krystall says, "This one's on me, baby," before running her hands down my chest and over my breasts, making a hiss escape my lips.

"Are you sure? He doesn't mind paying."

"He looks like he minds something," Krystall murmurs, a focused expression taking over her face as she drags her nails across my stomach, hooking on to a hole in the fabric to tease the naked skin beneath.

The urge to buck up into her has me gripping the bottom of the seat cushion, my knuckles screaming from the pressure. My breath grows unsteady as her fingers find the top of my leather joggers, then move to my thighs, gliding down between them to rub up and down the insides.

"Shit," I pant, not even remotely surprised how turned on I am already.

Her eyes on her hands, she says, "If you're gonna watch, at least hold her chair steady for me."

I finally glance at Julian, finding he's not nearly as interested in the woman grinding on his cock as he was just a minute ago. Those blue-bordering-on-teal eyes of his look downright haggard as he looks from me to Krystall, then the arm by my head flexes as he grips the top of the chair.

Krystall grabs both my thighs from underneath and yanks my ass forward, off the chair and into the air as she hoists my entire bottom half up. Her mouth goes straight for my pussy, and through the material, I feel her purr loudly, clicking that tongue ring at the same time. Each click is a shot straight to my core and the warm air from her mouth has me heating internally, like an inferno rapidly swirling inside me, begging to get out.

A little more of this and I might just come…

All at once the sensations disappear, then I'm hauled off the chair completely, crushed to a sinuous body that's definitely not Krystall's.

"That's enough," Julian growls, his alcohol-infused breath falling over my face as he walks us away from the table.

"I didn't say you could touch me."

"Fucking try to stop me. I dare you."

"Subtlety of a nuclear bomb," I tsk, hooking my ankles behind his back, and he mumbles something about exploding soon.

"I'll share her with you," Krystall calls after us, and Julian grips the hell out of the thighs she was just between, slowing his steps and meeting my eyes.

My chest tightens at the familiarity of it all, but then so clear the private rooms in the back can probably hear him, Julian says, "No," and I release all the air in my lungs.

Words do hurt, but that one doesn't. Not the way he said it. Like it wasn't even an option.

Julian carries me until we're back outside beside the McLaren. When he goes to unlock the doors, only to realize he doesn't have the key, I free myself from his grasp, placing my feet back on the ground. He's quick to cage me in on the passenger side though, bending down so he's eye level with me.

I park my ass against the futuristic door, regarding him silently, while simultaneously pushing on his chest to create a little more space.

"You get it now?"

"Get what?"

"You know what."

I bite my lips together. I do, but I'm not admitting it. I'm not admitting anything to him. Confessions are leverage, they can be used against you when you're least expecting it.

"You didn't like watching someone else on my cock, did you?"

My bare shoulder lifts, then falls. "You think I was jealous of her, but really, I was jealous of you. That's why I took matters into my own hands by trying to satisfy that want you smelled the entire drive over here."

His laugh is void of any humor as he straightens his spine, then starting at my toes, Julian drags his heavy-lidded gaze up my body, landing on my lips.

"The want Porsche douche got outta you, right? Or was it from Bodee?"

"Maybe both." I raise my eyebrows and he snarls, pushing into me again.

I hold him off with both hands, giving myself some breathing room. *Some* breathing room. Not much because Julian…he's trying. He's trying to get close, as close as I'll let him.

And I can't let him.

I let out my own laugh, knowing how much men hate being laughed at, and say, "Admit it. Your plan to punish me backfired. By bringing me here and making me watch another woman give you a lap dance, you were trying to get me as jealous as you were when I went on a date."

"Fuck your date," he spits. "I put an end to that before there even was one."

"And just what did you think would happen next, huh? That I'd be so overcome with jealousy that I'd spread my legs for you and let you finish what another man started?"

His nostrils flare as he says, "He didn't start shit," but I don't back down an inch. In fact, I lean forward, too, closing the distance until our noses are nearly touching.

"You mean they?" Because if we're taking this hypothetical plunge, we might as well commit. Neither Victor nor Bodee is responsible for my aching pussy, but that's another truth I can't let out.

"We both know it was my car that had you—"

"This isn't your car."

"But it was my cock that you were creamin' your fucking panties on top of."

"Mmm," is all I give in response. There's no sense in denying it. We both know the score on that front.

"Can I expect you to throw a fit every time I have a date? Because—"

"Stop talking about dates, goddamn it."

I shake my head at him as much as myself. "This isn't my first rodeo and you're not the first one to try to get in my pants." He's just taking longer to get the hint. "It won't work out for you though, just like it didn't work out for them."

"Who else tried?"

A bitter smile forms on my lips. "You wouldn't believe me if I told you."

"Why don't you tell me their names and I'll let you know if I believe it. Addresses, too. You know, for shits and gigs."

"And you swore I wouldn't be getting off tonight."

"You get off on torturing me, Collette?"

Our eyes taking in the other's, I stick my tongue to the corner of my lips and give him one minuscule truth by nodding. I don't know if it's his jealousy or just his protectiveness overall, but I do like it. More than I should.

His fingers creep up my breastbone before grasping my neck in a firm, yet somehow still gentle chokehold, and for whatever reason, I let Julian tilt my head to the side.

"That scene you just caused," he rasps against my cheek, making me sink my teeth into my bottom lip to keep from moaning. "That fantasy you created for me and every other motherfucker in the club, *that* was fucking torture. Tonight, I'm gonna replay that in my head, picturing it was my hands all over you, then I'm gonna fuck my hand, pretending it's yours."

I can feel myself melting. On the inside, the outside, everywhere. I'm like warm putty in Julian's hands, he just hasn't realized it yet.

Good. I have to keep it that way, by any means necessary.

I force a swallow down, the lump barely making it past Julian's palm on my throat to say, "So, now you know the next time you try to teach me a lesson, you'll be the one getting schooled. Now, get your fucking hand off me, and go back inside to find someone who'll actually stroke your cock and ego at the same time because like I keep telling you, it won't be me. I may enjoy winding you up a little, but that's all it is. All it will ever be because I don't fuck celebrities."

He releases me to step back, a scowl etched on his heartbreakingly beautiful face.

Getting my breathing under control again, I run my gaze the length of Julian, remembering the image I walked out on of him at the photo shoot. Gloriously naked with tight and toned muscles everywhere. Colorful tattoos on even more skin than I realized. Julian may be good-looking, but that doesn't change the facts, and the fact is, he is a celebrity. A clueless one, yes, but still, a celebrity just like me. Even worse, just like Bodee.

Eyes on the ground between us, he says, "I'm not just a fucking celebrity."

"What else are you?"

"I don't know. I just... Everyone wants something from me because I'm a celebrity, but you don't want anything from me because I'm a celebrity. They both feel the fucking same, like I'm..."

Please don't say like he's not good enough. I don't want to make Julian feel that way. I wish there was another way to do this without making it personal, but he's not leaving me many choices here. He's making me *melt*.

The silence grows sour, churning my stomach, and I reach out, lifting his face with just my middle finger under his jaw. For the first time, his heartbeat actually speeds up, pounding strongly under my touch.

"What does it feel like?"

His swallow jostles my finger momentarily, but then those turbulent thumps spring right back up, beating with wild abandon again.

"Like I'm free-falling."

That's exactly what being a celebrity feels like. You expect it to be some high honor, except instead of ever reaching it, all it feels like is falling with hundreds and hundreds and hundreds of hands thrust out at you. Not to catch you, or save you, only wanting. Always wanting. Something, anything. They're constantly pulling you in all different directions until you don't even know which way is up anymore.

Then one day a hand appears in front of you and they're not asking for something, so you grow even more suspicious because sometimes those are the most ravenous of all. I can handle the people that make their intentions clear, it's the other ones, the ones with hidden agendas and ulterior motives, that you really have to watch out for because they will take everything, and they'll do it without a second thought.

But that's just it, I don't want anything from Julian. At all. He doesn't know that though. Or if he does, he doesn't trust it.

"It's the comedown," I say, pulling my hand back. "The free fall from whatever high you're on, or think you're on, to a reality that's harsher than you were expecting, than you could've ever expected. This life isn't all glitz and glam, Julian. It's the fucking jungle, except during our fight for survival, we also end up killing ourselves." Our creativity, our happiness, all the things that makes us *us*—we shrink those parts of ourselves either until they're unrecognizable or they disappear altogether. Always with the same intention though—getting ahead, then staying ahead. Even the most innocent, well-meaning newcomers can turn into bloodthirsty hounds after their first taste of stardom. And the ones able to catch the scent of their own weakness early on, they're usually the ones that make it the farthest because they already hunted down and killed whatever was holding them back.

The last time I showed weakness was…just before I killed it myself. When I was forced to kill it. That or be killed by it because it could've ended me. It would've.

I made rules after that, rules to keep me from being in a position like that one ever again—way before Julian came along—and I refuse to break them. I have Holter to keep safe, and in order to do that, I need to be safe, too. No matter the risk, and no matter the sacrifice.

"That's what I'm counting on," Julian says, and I frown.

"Counting on?"

"You ever heard of The Twenty-Seven Club?"

"Yeah. I think everybody has."

It's not an actual club, it's an urban legend regarding all the celebrities that died at only twenty-seven years old. It absolutely reeks of conspiracy theories, and constantly has different numerology rumors clinging to it, but it boils down to an unfortunate string of coincidences. There are all kinds of artists on the list, from athletes to actors, but none more so than musicians. The celebrities on it, a lot of them led similar lifestyles riddled with addiction and depression. Which is no coincidence at all when you've seen it firsthand, the toll this lifestyle takes. Those are just the sad yet painfully accurate statistics of being a performer in this industry.

Without another word, Julian turns and leaves, going back inside like I told him to. I wait until he's out of sight to open my internet browser for a quick search.

Twenty-seven. Julian's twenty-seven years old.

I scroll until I find his birthdate. August fifteenth. That's next month. We'll still be on tour together.

"I just wanted to see you while I still could."

As much strife and disappointment as this lifestyle holds, there's good to be found, too. So much good. You just have to look for it, cultivate it, demand it outweighs the bad. Julian doesn't know how to do that yet. He could, and I could be the one to teach him. Not if he joins the Twenty-Seven Club though.

He thought I was a scrapper before, but he hasn't seen anything yet because if I'm not going anywhere, neither is Julian.

Chapter 11

Collette

After reuniting with Holter and Mary the next morning, we spend the day on the road, my dancers and I practicing a couple routines in the aisle of my bus, and we end up arriving into Sacramento just in time for one final run-through as well as a sound check. Julian shows up physically, but mentally…he's quiet and withdrawn during the whole thing, barely acknowledging me at all.

Just before I go out to kick the show off myself, he disappears entirely and it's not until after my set, my dancers rushing past me as I stand offstage while the stylist fixes my hair, that I let myself ask where he might be. I held off on asking because I didn't want my worry for him to derail my own performance. Julian can tank his career, but he's not taking mine down with him.

Bruce shakes his head, his jaw grinding back and forth on its hinges.

Our song is next and nobody can find Julian.

"Somebody should put a fucking bell around his neck," I say, accepting my stainless steel bottle full of water from Irelynn. "Maybe then you won't lose the headliner," I tell Bruce before taking a drink and handing it back to my assistant.

"He's not my—"

"Yes, he is your responsibility, Bruce. You should be looking out for him because without him, there are no shows. And without shows, you don't get paid." I've been on enough tours to know exactly how they work. Bruce won't even see a dime until *at least* halfway through this tour.

It's so fucking sad that even with money on the line, he still doesn't care. None of them do.

I rip my earpiece out, spinning around to ask, "Where the fuck is Julian?" My voice cracks on his name. He better not be dead.

"There. He's there." Irelynn points, and from the other side of the stage, Julian strolls out, going straight over to his mic stand. From the way he drags his feet to the way his glossed-over eyes skim the coliseum haphazardly, I know exactly where he's been—getting high.

I'm glad he's not dead…because I might just kill him myself.

Instead of greeting the fans, he opens with "Got anything to smoke?" and the crowd erupts into ear-splitting cheers. Dropping to sit at the edge of the stage, Julian reaches out and grabs a joint from someone in the front row, pausing to take a hit before blowing a cloud of white smoke above his head. He then proceeds to launch into an entire monologue about how much he appreciates the legalization of marijuana.

I rub my temples, trying to think of something to bring this back on track.

"Are there any chairs I can use?" I ask a passing roadie, and he pauses to consider it before scurrying off to see what he can find. A moment later he reappears with a fold-up chair and a shrug to his shoulders that says it's the best he could come up with.

Yeah, we're all compromising right now.

I have him run it out to the place marker I point out, then ask the stylist if any of my flats are close by.

Removing my sheer cover-up so I'm down to my studded push-up bra, I quickly change into the pair of knee-high flats she hands me. They're higher up my legs than I was hoping for, but they accentuate my booty shorts nicely, so I walk out with both my ass and attitude matching, and immediately start humming the opening notes of our song into my mic, effectively cutting off Julian's rambling speech.

At first, he doesn't react, then slowly shuffling to his feet, he turns to pin me with a glare. It's a glassy glare that does exactly nothing to intimidate me, and I crook a finger at him, sending a wink over to Axel already poised behind his drums. *Start the damn song.*

Unable to resist, Julian staggers toward me, and I grab the buckle on his belt as soon as he's within reach, leading him over to the chair.

With one strategic push, I get him into the plastic chair just as the beat kicks in, then I seduce the arena with my verse about needing someone who understands the assignment—get in, get *it* in, get out. Basically, what I was looking for with Victor last night, but that Julian ruined.

Our part comes and goes without Julian so much as lifting his microphone. His heavy gaze trails me everywhere I go, following my every move across the stage, so returning to him, I straddle his thighs, serenading him alone to try to rouse him.

While toking from the joint between his lips, the mic remains firmly in his right palm though, nowhere near ready for use.

Shit, shit, shit.

My wild eyes find Axel's, but he just gives a subtle shake of his head, keeping his drumsticks flying.

Arching backward, I press my own palm to the floor and do a slow backflip off Julian's lap, landing in a crouch in front of him. His eyes lift to mine, the mild curiosity I just saw in them spiking significantly.

With a coy smile, I start backing up, careful to maintain eye contact. Luckily, he stirs and leans forward, bending down on a knee to track my retreat as he stalks toward me.

That's it, little lamb. Follow me.

Still crawling in a slow game of cat and mouse, I bring my mic up between us, hoping he'll take the bait when it's time for our chorus, and with his forehead an inch from mine, he finally joins in, looking directly into my soul as we sing about the effort it takes to keep yourself detached from emotional connections.

The second we finish, he takes another hit and blows the smoke into my face knowing I'm sucking in lungfuls of air before it's my turn again. As much as I want to drive my palm into his nose, the crowd roars in the background, reminding me of our audience, so all I can do is inhale as little as possible, ignoring the sting in my lungs with a smile playing on my lips and a *fuck you* in my eyes.

We manage to get through the rest of the song together—it's sloppy, but we pull it off—then I practically sprint off the stage, completely forgoing a wave goodbye to the audience.

Unsurprisingly, Julian follows me, but I don't even bother turning around when I say, "Do that again and I'm walking."

Somehow he catches up to me, saying, "Do *that* again and you won't be walking anywhere for at least a week."

"Do what? Save your ass?"

He swings around in front of me, putting himself in my path, so I stop.

"The next time you climb on my lap, you won't be leaving it unfucked. I can guaran-fucking-tee you that."

A shot of adrenaline runs through me at his words. His *guarantee*.

"I remember a woman being on your lap last night and she walked away unfucked."

"Did she? You know that for a fact?"

The adrenaline is burned off with something much more potent.

"You're the one that made me go back inside. Wanted me to… What was it you said? To find someone that'll stroke my cock? Remember that, Collette? And with an entire hotel full of empty rooms waiting for me…"

"Can't say I'm all that surprised, but I am disappointed."

"Because I fucked someone else?"

"No." *Kind of.* "Because you took an order so *fucking easily*." His smug smiles drops. "Like a little lamb to the slaughter, you're happy to fall in line though, huh? Because at least then you have somebody else to blame for your demise." And he is banking on a demise. His comments last night said as much.

"Then tell me, Collette. What do you want me to do?"

What do I want him to do? I…don't know. What I do know, like the back of my fucking hand, is what we're supposed to be doing, which is putting on a show that at the very least is worth the price of admission, and at the most, has the potential to change lives.

"Stop being a puppet," I say like it's easy. I'm still under just as much pressure as he is, but as an indie artist without a record company telling me who to be and how to be her, mine comes from other sources.

"You're the fucking expert all of a sudden? How?"

I'm not. I'm not an expert at all. I'm just better at pretending to be. Julian's a bad actor, he couldn't act his way out of an open bag.

"For starters, you can go back out on that stage and prove to the fans you have what it takes to be up there." That, at least, is real advice stemming from a very real place. He has what I haven't been able to get ever since I walked away from Bodee—a record deal. Nobody would sign me after that, and even fourteen years later, they still won't. He's wasting an opportunity other people would kill to have.

I give his chest a push, saying, "Now."

"Fuck them. They can wait."

"No, they really can't. Those people paid money to see you, and if you don't get back out there, we're going to have to refund that money."

His bloodshot eyes flare. "That's what you really care about. The fucking money."

That's his takeaway from what I just said?

I don't even know what we're talking about anymore, and judging by Julian's response, he doesn't either.

"Doesn't matter." He shrugs. "I'm not going out there."

"Yes, you are. You have to."

"I can't."

"Why not?"

His lost eyes touch on mine before plummeting to the floor like a meteor. "Because I don't have anything to come back for."

The anguish in his gaze combined with the pure vulnerability in his voice guts me because I know exactly what he means. It's a feeling I know all too well. We all do at one point or another. The times when I can't bring Holter along with me, I leave my shows and return to empty hotel rooms filled with deafening silence. To go from thousands of people screaming your name, idolizing you, to just…nothing. And it's not just after shows, it's even worse after a tour wraps, each and every time. When a tour ends and all the adoration goes with it, you're left feeling sad and empty. Insecure, unfulfilled, neglected. *Not good enough.* It's another comedown, different from the one I described to Julian last night, yet similar in many ways. It can be fucking brutal. It's also incredibly hard to navigate in the beginning, especially alone. Craving that affirmation but getting none, sometimes it can lead to searching for it elsewhere. Avenues that are only temporary fixes, like drugs and alcohol—partying.

With Julian constantly surrounded with people, even when he's not performing, you'd think he'd never get the chance to feel lonely, but I'd be willing to bet lonely is all he ever feels. Because those people don't want him. They want *from* him. And he thinks I do, too. Still. I thought that by not taking from Julian, I was proving I didn't, but his pain runs deep. Nobody can pour from an empty cup. If I truly want to help him, I need to give.

"Hey," I say, lifting his jaw with my middle finger, then keeping it there when he meets my eyes. "How can I help? What do you need from me?"

The pulse against my fingertip is like a lightbulb sparking back to life after sitting dormant for too long.

"Do you know any of my other songs?"

"I can keep up."

"Let me show you my world."

My smirk matches his. "There's nothing I don't know about this world, little lamb."

"Then be my queen."

I pull my hand back a few inches.

He leans into my touch again, whispering, "Just for tonight."

I nod. "Okay. I'll go out there with you." Taking the roach from him, I drop it, then extinguish it with my boot's sole. "But only with *you.*"

"I'm not—"

"I know." I know he's not sober right now, but beneath the Julez façade, there's still a flicker of Julian—he wouldn't be talking to me like this if there wasn't—and that's enough. All I need is a flicker.

"Give me a minute to change, then I'll be out."

"You look perfect to me." I go to argue, and he adds, "Exactly how you are. I want you exactly how you are."

"Careful what you wish for," I tell him, shaking my head and turning around.

"The crop of all the other cream,
she actin' like a simple wish,
not knowing she's my number one dream."

"You're gonna get someone pregnant with lyrics like that."

He says something under his breath I can't make out, then we're back on stage…performing his rap songs…together.

"Mom, I didn't know you could rap," Holter teases as soon as I enter my dressing room, and I laugh, barely feeling my cheeks from the last hour and a half. I don't think I stopped smiling once. Julian really knows how to show out when he tries, and he's so damn charming doing it, too.

Not changing my shoes for an entire ninety minutes bit me in the ass though, and it takes the help of Holter, Mary, and Irelynn to get my boots off.

I'm just coming out of the attached bathroom, tying the drawstring of a pair of baggy sweatpants when they bring up what everyone wants for dinner.

"Are we going out or staying in? Because I can't wear this out." I don't even specify what "this" is. They know.

"Well…" Holter says, studying his sneakers.

"Well, what?" It seems pretty simple to me, either we're eating at a restaurant or we're getting takeout.

"There's this…"

"There's this what?" I look from Holter to Mary. "What's he trying to tell me without actually telling me?"

"You better make it quick like a Band-Aid," she says to Holter.

"It's the text messages, isn't it?"

Holter groans.

"I knew it. There's a girl."

"There's a girl," Mary confirms, nodding, and I sink down on to the loveseat, my eyes welling up with tears.

"I told you she'd overreact," he says to Mary like I'm not even here.

All I can do is sniffle, asking, "What's her name?"

"I'm not telling you."

"Why not?"

"Because you'll look her up and troll her on every platform."

"So? That's my right as your mother."

"That's not a thing, Mom."

"Yes, it is. It's my thing."

Holter groans again. "You're *so* embarrassing."

"I am not," I mumble from behind a tissue after blowing my nose.

A knock at the door barely even registers until Irelynn goes over to crack it the slightest bit.

I knew this day was coming; I just didn't expect it for another two or three…decades. I'm not ready for my little boy to date.

"She's, um, indisposed at the moment," Irelynn says to whoever's at the door. "Can I give her a message for you?"

"Indisposed? The fuck?"

Julian.

"My son hates me," I cry, flopping on to my back, vaguely aware of Julian squeezing past my assistant to come inside the dressing room as well.

"Mom, stop."

"Quick like a Band-Aid," Mary mutters.

"I tried!" Holter half-shouts, half-laughs before telling me, "I don't hate you."

"But you think I'm embarrassing?"

"On social media, yeah."

"How?"

"You post a lot of… You're not always wearing a lot of clothes in your posts."

"Those are the only part of social media I like," Julian murmurs from the opposite wall as he leans against it, taking in the room with clearer eyes than he's had all night.

"Gross. That's my mom," Holter says, making him chuckle.

"All right, can we stop with the body shaming now?" I give my son a disappointed look with the best mom-eyes I can muster from my reclined position. This body carried him for nine months, then birthed him. He usually never says stuff like this.

"I know. I'm sorry. It's not even you, it's…"

"It's what? Please just tell me," I say before shifting my attention to Mary, asking her, "Do you know what's he talking about?"

"The fight at the mall," Mary says, deliberately dipping her head at me.

"The one about the shoes?" He ran into a guy he knows from school at the mall and supposedly Holter spilled his drink on him, ruining the guy's shoes. It didn't sound like something Holter would ever do intentionally, so when I went to pick my son up from mall security, I was bracing myself for the worst. Because he was the one that got the crap kicked out of him, right? Except he wasn't. Aside from a set of swollen knuckles, Holter didn't have a single scratch on him. The other kid wasn't there, so I don't know what he looked like, only what Holter told me, which now I'm questioning was even the truth. *What is the truth?*

Nobody speaks until Irelynn of all people glances at Holter, telling me, "Some of the boys at Holter's school have…expressed interest in your more revealing posts."

"Expressed interest? What does that mean? They comment on them?"

"That and they send you DMs about them."

Occasionally, I'll check some of my posts' comments myself so I can personally respond to fans, but I leave my DMs for Irelynn to filter through in case there's something important that requires attention, otherwise I never, ever check those. Most comments are pretty draining to read as well, but DMs are usually where people shed their inhibitions entirely, and some things you just can't unread. Or see, because as revealing as my posts may be, my DMs are full of X-rated photos that'd get the senders banned if they tried posting them publicly.

"Okay, but what does that have to do with you?"

Holter's wounded eyes reach mine.

"The fight?" I ask quietly, and he nods. That's really what the fight was about, the boy said something to Holter about my posts.

"I didn't want…"

He didn't want to give me one more thing to feel guilty about. None of my team did, that's why they all kept it from me.

If mom-guilt was lethal, I'd be dead where I lay. Even knowing it's not, I'm still surprised the all-consuming guilt I feel on a daily basis hasn't killed me fifteen thousand times over already because it *hurts*, worse than any other pain I've ever endured.

"Block them all. Block them everywhere. And at the freshman meet and greet, you better point out the boys, Holter, so I can talk to their parents."

That is my right as his mother. He shouldn't be the one to protect me; I should be protecting him.

"What if you can't make it?" His voice comes out small, intentionally small.

I squeeze my eyes shut, swallowing as much of the guilt as I can to promise him, "I will."

Julian speaks up and forces a laugh to say, "Your mom's gonna kick some ass."

Automatically, Mary chastises him, saying, "Watch your language," to which Julian responds with, "Shit, sorry."

I'm not going to kick any ass. I'm just going to hold some brats responsible for their actions. Anybody can be brave behind a screen. I want to see how bold they are when they get called out in front of their parents.

Holter mutters, "It's okay. I've heard it before."

I open my eyes to study him and then Julian, who's bobbing his head, the hands at his sides alternating between twisting his many rings and clenching and unclenching.

"So, was that it? Is that all yinz were talking about before I came in? Or was there something else that had your mom all *indisposed?*"

"Yinz?" Holter questions.

"Yeah, yinz." Julian looks around like it should be obvious before telling us, "Man, yinz need some culture. It's the Pittsburgh way of saying y'all, or you guys."

"Oh, please. You don't even know what indisposed means."

He thins his eyes at me. "I know what it means."

I laugh, shaking my head against the loveseat's upholstery. He doesn't know.

"Anyway, since you asked, what has me all 'indisposed' is the fact that my only child is too embarrassed to introduce me to his *girlfriend.*" Holter makes a sound in the back of his throat. "And still has the audacity to want to take her on a *date.*" Now my throat's making a weird sound. "Probably with my money, and with my name on the reservation."

"She's not my girlfriend."

"Yet," Irelynn adds unhelpfully.

"Told you that word fucking sucks," Julian says to me.

"Language," Mary tsks, this time without even looking up from her e-reader.

"Fuck," Julian blurts, making all of us laugh.

"What word?" I ask him once everyone's quiet again, the mood rapidly improving.

"Date."

I roll my eyes, heaving myself up to sitting, my upper half swaying from the movement even when I'm stationary.

Am I stationary?

"What's wrong?" I hear Julian ask, but it takes me a few blinks to make both his bodies blend back into one.

"Um, nothing?" Right? I check around me, making sure I'm actually upright and everyone that was here a second ago is still here. It feels like I blacked out but didn't lose any time.

"Then what just happened?"

"I don't know. I must've got light-headed or something."

For the first time since barging in here, Julian frowns, pulling out his phone without taking his eyes from mine.

"When's the last time you ate?"

"When's the last time *you* ate?" I counter, then immediately follow up with a much softer, "I think I'm just worn out from the show." *I did perform twice as long tonight.*

Tearing my gaze away from Julian's merciless stare, I focus on Holter, asking, "How is that supposed to work? You want to take this girl out on a date, but I can't meet her. You're thirteen years old, Holter."

"Where you trying to go?" Julian asks my son.

"Alma."

"The Cuban one across town? I got some people over by there right now."

"You didn't rent another car, did you?" I know the McLaren was returned already. I was the one clutching the key this morning when the dealership came to collect it. "Because you can't drive," I say, but Julian doesn't acknowledge me, only smirks.

Thankfully he's much more coherent now, but that doesn't mean I want him driving, or encouraging my son to date. Why *is* he here?

"Was there something I can help you with?" I ask point-blank, and Julian laughs.

"I came to thank you." Meeting my eyes over his phone, his tone turns serious as he adds, "I thought I'd make it up to you."

"You don't owe me anything."

He looks down at his screen again. "At least let me take you to dinner."

I tilt my head, weighing my options.

"At Alma?"

Engrossed in his phone, Julian gives a single nod.

"Can we sit at the same table?" Not that I want to do a double date with my own son and Julian of all people, but I don't see any way around it.

"Please no," Holter begs.

I utter words I never thought I'd say, "You need a chaperone," then wince at how old-fashioned I sound. It's true though. I know better than anyone what can happen to unaccompanied teens in this world where money often talks loud enough to drown out objections.

"Done," Julian says suddenly, pocketing his phone.

"What's done?"

"All of it. The reservations. Our ride. His…chaperone. It's all taken care of. We leave in twenty." He points at Holter. "Is that what you're wearing or do you wanna borrow something of mine?"

Now I'm the one begging with, "Please no."

Chuckles around the room pluck at my already stretched too-thin nerves like a ten-year-old learning to play the violin.

"Can I speak to you outside?" I ask Julian, already off the loveseat and heading for the door.

Chapter 12

Julian

I pause next to Irelynn real quick, quietly telling her to forward me all those DMs those little shits sent Collette before she blocks them, then as soon as I'm near the door, Collette yanks my ass the rest of the way through the doorway, slamming it shut behind us.

"What do you mean it's all taken care of?"

A grin splits my face so fast. Goddamn. I haven't felt this high in a long-ass time and I get high every fucking day. I didn't think it could get much better than performing alongside Collette but spending time with her at her most vulnerable…fuck, it's a *close* second.

Guessing she's really only worried about the chaperone part, I say, "Don't worry. Your boy will be fine. I promise Bare won't leave his side."

"Your bodyguard? How is that less embarrassing than me?" Her hands flail at her sides while I hold back a laugh. Not even *The* Collette is immune to embarrassing her teenager.

Since meeting Collette, she's had her confidence in place like an iron shield, but just now, she let some of what's behind it show, proving she's just like the rest of us—human. Her son's the crack in her armor, probably the only one she's got.

"I can't believe this is happening." She sighs, propping her shoulder against the wall.

My eyes immediately fall down the rest of her, trying to judge if she's doing it because she really is tired or if she's wobbly. I don't care what she says, I know what I saw, and she was about to pass out in there.

Her eyes are a silverish green right now as she glances up at me, saying, "He's only thirteen. Were you going on dates at thirteen?"

Umm. "Not exactly."

"See?"

But that doesn't mean I didn't want to. I would've gone on dates, if I could. I just didn't have the money to. Plus, I had a lot of other shit going on during that time in my life. I'm not telling that sob story to Collette though. Instead, I say, "Don't take it personal. That's what we do. We push away from our moms to make room for our girls."

"Is that what you did?"

"Yeah," I lie through the pain in my throat, chest, and stomach. The truth is I never even got the chance to push my mom away. She was already gone before I made it to my teens.

"What are we going to do about paparazzi?"

"Ignore them?" That's what I usually do. Unless I'm forced not to. She scowls at me.

It was worth a shot.

"My name's on the reservations, so I'll go in the front while Bare takes you and Holter in through the back. That cool?" If anyone can make a scene, it's me.

Nodding absently, her bottom lip trembles, and with no makeup on and her short blonde hair on full display, she looks like a completely different person than the one I was just onstage with. Out there, she was a storm, affecting everything in her path. Now, she's the aftermath. A mortal mess. The most perfect one I've ever laid eyes on.

Without thinking it through, I pull her to me for a hug, and because I must be the luckiest motherfucker on the planet today, she actually lets me, relaxing her body against mine. I drop my chin to the top of her head, inhaling until my lungs sting.

Hugs, man…who fucking knew?

My text alert breaks the silence, the moment, and my fucking patience all at once.

"Shit. I need to get ready," Collette says, pushing away from me.

Fucking phone. If I ever get the chance to hug her again, I'm smashing my phone first, swear to God.

"Ayo?"

Collette freezes, her gaze locked on her hand holding the doorknob.

"Don't do too much."

"Yeah, I heard you. We leave in twenty."

"I don't give a shit about the time, Collette. I just…I want you exactly the way you are," I repeat, meaning it as much as I did the first time.

"You're high. You don't know what you're saying."

She thinks I'm still high from earlier. She has no idea my high right now has nothing to do with the drugs I took before the show and everything to do with her.

"Don't be sneaking any of that baby food shit in your purse either," I tell her. "You're fucking eatin' tonight."

She shakes her head, but I catch a hint of a grin before she escapes back into her dressing room.

I don't leave right away, choosing to stay and listen to the sounds coming from the other side of the door, committing it to memory, all of it, every second, even our performance tonight, from Collette straddling me in that rickety-ass chair to right now, hearing her and her family joke with each other again.

> Duckin' and dodgin' ain't enough to curb this greed,
> plain as day, it's straight taking over me.
> Still carrying the stench from growing up poor,
> now I'm paying to slip right past locked doors.
> Best watch out, Collette,
> soon I'll be coming for yours.

I should probably take her name out.

Or not. She said it herself, I'm as subtle as a bomb.

It's several minutes later when Bare finds me still standing here, chewing on my thumb.

"Ready, boss man?"

I drop my hand, sliding my All Souls' Day ring back in place, and admit, "Probably not." But I'll be damned if I'm gonna let that stop me.

Like a fucking bomb.

"Do you recognize her?"

I slide my eyes to Collette. "Girl's thirteen years old. Why the fuck would I know her?"

Seated on a tall stool at the bar, she's got her phone out with the camera open and zoomed in from across the restaurant, trying to get a clear shot of Holter's date.

"No, I mean does she look like anyone familiar?"

Holter told us on the way over his girl's parents are actors. He wouldn't tell us which ones specifically, just that they were pretty famous.

Standing next to her, I prop an arm on the back of her barstool and glance at the screen again.

"All I see is a dark pixelated mess, so unless one of her parents is a QR code, I got nothing."

Groaning, Collette finally gives up, putting her phone down for the first time since we met up in the attached bar. I told her nobody would bother the teens and I stand by that. Bare's at the table literally right next to theirs.

Besides, I got my hands full with worrying about Collette and keeping people away from her. People, gazes, everything. She's wearing a long-sleeve top with a back that dips down to the top of her ass and I know I'm not the only motherfucker in here to notice.

Still sneaking glances at Holter while pretending to look over her menu, she murmurs, "Get your hand off me." It's nothing like last night when she said the same thing though. That was…

Parts of last night I wish I could forget entirely, but the rest will haunt me forever, in the best and worst ways. I don't know what I was thinking taking her to the club like that. As soon as the word date came out of Collette's mouth, I lost all rational thought. After that I wasn't thinking at all; I was just reacting. Maybe even overreacting.

Maybe.

Actually no, I was reacting exactly enough. Collette was jealous, too, and not just of me like she was trying to make herself believe. That's the kind of bullshit I'm fluent in, so I recognized the lie before she could even finish spouting it. Why she lied though, I don't know. Something to do with her hang-up about celebrities and not wanting anything to do with them. Not gonna lie, they do kinda suck. All high and mighty and shit. A lot of big-dick energy in an industry full of small-ass dicks.

My energy matches my cock though, which Collette's seen with her own eyes, so I don't know why she keeps grouping me with all the other celeb jag-offs.

"Nah, I don't think so," I say in response to her suggestion. Her smooth, toned back is like a fucking magnet to my metal-covered fingers. There's no way she's wearing a bra. None. And her ass crack peeking out…I could do a lot to that ass crack. I *want* to do a lot to that ass crack, like dip my finger down between—

"Well, think again, because although I am in need of one of my slits being fingered, it's not that one."

"Jesus," I practically choke, my fingertips freezing on the last letter of her spine tattoo, *just* above her ass. "You can't say shit like that to me."

"I just did."

She side-eyes me, her cocky-ass smirk pulling sideways, too. God, she's a sadist.

Lowering my head until my mouth touches her ear, I say, "I'll finger whichever slit you want me to. Just give me permission."

Her ear warms against my lips and I rub the underside of my bottom lip back and forth, letting my dolphin piercings tease the shell.

"Back. Off." Her voice is breathy, just like I hoped it'd be. "It doesn't look good."

"It looks good from where I'm standing," I rasp, my cock swelling as I spread my feet farther apart.

"Because you're standing too close to me," she snaps, jerking her head away a few inches. "Which probably doesn't look good either. You should—"

"I ain't fucking moving. I'll be glued to your side 'til we leave this fucking place," I promise her, removing my hand from her back, but staying right the fuck where I am, standing half over her so anyone that bothers looking her way will get an eyeful of me, too.

"Why Collette?" I ask, changing the subject.

"Why what?"

"Why'd you get your name tattooed down your spine?"

"It's a reminder," she says without looking up from the menu in her hold. "The only person I can depend on having my back…is me."

Damn. That's depressing. And familiar as all fuck.

"What about Bodee? Does he have your back?"

Her eyes meet mine, but she doesn't bother answering, which is pretty fucking telling if you ask me.

"Did he ever?" I ask, only getting more silence.

Swear to fuck I couldn't hate that guy more.

She returns her attention to the menu, but I pluck it out of her hands, stacking it with mine before dropping them both behind the bar.

"I was reading that." Her eyes hold so much challenge all I can do is stare back, wishing I could kiss that smart mouth of hers.

The bartender comes over, keeping me from pressing my luck for what would most likely be my last time. Collette would kill me for pulling something like that publicly.

But privately…

Either way, I'd meet my maker with a smile on my face and the taste of Collette on my tongue 'cause if I'm tempting fate one final time, I'm going *all* in.

"Lemme get a vodka soda and she'll have a jalapeño mojito." I ignore Collette's scoff, telling him, "We'll share the papas rellenas and send over two virgin whatever-the-fuck kids drink these days to that table." I point out Holter and his *date*. "Put theirs and the table to their right on my tab, too."

"Yes, sir."

"Umm, no. Put them both on *my* tab."

I give Collette a long look, then meet the bartender's eye, giving him a small headshake.

After he leaves to put in our order, Collette says, "Since we're sharing, I'll let you pay for my meal, but—"

"That wasn't our meal. That was just the appetizer."

She returns my stare, telling me, "You're such a paradox."

"The word you're going for is enigma, Poohbear. I use the thesaurus app more than any other app on my phone. That and the dictionary app." I wink at her, memorizing the look of her jaw unhinged. It's okay. Once she gets some ropa vieja in her, she won't be using any words at all, just moans of appreciation.

Jesus fuck, my cock's 'bout to punch a hole through my jeans.

"And yet you didn't know what indisposed meant."

"You didn't know what slippy meant."

"Slippy's not a word!"

"That's it. I'm taking you to Pittsburgh, over to the Souside so we can get some eats, then Imma put your ass in a buggy, and buy us some chipped ham for hoagies. I'll get you a pop from Sheetz."

She puts a hand up, stopping me in my tracks. I could go all night.

"Okay… Souside sounds like Southside, but you dropped off a few letters like you did with slippy." I nod, making her smile widen. "Chipped ham is…sliced ham?"

"Close. It's shaved smaller, like in pieces."

"Right. For hoagies?"

"Yeah."

"Not subs?"

"No, not fucking subs. Hoagies. You can also get jumbo on them instead of ham."

"I don't think I want to know what that is, it doesn't sound very appetizing. Sheetz I've actually been to myself. It's a convenience store chain, but I didn't think it was exclusive to Pittsburgh."

"It's not, but we claim it as ours."

Thankfully she doesn't even bring up the word pop, otherwise I'd need to have a full-on debate here and now with her because it is called pop, not soda, and never, ever soda-pop. The fuck.

"What's a buggy?"

"A shopping cart."

"Why would you put me in a shopping cart?"

"So you don't have to walk while we're food shopping."

She throws her head back on the kind of laugh I'd record if it wasn't so fucking loud in here so I could put it on one of my tracks. It's purer than uncut cocaine. Probably even more potent, too, because instead of feeling numb like I normally do after doing coke, I feel all of my body, every single inch of it, down to the tiny hairs on my wrists standing straight up.

"You should come with your own dictionary. I seriously don't know what the hell you're talking about right now."

I look her face over, then lower my voice to say, "But I like telling you myself."

I'd take Collette to my hometown in a heartbeat. I'd show her everything, teach her all about the place I grew up and the reason why I talk the way I do. I'd introduce her to…*me*.

"Speaking of definitions, now that you know about my nickname for you—"

I flinch back from the reminder. I thought I wanted to know, but I didn't. Not really. I could've gone my entire life without learning my nickname's origin story. I was just starting to like her calling me little lamb, too.

Shit, I still do. She's the sadist, while I'm a motherfucking masochist through and through. Nobody can hurt me like me, but I'd let Collette try her best.

"—will you tell me why you call me Poohbear?"

"Probably." Just not right now.

Our drinks are dropped off and I freeze with mine almost to my mouth to watch Collette's reaction to hers. She takes a sip and hums, then sets it down. A second later, she picks it back up to take another drink, this one bigger. Grinning to myself, I drain half my own glass. *She likes it.* Of course she likes the combination of sweet and spice. Woman's got both in fucking spades.

"So…about tonight."

"Tonight was a shit-show. You can't do that again."

"Do what? We had fun together." Better than fun. It was fucking amazing performing with Collette. Before her, I didn't think that was even possible—legitimately enjoying this gig.

"Did you forget the part where you sabotaged our song?"

Not exactly. I just can't remember every second of it. I do remember Collette though. I blinked and she was there, right fucking there, sitting on my lap…until she wasn't and all I wanted was her body on mine again. I would've crawled through flames to get her back, too. And the confession that followed, the one about not having anything to come back to, felt like I had. I've never said that shit out loud before. I've thought it plenty, and I've written hundreds of lyrics about feeling that way, but I've never shared anything that honest before, not with anyone.

"I'm sorry," I tell her because I am. Not to anyone except Collette because I know how much she puts into this whole thing.

"Wow. Was that so hard?"

I lean into her again, my nose pressed to the hairline of her fiery-red wig as I inhale loudly.

"Is that…sarcasm I'm smelling?"

Her body shakes from a laugh. "You think you got all my scents pinpointed now?"

"A couple," I joke back. Her sarcasm might not have a smell, but her arousal sure the fuck does and *that* scent I could pick out in a crowd.

Not putting up with me one bit, she shoves my ass away to take another pull off her mojito.

"All right, Poohbear," I say, coming right back. "Let me have it. What else do I owe you an apology for?"

"There's a list."

There usually is.

"What's at the top?"

"Hmm. Maybe calling me a has-been."

Maybe? I definitely owe her an apology for that.

The next pass the bartender makes by us, I ask if there's a PA system I can use to play my new single to the whole restaurant for its world debut.

"You don't have a new single. What are you doing?"

I ignore Collette, taking the podium-looking mic from the bartender, then climb on the stool I wasn't planning on using tonight to say, "Ayo! If I could interrupt everybody's meals for just a minute. I'm Julez." I wait for the round of applause to die down before adding, "And I'm in town for my Family Julez Tour, where I'm lucky enough to get to perform with one of the best singers on this motherfucking planet."

I reach my hand down to her, helping her off the barstool while shout-ing, "*The* Collette!"

Collette stands, waving to both the bar and dining area, and the applause she gets in return puts the applause I just got to shame.

"Anyway, I said something stupid to her, so I was hoping yinz could help me out with my apology tonight 'cause a small one ain't gonna cover it." I instruct everybody to yell out the word sorry on the count of three before perching down on two so I can look Collette in the eye. Then on three, with the orchestrated chorus of sorries serving as our back-drop, I tell her, "I'm sorry." The truth is I was nervous to meet Collette. I was scared, fucking terrified, she'd take one look around and decide my tour wasn't worth her time. That *I* wasn't worth her time. For days leading up to her arrival it was all I could think of, so I got obliterated to the point that I couldn't think about anything.

I don't know why Collette didn't quit on the spot, especially after the way I treated her. She could've. Probably should've. But I'm grate-ful—so fucking grateful—she didn't.

"Do you accept?" I ask, my shaky voice echoing through the shit-ty-ass built-ins, making it sound even shakier.

With a smirk just for me, she cups her mouth to yell, "Yes!" in the air, reminding me of those over-the-top public proposals in movies.

The cheers and whistles do nothing to block out my pounding heart as I jump off the chair, waving a hand above my head in a silent thank you to everyone for their help.

Camera flashes threaten to blind us as we get Collette situated on her stool again, and when I hand the mic back to the bartender, he tries to give me a condescending look that I could give two shits about. His vodka soda's weak, too, so fuck him all around. I've gargled mouthwash with more alcohol than this shit.

If I trusted my voice, I'd tell him as much.

"Where are your friends, by the way? Didn't you say they were nearby?"

"And?" I ask, leaning an elbow on the bar so I'm closer to her. I bet with her red hair and my blue tips, we look like fire and ice in the pic-tures everyone's taking right now. I kind of wish I had a copy to keep. I've been needing a new tattoo…

I can get some off one of my socials later, easy. I just gotta get my newest passwords from Slade. I'll be tagged in photos and videos of myself at least two hundred times before the end of the night 'cause, you know, I fucking love watching other people record me without my permission. Nothing creepy or invasive about it.

"And would you prefer to be with them—"

"No," I say before she can even finish. Like it's even a question.

Collette's quiet for a while, then asks, "You know what my favorite part of performing with you is?"

"The free contact high?"

Still not taking my shit, she says, "Your charm." *Charm, huh?* "You can be so fucking charming when you want to be. You could steal so many hearts if you bothered to try. You steal hearts without even trying."

I think she's gonna say more, but she just picks up her drink with both hands, frowning at the clear liquid with green bits floating around.

Stealing hearts. Stealing hearts.

I snag the napkin that was under her mojito, flipping it over to scribble out the lyrics before I forget them.

All these hearts I'm said to be stealin',
keep lining my pockets with the deals I'm signin' and sealin'.
Never wanna let that ink run dry
just like the tears they pretendin' to cry.
One by one, they weighin' me down,
not gonna stop 'til I'm good and drownin'.

The sweat ring from the other side seeps through, making some of the words bleed, but I fold it in half anyway, sticking the napkin in my pocket along with the marker I always keep on hand.

"Can I see what you wrote?"

I chuckle, downing the rest of my watered-down soda. "Probably."

Collette stares at me like we aren't both trying like hell to ignore the phones pointed in our direction. The public apology backfired because now everyone, even the dishwashers, know we're here. I should've filled her bus with roses or something. *Does she even like roses?* Peonies. I should've filled her bus with peonies. Roses are too basic.

Slamming the glass down on the bar, I take her hand and help her to standing again. "Let's get out of here."

"What do you mean? Holter's here."

"We're not leaving. I just need some air."

"What about our food?"

"We'll be back in a minute. I need to talk to you without all this."

She arches an eyebrow. "Just talk?"

"Unless?" I arch one right back.

"I'm kidding," I tell her, placing my hand on her lower back to nudge her forward. I'm mostly kidding. My plan is to talk to her, but if she has other ideas, who the hell am I to turn the woman down?

As I steer her over to the emergency exit, she strains to catch a glimpse of Holter up until the very last second, but she pushes through the door without hesitation, finally turning a questioning look over her shoulder once we're inside the stairwell.

I lift one finger, pointing above us.

"You didn't say anything about stairs. My feet were already killing me before I squeezed them into six-inch heels."

"Then why'd you even wear six-inch heels?"

Yeah, okay, that's a dumb question. Collette doesn't do dressed down very well. I mean, she does—she really, really does—but she chooses not to.

Bending down, I scoop her up with one arm behind her exposed back and the other under her knees.

"It's like," she counts, "four flights of stairs."

"Then maybe you should stop moving."

She's wiggling like a worm on the sidewalk after a rainstorm and I have to readjust my hold every three goddamn stairs just so I don't drop her. I'm usually strong, but damn, help a guy out.

We reach the top level and I put her on her feet, keeping a hand on her back so she's still in my reach.

"So much for you getting some air," she says, looking around us. "There's not even roof access up here."

Honestly, I didn't know that until now, but I'm not about to give myself up. This is enough air, so instead, I say, "I wanted to be alone with you for a minute." Which is true. Even if someone follows us in here, we'll be gone by the time they reach the second floor. No pictures, no story.

I can be myself and Collette can…relax. I want to know her smiles are smiles I put there, not ones forced because she knows we're being recorded.

"You know what I like best about performing with you?"

Collette lowers herself on to a stair, saying, "If you had to carry me four flights of stairs just to tell me, I probably don't want to know."

"Your ass."

One of her six-inch heels kicks out so fast I have to jump back to avoid being pierced by it.

I guess relaxing is out.

"I'm just fucking with you." I take a seat next to her, leaning back to put an arm behind her. "I mean, it's great, don't get me wrong, especially when it's floating on my cock."

Her gaze shifts to my crotch and I have to fight the urge to cover myself with both hands. She wouldn't…*would she?*

"Is there a point in the near future? Or am I going to die in this deserted stairwell waiting for you to—"

"It's your smile. Everything you do out there, you smile through it like you're having the best time of your life. It's so fucking contagious." It's so fucking addicting. Maybe too addicting because I'm already hooked and we've only done three shows together.

The smile on her face stretches wider as she turns to face me, and I know without a shadow of a doubt, that baby's real.

"I thought I made weird faces when I'm singing, at least in the pictures I've seen."

"Nah. Not weird." Not to me. "I want us to do tonight every night."

Her smile dips.

"The show. I want you to stay after your set's done and help me with mine. Every night."

"You don't understand. I couldn't even if I wanted to. My vocal coach will probably kill me for tonight alone. I can't sing that much in a night without my voice rebelling on me. I've had my voice go out from overuse before."

I thought singers losing their voice was an urban legend. I've never had any issues and I smoke like a chimney on a cold, winter night.

"It's not worth risking it," she says, then winces. "I'm sorry, I didn't mean like that. I just…it's a lot, Julian."

I know. I fucking *know*. But she asked what I needed from her, and this is it—her. I never want to perform again without Collette by my side. It's…not the same.

"You don't have to sing."

"If you're looking for a backup dancer, I have four and any one of them would jump to add your name to their résumé."

"I've seen 'em. They're good. I don't want them though."

"I can get you some other names," she says, trying to shut the conversation down by not meeting my eye anymore.

I scoot my ass to the edge, turned toward her, and place a hand on her back as I cage her in, hoping she'll listen to me even if she's not willing to look at me.

"I don't want other names. I just want to see your smile while I'm performing my set. I don't care what you do. You can dance, sit your ass in a chair, or even mime for fuck's sake. Just…be with me. Out there."

Through the fingertips tracing over her ribs, I feel her breath heave inside her lungs even though she stays tight-lipped.

It's not a no. It's not a fucking no.

Chapter 13

Collette

We play in Colorado, Utah, and Arizona, and for each show, I remain onstage almost the entire time. Instead of pushing my voice past its very clear, very thin lines, I don't sing once my set's done. I try not to even yell. I do keep Julian company though by either engaging with the crowd or I play around with him in a couple little choreographed pieces I put together. They're nothing like the time I straddled him, but still flirty and fun, enough to get the fans' tongues wagging while *mostly* keeping Julian's hands to himself—as impossible as that is. He's been diligent about being on time for everything, and even though he pretty much always smokes throughout his performances, he's been mindful not to do it in my face again.

They added a show in Los Angeles for tonight, and the closer we get to showtime, the more anxious I feel about performing in California again. Julian's been a completely different person since our first few days together. Even during the long stretches on the road over the past week, he's been hopping on my bus instead of his own. Along with Holter and some of my other team members, I get him to play cards or watch movies or have blindfolded drawing competitions that I swear Julian cheats at because his are always so good.

I kind of like it, the routine we've established. There's a synergy between us finally that I didn't think was possible when I first joined The Family Julez Tour.

But now, I'm nervous. I'm nervous he'll revert back into the person he was the last time we were in this state because that person, I don't like at all.

"What are you doing after appearances today?" Julian asks around a bite of Jell-O—from the sound of it.

They added the LA show last minute, then were surprised it didn't sell out immediately, so now Julian and I have to go out and do a bunch of publicity to try to sell more tickets. We have a couple radio shows, a ribbon-cutting at a grand opening for a record store, and they want us to swing by a fashion show some reality star is putting on. We don't have to sit for it luckily, just take pictures on the step-and-repeat outside.

I lift my head from the portable massage table, smiling at Julian's half-empty cup of his beloved strawberry Jell-O as he bites another spoonful into his mouth.

"I have a thing."

"What thing?" The suspicion in his voice fills the bus with an additional tension I really don't need right now.

"I'm going to the children's hospital."

"How long will you be?"

"Why? Are you gonna miss me?" I tease as I lower my head to the headrest.

"Yes."

I push my face down a little deeper to hide the blush now burning my skin. He has to be lying. There's no possible way he could miss me. He'd have to be away from me to actually miss me and we've been together almost nonstop lately. Except at night. I don't let him stay on my bus overnight and he doesn't ask to.

"You could come with me," I say muffled.

"That might just feed the rumor mill even more," Irelynn says. "Jollette was the number one trending hashtag for like twenty-four hours after your dinner together at Alma."

Our little private escape to the stairwell to talk didn't help either. It looked like we snuck in there to fuck. We didn't, but that doesn't matter. The truth rarely does anymore. Photos show projections now-adays, not facts.

"Jollette," Julian sneers. "Is it too much to ask that we get a decent couple name like Culian?"

"Good luck. The simps have spoken."

"You're thinking of stans. They stan us."

With my head cranked to the side, I give Irelynn a look, asking her, "Would you please tell him they're called simps?"

"You're both wrong. They *ship* your relation*ship*."

"Alleged relationship," I say, just to be clear, because Julian and I are not a couple. Far, far from it. If anything, we're co-workers.

Who spend most of their off-time together.

But not their off-time during nocturnal hours.

Except sometimes after a performance when we all go out to eat together.

Or when we get lost in conversation and next thing I know it's after midnight and I have to say a very awkward goodnight to Julian because although he doesn't ask to stay the night, he doesn't not ask either.

I don't even know what not asking is.

"Alleged," I repeat. "That's all they ever are—alleged. Any man I'm photographed with gets their name blended with mine for at least a week. People will lose interest in Jollette when they realize there's noth-ing between us, then there'll be another made-up couple name trending in no time." And on and on it goes.

I glance at Julian again, seeing him studying his Jell-O cup with furrowed brows.

Is he getting it yet? Why I avoid dating men in the public eye. And why I sneak around so much. Julian lives his life so…unfiltered. He has no idea what happens when the tide he's been riding turns, because not everyone is contractually obligated to Julian, and it *will* turn. Sooner or later, it always does.

"Well, the offer still stands, if you want to join me," I tell him, re-turning the conversation to the hospital instead of a relationship that's not even real and will never be real.

"What do you do? Autograph hats?"

"Hats?"

"Yeah. Aren't the kids missing their hair?"

I consider his question. Though innocent, it's also incredibly ignorant.

"Some of them have lost their hair due to chemo, but not all the kids staying there are being treated for cancer."

"Why are they there then?"

"How about you see for yourself?" Experience is life's greatest teacher.

"I don't know. Kids freak me out," he says, getting up to throw his Jell-O cup away. My bus's fridge is now stocked with it, too, because Julian has to have at least one cup a day.

"You've been doing fine with Holter."

Holter, busy on a FaceTime call, tips a hand side to side from his bed.

"Meh? That's all I get? I gamed with this kid for five straight hours yesterday and I get a *meh?*"

Julian looks genuinely offended and I snatch a pillow off the couch to toss at him, laughing when he catches it to immediately throw down the hall into Holter's bedroom.

"He's just showing off," Mary says on her way to the back to close Holter's door so he can talk to the girl he took to dinner without too much interruption. He still maintains she's not his girlfriend, but…they talk every minute that I don't keep him busy. Probably even then, too. He's never not on his phone now.

Suddenly, Julian shoots over to the massage table, saying, "Hey, man. Do you need to be up in her shit like that?"

The travel masseur rubbing my upper thigh stops what he's doing to look at Julian, and the two of them seem to have some sort of silent stare-off above my head.

"Irelynn, can you ask Antonio to pull over? Julian needs to take a walk." *Back on to his bus.*

"If I take a walk, I'm taking this motherfucker with. He shouldn't be touching you like that."

I roll my eyes. "Have you ever had a massage?"

Thankfully, the masseur returns his attention to my leg, kneading a particularly sore spot on my inner thigh. It's been tight the last three days and no amount of stretching has helped.

"Are you offering?"

"No," I half-moan.

"I swear those fingers…" Julian's voice is coiled tight like a snake preparing to strike, but I rise onto my elbows, covering my bare breasts with a forearm before he can ruin my massage with a fight. Would he actually fight the masseur? Over a simple massage?

I don't want to find out.

"See the sheet?" I ask, feeling like a schoolgirl defending my skirt length to the principal all over again. "He doesn't go above the sheet."

"It's hiked up to your ass cheek!" Julian argues, and I flop back down, sighing, "No, it's not." It's just below my ass cheek.

"Jeez. Haven't you ever heard of a happy ending?" one of my backup dancers teases, making me laugh into the headrest, my shoulders bouncing.

The sheet covering my back gets yanked down until it stops mid-thigh instead, then I hear Julian threaten, "Don't touch the fucking sheet."

He's unbelievable. Not that I was actually planning on getting a happy ending—in front of nine other people no less—but I'd bet my life Julian himself has gotten his own happy endings before.

"You know what? Never mind. You're no longer invited to go to the children's hospital with me."

His chuckle is deep, but not authentic in any way.

"Why'd you make me come here?"

We're sitting in conference room while the hospital staff get everything set up, and Julian's turning a very interesting shade of green the longer we wait.

I tell him plainly, "I didn't. You tagged along, remember?"

"I remember you trying to get one of your slits fingered by that fucking—"

"For a man with such filthy lyrics, you're a prude, you know that?" At least when it comes to me.

He lowers his face, saying seriously, "Collette, this place isn't for people like me."

"Prudes?"

His head snaps up. "I'm not a prude, smartass. Anytime you want me to prove it—"

"You were saying?"

"I have tattoos." He checks over his shoulder as if he's expecting to get arrested any minute.

"So do I."

"But some of mine require parental supervision." He slips his arms through his leather jacket, covering up most of the tats that are definitely intended for a more mature audience.

"What are you planning to do when you have your own children? Wear long-sleeve shirts until they're eighteen?"

"I just won't have any," he murmurs, still glancing around, and I lean forward, my arms dangling between my now spread thighs.

He won't have any *what?*

Julian notices me studying him, and shrugs, saying, "I got fixed."

"You got a vasectomy?"

He nods.

"Already? Why?"

"You know..."

No, I don't. Was it voluntary? Involuntary? Was it for medical reasons?

"Look, whatever," he says when my face hasn't changed. "That shit happens all the time. I've already had three paternity suits filed against me and not only do I never fuck bareback, my spunk don't even got swimmers. You know the deal. Groupies looking for an eighteen-year-long paycheck."

I scoff, sitting back abruptly. Yes, that's a legitimate concern in this industry, but holy shit. What a sacrifice to make yourself. And so young. He's only twenty-seven years old for Christ's sake.

Except this might just be as long as he was prepared for his life to last.

At night, I do make Julian leave my bus because I know it's what's best, but the worry I feel in his wake never leaves. The worry isn't just for his sake either; it's for mine as well. I like Julian. He's a good person, much better than he lets on. He's funny, protective, and talented—so talented it's not even fair—and every morning I find him still alive feels like a gift. I wish he saw it the same way.

"Do you *want* kids?"

"I don't know. I never thought about it."

Never? Before he made that big of a decision, he didn't even consider the idea of having children?

"Do you think you'll ever get married?"

He lifts his fist to his mouth, biting the ring on his thumb.

Is that a *yes?*

"What if your wife wants kids?" I don't know why my voice rises or why I'm pushing this. It's his decision. It's his wife. His. Wife.

Assuming he lives long enough to get one.

"What about you?"

"What about me?"

"Do *you* want more kids?"

"Yes," I say automatically, and his head whips back like he was just in a car accident.

"Then why haven't you?"

And now I feel like I'm the one in the crash.

I push out of my seat, going over to the floor-to-ceiling window. "I *wanted* more kids. It's probably not going to happen now."

"Why? Because you're not married?"

I wasn't married to Bodee when I got pregnant with Holter, but I wasn't trying to get pregnant then. I was just young and stupid. Two things I'm not anymore.

"Because..." Because I haven't found anyone I even like enough for a second date, let alone tie my life to by making a baby with. Because I'm constantly traveling and any spare moment I have goes to the child I'm already failing. Because I. Because I. Because I. "Because I'll be thirty-four in September," I say, settling on the one reason that isn't my own doing.

I should've considered my words more carefully before answering

Julian. It's just…I have always wanted more kids. Ever since I was one myself, I've dreamed of having a houseful of kids. Then my parents surprised me with tickets to that Bodee Keys concert for my sixteenth birthday and my life took a sharp left turn on to the road that ultimately led me here today. I haven't taken my foot off the gas once and that's why I don't have more children. Because I've been too busy outrunning my past to even consider my future.

Now I'm on the cusp of thirty-four with zero romantic prospects and even less of a chance of slowing down to find one. The truth is I wouldn't know *how* to have more kids while touring still. Touring is all I know how to do, so I try to make sure I do it really fucking well. It's why I'm such a failure as a mother.

I catch the tears clinging to my bottom lashes with a knuckle.

"So what? There's some kind of cut-off?"

"What?" I spin around, finding Julian's watchful eye trained on me. "Oh, um, not exactly a cut-off. For women, having kids past their thirties can be…riskier, I guess. In some cases, anyway. Pregnancies have the potential to be more complicated the older a woman gets." It's not just Hollywood trying to tell me I'm old, it's science, too. At only thirty-two, women's chances of getting pregnant already start to decrease.

Just one more example of how double standards rule over our entire fucking existence.

"Would you even want to get married again? Or did Bodee—"

"Bodee was no husband."

"He was yours." Julian's voice is low and gritty, like worn sandpaper that can still rub you raw at just the right angle.

"For one day." Which was one too many.

"Long enough to get you pregnant."

"Me having kids has never been, and will never be, dependent on if I'm married or not. That's an outdated belief that I didn't even buy into back then." I'd *like* to be married again one day, and I'd *like* to have more kids, but neither concept is reliant on the other. Even separately, they're unrealistic. Together? I won't be holding my breath, not when I have sold-out concerts to perform in.

"But then…"

"I was pregnant before the wedding. That's why we moved the date up, so the pictures wouldn't show my growing belly," I relay exactly like I've done numerous times before.

Why are we still talking about this?

Just because I'm still outrunning my past, doesn't mean I check the rearview mirror. I know what I'll find in its reflection. I'll always know.

"And he still tried to divorce you?"

"He tried to do a lot to me in that time."

Julian stands to his full height. "What'd he do?"

"Something that cost him his wife, and almost his child, in the blink of an eye." Or the swipe of a knife if we're being precise, because I couldn't afford to blink while I was clawing my way out of hell by fighting the man who was trying to drag me there—Bodee's manager, who I call Jack. I refuse to use his real name. Scum of the earth don't deserve that luxury. Bodee's lucky I use his. If it weren't for the son we share, I wouldn't.

Framing his hands on the polished conference table, Julian leans forward to say, "The Collette I've gotten to know wouldn't let anyone or anything tell her when she can or can't do something. If you want more kids, you should have more kids. Whenever the fuck you want to."

"Hmm. Maybe it's for the best," I say more to myself than anything. "I'm not doing too great with the one I currently have."

"What do you mean? Holter's awesome."

"Mary probably has a lot more to do with that than me."

"Mary loves Holter and he loves Mary, but you *love* Holter and he *loves* you. There's a big difference."

"No, there's not. Love is love." I haven't given Holter everything I wish I could've, but at least I've given him love—mine along with Mary's. Nannies get paid to take care of their charges, not love them, but I interviewed nannies until I found one that would do both. I questioned if my love would be enough and I knew Bodee was incapable of loving someone else, so I tried to give Holter the next best thing. That's what I've been telling myself all along. Love is love, and at least Holter has that.

"There are different kinds of love like there are different kinds of rainstorms."

"Rainstorms? They all result in the same thing though, getting wet. It's the same with love."

Julian shakes his head. "Some rain can be seen by anybody looking for it. Big, fat drops that splash against your clothes. Your brain tells you you're wet as you're getting wet. Some rain is so fine, like mist that penetrates silently, there is no need to look for it because you're already drenched past your clothes and into your skin before your brain even gets the chance to tell you anything. Some love is seen *and* felt, but some doesn't need to be seen to be felt at all."

"What sets them apart?"

"Sacrifice."

My eyes fill with tears for the second time, so I blink them back as fast as I can.

Even after my vision clears, Julian's still focused intently on me, nodding like he's got a song in his head only he can hear.

He probably does.

Julian's always writing down lyrics, whether he can find paper or not. It's actually kind of funny watching him scribble words on any available surface. Yesterday it was his pants. This morning it was mine. The entire left knee now has his handwriting etched on it…upside down. He had to sit on my stomach just to hold me down so he could get them out which at first annoyed me, but then when I saw the final result, I vowed to never wash the pants or get rid of them.

Julian's like a waterfall of inspiration—it just pours out of him unchecked. One day he'll figure out how to harness that rare talent, so it's not quite so overpowering, and hopefully make some songs with them because the songs he puts out now, are nothing like the lyrics I see him write down.

"What does your love look like?" I ask him.

"Ever seen a thorny devil lizard?"

"I don't even know what that is."

"They're these spiny lizards in Australia that draw water to their mouths from other parts of their body using grooves between their thorns. So, one can literally stand in a puddle and absorb every last drop of the water without ever opening its mouth. I drain other people's love until there's nothing fucking left."

"I asked about your love, the kind you give, not take. What kind of rainstorm are you, Julian?"

"A megadrought."

A drought that lasts for decades.

Damn it, Julian. What happened to you?

Eyeing him, I whisper, "I don't believe that." Something, or someone, caused Julian to believe he's unworthy of receiving love, or even giving it. In just over a week of being around him, I can see and feel quite clearly how caring of a person he is when he's mentally present and putting in effort. If his love feels anything like his care, he's more like a cloudburst—sudden, violent, and has the potential to flood a person's heart within seconds.

"Are you two ready?" I hear behind me, and turn around to face the woman, Sue, in the doorway.

Coming to stand beside me, Julian looks like he's about to throw up as he admits, "No."

While experience is life's greatest teacher, perspective is the clearest lens you could see your lessons through. We're about to get both.

I take a deep breath, mentally shaking myself. Here I am crying over not having more than one child and I'm preparing to meet parents losing their only child.

With my elbow propped on Julian's shoulder, I tuck the side of my middle finger just under his jaw, seeking out that heartbeat of his. It pounds against my skin instantly, and just as quickly, he leans into my touch, seeking…something as well.

It's called capillary action—the thing that lizard does. I learned about it in one of my college courses, during a study on groundwater. It's the spontaneous flow of a liquid into a narrow tube based on levels of cohesion and adhesion. Each time I've pressed a finger to Julian's pulse, I've done so selfishly to console myself that he wasn't dead. But what if… What if through my finger, he's been taking *something*—I don't know what exactly—from me, too? I'm not offering Julian love, but I can provide him some sort of solace, at least temporarily.

I tell Sue, "We're ready."

Celebrity status comes with *some* perks, this being one of them, and I can't wait to share it with Julian.

Chapter 14

Collette

"Thanks again for fitting us in on such short notice," I tell Sue as Julian and I follow the event coordinator out into the hallway.

I met Sue several years ago when my agent booked me a charity photo op here. I was slotted to be here a grand total of fifteen minutes, but once I met the kids in person, I ended up staying longer—much longer. I stayed until they kicked me out actually. Sue gave me an open invitation to return, and I try to take her up on it whenever my schedule allows. I may live in the area, but unfortunately, I'm rarely home long enough to make it over here. I thought today would be the perfect opportunity to squeeze in a visit, even if it won't be as long as that first time. Holter's at his best friend's for the day, with plans to stay the night, or else I would've brought him along, too.

As soon as we get closer to the noise, all the tension starts to leave my body, like waves being pulled away from the shore for low tide. There can be a lot of toxicity in this world, but here, there's no room for that shit. None. Every single day of life is a gift to these children and their families, and simple pleasures like bubbles are treated like gold. If I can give them the magic of a song or a smile or a signature, I will. I will for as long as they still think it's magical.

The ironic part is that although these kids have only ever treated me like a superstar, I'm the one always left awestruck by them—their courage, their drive, their positive outlook on a world that hasn't been the best to them. These kids, they are the magic, and if Julian doesn't think life is a gift after this, he never will.

"Thank *you*, Collette. We're always happy to have you stop by. And, Julez, the kids are really looking forward to meeting you."

"Really? Sweet." He looks pleased with himself for all of two seconds before he falls back into his pit of uncertainty, asking, "What am I supposed to do? You know, with the kids?"

Sue smiles, giving him the typical list of instructions, the dos and don'ts, and what terms to avoid.

"Especially curse words," I emphasize. When his frown sinks even lower, I add, "Don't worry. You'll be great. Just let them lead you."

"That sounds dangerous," he jokes a second before two glitter bombs explode in our faces.

"A little dangerous." Sue cringes through the cloud of sparkles. "Sorry. They're right in the middle of art exploration."

Julian nods, wiping both eyes with his palms. "I'm down with art."

A tiny girl that I'm almost positive has no idea who Julez is skips over and grabs Julian by the hand, leading him over to a table with an authority even I don't possess. Before I can offer him so much as a reassuring look, I'm whisked away as well to the opposite side of the room.

An hour later we meet back up at the carpeted section littered with small slides and various toys, next to a long bookcase full of well-loved books. Two small braids stick out from the top of Julian's head now, and there's so much glitter on him, he'll probably be washing it off for weeks.

"Glitter works on you."

"Yeah? Think I should add it to the show?" he asks with a genuine smile, all traces of insecurity long gone, smothered by either a pound of glitter or delight. Maybe even both. Truthfully, he's never looked happier…or sexier.

I angle my body toward his, my voice for his ears only. "I was wanting a disco ball during my set, and now, I have one."

Julian breaks into silent laughter, turning to face me, too. "You got jokes, Poohbear?"

All I can do is nod, trapped in amber-flecked blue eyes made even more hypnotic by the sparkles accentuating them—not trapped like the bear blindly stepping into hidden steel jaws, trapped like the fish that spies the shiny glint of the hook and decides to swallow the worm whole anyway.

"A story! A story!" a little boy with thin red hair shouts, breaking the moment.

"A story?" I ask him. "How about a song instead?"

A collective "Ooh" spreads around the room and I smile, honored I get to provide a little slice of the same escape they just gave me.

The same tiny girl from before comes over and tugs on Julian's shirt twice until he bends down to her level, asking her, "What's up, sunflower?" She whispers something in his ear, then he says, "That's right, I did, huh? Will you help me out?"

She glances at an acoustic guitar sitting in front of the wall of windows, nodding shyly. Going over to it, Julian lifts the Yamaha off the stand before taking a seat on the floor while the girl settles in next to him.

The sight needles its way into my psyche, sewing a clean little stitch of an imprint of itself to my memory.

"You're going to play?" I gesture to the guitar he's already mindlessly strumming, and he nods. "Anything in particular or do you just make it up as you go?"

"Both," he says on a chuckle, making me laugh, too.

I know he's got lyrics just waiting to come out, he just has to make sure they're clean.

As if just remembering that fact himself, Julian's eyes fly to mine. "None of my songs are appropriate."

Well, yeah.

"Make something up right now then."

Gazing down at his helper, he hums as his fingers float across the strings. "What should I sing about, sunflower?"

She lifts the doll in her hold, giving it a suffocating squeeze that only comes from love—the kind you can see and feel.

Julian smirks up at me. "A dolly?"

"Hey, you asked."

Bringing his attention back to the guitar, his eyebrows crease as he concentrates, and I walk closer to get a better look, planting myself on the other side of the little girl and her doll.

The rest of the room falls into a sort of trance, lulled by Julian's clever handwork until his raspy voice blends with the chords, captivating everyone all at once.

"Sifting through the dozens just to find that one true dime.
Right out the box, she's got that sparkle and shine.
Promise not to let it dim long after she's mine.
Her 'fit's so fine, got these other girls claimin' it's a crime."

With a smirk, Julian looks at the little girl between us, then shifts his focus to me.

"The day she came into my life,
right in through those eyes,
I felt myself drop, on for miles and miles.
Down, down, down,
powerless to stop the fall, not that I'd even try.
'Cause ain't nowhere else I'd rather be,
than right beside that glowing smile."

Julian doesn't typically sing, more so talks his raps, but on our song he does a kind of mixture of the two on the parts we do together, so this is the first time I'm hearing his actual singing voice all on its own and it's…incredible. I don't know why he doesn't sing more often. Or play guitar. He should be doing both.

"Didn't think I'd—"

He pauses, redoing the chords he just played.

"Hoped I'd stand a chance,
Not realizing she'd already crushed it between her hands,
Hard plastic molded to capture countless hearts,
She's done caught mine, my sweet little…"

Julian stops suddenly to whisper to the little girl, "What's your doll's name?"

"Ruthie."

"Ruthie? Does she have a middle name?"

The girl shakes her head, and Julian starts the bridge over.

> "Hoped I'd stand a chance,
> Not realizing she'd already crushed it between her hands,
> Hard plastic molded to capture countless hearts,
> She's done caught mine, my sweet Ruth Ann."

"There," he tells her after finishing a complicated strumming pattern. "Ruthie can have my grandma's name as her middle name. It's special because she's the one that raised me."

She did? When Julian said he pushed his mom away as a teen, I assumed she was the one who raised him, or the very least was around. *Was she even around?*

The kids clap and Sue catches my eye, reminding me my time today is limited. I'd love nothing more than to stay right here in this moment, watching Julian play the guitar while singing to a little girl about her doll.

"Will you sing, too?" the boy from before asks.

"I'd love to…if Julez joins me." I know I'm putting him on the spot, but only because I know he can handle it.

"What did you have in mind?" he asks, and I tell him the title. It's not one of my songs because mine aren't exactly kid-friendly either, but it's one I think most people will recognize. It's got a great message and always makes me think of the kids here whenever I hear it. Originally it was performed by the artist and her young daughter, but today it's just me, with Julian on guitar.

After a couple failed attempts, Julian finger-plucks the intro riff just right, allowing me to sink effortlessly into the lyrics for "Cover Me In Sunshine" as I weave my way around the room so I'm looking directly into the eyes of each and every child as I sing the meaningful words out loud.

By the time I get to the last line, I'm fighting tears, and I slowly return to Julian. He doesn't end where the regular version does, instead prolonging the song by repeating the outro riff a second time before finishing flawlessly.

Our eyes find each other when his fingers finally come to a stop, blurring the edges of reality around us.

Sue appears, telling me, "You have time for one more song, if you'd like."

"Of course." I swing my gaze from Julian's to our audience. "This next song I wrote for my son."

One night after a show during a particularly grueling tour—one I couldn't take Holter along on—I found myself lying flat on my back in the walk-in shower of my hotel room, staring at the pockmarked ceiling for answers. Answers, like sleep, eluded me that night. Instead, I came up with this song, an emotional melody about wanting to see the person that means everything to you, even if just for one. More. Minute. Because when you're apart from the person you love most, no amount of time with them feels like enough, so you try to stretch what time you do get together out, for a day, an hour, another tick of the clock.

I wrote the lyrics on one of the hotel-provided, bleach-smelling white towels, my tears soaking the cotton quicker than the marker's ink, then I kept the towel just like I kept the guilt written into its fabric. Now the words written long ago burn their way up my windpipe before flowing from my lips like molten lava, the pain from it all churning my gut as if I'm still on that terra-cotta-tiled floor. Soon, Holter will be out of the house, off to college or whatever else he might be interested in, and that one extra minute won't even be an option. I really am failing him right now.

My voice catches on the verse, then I hear the G chord strummed by Julian, and look over to find him with his eyebrows knitted together, now playing the guitar loud enough to cover my mistake. He dips his head, telling me to keep going, and I do. Thinking about this tour and the quality time I have gotten with Holter lately, I pull from that pit in my stomach, gathering the bubbling ache there and channeling it into my vocals until it's power I'm drawing on, not pain.

When I close out the song, I feel lighter, yet stronger. After a standing ovation that brings more tears to my eyes, Julian and I walk around, giving out as many hugs as we can before Sue is calling us back over to another set of double doors. She immediately points us toward the bathroom, explaining how to wash our hands properly since the children in this next section aren't able to congregate in the common rooms like the ones we just saw, due to a variety of reasons, anything from lack of energy to recovering from a recent surgery to not wanting to risk exposure to certain germs other patients might be carrying. Luckily, we still get to visit them individually, but only for a small amount of time per child.

It's the part I always wish I had more time for. It goes so much quicker than you think and some of these kids don't have much time as it is.

"Thanks for saving me," I tell Julian once we're alone in the bathroom, washing our hands in the same sink.

"I owed you one."

Our eyes meet in the mirror.

"Why'd you call that girl sunflower?"

"Sunflowers absorb radiation."

Ah. "She has cancer." Even though it's not a question, he still nods. I drop my eyes to my hands, scrubbing between my fingers.

"You lied."

"Yeah, I do that a lot."

"You said you don't read. You didn't go to college, you barely graduated high school." During one of our late-night conversations, he told me he struggled in school but didn't explain why. "If you don't read, how do you know so much? Do you watch documentaries?"

His amused laugh bounces off the tiled walls.

"I look up stuff on my phone. One thing leads to another, then two hours later I'm learning about a horny lizard in Australia and sunflowers planted at Chernobyl."

"That's reading."

"Okay, Poohbear."

"Why do you refuse to give yourself credit? For anything?"

He looks up through his lashes, and I shake my head, telling him, "Besides your sexual…competence."

"Competence," he mocks, laughing. "Shit."

"Seriously, you read, you play guitar, you sing, but you hide all of it. Why?"

"It's not who they want me to be." He shrugs, grabbing a paper towel.

"Who's they?"

"Everybody."

"Not everybody. I want you to be—"

"They want what they see, Collette, and what they see when they look at me is a rapper."

They. The fans? Or his label? The ones managing his career and life by stuffing them both in the box he's suffocating in.

Grabbing a paper towel myself, I turn off the faucet with it, then wait until his eyes return to mine.

"Because you told them to. You're *telling* people what to see."

He holds up his still-dripping hands, saying, "I lie."

"It's not our job to give people what they think they want. It's our job to show them what they never realized they needed."

"And what is it they need?"

"They need to see the narrative that people can only be one role, only check one box, to be silenced already. Rappers. Popstars. Professional athletes. Providers. Mothers. We all can, and should, be complex human beings, with feelings, and emotions, and a full range of what makes us *us.* Everybody's allowed to have hobbies, interests, other talents, outside the role the general public sees. Just by escaping the confines we all feel on a daily basis and living authentically, you can show others that are currently hiding what might be the best part of themselves how to live authentically, too."

"You're indie. No one's holding your reins."

"You'd be surprised."

"Would I?" He lets that hang in the air while we both wipe our hands dry. "Why the wigs, Collette? Why don't you let anyone see the real you? Maybe you're hiding."

That was never the intention. Women in this industry are expected to constantly reinvent themselves if they want to stay relevant, and changing my hair every day gives me that edge, that newness everybody's always looking out for. The wigs were only supposed to set me apart, not make me blend in, or hide myself entirely. I didn't know that's how they came across. My fans even wear them to my concerts, and

I've always felt a sort of camaraderie seeing all the different colors and styles staring back at me. Are they doing it as a way to hide? To mask who they really are? Is that the message I've been sending?

Is that the message I want to send?

"Exactly. Don't preach about being authentic when you're as fake as the bubblegum-pink hair on your head."

He tugs a strand, and I slap his hand away, telling him, "It's rose-quartz pink. And now you have to wash those again."

Without taking his eyes off me, Julian turns the water back on and starts washing his hands aggressively—so aggressively water sprays all over the place, dousing the front of my navy-blue jumpsuit.

"Stop," I practically shriek, pushing the handle down again.

Abandoning the sink, Julian lunges for me and grabs my arms, dragging me forward with his soaking wet hands.

"I hate you."

"I don't think you do," he says as he looks down at me.

"I'm not the liar here."

Heavy breaths entangle between us, pushing, pulling, goading.

"What am I supposed to do now?" I whisper. "I don't have another outfit to wear."

"You're gonna go out there and you're gonna be you." His head lowers as does his voice. "The you that I know, the you that isn't dressed for appearances all the fucking time. And everybody's going to fall for you just the same, because while I steal thoughts, momentary thoughts that mean next to nothing, you… You're the one that steals hearts, Collette, and you don't need a wig or dry clothes to do it. You're perfect exactly as you are."

I shake him off, frowning at the large handprints now staining my sleeves, and tell him, "Don't even think about touching my hair again. I'm keeping it."

"Today."

"I'll take the wig off when you play the guitar…"

Julian shrugs arrogantly, grinning.

"…during a show."

The smug smile melts off his face so quick I'm surprised he's got any lips left to frown with.

I sidestep him and go back out into the hall—wet, but at least I'm not the only one. Julian's shirt and leather jacket are spattered with water, too, as he follows close behind.

Sue gives us an assessing look but doesn't mention the state of our clothing. After last week's headlines about us, she's probably just relieved to see us still wearing clothes.

With a swipe of her keycard, she leads us through the double doors and everything before this moment becomes utterly inconsequential. Nothing else matters when you're about to face an innocent child that may not make it to adulthood.

Chapter 15

Collette

"Mine? You like my hair? Collette's got bubblegum hair, but you like mine best?" Julian asks, pointing at the two little braids bouncing around on his head as he moves about, sketching a picture on the dry-erase board by the door.

"It's rose quartz," I correct through a smile so wide a clothes hanger could fit between my cheeks with room to spare.

The young girl we're visiting, Paisley, nods faintly, trying to smile just as big. She's exhausted though. She can barely lift her little head off the pillow, but she's been giving it her best since Julian and I strolled into her private room. Julian continues talking to Paisley like they're old friends as her mother and I sit and watch. Even though Paisley's one of the sickest ones here, Julian hasn't treated her like it once. For the past couple hours, he hasn't pretended to be the bad boy he's reputed to be either, nor has he been morose, lethargic, or adrift. He's been…effervescent. Absolutely teeming with life and fun and charm. So much damn charm.

This is what I meant about him stealing hearts. Nobody's safe from this Julian. Nobody.

He finishes with his drawing, then takes a step back, revealing two stick figures. They're better than any stick figures I could ever come up with, but they're pretty basic compared to what else I've seen Julian draw, even with only using a dry-erase marker. He's *that* talented.

"It's us," he says, glancing at me.

Sure enough both stick figures have microphones in their hands and they're on a stage, facing each other. The one I'm assuming is me has a big mass of hair on its head and extremely long, pointy high-heeled shoes. The one supposed to be Julez has gigantic muscles that make me laugh out loud. Julian is surprisingly strong for his build, but…a bodybuilder he's not.

"Since you can't come see us in person, Paisley," Julian starts, and I hold my breath until he adds, "because you're not old enough, I drew you this so you can at least see what Collette and I look like onstage together."

"I don't know," I say, leaning toward Paisley conspiratorially. "Don't you think Julez drew himself a little…larger than real life?"

Julian gasps, then proceeds to flex dramatically. His leather jacket doesn't so much as budge which makes us girls laugh even harder.

Paisley's eyelids flutter like a butterfly settling on a leaf, so I stand, saying, "We should get going."

Gazing down at Paisley's frail form, I consider how short life can be. Not just in general—eighty, ninety years is nothing in terms of time overall—but how much shorter it is for some, like Paisley. Why her? Why not someone who doesn't give a shit about the life they were handed? Paisley hasn't even started her life, not in comparison to almost a century, and here it is slipping from her grasp before she gets the chance.

I look up at Julian again, wondering if this is all sinking in yet. I hope so. His life is too precious to throw away. All life is.

Julian comes over to join me, and we give Paisley and her mom a final goodbye, knowing we'll never see the little girl again. Not because she'll make it out of this hospital bed and go on to live a full life where a random encounter with a rapper and a popstar barely register, but because she most likely won't.

After leaving Paisley's room, Sue informs us our car is already waiting downstairs, leaving Julian and I to take the elevator alone. Before the doors are even fully closed, he's got his palm up to his mouth. I expect it to be there a while since that seems to be his habit when he's nervous—chewing on his ring—but his hand comes away just as quickly and I see his Adam's apple bob from a swallow. He took something. After watching with his own eyes, innocent, selfless children fighting for their lives, he's still willing to jeopardize his.

He didn't learn anything.

Usually I leave here feeling grateful—sad, but grateful. Now I'm just aggravated. No, I'm pissed actually.

Julian guides me to the back of the town car, meanwhile mobs of paparazzi surround us, screaming out the stupid couple name the media's given us. There are families upstairs taking out second and third mortgages this very minute to extend their children's lives by days—*days*—and these dipshits are down here more concerned with finding out if two people famous for using their voices in an impressive way are together or not. Clickbait's the biggest motivator anymore, not human decency.

As I'm getting in the back seat, questions pelt me from all sides about my "pregnancy" with Julian's baby and I flinch as if I've been slapped across the face. I figured they'd find us at the hospital, but I didn't anticipate them alleging I'm pregnant because of it. And with Julian, someone that took that opportunity away from not only himself but any woman in his future who might want to have his children. The same someone that can't even manage his own life, let alone the life of a baby.

"Jesus fuck. That was rough," Julian says once the doors are closed and the car is moving. "You okay, P—"

"I'm fine."

He scoots away from me like he's scared, like I just uttered the code to a nuclear weapon, and maybe I did. I feel volatile right now.

I feel…disappointed. In Julian. In myself. In humanity.

I need a break from all of it.

On the highway, Julian points out the window at a billboard, saying, "Aw, shit. Look at that."

I barely glance at it. It's us from the promo shoot. The pose where Julian's naked with both of us "holding" his package as my back is to the camera and my head's cranked over my shoulder.

"Damn," he says under his breath, so I look again, longer this time.

Julian's not looking at the camera in the billboard photo; it's a shot of him staring directly at me. At my lips.

"I'm not staying for your set tonight," I tell him suddenly.

Julian finally tears his gaze from the billboard to study me, his hand coming up to hover near his mouth.

"Why?"

"Because…" Because on a day where the world feels desolate and everyone on it appears broken, performing with Julian—something that makes me feel whole and happy—seems wrong. Because the more I'm around him, the more I *want* to be around him, but I don't even know who he really is. And neither does he.

With his hand still in front of his mouth, Julian threatens, "I'll shut every hotel in LA down, Collette." It comes out low and menacing, reminding me of the night at the strip club when he lost his temper because he thought I was going to sleep with someone…someone *else*. Of course, that's what he assumes now. That's what everyone's always assuming about me.

"You can certainly try," I murmur just loud enough for him to hear. "But by my estimation, your motor skills should be slowing down any minute."

"They're working fine now, so if you need to catch a dick that fucking bad—"

My gaze flies to his, and without blinking, I say to the driver, "Sir? Would you mind pulling over? I'd prefer to find my own ride."

Julian doesn't break the connection either when he tells the man, "Merge outta this lane and the next car you'll see the inside of is a hearse."

"Please excuse my associate. He has the manners of a feral cat thrown in a bathtub full of water."

Julian's head jerks back. "Associate?"

"What's the matter? Are the drugs kicking in already? Or are you just unfamiliar with the term? If that's the case, allow me to enlighten you. An associate is a fucking work colleague. That's. It. It's *just* business."

"What was today?"

"A mistake."

"Collette."

I shake my head as I return my stare out the window. As well-intended as my attempt to help Julian was, it was misdirected. There are other, far more deserving people in need of help right now. I should put my efforts there.

I use the rest of the silent ride to send out a few emails. The first to my board of financial advisors asking if my idea is even possible, then one to Sue and the hospital director to get their opinions as well. The last one goes to my producer, David Yonko, who also happens to be my landlord. Holter's at his house right now, hanging out with David's son, Tai, so I make sure to send the email to his work address in case he's busy entertaining the boys. David's a huge producer in the music industry, but his main priority is family, so he works from his home studio and shapes his hours to fit around his family's schedule. I can't think of a better person to co-chair a charity for the children's hospital with.

The tour buses come into view as soon as the driver pulls into the abandoned mall's parking lot where we're parked for the night, and my hand's already on the door handle.

The moment the town car slows enough, I'm out the door, slamming it shut behind me.

"Collette?" Julian roars, but I ignore him in my dash up my bus's steps, slamming that door, too…and locking it.

Chapter 16

Julian

I can hear the crowd and feel their weird-ass energy as soon as I pull up to the outdoor venue. It's restless, like mine. I know what my problem is though. I'm about to go out and listen to my *associate* sing her dumb fucking lyrics about getting railed, knowing she has every intention of actually getting railed afterward. And I'm supposed to keep performing after she walks off to get said railing? I'm supposed to lean on my own dumb fucking lyrics about fucking someone else to make me not think about Collette getting railed?

Fuck. That. Shit.

This day fucking sucks. So does Collette. I hate her and her lyrics and her ditching me to go do who-the-fuck-knows.

Who the fuck cares?

Not me.

The bottle of vodka in my fist knocks my front teeth when I try to take a swig and walk at the same time, and after a long drink, I throw it against the partition keeping me out of view, laughing when glass shatters everywhere.

Someone flinches beside me, and I do a double take, making sure it's really who I think it is.

When'd she get here? I missed sound check completely—whoops—but

I tried to get over here as soon as I could to catch the last of her set. She didn't finish already, did she?

How late am I?

"You done then?" I ask, but she doesn't say a word. She doesn't glare at me, threaten me, hit me, nothing. Just full-out ignores me like she did earlier, which makes me hate her even more.

She hates me, too. That's why we're fucking perfect for each other.

The king and queen of scorn.

Scorn me,

adorn me,

just don't fuckin' ignore me.

God, she's such a stuck-up bitch. She talks like she isn't, but she is. I should fuck someone right in front of her just to see if I can get a rise out of her. I think she'd have a pretty hard time ignoring me then. It almost worked at the strip club.

Almost.

Maybe.

I don't know. Shit's confusing.

This woman's got me fucking spiraling like I'm on a ride at an amusement park. One I wish she'd stop trying to kick my ass off of.

Stumbling the few feet to the stage, I rake my eyes across the front row of fans, the faces blending together like some sort of giant swamp creature from a forgotten lagoon.

Sick.

A tank top lands next to my feet as I approach the center of the stage, but I can't even tell whose tits might be showing. Everything is just…dull. Muted. Ugly.

I flip the crowd off, making the ground beneath me tremble. A look over my shoulder, I can make out Collette talking to Irelynn. Her hands are flying around her like crazy, then swing in my direction, so I turn my middle finger on her instead.

Fuck you, Collette. Fuck you and the things you make me feel.

She made me feel so fucking much today. Everything. Every-fucking-thing. She made me feel every emotion in the book and I hate feeling. I avoid feeling anything, but Collette, she makes me feel things I never even knew were possible. Things I don't want to be possible.

I'd already made the choice to get a vasectomy—already got my shit snipped—then here comes Collette making me regret even getting the procedure to begin with.

If I hadn't, I'd give Collette hundreds of kids myself, because if anyone should have more, it's her. She fucking cares so much. She loves so openly. Fuck a rainstorm, Collette's a tsunami. You couldn't outrun her love in a Bugatti. Those kids today sure didn't.

And if I was capable of loving, I would've given them mine, too.

I'm not though. I'm not built for that kind of shit. I'm built for… fuck, I don't know.

I wish I did. Now. Now I wish I knew. Before Collette came along, putting ideas in my head, putting emotions in my chest, I was motherfucking fine, great, fantastic with being exactly what I was.

I was.

Wasn't I?

I don't know anymore. I try so hard to forget, I'm losing control of what stays and what goes.

All I used to want was to forget. Now I found something I want to remember, and I wish I could replace every memory I've ever had with one from this tour because I never want to forget what's happened so far. I want to remember the days I sat on Collette's bus, watching her with her boy, teasing him, kissing the top of his head. I want to remember the time Collette fell asleep with her head on my shoulder and I spent forty-five minutes with a cramp in my ass just so I wouldn't disturb her. I want the smiles she gives me when we're performing together like we're the only two people that exist. And the look on her face today when she sang her fucking heart out to a bunch of sick kids, giving them hope, giving *me* hope. I want all of it, every minute of being around Collette locked in my memory for-fucking-ever.

Since the day she pierced my back, I swear Collette's infected me with this feeling bullshit. All these feelings and I got no clue what the fuck to do with any of them. That's why I took that Xanny—to try to gain back some of that control, so I could forget. Forget those kids, and their parents, and everything they made me feel.

Then when Collette called me her associate and locked her bus door in my face, I decided to drown myself in booze to see if I could forget her, too.

But she won't let me.

I won't let me. Something deep in my subconscious will not allow me to forget her. I tried. I'm trying.

I don't want to try. I never really did. I just like being numb. It makes everything hurt less. Even now though, I'm totally numb, numb to all of this…except her.

The indifference in her gaze when she finally stops talking to Irelynn to meet my eyes flays me wide open, and I stumble again. Nothing mutes Collette or the pain she inflicts with her apathy.

The sky opens up, and with no overhead coverage out here in this field, rain pours down all over the stage and everything on it.

Maybe Collette's love isn't a rainstorm, but her apathy sure the fuck is.

I'll soak that shit up, too. Straight drain her dry. I'll take *anything* she's willing to give me.

Zeroed in on Collette, I bring my mic up to my mouth.

"Sliced to my core, your blade cut so clean.
Whispered threats miss their mark, sending me back reeling.
Together, you and I, we'd be a fucking catastrophe.
Calamity.
Tragedy.
Drippin' from head to my bones in the agony,
soak me good, baby, because without you, it's straight misery."

The words aren't from our song but they're more real, more true, than the lyrics I consider rewriting every minute of every goddamn day. The song we "made together" sucks, too, and I hate singing the lyrics anymore. I'd have no issue singing them with literally anybody else, but with Collette, I *hate* them. More than I hate myself. More than I hate Collette.

I don't hate Collette.

It'd be easier if I did.

A dare in her eye and a pep in her fucking step, Collette joins me onstage, the shoulder-length blue hair she's wearing turning wavy around her own stormy expression as the rain infuses the strands.

Here we go. Punish me. Show me I'm worth punishing.

Her own mic comes up when she's a foot away from me, and amongst the rain and the screams and the chaos of my head battling my heart for dominance, she sticks a finger in my face and raps, actually fucking raps.

"These girls might be calling you Daddy,
But you should know I ain't your baby,
You want me at your feet, yet I got you between my knees."

With her hand on my head, she lifts a bent knee, pretending to guide me to her pussy, and it takes everything in me not to fall and worship her here and now. A king kneels for no one, but I'd drop to my knees for Collette—my queen.

"Praising me good, buried deep beneath the sheets,
Coming up for air just to catch a peek.
I know you like to watch, but trust me when I say,
you ain't seen nothing yet.
Might wanna wipe your upper lip, Julez,
we both know it won't be sweat."

She takes a swipe at my top lip and I chase the move with my mouth, wanting to bite her so fucking bad. I'd pray for lockjaw and never let go. Never.

"'Cause when it comes to who's on top,
please believe it'll always be your girl, Collette."

Ending with a hard glare, Collette moves toward the crowd, but I snatch her ass up with an arm around her waist, pulling her attention back to me. Doesn't she see? This is all for her.

My hold on her tight but not tight enough, she pulls from my grasp, facing off against me like we're in a real battle. *My specialty.*

"We ain't gon' talk about it?
Shit, say the word and I'll straight scream about it.
Why can't we just be about it?
Got me spinning in circles just thinking about—"

A loud crack of thunder rattles the stage, cutting my mic off mid-sentence, but I step into Collette, still going without it.

"Let me off the ride, but never the high."

Before I can get another word out, the crowd starts booing, bringing me back to the moment and the fact that we're not alone. Collette makes me feel like no other, but she also suppresses like no other. She's my new drug of choice, and just like everything else in my life, I'm gonna over-fucking-indulge.

Bruce rushes out with a megaphone, probably to tell everyone the show is cancelled, but I'm not about to stick around and face that wrath, so when Collette turns to leave, I follow.

I would've followed her anyway. I'm used to boos. It's silence I can't handle.

My steps don't take me as fast as hers and I get frustrated watching her speed up so easily, leaving me behind without a single care whatsoever.

"Fuck you," she says, and I don't have to guess who she's talking to.

"Don't threaten me with a good time," I smart off because I can. It feels too good to have her attention on me. I don't care how I go about getting it, as long as she gives it.

She mutters, "You wouldn't know a real good time if it sat on your face and rode your tongue to ecstasy," but I hear it and bark out a laugh, stopping her.

Finally.

Stay. Stay and fight. Stay and hate.

Just fucking stay.

I crowd her back, telling her, "You're right about that, Poohbear."

It takes her a minute to put the pieces together, giving me time to memorize her body against mine. I've played around with her a few times, and even gotten a hug out of her, but nothing like this. I want to be able to draw a map of her body from memory. Like an early explorer, I want to conquer it *all*.

"You've never gone down on a woman before?"

My scoff feathers over her neck, making her shiver, and my cock swells instantly. Fuck, I want to make her shiver a thousand more times.

"Never needed to. They come for me on command. I don't need to coax shit from anyone."

"Well, you must be really…"

Her voice dripping in sex, she spins in my arms, running her hands up my chest to my shoulders, then almost to the spot on my neck she's always dabbing at.

"…really…"

Her breath strokes my lips and I groan, growing ten times harder.

"…lazy in bed." With an arctic draft of a tone, she pushes me away and I stagger back a few steps.

What the fucking fuck was that?

"Typical spoiled celebrity."

God, I want those ruthless lips on mine already. *Eat me alive, Collette. Fucking please.*

But she won't. She ain't having it. I wasn't born with a sliver spoon on my tongue, but because I've never had pussy on it either that somehow still makes me "spoiled." And lazy, too?

The fuck?

"So you only fuck guys that eat you out first?" I didn't say I wouldn't, just that I haven't had to. I can get my knees dirty. Shit, I was already bending 'em the second I heard her rapping about me tonguing her pussy.

"Among other things, yeah. Haven't you ever heard the best things come after hard work?"

"Are you saying you're hard to make come? Or that you're the best? Because I could—"

"When a man falls to his knees for me," she starts walking backward, "it's not because I challenge him to, little lamb. It's because he can't imagine being anywhere other than having his face buried between my thighs. He *begs* just to get a taste, but I don't let him until that happens, because just like you, I don't coax shit from anyone either."

"You're talking about a man. Leave your bus unlocked tonight and I'll show you how a king eats." I almost—*almost*—say *your* king, but don't.

Collette smirks the ugliest fucking smirk I've ever seen because it's cruel, deliberately cruel, as she says, "I'm not staying on the bus tonight," before following up with the ugliest fucking wink imaginable. I swear this shit'll haunt me for the rest of my life.

"You ain't finding a hotel with availability," I lie. In the process of trying to forget everything, I forgot everything, including my plan to buy out every hotel in the city. Not that I could afford to, but I would've booked as many as I could before my cards shut off because unlike my credit cards, my pettiness has zero limits.

"I'm not staying in a hotel either," she says as she climbs into a waiting golf cart.

She's leaving. She's leaving me. She's leaving me to go be with someone else.

I should've said "your king."

Not sure what to do or say, I flip her off again, hoping she'll come back and hand me my own ass because at least when she's pissed, she doesn't ignore me. Or leave me.

Don't leave.

All she does is return the gesture with her own middle finger as the golf cart pulls away though, leaving me standing here feeling more like a clown than a king.

Axel finds me stuck in the same spot, asking what the hell we're gonna do now.

"After-party," is all I say. I mean, what the fuck else is there to do? Collette just left to do whatever the fuck she wants, so Imma do whatever the fuck I want.

What I want just left me.

"After-party?" Axel parrots. "There wasn't even a full show tonight."

"Remember Miami?"

He chuckles, telling me, "We can't do that this time."

"Why the hell not?" It was the early days, but who cares? We could pull that shit off again. Instead of surf and sun, we got rain, which in Cali should be celebrated.

"Uh, Collette. And Holter."

I've always thought of Axel as a brother. We've been playing together for fucking years. Even when I couldn't afford to have my own drummer, I still found a way to keep him with me. He was too talented not to use and too important for me to let go. But hearing those names slip from his lips so easily, like he's the one that gets to worry about Collette and Holter, like he *cares* about them, it does something to me. Makes me want to pull each and every one of his teeth out, from tip to root. He doesn't get to just care for them. They're not his to care for.

"Holter's around?" I ask, side-eyeing him.

"I don't know. I haven't seen Bare for a while."

I catch sight of Slade and call him over to ask where Bare is. He's supposed to be with Holter any time Collette isn't, but I've been out of touch for the last few hours—ever since Collette closed and locked the only door that's opened for me without having to pay a price for admission.

"He should be here soon."

"With Holter?"

"No. I called him off Holter."

"Why?"

"Are you kidding?"

I stare at him blankly because, would I be fucking asking if I was kidding?

"Fuck. With the weather turning, we need him here, covering you—"

"I don't give a fuck about me!" Jesus Christ. Out of everyone, he should know that. "You don't get to make those calls. That's not your place."

"Yes, it is," he says, pushing into my personal space.

"You know what?" I shove his face out of mine, pointing at him with a shaky hand. "I let it slide when you put Collette in danger in San Diego." His eyes go wide and I smirk. *Motherfucker thought he was slick.* "And now you're making calls that aren't yours. Bare stays with Holter. Period."

"You're my client. My job is to look out for you, not some bitch and the pup she doesn't even bother protecting herself."

My fist collides with the left side of Slade's nose, making his face whip sideways and blood splatter on the darkening ground. After only a brief hesitation, Axel sees himself the fuck out of my way without me having to say a word 'cause he already knows.

I don't particularly care what the fuck goes on around me or who's involved, but I'll be goddamned if I'm gonna let *anybody* talk shit on Collette or her boy.

She doesn't bother protecting Holter? Shit, I got a scab on my back that says differently. I know Collette's got her boy's best interest in mind, and I'm sure they've got this shit down by now, but that doesn't change the fact that I *want* to make sure she's taken care of. Her and the son she loves more than anything. Hell, after spending the last week around Holter, I even like the kid, too, and as long as I have the means to ensure he's protected outside of his mother's care, I motherfucking will, and fuck anyone who tries to get in my way, including this bitch-ass in front of me.

I grab a fistful of Slade's greasy hair, lifting his head to look him in the eye. "You got a long leash. Have for a long time, too." I squeeze the hair near the scalp, making him hiss. "As of now consider that shit shortened. Collette and Holter? You keep their names out your fucking mouth and your path from crossing theirs. Got it?"

After Slade jerks out a nod, I look at Axel, telling him, "That goes for both of you."

"Are you serious?" Axel sputters. "I was just trying to help."

Was he just trying to help when he offered to show Collette his cock? I think the fuck not.

"That's not your place either," I say, releasing Slade's hair, then standing up straight to wipe my palm on my jeans. Fucking oily prick.

"How is it yours?"

Axel's right. It's not my place. They're not mine to care about any more than they're his, but that hasn't fucking stopped me from caring anyway. I don't let myself love anyone anymore, but when I find someone worth caring about, I let my care run like water torture—once it starts, it never lets up.

Fuck if I'm gonna tell him that though.

"Are you fucking her?" Slade accuses, and this fucker must have a death wish because I'm about to—

"Not yet he hasn't," Axel says. "He would've moved on already."

First, they mistake me for a comedian with all this "Are you kidding?" and "Are you serious?" bullshit, and now they're confusing me with Bodee fucking Keys moving on from *The* Collette.

I mean, yeah, I wanted to fuck Collette. *Want* to, because I still want to fuck her. Goddamn do I want to. But today I fucked up any chance of that ever happening. I fucked up a lot today. And the days leading up to it.

I'm a master at making bad decisions.

Even if by some miracle-on-earth type shit Collette actually did let me fuck her, would I really move on afterward like usual? Could I? That'd put a stop to all the time I spend over on her bus with her and her family—the family I was just starting to feel like I might fit in with, even if it's as the inappropriate uncle who doesn't say much other than curses that make the room squirm, but is content sitting in the corner anyway, watching everyone else interact because it's the only family he's ever wanted a place in.

The gravity of that scenario sits like a lead weight in my stomach, and if I wasn't on land right now, I'd sink to the bottom of the fucking ocean.

Doesn't matter. Collette would never let me be anything to her. I thought maybe…maybe. But if I'm being honest, I'm not so sure. Not anymore. Especially not after today. She could hate me for real now— easily. I flipped her off as a goodbye which might've been *our* goodbye now that I replay it in my head.

I flipped her off as a goodbye.

The knot in my stomach grows even heavier, and I glance down at my feet to make sure they're still firmly on the ground, not sinking below the surface.

Maybe I should disappear somewhere deep where I'll never be found.

I thought I already had, then Collette arrived and brought me back to life. Or whatever this is. In purgatory I knew what I was getting—the same day on motherfucking repeat. This though…I don't know what the fuck's going on. It's both heaven and hell. Heaven's within reach, she's just not in my reach.

"Where was Bare when you called him?" I ask Slade instead. I don't have to answer to these dickheads. I can't even answer to myself.

"Some Hollywood gated community. Security made Bare sit outside the gates while Hol—"

I tilt my head at him, prepping my fist, and eyeing his jaw this time.

"The *kid* visited a friend somewhere inside them."

"Was Mary with Holter?"

"No. Bare said she dropped…the *kid* off, then left."

What the fuck? I hate that Slade knows all this and I don't. I need to talk to Bare. Shit's gotta change going forward.

I call Bare myself to get the rundown straight from him.

"I don't know, boss man. It seems legitimate to me. I think he's just staying the night with a friend. After dropping Holter off, Mary drove out of there like she had a hot date. No hesitancy at all about where she was leaving him for the night."

Date. She's not the only one. I'm sure Collette's on her way to hers right now.

"All right, meet us at the buses. And call as many buddies as you can. We're gonna need 'em."

"For what?" Slade asks at the same time Bare does.

I tell them the only word I need to, "Miami." Hanging up, I hop in a golf cart with a driver ready to take me offsite. This'll keep me both occupied and out of jail…probably. I let that fuckhead in the Porsche off easy. I won't be so generous next time Collette tries bringing around another *date,* and if I'm not busy with something, I'll go looking. Or drive myself insane wondering.

I'm already halfway there now.

"Get everybody."

"Everybody?" Slade asks while Axel blows out a breath, running a hand through his hair. Dude's so emo. He's still my brother, but he messed up propositioning Collette. I'm the only motherfucker who gets to do that.

"Everybody," I repeat, tossing Slade his phone back.

Chapter 17

Collette

What's that sound? It's like bees, a swarm of them, but louder. So much louder.

Coming from the back bedroom, I peer out one of the heavily tinted windows, sucking my breath through my teeth as an entire fucking mob of people rush toward both buses. I immediately bring my phone up, dialing Holter to…I don't know. Is this an angry mob? Or a happy one?

Why is there a mob at all?

Luckily, it's just me here since I gave my team the rest of the night off. Well, me and Antonio. He insisted on staying with me until I finished packing my bag for the night. Even though I'm going home, I still needed a couple things.

When Holter doesn't answer, I hit redial, calling out to Antonio. The driver's weathered eyes meet mine in the rearview mirror.

"Can you get us out of here?" Do we even have time to get out?

Pounding against the outside of the bus gives me my answer.

As if today couldn't get any worse.

Antonio has the radio up to his mouth, speaking into it when I join him at the front.

The voice on the other end comes through somewhat choppy as the driver from Julian's bus says, "They're putting on a concert."

A concert?

"Who?" I ask Antonio.

He looks up at me apologetically, saying, "Julez."

"Where?"

"Here."

A concert here? It's raining. And there isn't any equipment. Or a stage.

Finally, Holter answers, asking, "What's up, Mom?"

"Oh my God," I say, jogging back to the bedroom and closing the door. Pressing the phone to my ear as hard as I can, I have to stick my finger in the other one to even hear myself. "Please tell me you're still at Tai's house."

The pounding is amplified by the screaming and chanting now, making it hard to focus.

"Yeah. Why wouldn't I be?"

"I don't know. I just…got worried. Why didn't you answer the first time I called?"

"We were out back watching David cook pizza in their new outdoor pizza oven."

Even through the madness of whatever's happening outside, my heart still aches at the mental image that one sentence creates. A stable full-time home with a loving, hands-on father—things I wish I could've given Holter, but didn't.

"You're still coming for dinner, right?" he asks, and I shake my head even though he can't see it.

"Something came up and I'm not sure when I'll be able to get away now. You guys go ahead and eat without me, okay? I'll let you know when I'm at the casita, in case you decide you want to sleep there instead." The casita we rent is a guesthouse on David's estate. He was the only producer that'd work with me after my fallout with Bodee, and for as long as we've been making albums together, our families have been close. David and his wife, Kim-ly, became good friends when I had none, and our boys, only three months apart in age, basically grew up together. Living a driveway away from each other, they're more like brothers than best friends. Although I'm eternally grateful for all of David's help—he's done so much for not only me, but Holter as well— sometimes living so close to him and his family makes me…sad. It makes me envious. Extremely envious. And I'd never admit this to any- one, but it makes me ashamed—ashamed for not being able to achieve the same setup for my son, ashamed for even being envious in the first place, just ashamed overall.

"Hey?" I swallow down some of my nerves. "I love you."

"Love you, too, Mom. Will you tell Julian I finally beat the level we were working on yesterday?" He says something away from the phone, then, "Fine. Tai and I beat the level." I can practically hear his eye roll.

Again, I shake my head without him seeing, but say, "Yeah. I'll tell him." I don't even think Julian and I are speaking right now. We left on bad terms—again. I need to kick my habit of dramatic exits already.

I need to find somewhere worth sticking around for first.

We hang up and I stare at the closed door, listening to the ruckus outside grow louder and louder.

Why is Julian doing this? Even with an impromptu concert, we still have to give out refunds for tonight's cancelled show. I played my set, sure, but the headliner didn't. At the very least partial refunds will be given. So, why bother with a free concert? And a dangerous one at that?

With my phone still in hand, I plug in different hashtags, finding what I'm looking for after only three, and someone's livestream of what's happening just outside fills the room instantly. Standing on top of his bus is Julian. No, not Julian. It's Julez up there. I can see it in his eyes even with his hair partially covering them. He's shirtless and soaked, pointing at the crowd below, encouraging them to rap his lyrics along with him. His lips are moving so fast, they're a blur on the screen, and for a moment, I forget I'm mad at him and get caught up watching him like a fan would.

Julian's songs may not be all that impressive, but the way he delivers them is. He's quick and accurate when he raps, and when he's sober— or at least partially so—he could charm the gown off a nun with his charisma alone.

I was busy touring with another artist at the time Julian's label wanted our song recorded, so we had to do our own separate parts individually. I'm glad it worked out that way because the lyrics of our song…they were written for market. Right now, that's what sells and sells well—sex, individuality, and answering to absolutely no one in the pursuit of both. After getting to know Julian better, I don't think that's the song I'd write for us now. I'd write something much more personal, more meaningful. A slower, raspier melody about the constant juxtaposition between the Julez everyone else sees and the Julian I see, and how undeniably jarring it is when the side of the coin flips to reveal one extreme personality to the next.

While most of today was Julian in his best form, tonight was all Julez. Drugged up, harsh, pissed off at the world. I don't blame Julian for being pissed off, just how he handled it. Or more accurately, how he chose *not* to handle it. Today was just a lot. A lot of emotions, with no real resolutions.

He found his resolution—escapism via drugs. He got to disassociate while I was left on my own, feeling…helpless. I felt so helpless today, not only at the children's hospital but also with Julian. Being helpless is a feeling I hate with a passion. A feeling I took back fourteen years ago and fight like hell not to lose myself to anymore.

Faced with that helplessness again, I retreated to my safe place the only way I know how—alone. Pushing Julian away earned back some control, but then when that wasn't enough, I lashed out. Facing off against Julian onstage like I did wasn't my smartest idea, especially using those lyrics. People already think we're fucking. I didn't need to fan the flames stoking the rumor mill. Not those flames or the ones brewing between me and Julian because there is *something* there. Something even I can't deny. If there wasn't, he wouldn't get so damn angry at just the idea of me having a date. The only date I have tonight is with my own bed. A bed I would've tossed and turned in thinking about Julian, worrying the whole time about what I'd be coming back to in the morning. If there'd even be anything to come back to.

And that was before this whole concert-on-top-of-a-wet-bus situation.

"How close can you get us to the other bus?" I ask Antonio, tucking the smallest folding pocketknife I own into my front pocket on my way up the aisle.

"Less than an inch," he says confidently, so I have him do it, helping guide him through the tightly packed crowd to close the several feet separating the buses.

We work together to open the emergency exit window in the roof, then before I pull myself up through it, I tell him to lock it after me so no one can get in. It's not like anyone can actually climb the bus, but just in case.

Once on top of the bus, I stay perched down, scanning the massive crowd of drenched fans singing, dancing, and drinking in the rain. Everybody's having a genuinely good time and I can understand why Julian did this, because sometimes people just need to let go and have fun in the simplest of ways. Money isn't everything, and although it helps make life easier, it definitely doesn't make you happier.

Surfboards and inflatable boats—some empty, some with people in them—all gyrate aggressively as they're shuffled between different hands over people's heads. I shake my own head, getting lost watching it all. They're fucking crazy.

We're all fucking crazy. I should've left when I had the chance.

With Julian's back to me, I remain still, secretly watching him as he continues rapping acapella.

He's why I stayed. Even now, I can't leave.

I can… I just don't want to.

Slowly and carefully, I push to standing, smiling when the crowd thunders even louder than the rainstorm overhead.

"Collette! Collette!" they chant, and I wave, spinning in a tight circle to take in the sheer size of the gathering. It's ten times bigger than I imagined. Did he invite the entire concert?

A drone hovers nearby, daring to come in dangerously close, so I blow it a kiss since it's undoubtedly streaming this whole thing somewhere. Two more pop up right behind it, zooming over as well, and I do the same to them, blowing each a kiss for whoever's watching.

Past the drones, beach balls bounce wildly in the air, the people beneath just as frenzied when Julian's voice cuts off.

Across the tops of the buses, I'm barely able to make out Julian say, "You came." He's staring at me like he sees me, but doesn't really *see* me. He was drinking last I saw him, and who knows what other influences he's under right now. I doubt he even knows. He consumes blindly, ignorantly. He doesn't want to know what'll happen to him when he takes something because he doesn't care.

Or he does and is just hoping for the worst.

I take a step toward him, calling his name.

Not hearing me—or choosing not to—he turns, lining the backs of his shoes up with the edge of the roof, inadvertently revealing Axel on the other side of him. Axel's sitting at a much smaller drum set than he usually uses and his eyes triple in size a second before he's off his stool, standing and pointing at me with one of his drumsticks.

His eyelids now closed with both arms stretched out to his sides, Julian either says, "Follow me," or "Fall with me." At the same time I take a step toward him, my right foot slips on the wet metal under me, my whole body jolting backward to counteract the movement. I catch the moment Julian falls straight back, *off* the side of his bus, and stop, my body going cold at the sight. He crowd-surfs at every single show we do, but this…this feels wrong somehow.

Axel shouts, "Collette! What are you doing here?"

Julian's eyes fly open to seek out mine again. His arms windmill in front of him as he tries to stop his fall, but it's no use. He lands in the ocean of bodies below in the next breath and is immediately swept up by the swell, mixing with the others already riding the human surf. At first, he attempts to sit upright, yelling while scrambling to remain above the bouncing heads and hands, then all at once, he's ripped away as both his body and voice disappear beneath the surface entirely.

This whole thing feels wrong. Not just Julian's odd behavior, but also the claiming I just witnessed. Even with the main attraction himself down there now, the undertow doesn't seem to be satisfied. It's like the tide's leveling up, preparing to add to its collection of victims.

The emergency window on Julian's bus opens and people start piling out onto the roof through it. Julian's bus is always packed with people. With partiers. *Remoras*. Remoras attach themselves to bigger fish around them—the bigger, the better—then feed off their leftovers. They live off the rewards, whether from hard work or good fortune, that they had zero help in obtaining themselves. They're essentially success leeches and they'll bleed you out if you let them.

On the other side of the remoras, Axel yells for everybody to go back inside, but nobody listens. More and more lift themselves up through the window until they're spilling on to the roof of my bus as well.

Behind me, I reach a leg out to tap on my own emergency window, hoping Antonio is nearby to open it for me. I hear the latch disengage, then a shoulder bumps into mine, sending me sideways. Unfortunately, two pairs of arms reach out, steadying me before I fall. *Unfortunately* because they're overzealous, twitchy arms. Arms that are impatient for no other reason than self-satisfaction. My heroes aren't heroes at all. They're remoras, trying to get their suction cups placed anywhere they can.

"I'm good," I tell them, thrusting their hands off. The exchange causes me to trip over the now-ajar window, landing directly on top of the glass with a hard thump, closing it again. *Shit. That's going to hurt tomorrow.* Thank God the glass didn't break, or else I would've fallen all the way through to the floor of the bus and possibly cracked my tailbone, or worse.

"Hey!" I hear Axel yell again except in another direction. "Get Bare! Hurry!"

My pants and underwear soaked straight through, I start to crabwalk backward, off the window.

"Oh, I remember this skit," one of the remoras says, elbowing the taller, bulkier one. "That show was so hot. Think she'll give us lap dances, too?"

Lowering himself, he follows after me in a sort of bear crawl, identical to how Julian did when he was baked out of his mind and I was just trying to rouse him enough for our performance. Except this is much more predatory. Much more intentional. This time my heart pounds at a rapid speed I can't control any more than I could the last time something like this happened.

No, no, no.

Keep your head up, smile on, and don't show weakness.

"That's not what I'm doing, guys," I say through chattering teeth. "I just want to get back inside my bus."

With my ass almost clear of the glass, the very real concern shifts from if I can make it inside to if I can make it inside alone. If someone, or multiple someones, follows me inside, I'd be endangering Antonio, too.

In a split-second decision, I straighten my legs out in front of me, and bang a fist on the glass, yelling for Antonio to lock it again. I don't know how or when he'll be able to get out, but I have to believe he'll be okay as long as nobody else makes it inside with him.

Why did Julian do this? This is where our teams sleep. At least my team does. He got lucky that they weren't here.

Axel's question comes back to me. *"What are you doing here?"* Like he was surprised I was. I can only hope that Julian assumed everyone from my bus was gone.

Hands latch on my ankles, then jerk me forward, my ass sliding easily across the slippery surface to the smaller of the remoras. In an automatic reaction, my hand flies to my pocket, but before I can get it inside, the larger remora drops from standing into a plank over my body in one smooth motion, his torso landing on mine as his arms give out, crushing my arm between us.

Breathe. Just breathe.

The problem is with the extra weight on me, it's hard to breathe. And with the hands still holding my ankles down, it's hard to move. No, it's impossible to move. Three of my limbs are restrained for Christ's sake.

"We're not gonna make the same mistake Julez did. We're not letting you cock-tease us."

His rancid breath heats my already clammy face as his erection digs into my abdomen, and a scream tries to make its way up my throat. Last time this happened, I let the scream out and help never came.

You've been here before and escaped. You can do it again.

Right?

I have one arm left. *I just have to use it correctly*, I think as I eye the side of the bus.

They can't do anything too bad in front of all these people watching. In front of Julian watching. Is Julian watching? He'd never let this kind of thing happen.

The problem with that is…Julian isn't here. Julez is, and Julez is unpredictable, unreliable, and…he's not actually here at all.

It's not like expecting a man to come to my rescue ever did me any good anyway. My name's tattooed on my back for a reason. Because in moments like this, I can't trust anyone but myself.

Wrapping my free arm around the foul-breathed remora's neck, I pull him against me even harder, blocking out the feel of his body against mine, then roll with all my might, twisting my legs so quickly and tightly into a tangle, the other remora's forced to release them. The two of us roll off the side of the bus together and into the pulsing crowd below. The dozens of other hands that catch us help pull us apart as I kick out at the remora, getting him as far from me as possible, but then they turn on me, too. Strange hands groping my crotch and breasts feel as invasive as the remoras' attack, but I have to block it out, drawing on the arsenal I always keep at the ready, and bend myself in half so my ass sinks. I manage to shake one of my legs free, dropping it under me. Once my foot touches solid ground, I push as hard as I can, trying my best to part the sea of limbs and smoke and desperation. I just want out.

A large hand breaks through, grabbing one of mine, and yanks me past everyone else's. Bare's face appears a second before his apology does, followed only by another, and another.

"I gotta get you out of here. He's gonna kill me. He's gonna kill everyone. Fuck."

He tucks my trembling frame against him like a football in a wide receiver's hold when he books it for the end zone, then pushes through the throng of people until we eventually come upon a blacked-out SUV idling just past the thickest part of the crowd.

"Thank you," I tell him through cold lips as he places me in the back seat, buckling me in.

"Please don't thank me. I didn't do my job."

"You weren't able to get Julian out of there?"

He shakes his head once. "I was trying to get to him when Axel got me."

"And you left Julian to help me?" Bare is Julian's bodyguard, not mine. His job is to keep Julian safe and alive. He lost his boss in a mob of crazed fans and just…abandoned him there…for me.

Bare gives me a confused kind of stare, then sighs, rubbing a hand over his beard. "Per Julian's instructions."

"What instructions?"

"Julian made it very, *very* clear that if it were to ever come down to him or you, that I'm to go for you first. And if Holter's present, then I'm to help Holter first because Julian knows you'd choose Holter over yourself."

Of course, I would. I love Holter more than life itself.

"When he kept repeating your name from the crowd, I didn't realize it was because you were here. I thought he was asking after you like he always does."

"Always?"

He nods slowly, glancing behind him, and saying distractedly, "I assumed that's all it was because everyone thought you'd left for the night. It wasn't until Axel got my attention that I saw you hadn't." Bare looks back at me. "I'm sorry I didn't get to you sooner and I'm sorry for what happened. If Julian lets me live, I hope you can forgive me."

There's nothing to forgive because it's not Bare's fault. The only people responsible are the aggressors.

The sympathy in his eyes brings tears to mine, and all I can do is whisper, "Find him." Julian putting me and my son first doesn't change the fact that he's still in need of saving himself.

With a final nod, Bare tells the driver, "Make sure you get her to a hotel safely." Then he closes the door on the noise but not the memory of what just took place.

One memory leads to two, then enough to burst a hole in the dam I've kept in place for well over a decade.

"Which hotel, miss?"

I don't need a hotel. I need my son, the reason I learned how to fight so hard to begin with.

Through a sob, I give him the address to David's estate, then press my head to the headrest, letting the memories flow as freely as the tears streaming down my face.

Being with Bodee was like being on a roller coaster except there were no rules, seat belts, or safety precautions. And there was no finish line. You never got a rest or a chance to get off. Once you sat down, you were locked in by the gravity Bodee himself created.

When he picked me out of a crowd, crooked a finger while

whispering to one of his guards to collect me, I thought I was scouted for my talent. I'd been singing along to his set, hitting every note, so when I joined him onstage, I had no idea he would want me for anything else. I was sixteen, of course I fantasized about Bodee Keys falling in love with me and asking me to run away with him. I never imagined it'd actually happen. In the beginning, it was all so surreal and exhilarating for me to even question why it did. Having Bodee pursue me was the biggest rush I'd ever experienced. Even bigger than opening for him after that first night because *he* was exhilarating.

It wasn't until years later that I realized I'd been picked, not for my singing ability, but to be groomed. From the time I was sixteen and joined his tour—handed over with my parents' handsomely paid-for blessing—I was expected to do whatever Bodee wanted, whenever he wanted. If I objected, he'd find someone else who wouldn't, and there was never a shortage of volunteers in that department.

At first, I didn't object because it was fun, enjoyable. Mutual, consensual. Threesomes, foursomes, orgies—usually with Bodee and people I'd only ever caught glimpses of on television.

I was young—too young—I was attractive, and I had what people kept calling "stage presence," but only when Bodee wasn't in earshot. He had a jealous streak that rivalled Julian's except in a completely different way. Bodee didn't have the same reservations about me being with others; he shared me regularly. His jealousy revolved around one thing only—stardom. He was the star, the biggest star, the fucking sun, and the rest of us were just lucky enough to be in his orbit.

Right around the time I started voicing my objections, I also started outshining Bodee in the public eye. Our relationship had been top news as soon as he let us go public with it, but my singing career was suddenly getting more attention than Bodee's. Maybe because I was getting older, more mature, more confident in both myself and my abilities. I don't know why things kicked off at that exact time, just that they did, and I wasn't going to miss the opportunities headed my way. You learn very quickly that lightning doesn't strike twice in the entertainment business, so when it does—*if* it does—you grab hold, grit your teeth, and ride out the shock for as long as you can. I knew I had to hone my talent if I was going to be a solo artist, so I hired a vocal coach. I was done performing for Bodee, onstage and off.

With my online schooling, I was gaining access to more information, as well as better resources, and I didn't like Bodee's requests anymore, or the reasons behind them, especially when I declined and he kept pushing. It's one thing when both parties agree to be polyamorous, but it's a whole different story when one doesn't. That's coercion and a form of abuse. Sixteen-year-old me didn't know that, but eighteen-year-old me was catching on.

I still loved him though. Everybody romanticized the man Bodee Keys pretended to be and it was hard to get past that false persona to see the real monster it was masking.

To add to confusion, Bodee surprised me by being supportive of my budding solo career. He became involved in every aspect, helping me with anything I needed. He even jumped headfirst into monogamy. I thought it was all for me. He made me believe it was all for me.

Really it was all for show. Bodee's entire life is for show and everything he does is for his own benefit. He was building me a career so that he alone could knock it down. I was getting strong; he preferred me weak. I was growing brave; he needed me meek. So, he started chipping away at my confidence, always making remarks about my body, my vocals, my everything. Nothing about me was good enough all of a sudden.

Then came the relationship manipulation. He didn't just try to share me anymore, he wanted to hand me out, because with Bodee, if you don't bend the way he wants, he'll break you in half, then bend the pieces himself.

Luckily, I'd just found out I was pregnant, so I was glued to the toilet with morning sickness that lasted around the clock and managed to avoid the brunt of Bodee's planned punishment.

Once the nausea subsided weeks later, he planted a story in the press about his big proposal, that way if I tried to leave, I'd be public enemy number one for breaking Bodee Keys's heart right after he promised me a storybook wedding and a matching happily-ever-after to follow.

Technically, Bodee never asked me to marry him, but I agreed to anyway. I didn't have any other options. Bodee held my entire life in his perfectly manicured hands and the news around our engagement had become an absolute circus. We were everywhere. There wasn't any room or time to do anything other than be Bodee Keys's fiancée. My only hope was that us having a baby together would change things, would change *him.*

Another quality of Bodee's I made the mistake of underestimating was his patience. He doesn't abandon his schemes; he prolongs them for harsher outcomes.

He moved the date up so there was no chance of my pregnancy overshadowing the wedding he manufactured into existence before seeing it through to a flawless execution, and we got married in one of Hollywood's most televised nuptials the world had ever seen.

Hours after we said, "I do," he sent his manager into our room… to fuck me, his new wife.

On my wedding night.

While I was pregnant.

And sleeping.

Thank God I woke up in time before actually could. It wasn't enough to deter Jack though. Even pregnant, I still had to fight him tooth and nail to avoid being raped. I fought him harder *because* I was pregnant. I was overcome with a primal urge to protect my unborn child, and my body was the vessel responsible for keeping Holter alive, so I did what I had to.

During the altercation, I broke off one of the handles from my nightstand's drawer, and I used it as a knife to get myself out of both that room and Bodee Keys's clutches. I hobbled out of Bodee's mega-mansion naked, bruised, covered in blood, and alone. By the time I reached the bottom of the driveway, both my marriage and career were over. That night, I left with nothing except my arsenal of weapons, not just the physical kind I was wielding in front of my battered pregnant body, but mental ones, too, and I've remained armed ever since.

Tonight proves why I've had to. There are monsters at every pay-grade. From the Bodees of the world to the remoras, they exist everywhere you look. The richer the monster, the more elaborate the mask, and sometimes the wealthiest are the ugliest of all.

Chapter 18

Collette

The next two days all my calls and emails are auto-directed to Irelynn while I bunker down with Holter at our rental. In between studio sessions together, David and I also discuss my proposed charity idea. We agree on hosting a gala to benefit the children's hospital in LA, and thankfully, Kim-ly offers to help with the planning portion since neither of us are very experienced in that area. David is one of the biggest names in producing, but he's incredibly private, choosing to stay close to home night and day to be with his family, and he rarely does public appearances. Excluding the extreme wealth, David's the exact opposite of Bodee Keys.

Saturday morning, both tour buses are already in Washington, and since David has business in Seattle, Holter and I tag along in his helicopter to meet up with everybody. It's not like me to disappear in the middle of a tour—at the end, yes, but not during. Never during. The break helped clear my head though, and I'm happy I took it. I'll see the rest of The Family Julez Tour through just like I would with any other tour; I just…needed a little space. And time. Time is one of the only luxuries you can't buy more of. It's priceless and it flies by faster than you realize. As much as I hate to admit it, it's gone quicker than I thought possible. I wish I could get it back, but since I can't, I need to make the most of the time I have now. It's as simple and as hard as that. The biggest gift Bodee gave me was our son, but the second biggest gift was time. Time that belongs to me and only me because if I'd stayed with my ex, nothing in my life would've belonged to me, especially not time.

As soon as the chopper lands, Holter and I part ways with David with a promise to meet up before he leaves again, then I hire a car to drop Holter off with Mary at the buses. With Julian nowhere in sight, I decide to turn right back around and head into downtown. We're scheduled to record a podcast, but it looks like he's paying me back for ghosting the tour. I didn't miss anything important, only travel days.

Doing my own hair and makeup on the ride over, I leave my large, dark sunglasses on, then I walk inside the building where the studio's located with my head up, a smile on, and not an ounce of weakness to be seen.

Seen…because while it may not show visibly, it's definitely felt. After spending the last couple days in near-seclusion, it feels strange being around others again. After everything that's happened, I feel strange—vulnerable.

I don't want to be here.

I push the sunglasses closer to the bridge of my nose, stretching my lips even wider as I enter the elevator, then lean back against the handrail inside, clenching my tight, swollen fingers around the cool metal. The numbers rapidly increase before the loud *ding* announces the floor I selected.

Time to face the music. The same music I've been facing all along. I've done this before and I can do it again, just like I always have—alone.

The second the doors open, I'm greeted by loud voices that make me hang back.

Actually, only one is loud and its owner is absolutely furious.

"Where the fuck is she? It's been how many hours, how many fucking *days*, and nobody's seen her? Nobody? Fucking find her already!"

Right away, I know it's Julian, so I step off the elevator, purposely keeping a slow pace to gauge the situation.

Slade looks up from his phone with a bored expression, telling his client, "You don't need her. You're the most interesting part of the whole tour anyway."

"Julez, we're live in ten minutes," a producer says. "We need you to go on whether Collette's here or not."

"If she's not here, I'm not going on. Yinz can kiss my ass."

"Julez. Dude," one of the show's hosts, Scott, says with a scowl. "This isn't what Slade said when we spoke last."

Slade straightens his spine, glaring at Scott before swinging a worried gaze to Julian.

Julian's too busy freaking out to notice though as he booms, "Fuck you! And fuck your pussy-ass show!" He turns my way, finally spotting me, and time—the same time that usually passes too damn fast—actually slows for once as we regard one another.

He looks like a fucking mess—the most beautiful mess to ever exist. He's got dark circles under red-lined eyes and a small cut on his right cheek. A new tattoo that's still raised covers the side of his neck, and as much as his heavy gaze tries to hold mine captive, I can't help but run my eyes over the tattoo, mesmerized by it. It's a pot of what looks like honey with two dead bees lying at its cracked base as the thick, golden liquid oozes out.

The moment's broken by Julian's low demand—he's *not* asking—as he says, "Where the *fuck* have you been?"

Everybody, even the delivery guy holding a stack of boxes at the front desk, is tuned in, watching us.

Lifting my chin, I say with the tone of a true professional, "Working. Ready to get back to it?"

"Work," Julian repeats with a shake of his head before strutting into the soundproof room.

Slade bolts right for me, whispering, "Remember, you signed—"

I put a hand up. "I know what I signed, Slade." Thanks to the NDA I signed before the tour, I can't talk about what happened—what really happened—with anyone, not even Julian. Especially not Julian. "I also know what Julian told you about me, so stay the fuck away from me, unless you want me to start causing problems you won't be able to sign your way out of." Asshole.

"But you can't—"

"Six minutes!"

"He'll—"

"Do you mind?" I give Julian's agent a look so hard he stops short. "I have to focus."

Bypassing him, I go in to take the seat next to Julian, murmuring for his ears only, "Professional as always."

He ignores me, putting his headphones on.

I shake hands with both Scott and his co-host, Lon, speeding through the usual small talk. I've been interviewed by them a few times over the years on their podcast, Lon-Awaited News. It should be called Lon-Awaited Gossip because they like to stir up trouble with any tidbit they can get their hands on, whether it's true or not. You have to be on your game at all times with them, and I'm really hoping they don't bring up whatever the hell Julian just pulled while we're on-air because I honestly don't know what I'll say. They're supposed to give us a list of questions they're going to ask ahead of time, which I studied on the flight up here, but these guys are notorious for going off-script, so I really do need to focus. Press of any kind can be a total mindfuck, but interviews like this are even worse.

"And we're on in three, two…"

"We're here with popstar sensation, Collette, and rapper, Julez," Scott starts, speaking into his microphone as I toy with my headphones. With my sunglasses still on, they're not sitting flush against my ears, so I'm getting a lot of background noise, making it hard to hear clearly.

"…your Family Julez Tour?"

Luckily, they're both looking at Julian.

Julian hesitates, then says against his mic, "Yup."

Christ.

Just what every radio interviewer wants to hear—one-word answers.

Their eyes turn toward me and I take a stab in the dark, saying, "We're having a lot of fun. This is my first time touring with a rapper, and I have to say, the energy on The Family Julez Tour is unmatched. It's been pretty amazing to be a part of. I'm really looking forward to our show tonight." That's why we're here, to promote tonight's show. I just need to keep them on-topic and keep Julian…off-air. He's got his lethargic vibe going and nobody will want to buy tickets to sit and watch *that*.

"What—"

Static.

"—part—"

More static.

"What part?" I repeat, making both men frown. Lon points at my glasses when he notices my headphones sitting askew and mouths for me to take them off, but I shake my head, cupping the headphones with my hands so they're pushed against my skull.

"What part exactly has been amazing for you, Collette?"

"Oh, well, watching Julez perform has to be the front runner." I force a laugh, still trying to keep tonight's show the focal point. "I've never seen anyone keep a crowd so captivated while on stage before."

"Wow." Scott rears back, glancing at Lon who lifts his eyebrows. "Not even Bodee Keys?"

Out of the corner of my eye, Julian's head twists in my direction, but I don't dare look at him as I say, "Not even Bodee Keys." A real smile tugs at my lips. They're not supposed to mention my ex's name to me, nobody that interviews me is, but this one time I'll allow it. Only because it's true. When he actually gives it his all, Julian's passion for music translates to his fans, making them love it, too. Bodee's passion for music was replaced by greed for money and power a long time ago, and it translates just as clearly. He was a lazy performer then, and from what I've seen, he still is. He doesn't need to wow anybody, his name alone does that, so he doesn't bother putting in the effort.

Scott and Lon ask me a couple more questions before bringing up the fans.

"Knock on wood, Julez's fans have been very accepting so far. When I first walk out, I think some of them are taken aback—"

Julian scoffs far enough away from the mic it doesn't pick the sound up.

"—but as soon as my music starts, they've been pretty good about giving me a chance to show them what I'm about."

They share a laugh that has the hair on the back of my neck rising.

"And what are you about?" Scott asks.

Lon immediately follows up with, "Who cares? I'd give her a chance to show me anything."

"Watch your fucking mouth," Julian rumbles beside me, not exactly into the mic but not away from it either.

My smile returns to the fake one again as I redirect them as delicately as possible. "I've always believed the fans are the best part of this whole job, and I'm grateful I get to meet so many new ones."

"Up close and personal?" Lon asks.

"Unfortunately, due to the rigorous travel schedule along with a lot of our shows being held at outdoor venues, we haven't been able to do many meet and greets on this tour. We're always happy to meet our fans out and about though. Julez has extra-long arms, perfect for taking selfies," I joke, hoping to lighten the quickly darkening mood. I can feel the wheels turning, I just don't know which direction we're headed.

"What about—"

More static interrupts.

"—on top of the bus, right? When was that? A couple days ago? That was an outdoor concert, and you were able to get very close and personal with fans."

"Or should we say one fan?"

"Was it one though?" The hosts exchange looks, then Lon pretends to think about it.

"Let's ask Collette."

A moment of silence hangs in the air, which is never a good sign. We're literally here to talk. I don't want to talk about the night on top of the bus though. I can't without breach of contract.

"Julez is a big fan of crowd-surfing," I say before holding my breath.

"Yeah, he sure is." Scott nods like he's throwing me a bone, which he kind of is. I need to get us off this train of thought.

"That shit got a little crazy…wouldn't you say, Collette?" Lon says, watching me closely.

Leaning forward so he's against the mic, Julian interrupts with, "My shows are always crazy. What are you getting at? And why the fuck are you looking at her like that?" His shoulders scrunched near his ears, he rotates his head my way.

Avoiding both men's penetrating stares, I say, "I'm just happy we could give the fans in LA *something*. We were disappointed part of the show got cancelled just as much as they were. Fingers crossed tonight's show has clear skies." I tell them more about our show in the heart of

Washington tonight as well as where people can purchase tickets. It's at an outdoor music festival in a gorge, overlooking one of the rivers that snakes through the state, which I think is a big enough selling point alone, so I make sure to mention it.

The subject change doesn't work, and Lon lowers his voice, only responding to the first part of what I just said. "You definitely gave them something."

Julian's out of his chair, pointing at Lon as he says, "You're doing a lot of insinuating right now, motherfucker. You got something to say, fucking spit it out before I put your head through the wall."

"You didn't know?" Scott asks Julian before looking at me. "—doesn't know?"

"Know what?" Julian snaps, his jaw twitching.

Lon shrugs. "To be honest, we thought you were in on it. Like an open relationship."

My heart starts racing so loud I swear the mics are picking it up.

"Yeah, the rumors have been nonstop since The Family Julez Tour started with pictures of you two everywhere and the performances onstage." They both pretend to fan themselves, and I drop my gaze, staring at the dusty wires running across the table's surface. "So, when Collette gave a little extra *something* to those 'disappointed fans' to make up for the cancellation…"

I tune out the rest. So it's on me. I *gave* to those remoras, did I?

"Collette? What the fuck are they talking about?"

I just shake my head. I know I'm not allowed to tell Julian certain things and it looks like nobody else on his team is either. How does he not know *anything* though? Slade keeps Julian's social media passwords from him because Julian loathes social media, but doesn't he hear the news from anywhere? Or anyone?

"Here. We'll show you, Julez. We have the clip."

A TV mounted on the wall beside our heads springs to life, then the black screen is replaced by a video of the remora lying on top of me with my arm clenched around his neck just before we roll off the side together. With absolutely no context, it looks like I'm pulling him to me to kiss, to fuck—willingly. It doesn't show the other remora holding my feet in place just seconds before the fall. It doesn't show the fear churning inside of me during the entire ordeal. It doesn't show the truth at all.

I watch the video once, only once, because it's enough. I already know exactly what went down, and it's nothing like what these men are trying to make it out to be.

Releasing my headphones, the headband portion slides forward to hang loosely in front of my face while the clip plays on a loop, the hosts narrating every sickening second to their audience.

Julian curses, turning to leave, but I shoot a hand out, blindly catching his wrist. If I can't tell him, I want him to at least see. I feel like he's the only one that could understand without me needing to tell him at all. Maybe I'm a moron for wanting him to see that I wasn't ready to fuck some random guy the second he was out of my sight. Maybe I'm a moron for thinking he even cares in the first place.

But he wouldn't be reacting like this if he didn't. So maybe…I'm just a moron for liking the possibility that he does care at all.

Julian watches it through one more time, then barks, "Shut it off." He pulls my mic to his mouth, and says, "The interview's over. Yinz can go fuck yourselves." He helps me to standing, carefully removing the headphones still trying to cling to my ears, then he overhand throws them at the TV, splintering the glass.

Our hands clasped, he pulls me behind him out the door, away from the hosts' angry shouts. Slade immediately attempts to intercept us, but Julian just shakes his head at his agent, taking me down a hall until we reach the men's restroom.

Pushing the door open, he makes sure it's empty, then tugs me inside and flicks the lock behind us.

Stopped in front of one of the sinks, he reaches up to grab my glasses, but I stop him, shaking my own head.

"Let me see."

"Let you see what?"

"What he did." He winces like he's in pain. "Were there more?"

I give a small nod. Nodding isn't telling, per se.

"Then let me see what they did to you."

He did notice. He noticed what the other two men in that room didn't. Wouldn't. They chose to view me like that.

I take the sunglasses off, staring at the floor between us.

"They didn't leave any marks around my eyes."

Soft as cashmere, Julian whispers, "I'm not looking around your eyes. I'm looking *in* your eyes."

My eyes lift to meet his, then his face blurs behind a sheet of tears. The next instant, I'm pulled to him in a hug as he rubs soothing circles on my back.

"I'm so fucking sorry. I fucked up. Again. I'm always fucking up."

He hangs his head until his chin rests on my shoulder, his strong front holding up mine.

"You didn't do it. They did."

He pulls back to look me in the eye, and drops his hands to the sink, framing my hips. "Why didn't you call me? Why didn't you tell me?"

"I… I thought you knew."

"How could I?"

"Because Bare—"

"Bare knew?"

I regard Julian, my chest aching for him more than myself in this moment. His own bodyguard couldn't tell him. Slade made quick work of cleaning the whole thing up…for Julian only. Slade never checked on me to see if I was okay.

"No one told you?"

"No, they fucking didn't."

We're both quiet for a minute, then he asks, "Where'd you go?"

"Home. Spent some time with Holter and a couple friends."

"Were you okay? *Are* you okay?"

"I'm okay."

He stares into my eyes, not saying anything until slowly, so slowly, he leans down to press a kiss to each eyelid as they flutter closed.

With my eyes shut, I don't see it coming but Julian's lips hover over mine just barely, and we hold the position, neither of us stopping, neither of us pushing for more.

This response is unusual to me, foreign even. Not only because it's Julian, but because it's nothing like what Bodee would've done. He was never like this. He never treated me like this—like I was precious.

"Bare told me about your new hierarchy…the one with me and Holter at the top," I say without opening my eyes.

"So you know." Julian's warm lips tickle mine, and I almost moan.

"Know what?"

"What I'd do for you. What I'll do for you."

I go to open my eyes, but he places a hand in front of them, saying, "Not yet."

"Julian," I say, squeezing them shut.

"Collette."

Our names and breath mix between us in a combination of want.

Nothing on our bodies is technically touching, only his lip piercings grazing my skin every time I inhale, yet it feels incredibly intimate. Maybe because we both want to touch, and we both know we both want to touch, but neither of us is breaking that line; just making it stretch taut. One way or another, it's bound to snap if we don't pull back soon.

I'm just not sure I have the strength to do it right now. I've been fielding Julian off since the night he barged on to my bus.

For the first time since vowing to myself that I'd never get involved with another celebrity, I've started questioning it. Julian makes me question it because when he's like this, he's almost believable. Almost, because while I *want* to believe Julian is who he's showing me, it's when the coin flips and his other, meaner side comes out that I remember why I made the vow to begin with.

"Let me finish first."

"Finish?" I ask.

"Got me spinning in circles just thinking about it."

I recognize the line he used the last time we were on stage together, but where my lyrics were just talking shit, his seemed a bit more personal. While I don't know for sure that they were inspired by me, I don't know that they weren't either. Me saying he goes down on me was obviously not about Julian specifically. He doesn't go down on anybody.

Julian grabs one of my hands, lifting it above my head to spin me around so I'm facing away from him, then his deep voice envelops me.

"Let me off the ride but never the high.
The view from up here look different through your eyes.
Never need to chase that rush with you by my side.
Baby, you're the only drug I haven't done tried
Yet here we are together, ruling the fucking sky.
Gimme the cover beneath your wings,
And I'll promise to keep you lifted long after I die."

Finally, I open my eyes, considering Julian as he stands behind me. If he wasn't wearing a shirt, I'd search out that broken angel wing tattoo of his. Is that who these lyrics are for? Whoever he got the tattoo in honor of?

If so, why is he singing them now?

"Nobody will ever hurt you again. I swear."

"You can't promise that."

"I just did."

"You can't keep it." Nobody will hurt me *ever*? No one can guarantee that. Even parents to their children. Of course, we want to keep them safe forever, but unfortunately, we can't.

He lowers his head until his chin is almost touching my shoulder again, and says, "Watch me."

The intensity in both his stare and his words makes me question everything, even my sanity. This can't be real.

I busy myself washing my hands, then splash some water on my face, bringing reality crashing back into me—the actual reality I'm stuck in, not the one I wish I could escape to. Sadly, this entire experience is nothing new. Misogyny runs rampant in this business. It's tightly woven into every bit of the entertainment industry, making it the Kevlar of patriarchy—stronger than steel. Men may provide entertainment to the masses, but to the entire world women *are* the entertainment. And by any means necessary.

I feel the shirt at my back being lifted slowly, carefully, then something is written along my backbone. When I glance at Julian in the mirror, he's focusing intently on whatever he's writing with the marker he usually carries in his front pocket.

"What are you writing?"

"My name." He traces the letters with the tip of his finger when he's finished, eliciting a shiver that follows his every move. "I've got your back now, too."

Something inside of me thaws, a small piece of the ice casing around my heart that I've been cultivating since the night I left Bodee's house.

What if this could be real?

The scarier question is, what if I want it to be?

Chapter 19

Julian

"What the fuck, Julez? I thought you didn't care." Blood spews from his lips as he glares up at me from the floor of my bus.

Usually, I don't care. About any of it. Not about my money. Not about the dumb fucking overpriced material items I've accumulated. Not about my bus, my bed. Nothing. There's nothing in my life I actively care about anymore. Not when it all feels like it's on loan anyway. This all just feels temporary. Pointless. Everything around me is based off the public's opinion of me, and not even the real me but the version I give them because people who are smarter, richer, more experienced, and more powerful than me tell me who to be now. And that opinion can change at any time. I'm a puppet on someone else's strings. A pretzel being molded by someone else's hands. *I'm* temporary. *I'm* pointless.

But Collette? There's nothing pointless about Collette. There's nothing anyone can tell me about her. Or how I'm supposed to act around her. With Collette, my true self just comes through naturally because I care about Collette. I care about Collette a lot. And I guess I'm to blame for not letting that be known sooner. Doesn't mean I'm not gonna fuck him up though for putting his hands and his fucking cock on Collette while his buddy held her down.

I grab ahold of his foot—no clue where the fuck his shoe went, probably in my bedroom where I found him hiding in the closet—and drag him to the front of the bus, continuing down the stairs, making sure his body hits each and every step.

"You're acting like it's serious. Who fucking cares?" he screams like the pathetic piece of shit he is.

"I care!" I bellow, loving the way it feels to be honest for once, then kick him in the side. Fuck, I want to kill him. I want to kill every motherfucker that had a hand in this.

I asked Bare what happened as soon as he got me out of the crowd that night, but the only thing he'd say was that I needed to ask Collette myself. Yeah, well, how fucking could I when she took off? He should've told me. I would've torn the entire West Coast apart to get her back if I'd known. I wouldn't have sat around, blitzed out of my mind, feeling sorry for myself because I thought Collette finally came to her senses and quit my tour.

Then there's Axel… Why didn't he tell me? He's my brother. He knows I would never let anyone hurt Collette. I knew he got into a fight with someone that night on the buses, but he wouldn't tell me who or why.

Now I know why and part of the who.

"Go get the other one," I tell Axel, and he disappears on to the bus.

It'd be really nice if someone could explain to me how the fuck everyone knew what these motherfuckers did to Collette and still let them stay on my bus. They've had a free ride this entire tour, just like everyone else filling this goddamn bus right now, but theirs ends today.

Pressing one foot on his right hand, crushing it to the asphalt, I call for someone to get Collette, too.

I don't even know this one's name or where he came from, just that he fucked with the wrong person, and now he and his shitfuck of a friend are permanently banned from anything my name's attached to. Collette's name, too. They'll never get close to her again. They shouldn't have been that close to begin with.

Fuck.

I look down at my hands shaking with anger, so much anger. I'm angry at myself more than anyone else because it *was* my fault. All of it. I had the concert. I got fried out of my fucking mind. I jumped off that bus, leaving Collette up there by herself.

I saw her and I thought I was hallucinating. I thought… I thought it was all coming to an end and I was getting my final wish of seeing Collette's face one last time.

It wasn't until I was already over the ledge that Axel's reaction tipped me off that she was actually there. If only I hadn't been so wasted, then I wouldn't have needed my eyes at all because I would've felt her.

Collette appears at the door to her bus a moment later, then she skirts a look over to Slade and they have some kind of silent conversation that I watch through narrowed eyes until he gives her a subtle nod.

What the fuck was that?

Looks like I need to have another talk with my team and make sure they understand the rules I thought I already made crystal clear. I'm sick of the confusion I keep finding out about after the fact—if I even find out at all.

Makes me wonder what else is being kept from me.

Collette descends her steps, coming to stand by my side. I feel the slightest pressure of her arm against mine, and almost close the gap. It's been a *long* few days without her near.

"What is this?" she asks with a curl to her lip.

"My gift to you."

She blinks up at me, ignoring the protests below us. "I don't want it."

"I know you don't." Nodding, I put more weight on the leg pinning him to the ground before putting my other foot on his free hand as well. "That's why we're throwing him out. Got your knife?"

Collette's got different hiding places all over her outfits for knives—a fact I've learned the hard way.

She mashes her lips together as she shoves a hand into her back pocket, and I tell her, "Strip him."

The swish of her blade punctuates my order as she perches down beside the guy under my feet. In a flash, she swings the blade down, piercing his shirt just below his armpit and making him jump with more curses. Dragging the knife, she cuts down the side of his shirt before doing the same thing with his pants. They're thin joggers, so the fabric separates like ripped paper. She goes to work on the other side of both pieces of clothing, then I lean down and pull them straight off his body with a couple of hard tugs.

With him down to his raggedy-ass boxers, I step off him, hoping to God I broke at least a few bones, and he curls up on his side to cry like the little bitch he is.

Slade coughs somewhere behind me but fuck him. *He* should've told me. I know his ass knew. His face is glued to both his phones 24/7. Even if he didn't see Collette getting assaulted with his own eyes, he saw it on social media.

Shit, I don't even have access to my log-in info, but it only took me a few seconds to find what I was looking for after Collette and I left the podcast. Within minutes, I was able to see what happened on the top of that bus from all different angles. Two scumbags went after Collette like wolves cornering a deer until the deer escaped by outsmarting them both. Axel tried getting Bare, then gave up when he didn't see the body-guard, and pushed through the rooftop party himself to tackle the one remaining wolf. My brother did a good job beating the shit out of him, I will give Axel that.

Speaking of, Axel's got the still-bruised friend in a headlock, dragging him down the stairs, so when he deposits him in front of us, Collette and I give him the same treatment we gave the first one.

They're both standing in nothing but their underwear when we're finished, and with a jerk of my chin, I tell them, "Start walkin.'"

Collette crosses her arms over her chest, but not before I catch the shake in her own hands. She's angry, too, but she's scared.

That's okay. I'm not. If this gets out, I'll take all the blame. This feels more personal than anything that's ever happened to me directly and I've had people legit empty entire bank accounts of mine before.

"We don't have any money!" the first scumbag yells.

Money. Their first go-to. His shriveled up nutsack's literally hanging out and all he's worried about is money.

"Where are we supposed to go?" the other one asks a little calmer. A little nicer.

Too late for that.

"Don't know. Don't care. But you got fifteen seconds to get the fuck outta my sight before I have Collette use her knife on you again." I give

Collette a sideways glance. "Since you're almost out of clothing to cut off, she'll start with the first thing that sticks out…"

Every man watching the exchange sucks in a breath.

"Fifteen," I count aloud, my focus on Collette now.

"Fourteen," comes out automatically.

Thirteen never comes because they make a run for it, pushing each other in their panicked getaway.

Collette turns her head to the side, not quite looking at me, and blows out a wobbly breath. "This will look bad."

"It's a damn good thing you weren't here to see it then, huh?"

Her eyes fly to mine and something unreadable passes right through them, as bright as a shooting star streaking across the midnight sky and just as mysterious.

"I don't give a fuck what anyone thinks, Collette. I'll brag about what I did onstage tonight for everyone to hear, and I'll take my beating from the press for it. I could've done this myself." *I would've.* "But I wanted you to have the choice to strip them of the same dignity they tried taking from you." And I'm so fucking proud she did.

"See you tonight," she murmurs, before running back on to her bus. But, uh, what the fuck does she think she's doing? She was just away from me for how many days? I'm not about to spend another without her. Hell can wait.

I'm on her heels the next second, making sure there's no fucking way she can lock the door on me again, and as soon as I'm inside, I say, "Everybody off."

Collette spins around, her eyes wide as hell and…watery?

"What do you think you're doing?"

Ignoring her, I pull out several hundred-dollar bills, handing them to Irelynn. "Go get everybody lunch."

"But you guys—"

"If we're late, we're late. I'll take the fall for that, too." Collette's too busy pretending to be strong for everybody else, even me, and I need to know she's okay. Nothing else matters, especially not the festival we're supposed to be headed to right now.

"You want me to take everyone?"

"Yeah. Get Bare." If she's taking Holter, I want Bare with them. No exceptions anymore.

Collette shakes her head, snatching her purse off a table to pull out bills of her own. Handing the cash to Irelynn, she takes the Benjamins I gave her assistant and shoves them into my heaving chest. She never wants anything from me.

She never wants *anything* from me.

"Just pick something up and bring it back here. You can all eat on the way."

There's not a restaurant on this planet that has what I really want, but after what she just went through, Collette's eating, and the quickest way to get her to do it is if I eat, too, so I tell Irelynn, "Get us both burgers. *We're* eating on the way."

We both watch in silence as everybody files past us until Holter gives me a shy grin, then I ruffle his hair, telling him we'll catch up later. I don't want him to think I'm ignoring him, I just gotta take care of his mom first.

Once we're alone, Collette turns for the kitchen, acting like I didn't just empty the bus for us to talk.

"Collette?" I try, but she doesn't acknowledge me as she opens and closes the microwave. It's empty but she opens it and closes it a second time, stalling. Avoiding. *Another one of my specialties.*

"Collette," I say firmer, and something about my tone gets her to stop. Quieter, I ask, "What are you feeling right now?"

One second her back's to me, the next her lips are pressed to mine, not in the teasing way we've done before either. This is full-on motherfucking kissing.

Kissing? She's really kissing me?

It takes another second for my brain to catch up to what's actually happening. *Collette's kissing me.*

She tastes exactly like that first time stepping foot on her bus… like home. My home. That's why I didn't recognize it. I've never felt like I had one to really know.

Until now.

I drop the cash in my hand, wanting to deepen the kiss, wanting to hold her to me, but she pulls back just as quickly. All I do is freeze—everything—nervous if I even move, I'll break whatever spell she must be under.

Her own hand comes up and she runs her fingertips over my jawline, up into my hair, gripping the strands roughly. My eyes close, savoring the shit out of the feeling because I've never felt anything better… until… Until I feel her tongue lick from my chin up to my nose, making the saying "I licked it, so it's mine" come to mind, then I have to lock my muscles up to keep from returning the gesture because I wouldn't settle for just her face. I'd lick Collette from head to fucking toe. Twice for good measure. Thrice just because.

> "Looks like trouble, tastes like fun.
> Sweet and sour against my tongue."

Her voice is raspy, then she repeats my words from earlier, whispering, "Let me see."

I obey her command as if I was born to serve her every whim.

"See what?"

"Your new tattoo."

I go to twist my head so she can get a better look, but her hold on my hair keeps me from moving.

"Why a honeypot?"

Fuck.

"Do you know anything about Egyptian mythology?"

"They liked honey?"

"I don't know about that." I chuckle through the tightness in my chest. *How's she gonna take this?* "I'm talking about the goddess Isis and her husband, Osiris. Their brother—"

"Their? They were siblings?"

Another strained chuckle. We're not off to a great start here.

"Twins who fell in love in the womb, but that's not the important part." It's not even the craziest part. "The important part is Isis was this fucking badass that didn't let anything stand in her way. After her brother, Set, killed her brother-husband, she went around and found every piece of Osiris's body that Set had chopped up and spread out all over Egypt. She reassembled the pieces and brought Osiris back with her magic."

Her eyebrows crease. "What does that have to do with honey?"

This is it.

"You know my nickname for you? What's the one thing that little bear never stops reaching for?"

"Platonic friends," she says, half-laughing.

"Honey. Nothing keeps him from searching for his pot of honey… or finding it."

Her eyes drop to the tat for a split second before coming right back.

"Why the crack down the middle?"

"Isn't it obvious?" I ask after a swallow. "I'm broken."

We stare into each other's eyes. Hers give nothing away, but she doesn't let go of me either. Maybe I didn't freak her out. Maybe—

"What happened to Osiris?"

She didn't ask about Isis, only Osiris. She cares about me, too.

She. Cares. About. Me.

"Isis brought Osiris back, but she couldn't keep him with her for long, so he ended up in the underworld where he became the king of the dead."

"Do you want to be found?"

"That's not why I got it," I tell her instead of answering. Wanting to be found and thinking I deserve to be found are two different things.

"Why did you get it?"

"I got it so you'll always have a reason to reach for me."

"I don't have magic."

"Then what'd you use to bring me back to life?"

Using her free hand, she places a finger where she usually does, which is now the top of the tattooed pot, the lip overflowing with thick honey, and I know my pulse is a fucking wreck under her touch.

"This," she whispers. "I touched you here and everything changed."

Everything?

"You're a hell of a deity."

Her smirk slips when I drop to one knee, then the other, keeping eye contact the entire time.

"They didn't deserve to touch you. I hate that they did," I say, pressing my forehead into her stomach. "Give me permission, Collette, and I'll erase every touch of theirs until only mine is left."

I'm not begging…yet. I will though. I'll beg 'til my voice gives out.

The hand in my hair jerks my head back so my throat's exposed to her.

Just when I think she might let me, she says, "I'm tired of being touched. Since I was sixteen years old, I've been touched every single day by hair, makeup, stylists, fans, strangers… Most days my body doesn't even feel like my own."

Compared to her, I've only had a small taste of that. Not only have I been at this gig for a lot less time than her, but I can jump into crowds without being molested every time. It has happened but nothing like what Collette's suffered.

"What *do* you want?"

She takes in my position at her feet, and says, "To be worshipped."

Neither of us closes our eyes as her lips lower to mine. Even though I always thought it'd be awkward to watch the person you're kissing, with Collette it feels completely normal. Like we were built for exactly this.

Her tongue slips past my lips and mine chases hers automatically, matching her move for move.

My swollen cock leaks inside my pants, but my hands stay at my sides as I keep it to just kissing. Collette doesn't need to be felt up right now. She needs to be reminded she's not an object, she's a woman, a goddess in charge of her own body and her own desires.

This close to her pussy, that desire—my favorite fucking scent—fills my nostrils, making me kiss even harder as our mouths explore the other's in one of the most possessive kisses I've ever experienced, and I'm not even talking about my intentions. Collette is laying claim with this kiss.

Slowly, she pulls back, taking my bottom lip with her until it's stretched as far as it'll go, then she releases it with a smirk.

Fuck, that's hot.

"Let's pull out of tonight's show." Anything to stay here, with her in this moment.

Her face above mine softens as she gazes down at me, and I grow warm and full from the look in her currently blueish-gray eyes alone.

What is that? I haven't felt it before.

"I don't quit anything," she says.

I loop an arm around one of her knees, then pull so it gives out, making her fall on to my thighs as I sit back on my heels.

"You are more, Julian."

More? Than what?

"This isn't even me at my best," I tell her honestly.

"Yes, it is," she argues before pressing a soft kiss to my mouth and whispering, "If I did have magic, I'd make you see yourself the way I do."

The door to the bus opens and Collette's off my lap before I get a chance to ask how she sees me.

After collecting my money from the floor, I stand to greet everyone, and we all slide right back into our normal—the normal from before, when I was just an intruder in both Collette's bus and her life, but she allowed it…for some reason.

I don't feel normal though. It's like what Collette described when she touched my throat for the first time. She kissed me and now everything's changed. I feel changed.

Does she?

Chapter 20

Julian

"Since I've still got Collette out here, I thought I'd try something new," I tell the packed hillside, the sky above them full of thousands of colorful bubbles.

The festival's named after the region's obsession with Bigfoot and has a good mix of talent on the cards. While Collette went to meet some of the other acts, I went in search of my guitar over on my bus instead. I always keep it with me even though I don't play anymore. After playing at the children's hospital and Collette's follow-up challenge, I thought tonight would be a good time to pull it out again.

One of my roadies brings my electric guitar out to me, and I slip the strap over my head while he connects my Fender to the amp.

Collette ventures closer, turning so her back's to the fans, and gives me a surprised look.

"We've never done this before," I say into the mic, staring into Collette's eyes. "*I've* never done this before." I scan the people spread out across the lawn and beyond to the path leading to the campsites in the distance. "So, uh, I hope you like it. Here it goes."

Using my pick, I strum the opening chords to Billie Eilish's "You Should See Me in a Crown," singing the first verse, then Axel brings in the drums halfway through it. As soon as we hit the hook, we both pick up the pace with a rock, almost metal twist, like what Clio Cadence did in her cover of it.

Collette hypes the audience, then turns back around to watch me. She doesn't usually sing with me after our song together, only stays onstage with me for my own songs, but I'm hoping she'll humor me this once.

When I get to the bridge, I jerk my head at her, beckoning her over as I sing the first half with a smile splitting my lips, and even though she rolls her eyes with her own smile, she brings her mic up and sings the second half back to me with enough attitude to get me hard all over again.

She doesn't stop there either. She sings the chorus with me, too, then pauses while Axel and I jam out together for the instrumental break. We finish the song sharing my mic, my balls feeling so fucking big from the rush.

A sudden fight in the crowd can't even compete as everyone else goes nuts. Collette twists her head to survey them, and even though I hear it, too—the adoration—I study her instead, only interested in her reaction. Did she like it?

Facing me again, she gives me one of those smiles of hers that says there's nowhere else she'd rather be—the smile I fucking crave more than air itself. *She loved it.*

Since we're sharing the stage with so many other acts tonight, we're not doing our full set, but I want to do one more song with Collette, so I ask into the mic which song she wants.

She just shakes her head, laughing.

My smile matches hers as I start thinking of the one I just wrote last night. It's about her, of course, but the lyrics might scare her. They scare me.

"How about 'Your Bedside'?" some dude in a suit past Collette's shoulder calls out, naming one of my most underrated songs, and some of that warm feeling I got on Collette's bus disappears. Who's he? And why the fuck does he think he has a say here?

Collette turns her smile to him, sending him a wave, too, and I swear I almost puke up my intestines it hurts so bad.

A bottle of cheap vodka held in the air near the front of the stage snags my attention, and I follow the arm holding it to see a broad doling out sloppy shots to whoever opens their mouths for a pour. She's wearing a white see-through bodysuit and shorts that have the ass cheeks shredded completely out, so she's got a long line of people waiting.

I mean, I can see why. She had me at the vodka, and the eyeful she's providing as a backdrop only increases my thirst.

"Ayo! Get me next!" I yell out to her, not really seeing the girl's face, just the opportunity she's presenting with quick, easy booze. If I could get a vodka drip to my veins right now, it still wouldn't be enough. I'm *that* desperate up here. I just need something—any-fucking-thing—to take this edge off. Shit hit me outta nowhere.

The laughable security helps her on the stage, and she takes her sweet-ass time to pump her arms at the crowd. *Yeah, yeah. It's great… until it's not.*

I'm too tall for her to waterfall the alcohol into my mouth so I bend a knee, which makes the crowd go even crazier. I glance over at Collette to see her smile long gone. Honestly, I just want to drown, but if me kneeling in front of another woman pisses her off…

Does it piss her off?

The vodka burns all the way down my throat, but I fight the sting, taking huge gulps to numb as much as I can. At least three shots swallowed, I stand, spitting the rest in my mouth out in front of me in a wide spray. The girl beside me squeals from getting some on her before pulling out her phone to take a selfie with me. I'm soaked in sweat and vodka and rage, but yeah, I wanna be her phone's wallpaper for the next year.

Instead of looking at the phone, I watch Collette, catching the moment she turns toward the suit again, giving him an apologetic side head nod. He shrugs, grinning all pleasant and shit, and I sneer loud enough to get Collette's attention again.

I end up missing security escorting vodka girl away, then I'm staring after her, wishing I'd taken the bottle off her. I need more than three shots. A blackout is in order—quick.

This is why I don't resurface all that often. This shit is *hard*, especially when Collette's involved, her and the goddamn feelings she brings out of me.

My eyes cold but my blood fucking boiling, I start strumming some chords as I stand back up. At first it could pass as any other track, a fucking country melody about a rocking chair or some shit, then I pick up the tempo, riffing even harder, and I start singing "Or Nah" by Ty Dolla $ign, The Weeknd, Wiz Khalifa, and Mustard.

The lyrics are fucking filth and match my mood perfectly. Collette had the motherfucking nerve to kiss me like that, like fucking *that*, then bring this fucking suit to our show? And *smiles* at him? That was my smile. I fucking earned it, not him.

Just when I was starting to think that maybe she felt what I do… Goddamn it. I thought the kiss on her bus meant *something*. It did to me.

Obviously not to her though.

Fuck it. Let's get this out of the way now. I'm my own worst enemy. If anyone's gonna rip my heart out, it's gonna be me.

Collette's already hard gaze turns murderous at the first verse, especially since I refuse to take my eyes off hers as I recite the lyrics.

During The Weeknd's verse, she scoffs at the line talking about getting your face ridden which pisses *me* off because I was willing to eat her pussy. I offered. She left me though. She fucking left me, showed back up long enough to confuse the fuck outta me, and now she's trying to leave all over again, except with another man.

One line in particular hits close to home considering where we just had our first kiss, and Collette bites her bottom lip into her mouth, her fists balling by her sides. Seeing her flinch at the last line of the verse, I drop the guitar, letting it hang loosely as I spit the next part acapella directly to her.

Third line in on the chorus, Collette spins on her heel and runs off the stage before the lyric about bringing someone else into the mix even leaves my lips fully. Abandoning the rest of the song, I take off after her, handing my guitar to the same roadie as before.

The suit turns to watch but doesn't try following which proves why he doesn't deserve Collette. *Pussy.*

Behind the stage is a bunch of pop-up tents housing the talent, and Collette weaves through them, not slowing down for a second even as her hand shoots out, snatching up handfuls of something along the way—weapons probably.

"You're a liar," she says when I catch up to her in one of the back tents overlooking the river. An apple is thrown at my head next—*predict-able*—and I manage to dodge it just in time to watch it sail past my face.

"Why are you trying to hurt me?" I told her myself I'm a liar. That shit ain't new.

"*You're* trying to hurt *me!*"

"You started it!" I yell back, instantly feeling so dumb I almost take it back. She did though.

"You were supposed to be different, Julian." She paces, shaking her head, like she's talking to herself, and if she hadn't used my name, I'd think she was. Suddenly she stops to face me, and shouts, "I thought you were more!"

"More than what?"

"Him!" Her face turns red, and she looks around like she's worried he might hear.

"That suit?" I question openly because I don't give a fuck if he hears me talking about him.

"Suit?"

"Yeah, the motherfucker you brought around right after you shoved your tongue in my mouth. What? You couldn't wait 'til I finished my set to get your clit sucked, Collette?" She didn't know I'd be keeping her onstage tonight. She planned ahead. I just don't know how far ahead. Was it before or after she tongued me down in the kitchen of her bus though? Because neither option works for me.

Another fruit is chucked at my head—a peach maybe—but I bat it away, fully expecting it now.

"You have no idea who that is, do you?"

I cross my arms over my chest, biting my tongue. I didn't get that good a look at him. I saw Collette's reaction to him and that was enough for me to hate him.

"Does the name David Yonko ring a bell?"

"Your producer?"

She nods, turning to approach the river's shoreline.

That's how he knew the song my label tried to bury by not giving any money to its marketing budget whatsoever. His job is to know and memorize and make music. His whole life is music.

How was I supposed to know that was him? I've never seen David

Yonko before. He's a legend in this biz, but he's a faceless legend because he's a hermit.

Or so I thought…

What the fuck is he doing here, watching Collette perform in the boonies?

I go over and stand next to her. "Are you fucking him?"

Her eyes on the fast-moving water in front of us, she asks, "Why would it matter?"

"Because I'm a jealous fuck." Which I've also been pretty fucking upfront about.

"If that were true, you wouldn't keep all those people on your bus. They're remoras, Julian. They're going to take everything from you because you're okay *sharing* everything with them."

I remove the chain around my neck, sidearm throwing it into the river. It doesn't skip like a stone though, just makes an audible ring of bubbles on the surface where it sinks.

"They can have it."

"You could've made your point without throwing away thousands of dollars' worth of diamonds," she says nonchalantly, and I almost scoff. Didn't she throw a couple grand of my money out the window to prove a point?

"Those weren't diamonds. It was fake. It all is." I shake my head. "I don't give a shit about that stuff."

"What do you give a shit about?"

"The only thing I'm not okay sharing. You."

Collette doesn't say anything and neither do I until I repeat, "Are you fucking him?"

Spinning to face her, she looks at me head-on and says, "At least he'd be sober for it," gutting me so quick and efficient I know Imma bleed out. That's twice now she didn't deny it.

As usual, I bring out my anger to jam the wound and mask the pain as I bite out, "What the fuck's that supposed to mean?"

"You know what it means. You drink and get high—"

"So?"

"—all the time."

"Not all the time." *Most* of the time. There's a slight difference.

"You drink and get high—"

"So?" I shout, my arms out wide. That doesn't make David Yonko better than me.

"—to hurt me!"

Jerking back like I've been hit, I drop my arms by my sides. That's what got her mad? How could she even…

I do drink to punish, but the punishment is only ever aimed at myself. Not her. Never her.

I glance down at MAMAS BOY tattooed across my knuckles. My mom did the same thing except she punished *me* with her drinking. At least that's how it felt at the time because I loved her so much it hurt to see her hurting.

"Me taking shots, that hurt you?" I ask, my voice low. The shot girl, the lyrics—I was trying to hurt Collette up on that stage, but I was trying to hurt myself more because I've never felt pain like I have seeing hers. I never considered it'd work the other way though. I didn't know my pain hurt her. I didn't know my drinking hurt her.

"Yes."

With a shake of her head, she goes to leave, but I hook her elbow, stopping her. She does feel something for me. I don't exactly know what or how strongly, but goddamn, that shit's enough for me.

The words "I'm sorry" rush out of me as I close the distance until there's only inches separating us.

She meets my eyes but they're guarded still. She doesn't trust me. I lied. Worse than that I broke a promise. Less than twelve hours after promising her I'd never let anyone hurt her ever again, I went and hurt her myself. *I* hurt her.

"You don't even know what you're apologizing for."

"I don't need to. I hurt you, and for that, I'm sorry." So fucking sorry.

"Because you drank…"

It sounds like a question, so I nod.

"Okay."

"Okay?" *That's it?*

"Yeah." She sighs, breaking eye contact with me. "I need to go. David and I—"

David.

My grip on her arm tightens. "Don't get it twisted, Collette. I'm apologizing, but I'm not backing down. If that suit lays one finger on you, I'll fucking end him. One. Finger. Mark my words."

Her eyes find mine again, creating more warmth than the vodka ever could. "One finger? Not even you could get me off with only one finger."

My eyebrows about fly off my face.

Wanna bet?

Pulling her closer, I spin us so her back's to the water and mine's to the tents.

"Julian," she warns.

I shush her, saying, "Don't worry. I'm done hurting you, Poohbear."

"What are you doing?"

"I broke one promise to you. I'm about to make good on the other."

"Which—"

"The one where I erase everyone else's touch. Say I can, and I will." I drop my forehead to hers, begging, "Say it."

"With one finger?"

Stroking her middle finger, I bring it up to place on my new tattoo. "You proved what one of your fingers could do. Now let me show you what one of mine can do."

Her throat moves with a swallow.

"Say it." I want to touch her, but she has to be ready. She has to want it. She has to let me.

"Erase it all."

My cock swells, and my throat goes dry as a groan rips from it. Shit, yes.

There are people behind us…somewhere…so with me in front of her, I cup the back of her head and walk us closer to the river's edge for more privacy. I'll pretend I'm pointing out, like, rock formations. Collette just needs to stay in front of me with her finger on my pulse. She's gonna want to feel this.

"Don't let go," I tell her, lifting the front of her skater-style skirt with my free hand. "That's the only thing I want you to do. Got it?"

"You really think—"

"Normally I can't get enough of your voice," I cut her off, saying, "but right now I need you to shut up."

"What—"

I shove my hand into her panties, finding her waxed pussy already soaked for me. *Jesus…*

"Christ," she pants, her forehead pressing into mine as she looks down to watch.

"Collette." I glide my middle finger down her pussy lips, spinning it around to gather wetness like a paper stick collecting cotton candy, then I bring it back up to swirl around her clit. "Do as you're told for fucking once."

"I don't take orders," she says, her eyes fixed on my finger work.

"You don't want anyone to know you're getting finger-fucked by Julez, a *celebrity*, do you?"

"You're not Julez."

"Oh yeah? Who am I?"

"Julian."

My finger slows.

"Who are you?"

Her eyes lift to mine. "Collette."

"No. They get Collette." I jerk a nod over my shoulder. "You give them Collette. I want—"

"You want more, Julian? Then *be* more."

I didn't know what she meant when she said it the first time, and I'm not sure what she means now. More than who? The suit?

Or just more in general?

I want to be more. I want to be more for her.

Collette's other hand drops to mine, and she tries to press me against her clit, wanting to chase her own orgasm but, nah, that's my job. I pull away, making her groan.

"One finger," I remind her…and myself. Fuck, I hate rules.

"Then use it already!" she whisper-shouts. "Enough of this teasing bullshit."

Teasing her? Me? Is she serious?

I slam my middle finger between her pussy lips until I'm palming her clit like a basketball.

"You don't listen for shit."

"I told you." Her chuckle turns into a moan against my lips as I start to pump in and out of her, and I seal my mouth to hers, forgetting to refill my lungs. I'll breathe when I'm dead. Or is it when I'm sleeping? *Who cares.*

I hear footsteps behind me and break the kiss to spin her around in my arms until she's facing the river, too, then bow my other arm out so she's blocked even more. There's at least one or two pictures of my cock floating around the internet, but I'll be goddamned if anyone so much as catches a glimpse of what's under Collette's skirt. I'd be putting that knife of hers to use before I let that happen.

Not hearing the same thing as me, Collette rolls her hips forward, meeting my every plunge into her pussy.

She returns her hand to my throat over her shoulder, and I breathe out against her hair, "Be quiet." I kiss the strands, a few of them sticking to my lips when I part them on another labored exhale.

I drag my curved finger out from her slit to flick her clit with my nail, then I'm back between her slick walls, palming her pussy again as I crook my finger inside and massage, searching for that G-spot.

Pulling her against me so our bodies are flush, I thrust into her ass. "You wanna be worshipped, Collette?"

The back of her head moves against my face in a nod.

"By me?"

Another nod with a stifled scream in her throat this time.

"Why?" I ask a little softer.

"Because I'm…" Her whisper becomes a moan as her mouth falls open.

"You're a motherfucking goddess," I finish for her.

She grips the hair by my ear, and I twist to bite her wrist, keeping her there even though I shouldn't. A feminine hand on my head is a dead giveaway I'm doing more than looking at fucking rocks.

Her breathing hitches as I suck the skin on her wrist, making damn sure I leave a hickey before letting go with a *pop.*

"I'm…"

Her walls clench around my middle finger just as her pussy lips twitch against my hand, and I have to fight not to give in and slip another in. Instead, I bend my finger even more, rubbing just as hard as my palm pushing from the other side.

"You're what?" I demand, keeping up the same pressure.

"Coming."

My laugh blows her hair away from my face. "With one finger?"

For answer, her walls convulse around that one finger, then she starts to droop forward, but I snake my other arm around her middle before she can get too far.

"Will anyone else be touching you with *one finger?*" I ask, trying to catch her in that post-nut bliss, but she doesn't say anything, and I have to shake her. "Collette? Anyone else?"

"Just…fuck."

No. Damn it. That's not what I wanna hear.

The spasms rock the rest of her body as she slumps back against me, breathing hard. I don't remove my hand though. In fact, I slide my finger further into her pussy, burying it to the hilt. My palm grinds ruthlessly against her still-throbbing clit, and with her shoulder blades at my chest, Collette starts rolling her hips again, picking up the pace now that her first orgasm is dying down—her first orgasm because we're definitely going for two.

"Hitch your knee up," I tell her, then grip under her bent leg and pull until her knee's mashed to her rib cage.

"Will *David* be using a finger on you?"

Collette mouths off by saying, "He's not just my producer. He's my…" and my mind goes blank at the rest. *Excuse the fuck outta me?*

I try to rip my hand from her panties, but she beats me to it by releasing my hair to slam her hand on top of mine, keeping it in place as she rides my palm.

"He's your what?"

"Landlord." She laughs.

Laughs.

Fucking laughs.

How's she even laughing right now? I'm knuckles-deep in her pussy and she's laughing?

"How good a landlord is he?" I ask slowly, my finger regaining movement again.

"Good," she groans, holding me to her.

Several hard pumps into her hot pussy where I alternate grinding into her swollen, juicy clit, I rasp, "Don't fuck with me, Collette." She said she went home… Was she with him?

"He's…"

"What?"

"He's…"

Collette curbs another scream—just barely—as her second orgasm rips through her, her pussy contracting on my finger and hand and head. Holy fucking shit.

Without letting her recover, I drop her leg and spin her around, cementing her flushed face to my memory. Fuck everything else, this is the memory I want to carry for the rest of my life.

She blinks up at me and says, "He's also my good friend's husband. And the father of Holter's—"

"Best friend?" I guess, remembering Holter saying how close their houses were to each other's.

She nods. "He flew us up here this morning and we have some business to attend to before he gets back to his family."

"You played me." And that's no guess. She knew what she was doing, winding me up, challenging me.

"Yeah, but you deserved it. You bow for me, you bow for *only* me."

"So you were jealous?"

Her hand disappears behind her back only to reappear holding her knife, the blade already out and ready for damage as she lifts it to my throat. *Now where was she hiding that?*

"It hurt watching you drink…but it pissed me off more to watch how you did it."

The shot girl. I knew—

She makes a cut at the seam of my neckline.

"The fuck are you doin'? I like this shirt." It's a vintage band tee of Collette, and when I bought it online, I had to pay triple for shipping to get it in time for the tour.

"It's a knockoff, little lamb. Surround yourself with enough phonies and you'll forget what's real."

Meeting my eyes, she slices all the way down the shirt, the tip of the blade nicking me several times in the process.

"Shit, Collette," I say, glancing down at the beads of blood now dotting my abdomen.

Her eyes glued to mine, she guides the useless material off my shoulders before balling it up to tuck under her skirt, cleaning herself up.

"I thought you were supposed to come on my face, not your own," I say, gesturing to the shirt with her face on it while stroking my cock through my jeans.

"Speaking of cum…" She pulls the shirt back out. "We're going to redraw the lines we just blurred."

"Redraw? Nah. Let's erase 'em."

She doesn't go for it though, just ignores me to say, "My cum's on your finger."

Trying to give me the shirt back to wipe my hand off, I shake my head at her. Sticking the same finger I just used on her into my mouth instead, I suck, tasting Collette in a way I've never tasted anyone before.

"And now your lips."

Said lips open so I can drag my tongue over each knuckle slowly like I'm licking around an ice cream cone, making sure I get every last drop.

"Now mark *my* words. Just like your little…request…"

She waves a hand around, making me beam. It wasn't a request and she fucking knows it.

"…you won't be using this." With one quick tug on my still-wet finger, she closes the distance between us. "Or this." Her lips crash into mine, and we both groan, the taste of her cum on my lips but now also on hers. Before I can tackle her ass to the ground and obliterate this line bullshit once and for all, she pulls back, saying, "On anyone else either."

What's that? I can't kiss anyone? Or even *touch* anyone? But…

But…

"Not so much as one finger, Julian. One. Finger. Got it?"

If "owned" had a face, it'd be mine right here, right now 'cause damn.

Chapter 21

Collette

What was I thinking?

I finally give up trying to read and put the book down by my side on the bed. I've been staring at the same paragraph for the last thirty minutes, yet I can't remember a single word.

Two days ago, I did something so stupid, I still can't believe it. Kissing Julian was a mistake made in a moment of intense weakness. I can admit that. Letting him touch me after—no, *telling* him to touch me after—was even worse. Understandable because, hello, I haven't had an orgasm that wasn't at my own hands for several weeks now, but that's still not a great excuse. I should've known better. I do know better.

I don't date celebrities. I don't sleep with them. I don't kiss them. And I sure as hell don't let them finger me next to a river in broad daylight.

Except I did.

And if I'm being completely honest, it didn't feel very stupid. Far from it actually. Both the kiss and what happened after felt like nothing else I've ever felt before. Letting loose with Julian feels…right. Being with Julian, period, feels right.

I groan, rolling to my side to press a hand to my chest, rubbing small circles. Why Julian? Why now?

I know why. Because he's proving to be more than just a celebrity.

He's already proven to be more than Bodee and I still don't even know him that well. The parts I do know, I like. The sober parts anyway. The rest…is what's causing all this heartburn. That and the fact that I kinda, sorta tried to make us exclusive…without us even…dating.

Are we dating?

I told Julian we were redrawing lines, but I don't know what lines are left, except the one barring actual sex, which I'm holding on to with a death grip because anonymous sex with a stranger is completely different than sex with a man I spend almost every waking minute with. A man that's integrated himself into all aspects of my life including the family I hold dear. Holter and Julian have some sort of bond that I can't quite define. I wish I could write it off as gaming buddies, but even I know that's not true. Holter likes Julian. David does, too. When the two men met, they immediately put their heads together talking music and became…friends? Maybe even collab partners in the future if them exchanging numbers was anything to go by.

If all that wasn't confusing enough, I also told Julian he couldn't fuck anybody else.

After getting into New Orleans earlier this evening, we parted ways like we do every night, and even though Julian has his own suite, I doubt he's using it. He's probably on his bus, disregarding everything I told him, fucking anything with a pulse.

Pulse.

His pulse while he made me come all over his hand…God. His heart's never beat that wildly, not under my watch. He was *alive*. So undeniably alive.

Where is he right now? What's he doing? We're in New Orleans, a city that's tailor-made for people like him, and there's no way he's not taking full advantage.

This is exactly why I shouldn't have messed with any lines regarding Julian. If you don't give someone your trust, they can't break it.

Sighing, I swing my legs over the side of the bed, padding into the living room to listen outside the door right next to mine. Holter's heavy breathing filters through the thin wood, so I decide to go out on the suite's balcony to get some fresh air. Even though the hotel's on the infamous Bourbon Street, my suite's at the backside of the building, so

I'm met by peaceful quiet when I step outside instead of the all-night craziness that assaults the front on a recurring basis. That's a classic rookie mistake—booking rooms in the front of any building on the main strip of downtown NOLA. The partying goes until three or four in the morning…every morning.

It'll be a miracle if Julian makes it for our early morning wake-up call for the parade we're in tomorrow.

Piano notes interrupt the muggy night air, and I have to strain my ears, trying to make out where they're coming from. A glance at the balcony next door reveals an open slider, but I don't know whose room it is. I didn't pay attention to the room numbers Irelynn listed earlier as she handed out keys to everybody. Mary and Holter are in the three-bedroom suite reserved for me, and Irelynn along with the rest of my team are spread out all over the hotel. Julian and his team…I don't know. I don't even know *who* his team is. There are too many remoras to tell honestly. Aside from Bare and Axel, and I guess Slade—unfortunately—I'm not sure who's here to actually assist Julian. Suck, suck, suck, they're all sucking him dry.

Similar to how Julian sucked his finger after…

Oh God, what was I thinking?

I was thinking about how sweet Julian was after I showed him what the remoras did to me on the roof of his bus, and about how tender he treated me afterward. He took care of me, not the damage control, but *me*. He didn't worry about how the rest of the world would take it, only how I was taking it.

Then I was thinking about him kneeling down in front of that girl handing out shots and how much I *wanted* him to take care of me… and only me. He kneeled for me like I was a goddess, somebody worth praising, before he went and did it for someone else, someone he doesn't even know. Someone he doesn't make sure eats regular meals every day. Someone he didn't get a tattoo for. Someone he didn't tell his bodyguard to protect first because he values her life more than his own.

Someone that wasn't me. That's what it comes down to. I was jealous—incredibly so. For the first time in my life, I was jealous, and I broke my rule regarding celebrities because of it.

I do like Julian, and I'd be sad, so fucking sad, if anything happened to him. I wanted to get him to his twenty-eighth birthday, but I never anticipated…this. This feeling. *These feelings*, because there are a lot, more than just jealousy.

I drop my head back between my shoulders to look up at the night sky. Sparkling stars shine like brilliant gems and they seem to pulse as the keys on the nearby piano are practically smashed by whoever's playing.

"Pretty night." Axel startles me and I whip my head over to find him on the balcony of the room the music must be coming from. He's not looking at me though, just gazing up at the same sky I was just admiring.

"It is," I say before asking, "No sleep for you either?" Axel is an indie artist like me, hired by Julian, so he doesn't have to do any of the publicity Julian and I get booked for. He comes along sometimes, but usually for moral support…I'm pretty sure that's why. I have seen him checking Irelynn out a few times, so maybe his motives aren't purely altruistic.

Chuckling, he says, "Not in New Orleans."

A sultry tempo builds as Julian's voice picks up, moaning out the lyrics for Lady Gaga's "Bad Romance," except he makes it into a sad yet sexy lament instead of a dance song.

I should've known he played the piano, too.

"He's good," I say.

"He is…when he tries." Axel's eyes drop a fraction, and he swallows. "He could be good at anything he tries."

"He's one of those," I agree, nodding.

Axel turns to face me, crossing his arms over his chest as he leans against the banister. "Could be. Problem is he stopped trying."

I consider his words, asking quietly, "When did he stop?"

"Right after he got signed."

I nod absently, following along while also keeping an ear to the tune being played inside Julian's suite. It's beautiful. Haunting, but beautiful.

"Julian pitched an entire new concept for a debut album. He was fucking pumped to stand out. Invested. Excited."

I can guess the rest. Brand-new artists don't have a say starting out. Seasoned artists barely even get a say. They have to fight, scheme, trade. They have to prove themselves time and time again, then maybe—*maybe*—record labels will take their suggestions into consideration, but not all of them because even then compromise is expected. In some form or another, the label will ultimately get their way. It's their money they're putting up, betting on an individual—a brand, an image, but still very much an individual—and they want a return on that investment, plus a hefty profit.

That's another gift Bodee gave me by taking away everything I'd worked for. With no labels willing to sign me, I became an independent musician. And as an indie artist, I do get a say in almost everything I do. I still have to mold myself for the public's perception, but I don't have a record label controlling my every move on top of it.

"They didn't go for it?" I ask anyway, and Axel shakes his head.

"They basically laughed in his face before handing him his script. The one he's expected to follow all day, every day."

I stare at my feet, wiggling my toes, and say quietly, "He doesn't do well with rules."

"No. He doesn't. He does a hell of a job with sabotage though."

I return my gaze to Axel. "Sabotage?"

"After that, he went on what I thought would be a couple-day bender to lick his wounds, but ended up being…well, here we are two years later. He's been hit with some shit during that time, don't get me wrong, but this is intentional." He shakes his head. "Or it started out as intentional before he lost control somewhere along the line. First, he lost control of his dream, then he lost control of his plan to get it back."

"Making music wasn't his dream?" It may not be the exact way he wants but he's still doing what he loves.

"Making music his way was his dream. Rapping's only a small part of what he's capable of. His record label took one look at him and branded him for what they thought would sell. He wanted to do it all. Music, it's not just a hobby for Julian. Or a job. Not even a choice really. It's…*him*."

The tattoo of the aux cord into Julian's veins bears a whole new meaning now.

"So, he's musically fluid?" I half-joke, and he laughs, rubbing a hand through his hair.

"Is that like sexual fluid?"

"I think it's called sexually fluid or sexual fluidity. Sexual fluid sounds—"

"Like it's time for you to leave," Julian cuts in, suddenly standing at the open sliding glass door. His tall, lean body appears to be twice its normal size as he fills up the entire threshold, staring Axel down.

Wasn't he just playing? I hadn't even noticed him stop.

Axel says, "I just thought—"

"You thought wrong. Get out." Julian jerks his head to the side. He has yet to glance in my direction, and I consider sneaking back inside my own suite before he can. He knows I'm here though, so if I did, I'd look like a coward.

Axel and Julian stare at each other, neither man backing down at first, then Axel shoots me an apologetic look, saying, "Later, Collette," and earning a scoff from Julian.

On his way in, Julian barely moves to let him by, then I hear him mutter, "What'd I tell you?"

Whatever Axel says in response is too quiet to make out.

Once he's gone, Julian turns to me, his gaze falling to my bare feet and rising up to my face.

"He didn't touch you, did he?" he deadpans, making me laugh.

I eye the space between the two balconies. "From this distance?"

"It wouldn't stop me," he says, and I barely get a full swallow down.

With a smirk as my only warning, Julian hefts himself up on the banister closest to my balcony, standing on the narrow handrail to hold out a hand. I eye it, then him.

"Come over."

"I'm in my pajamas."

"I want you exactly how you are."

My eyes roll on their own accord.

"I'll play for you."

The piano. Julian playing the piano for me alone…I could go for that.

"Fine. Get down so you can go open the door for me."

He doesn't so much as flinch.

"Fall with me, Collette."

So that is what he's been saying. What does it mean? The last time he said it, anarchy broke out.

"No. No falling."

"Why not?"

"Because I can't."

"Can't or won't?"

What are we talking about here?

"Both," I tell him truthfully. "Now, go open the door."

"We're not using the door."

"Then how am I…"

His chuckle crawls its way over to me.

"Julian?"

"Swing a leg over and I'll help with the rest."

"Are you out of your mind?"

When his eyebrows lift in challenge, I mimic the expression with my own. He can't be serious.

Bending at his knees, Julian stretches his arm out toward me as far as his long body allows.

Shit.

On a huff, I get one leg over, straddling the banister and feeling coarse wood flecks scratch against my exposed thighs.

"Now bring the other over and stand between the uprights."

"I hate you," I say as soon as I'm done.

"Hate me while you try to step over to do the same on this one."

"I thought you were helping!" My voice trembles like my legs.

"I am," he laughs. "Gimme your hand, then step out. I'll bring you over."

"You're not in a position to catch me, Julian."

Something has him tensing, his eyes glazing over. A gentle breeze blows past, ruffling his hair, and at this angle, he looks like an angel. A guardian angel sent to protect me.

Or a dark angel meant to lure me to my death.

"Julian," I groan, snapping him out of his daze, and he grips the handrail with his other hand, leaning forward even further.

That wood could snap in half from his weight alone. Doesn't he realize that?

He probably does, he just doesn't care.

"I don't trust this."

"Then trust me. I got you."

Does he? While Julian has no qualms endangering his own life, I do trust he'd never intentionally risk mine.

At least before this moment.

Coming down to mirror my pose on the outside of his balcony, he reaches across to me, putting him much closer, and with sweaty palms, I extend one out to him. He somehow manages to grasp my entire wrist, tugging me as I stretch a leg out. Before my toes can even touch down on Julian's balcony, the other leg is already off mine and for a brief moment it feels like I'm a ballerina flying through the air, waiting to be swept up by my partner. Julian's grip on me tightens as he pulls me the rest of the way, and I make it across unharmed. He helps me over the top, then follows immediately after, landing beside me in nothing but a pair of jeans, his pale skin between tattoos shimmering in the moonlight.

I wrap my arms around myself, hugging tightly to keep from touching him, and joke, "Long time, no see."

His lips brush my forehead at the same time one of his hands touches the small of my back, and he murmurs, "Too long, Poohbear. It's been too long."

"It's been three hours."

The charming smile on his face as he pulls back conjures up one on my own.

It feels so good being with him again. When Julian's coherent, he's infectious to be around, and when he's not, he's still compelling, but in the way a waterfall is—vicious, uninhibited…dangerous. One wrong move and over the precipice he goes.

But when he's like this, it feels like I'm the one about to fall.

Fall with me.

"Want something to drink?" he asks, heading inside to the bar on the other side of the living room space.

"No, thanks." My eyes trail over to the piano in the corner. "Where'd you learn to play?"

He doesn't look up as he pours cognac into a glass. "My grandma taught me. She was an elementary school music teacher for forty-two years."

"Wow. That's amazing." His head bobs in a nod. "How many instruments did she teach you to play?"

"As many as the school she worked at could afford to supply her with."

This time I'm the one nodding, but then Julian ends with, "So, not many." My movements halt.

"Oh," comes out quietly. "Just the guitar and piano then?"

"I might know my way around a triangle, too," he says, and I bite back my smile. I bet he could find his way around any instrument if he wanted to. Knowing how to read notes is the biggest obstacle. After that it's all trial and error, kind of like life. Once you have the basics down, you're on your own to figure out the rest.

Drink in hand, he moves to sit at the piano, but I don't break from my spot in the middle of the living room as I pivot to watch him.

"Did she teach you how to sing, too?"

"When I moved in with her, I only knew how to rap, but she wanted me to sing in the church choir, so she taught me how to use my voice in all different ways."

"Did it work? Did you sing in the choir?"

"Fuck no." His back shakes with a laugh and I feel mine do the same even as I try to hold on to every little nugget he reveals about himself. How old was he when he went to live with her? And why did he have to?

Instead, I ask, "What does she think of your performances now?"

Julian's body turns rigid. "She never got to see me on stage. Not a big one. She died right after I got signed."

The prolonged bender makes more sense. Julian doesn't share a lot about himself, but I remember him saying his grandmother is the one who raised him. If he lost her right after his new label rejected his idea, then he started off on worse footing than I imagined. You don't build an empire on an unstable foundation and expect everlasting results. Eventually it will come tumbling down; it's only a matter of time.

"She must've been so proud of you."

"I got signed to a bullshit label with a bullshit contract. That's nothing to be proud of." He takes a swig of his liquor.

"Do you regret it? Signing with your label?"

At first he doesn't reply, then finally he settles his fingers atop the black and white keys and he begins playing again, this time much softer than he was earlier. I recognize the melody instantly. It's the song we played together at the children's hospital, "Cover Me in Sunshine." His fingers float across the keys like a bird skims the sea's surface—confident, weightless, utterly fascinating.

"If I hadn't signed with them, we wouldn't be on tour right now," he says after finishing. "And I wouldn't have met you. So I *can't* regret it."

"But?"

Another brief hesitation, then his fingers are creating another song, this one much darker, more passionate. He punches the keys as if they carry the emotions he's fighting, and when he finishes, his back is heaving.

He does regret it.

My feet pull me forward, leading me to Julian by what feels like an invisible force, and I reach my hand out, running my fingertips over the inked skin of his shoulder pulled tight with each full breath.

He goes for his drink again, but I get to it first, swiping the glass off the piano. He watches the glass fall to the floor, shattering on impact, while I watch him.

"Stay," I whisper. Julian's an atomic bomb of raw talent. It's all restrained tight inside him, waiting to explode, and I want to feel the blast for myself. I can take it.

I can't take him running away though. I can't take him sabotaging what could be a breakthrough moment.

When Julian starts to feel like things are getting away from him—or being *taken* away from him—instead of fighting, he removes himself from the situation entirely with drugs, alcohol, or both. Because then it's him who's giving up control. But like Axel said, Julian lost control over his drug and alcohol use, too, and it's no longer a tool anymore. It's a weapon pointed at himself. He's causing more damage than if he were to just deal with his problems head-on. Whatever's happening right now, he needs to get it out, and if he's drunk, he won't.

I start singing Rihanna's "Stay," tracing his jawline before sticking my hand in his hair, gripping the strands until he looks up at me.

Pressing a quick kiss to the hickey on the inside of my wrist, he smirks at the lyric quoting the man, then his fingers are moving again as he faces the piano, playing the melody for me. He takes over on Mikky Ekko's part and duets me for the outro.

"Stay with *me*," he says quietly to the piano before sending me a sideways glance. "Tonight."

"I can't."

"Can't or won't?"

The same question as before. The same answer as before.

"Both." Just like when he asked me to fall with him, fear's holding me back. "Don't you want this time to yourself?" I gesture to the suite.

"No."

The vulnerability is his stare physically hurts to see but I can't overlook it for my own comfort. That's what everyone else in his life does.

"What are you feeling right now?" I ask him because that's what he asked me when I didn't know I needed it, and even though it's only six words, they carry so much weight when strung together. Enough to make or break a person.

His amber-flecked eyes touch every part of my face before he plays a song that borders on several emotions at once. My heart rate picks up like there's trouble, like there's danger, at the same time tears fill my eyes, begging for release—anything to stop this pain, this torture. Then the ending mellows and all I want to do is curl into a ball and fall asleep, take a break from this world and enter another, happier one.

Unwilling, or maybe unable, to take my eyes off him, I sit beside him, studying his profile as much as those confident fingers of his as he slips directly into another song. Some notes he smashes the keys roughly, others he barely taps them out. The juxtaposition reminds me of his personality. Copious amounts of zeal at times balanced out by his quiet, methodical side during others. He's a walking conundrum, one I can't get enough of.

His left hand falls to my leg and he continues playing one-handed while the other drifts up my thigh like a second set of keys, making every inch of skin on my body tighten in response to his touch.

Lyrics filter through my head and out past my lips before I can think better of it. Lyrics about Julian's touch and what it does to me. Lyrics about wanting that touch more than I should. Lyrics Julian matches with his own about being equally affected. We sing together, our lyrics coming together in a beautiful fusion of our own unique styles, and through it all, Julian's hand remains on the inside of my thigh, moving just as skillfully as the one on the actual piano keys.

The song comes to a close, and a heavy dose of melancholy settles on top of me like a weighted blanket as I find myself wishing I could live in this moment forever. With Julian.

Automatically, he begins again, playing a song that's different from the others. It's more upbeat; not quite happy but almost. It sounds inspirational. *Hopeful.* A perfect song to end the night on.

"That was a beautiful lullaby," I tell him as I stand.

"That wasn't your lullaby, Poohbear."

He smirks at me a second before he stands, pulling me against his front. In one quick motion I'm lifted off my feet, then deposited on top of the piano.

"What are you doing?" I ask, watching Julian carefully place my heels on the keys so my legs are spread open to him.

He takes a seat again and kisses each ankle. "Playing our lullaby."

"Our?"

"I'll play your lullaby, if you give me mine."

I tilt my head, leaning back on my hands behind me. I have no idea what that means, but… "You're missing keys," I say, flexing my feet.

"I learned how to play on a keyboard with seven keys missing. Four is nothing." He kisses the inside of my thigh, making my foot jerk onto another key. His laugh tickles my skin, causing goose bumps. "Five keys."

"Julian," I warn, breathy and aching already.

"That's it. That's my lullaby. I want to fall asleep tonight remembering the sound of you chanting my name."

His voice deep and raspy, and his fingers determined and precise, he jumps right into Hozier's "Take Me to Church."

It's a vocal-heavy song and fast-paced, but at the first break, Julian removes his hands from the keys to pull on my thighs, sliding my ass closer to his face before immediately picking up where he left off. His lips move against my inner thighs as he sings the lyrics, letting the inside of his bottom lip drag up my skin.

"Julian," I moan, grabbing a handful of his blue tips.

At the end of the second verse, he pushes to his feet, sending the bench skittering out behind him, and clutches one of my legs, hooking it over his shoulder.

"Julian."

Burning up, I arch my back so only my head and tailbone are

touching the piano top, my pussy straining for his touch, for him. Julian doesn't pause again, just croons to my center as he hits each building note perfectly until the final chorus, then his nose presses to the thin fabric of my shorts covering my folds. He rotates his head side to side against my pussy, the last line spilling from his lips like an actual prayer.

Suddenly the only noise in the room is our breaths, then the movement of fabric as Julian slides the crotch of my shorts to one side, baring me to him.

His voice thick, he asks, "You're not wearing panties?"

"Not for bed."

"Jesus, I need a…"

The feel of his tongue on my pussy has me jolting, my breasts high in the air.

"Julian."

"You like that?"

I squeeze the strands in my hold, nodding.

"Tell me what else you like."

"Anything." Literally anything right now. I am so close to losing it and he hasn't really done anything yet.

"Now's the time to use that voice of yours, Collette. Be more specific. If I'm gonna do this, I'm gonna do this right, how you want me to, so tell me *exactly* what you want."

Listening to him inhale loudly, then groan, my body quivers, and I manage to get out, "Fuck me with your mouth."

"Like this?" He licks from the bottom of my slit to the top before spearing his tongue into my pussy, dipping his head so his nose hits my clit with each bob.

"Harder."

My other leg is tossed over his shoulder, and his hands seize the top of my thighs as he buries his face in my pussy, his nose pushed against my clit and his tongue lapping me up from the inside. The cold metal balls of his piercing balance out all the heat, making it the perfect combination.

"Julian!" I scream, holding him to me so tight I'm not even sure he can breathe.

Every time he rocks into me, I counter the move, until we become one machine, barreling toward the same destination—fast.

"Julian," I warn when the ember deep inside me ignites to a full blaze, spreading so quickly, all I can do is hold on, my orgasm ripping through me, then out of me, down through my legs, feet, and finally toes.

My back slumps to the piano's surface, allowing me to see some of Julian's face. There's a sheen on his forehead but his eyes are locked on mine like a shark stalking his next prey.

He pulls back a few inches to say, "Gimme your hand." His top lip is glistening, just like I predicted during our rap battle. *I guess I wasn't just talking shit.*

Silently, he guides my pointer and middle fingers to my clit, helping me to pull back the hood of skin surrounding it.

"Hold it there," is the only warning I get before his mouth closes over my exposed clit.

The second he suctions his lips to the still-sensitive nub, he sucks, and sucks, and sucks, not letting up once, and it's not long before my abs tense and I feel a strong pulsing under my fingertips. His name along with some unnatural noise leaves my throat as my head's thrown back, the flame in me already burning its way throughout the rest of my body. The fire reaches my limbs, seizing all movement as my legs stiffen and my toes curl so hard my heels dig into Julian's back, then it all explodes into a backdraft sort of phenomenon as my body goes completely limp. My arms fall to my sides like dead weights, my legs wilt on Julian's back, and my eyes roll into the back of my head.

"Fuck. That was—"

"Not your first time," I pant.

I feel Julian shift so he's above me now, his straining erection beneath his jeans settling in the tender crook between my jelly-like thighs as he kisses up the column of my neck. Against my lips, he whispers, "Yours is the *only* pussy I've tasted." He deliberately emphasizes the word only, then he's kissing me, letting me taste, too. When the tang of my arousal melts away, I only taste Julian's own unique amalgamation of flavors. There's smokiness accentuated by a paper scent hinting at an earlier smoke session, along with intense alcoholic undernotes from the cognac that are a touch too hectic to be considered sweet, and then there's Julian himself, who tastes like a soft caress hidden under a pointed dare. Kissing Julian is what I imagine it'd feel like to jump out of an airplane without knowing for sure if the parachute strapped to your back is going to work. He's pure adrenaline. Scary, yet addictive adrenaline.

I crack my eyes to watch him for a few minutes, before his open to do the same. We watch the other as our mouths make love. It's a stark contrast to how he just used his lips and tongue but feels no less amazing. It should be illegal for one person to be as naturally talented as Julian. My scalp is still tingling.

Propped above me, he gazes down through heavy lashes to tell me, "You're fucking perfect."

Unable to hold the intensity any longer, I shove at his chest, saying, "I'm drenched." In sweat, in saliva, in cum, in questions…lots of questions. Surprisingly, not regret though.

"Same," Julian says, using the bottom of my shirt to wipe his face. "These, too." Tipping to the side momentarily to drag my sleep shorts down my numb legs, he returns just as quickly to help me sit up and remove my shirt as well.

His eyes drink in my naked form, not missing an inch of my bare skin while mine drop to his jeans, specifically to the head of his cock peeking out the top of his waistband. There's a puddle of precum pooled at the very tip, so I swipe my thumb over it, making Julian shudder as he pitches forward, caging me in. Once I get it all on to the pad of my thumb, I suck the precum clean off, tasting his want, too, and Christ, is it intoxicating.

"Mmm," I hum, swaying into him.

His face pressed to the side of my neck, I feel one of his hands sneak between us, teasing fingertips gliding up my thighs. "I was trying to be nice, Collette. Unselfish. *Better.* But it's fucking killing me not to fuck you raw right now."

"So you do have restraint?" I half-joke, and he chuckles below my ear, causing goose bumps to pop up like dandelions in the spring.

"A very, *very* small amount, but you're testing it," he whispers as two of his fingers find my center, nudging inside my rapidly heating-up entrance. My hips buck in response.

Shit. I want more. No, I *need* more. Fingers won't cut it, for either of us. We will be fucking in a matter of minutes, if not sooner.

The line, the very last one between us, shimmers in the distance, just inside my periphery, but soon to be just outside my sanity if he keeps this up.

"Um." I gulp, and instantly, he pulls back.

"Um? That's not a yes." His fingers disappear, allowing me to catch my breath.

Barely taking his eyes from mine, Julian removes his shirt, only to put it over my head, fitting my arms through the sleeves until the long material drapes down my torso, covering most of me.

"You really are better," I say, regarding him and wondering how he does it, how he manages to surprise me time and time again.

"I just wanna know that when I do finally slide my cock into you, buried until I'm balls deep in your sweet-ass pussy, it's because you want it as much as I do."

I hope he doesn't put that in one of his songs.

Grasping desperately for a subject change, I ask him if he has a pair of sweatpants I can borrow. "I can't go back outside like this," I say, gesturing to my exposed lap that's somehow growing wetter after Julian's words.

"You're going back? Jesus, I said I wasn't going to fuck you tonight, not that I wanted you to leave."

Julian's body heat disappears from mine entirely so he can stand several feet away, his eyebrows almost touching as he nibbles on his thumb ring.

"You know I have to. I can't—"

"Stay? Yeah, you told me. So? What? This was just a dine and dash?"

Here's that other side of his coin, the harsher, colder side.

He turns and heads for the bar, but I'm quick to hop off the piano, getting in front of him to plead, "Don't do this."

"Don't do what? I'm fucking parched after you just tried to waterboard my ass."

"Waterboard? You're acting like I squirted."

"Didn't you?"

"I'm…" Glancing over at the piano, I scan the evidence of what just happened. Did I?

I fold my lips between my teeth.

"What?" he demands, dropping his stare to my mouth. "What's so funny?"

My laugh spills out. "Honestly, I don't know if I squirted." I very well could've. My entire body went fuzzy, and it felt like everything on me was soaking wet, even now it still is. "But why would you be parched *after* being waterboarded? And what is dine and dash?" Next thing, he'll be calling me a has-been all over again. He's lashing out and he's doing a piss-poor job. At least I see it for what it is now.

"I don't know. I just… You're… I want…" His hands come up near my face like he wants to touch me, grab me, hold me, then he drops them with a shake of his head, muttering, "I need a drink."

He tries to turn away, but I twist with him, positioning my back against the bar.

"No, you don't. I know you're mad." Or upset, or scared, or any number of the other emotions that are currently buzzing inside my own body, too. "But don't hurt me because of it. I won't be so forgiving this time."

"You weren't forgiving last time. You tricked me into finger-fucking you."

I rear back. "Tricked you? You didn't want to?"

All at once it's like someone pulls his plug and his entire stance relaxes as he gathers my body against his, dropping his forehead to mine. "I want to do everything to you. With you. Even…"

"Even?" I whisper, terrified what he'll say but also needing to hear it, too.

"Even spend the night with you. Stay with me, Poohbear."

"I can't—"

His skin leaves mine, then he's pacing.

"Why did you ask me to stay then? I gotta stay but you get to leave? I got nothing to fucking stay for!"

"I have Holter."

Julian stops, returning to his spot in front of me, his eyes on every inch of my face.

"I know that. I *know* that. I'm not asking you to choose. I would never ask you to choose. Fuck, Collette, I want… Fuck!" He's moving again, staring at the floor and biting his thumb ring.

I narrow my eyes, seeing it's not his thumb ring at all. It's his actual thumb he's gnawing on.

"Julian."

He freezes, air pouring in and out of him, but doesn't meet my eyes, only tilts his head to the side. With him not looking, I grasp his hand and get the thick silver ring over his knuckle before he can stop me.

Red, scaly skin covers the bottom half of his thumb. I had no idea.

Looking the ring over, I ask, "What is this supposed to be?" The top is layered with cloaked faceless figures and it's an eerie, gaudy ring.

Swallowing, he grits, "All Souls' Day." He says it as if it's more painful than biting the skin off his own thumb.

"The day the lost are remembered?"

"All Souls' Day is for the souls stuck in purgatory."

Like Osiris waiting for Isis to find him.

I press a kiss to his raw thumb, and whisper, "Come back to me and you can stay."

His head whips my way. "What?"

I drop his ring on to the bar, its obnoxious *clang* an intrusion to the already tense moment.

"You can take my bed, and I'll sleep on the pull-out couch in the living room." Just like his bus, his suite has too many temptations waiting for him to use against himself, especially now that he feels rejected, cast aside, hurt, alone. "Leave purgatory…for me."

Of all the things Julian can overdose on, I'm not one of them. I won't even be around long enough for him to try. His birthday's approaching, then shortly after that the tour will be over. This will all be over.

"You'd give me your bed… Why?"

"Isn't it obvious?" I repeat his own response regarding his tattoo, and trace his honeypot, making sure I linger at the top where the honey is—where his pulse is. "To keep you in my reach."

Chapter 22

Collette

The basketball bounces off the backboard, landing in Holter's waiting palms under the net.

"Damn," he mumbles to himself, and I grimace, both at the curse and his inability to make a single basket.

Right after this morning's parade, Julian and I bought beignets and chicory-flavored coffee for everyone, and after making sure I ate two myself, Julian left, saying he needed to go shopping.

Holter and I decided to utilize the hotel's full-size indoor court so he could get some actual practice in, and it's…not going so well. Holter wants to try out for his school's team, but there's been very little time, or space, for him to practice real drills on the tour so far. Sometimes during dance rehearsals, he'll dribble a ball around, but without a hoop, he hasn't been able to work on his jump shot. Or free throw. Or whatever it's called.

I hold my hands out in front of me. "Want to work on passing instead?"

"I almost got it," he says with a headshake, sweat dripping from his hair on to his forehead.

A couple years ago I would've wiped it away myself, then stole the ball from him. I'd run down the court and he'd chase me, laughing, forgetting all about the technical rules of the game, and we'd just have fun.

Now though, he wants to shoot a three, holding his hand smugly in the air as the ball meets nothing but net—or something like that—while I sit here being impressed but not too impressed. Enough to raise my eyebrows but not enough to clap, because that'd just be humiliating. And if I even tried to wipe the sweat threatening to fall into his eyes, he'd jerk away and stare at me in disbelief like I'm some sort of alien trying to snatch his brain from his head.

How I long to play a made-up game with non-existent rules with my little boy again.

Holter tosses the orange ball, missing the hoop altogether, and it ricochets off the backboard, boomeranging right back at us.

I manage to duck my head out of the way just in time, turning to watch as it sails past our to-go cups from breakfast.

"I should probably throw those out before they spill," I say before returning the ball to him and grabbing the cups off the shiny hardwood floor. Holter's is empty but mine still has some inside, so I sip the now-tepid chicory coffee on my way to the door. I swirl it around my mouth and let the milky, slightly nutty flavor tease my taste buds. Mechanically, I spit it back out, then push into the bathroom just outside of the gym in search of a garbage can.

After throwing them away and washing my hands, I'm just returning when I hear two voices echoing into the hallway—Holter's and… Julian's?

Slowing my approach, I linger at the door, watching from the threshold.

"What's your why?"

"My why?" Holter asks as Julian easily sinks the ball in the net from the free-throw line.

"Yeah. Everyone needs a why. What's yours for basketball? Why do you wanna play?"

"That's what my school's known for. Everybody there plays basketball, watches basketball, talks basketball, eats, sleeps, breathes basketball."

Julian retrieves the ball to make another shot, then looks at Holter.

"That's not *your* why. If you're only doing something for someone else, and not yourself, then you're guaranteed to fail. You gotta want it."

The ball bounces over to Holter, and he grabs it, balancing it against his hip.

"What else am I supposed to do?"

"Whatever the fuck you want." Julian shrugs before rushing to say, "Don't tell your mom I said that. Or Mary. She scares me."

Holter laughs and shakes his head.

"I don't know, man. The people at your school… The *guys* at your school, they seem corny to me. If I were you, I wouldn't waste my time doing what they're doing, especially if they're your only why."

"Why do you say that?"

"The thing with your mom and their creepy little crushes on her."

Holter focuses on the ball as he switches it from hand to hand, but then Julian adds, "Plus, they messed with you. Of course, I'm gonna hate 'em."

Holter's head lifts to watch Julian's advance. Even from here I can see my son's smile.

Julian says something quieter next to him and grabs his shoulder, nodding.

"You did?" Holter asks wide-eyed. "I thought you hate social media."

Julian chuckles, stealing the ball from his grasp.

"I do, but I made an exception. They won't do anything to you again." He points at Holter. "But if they try, call me."

Holter's steps stutter. "Won't you be busy?"

"Probably." Julian dribbles the ball between his legs. "Don't mean I can't make the time though. Like today." He scoops the ball into one palm and holds it out to Holter. "If you're really gonna go out for basketball, we gotta get you ready."

"What about sound check?"

"What sound check?" Julian asks, a shit-eating grin splitting his face before he releases the ball, slapping it toward Holter.

"But—"

"I got all day, kid. Let's play."

Julian definitely does not have all day because we do have a sound check scheduled soon, but I don't dare interrupt and correct him. I couldn't anyway, not with my throat clogged and my eyes clouded over with unshed tears.

I finally get ahold of myself, stepping the rest of the way inside to watch them play against each other, the whole time Julian giving Holter pointers on how to improve his game.

Holter makes his first basket and spins around to get Julian's reaction. While I try not to let the image break my heart, I feel the fissure anyway. Not just for Holter, and not just for myself, but for Julian as well. Will he ever have someone in his life look up to him like that?

Eventually Holter glances over at me for mine, so I give him the biggest smile I can, the building of more tears making my lips tremble as my cheeks twitch.

His hands on his slim hips, Julian follows Holter's stare, and smiles when he sees me. "Hey, Poohbear."

"Hey."

The moment stretches until the ball flies past Julian's face, cutting the connection as he reaches out to intercept it.

"I think someone else has a creepy little crush," Holter says, I think for Julian's ears only, but I hear it and shift. I don't know if I'm supposed to act like I heard it, but under no circumstance am I going to cop to knowing what they're referring to, so I pretend I'm oblivious on all fronts, picking a piece of invisible lint off my wide-legged, corded lounge pants.

Julian's laugh echoes off the walls, bringing my attention right back to him. Looking directly at me, he says to himself, "Ain't nothing little about that."

Holter smacks the ball away from Julian before sprinting down the court with it.

Julian doesn't take his eyes off mine at first, so I mouth the words, "Thank you," back to him, making him shake his head with a secretive smirk.

He takes off after Holter, and for the next hour, every time he looks my way, I'm the one smiling, holding on to my own secret.

Chapter 23

Collette

My breath comes out in spurts as my dancers rush past me off-stage, the finishing touches on my wardrobe-change hastily being put in place by at least three pairs of hands.

"Done," someone says, and striding back on the stage, I reach up and take my wig off, shaking my natural hair out and teasing the sweaty strands so they're not stuck to my head.

At first, the audience is silent, then all at once they erupt in cheers. My true fans know this is not my usual, but even the ones new to my music will have noticed I was wearing a wig the entire first act of the show.

"In case it wasn't obvious, I like my wigs."

My short, wet hair tickles my exposed shoulders, and I bend down next to a group of teen girls in the front row, smiling from ear to ear. They laugh and scream, snapping so many photos I don't think their thumbs even release the capture button.

"But recently someone asked me if it was a way to hide myself, and it made me stop and think." I look out at the crowd, standing again. "I love that you all wear wigs to my shows. I think you're beautiful." I pause, letting the applause weaken before continuing, "But what if I told you you're beautiful without it? What if I told you you're perfect just the way you are?" I have to raise my voice to be heard, yelling into the mic, "I want you just as you are!"

I catch sight of Julian off to the side, standing with his arms crossed over his chest, and I shoot him a wink. They're similar to his words, and I don't think I realized just how powerful, how meaningful, they were until this moment. To accept someone exactly the way they are without asking anything of them, that's rare. Not everybody can do that. There's almost always an ask, an expectation. Julian's got none for me. I'm not sure why or how, but he doesn't. He's told me several times now; I'm just getting around to understanding.

Unfolding his arms, he turns away, disappearing somewhere backstage.

Is he mad? Did I break the contract by repeating his words publicly? I didn't say *who* said them.

Oh well. This is more about me than him. He helped me realize I was keeping myself hidden; I'm the one coming out from behind the smokescreen.

Refocusing on the crowd, I shout, "Let's all stop hiding!"

High in the air, wigs in hues of blue, pink, white, silver, and every other color imaginable are tossed along with the inhibitions they masked, and I drop my hands by my sides, taking it all in. Several people sob while others scream or laugh, everything tumbling out into a beautifully chaotic blend of truth. Raw truth. Pain, agony, love, life, loss, regret, bravery, celebration—it's all here, both visibly and spiritually.

A sort of therapeutic sensation settles over the superdome, reminding me of my why. The one I lose track of every now and then during the hustle and bustle of this lifestyle. I sing to shape and heal people with the same songs that've shaped and healed me. This is what *fills* me.

Some wigs make it on the stage, followed by hats and what I'm hoping are fake necklaces. Laughing, I have to dodge a few, kicking chunks of false hair out of my way so I don't slip and fall on my ass.

Julian steps in front of me, his body replacing the rest of the superdome. He motions over my shoulder for the DJ to play some background music, then I flick the power button on my mic to OFF.

"Watch your step," I warn him, clutching one of his taut biceps before joking, "It's slippy out here."

With a grin, he asks, "You got some Pittsburgher in you?"

"Not currently, but I did last night."

He licks his bottom lip, flicking his piercings with his tongue, the memory of feeling the metallic balls on my pussy leaving me feverish.

"Fuck, Collette. Lemme fix that for you."

He leans in, and I warn, "Don't," quick as lightning, just as harsh. The way Julian blocks everything out with his presence, it may feel like we're all alone up here, but that couldn't be further from the truth. We are literally surrounded in every direction.

His gaze runs the length of me, and he asks, "Anything hit you?"

"Nothing physical."

He doesn't ask me for an explanation, and I don't offer one. Tonight, today, this all transcends description.

Nodding like he understands, he glances down at his hand before meeting my eyes, holding them. "I got you something."

"Can you give it to me after? I'm trying to uphold my end of our agreement here."

"I noticed." Eyes touching on my hair, he grins. "It kinda goes with this whole 'show your true self' theme you got goin' though."

"Okay…" My eyes fall to his closed fist, clenched around a large gold…headband? "Is that a—"

"Their hands be grippin' and rippin',
always hoping to catch me up slippin'.
Open mine, baby,
find it holding your crown,
even after I'm buried, six feet under the ground."

He brings his hand up to reveal a crown, an actual fucking crown, and places it on my head—a head with his words, his threat, his *promise*, running through it. *"You're talking about a man. Leave your bus unlocked tonight and I'll show you how a king eats."*

"When did you get this?"

"Earlier today." That's what he went shopping for. A crown. In New Orleans.

"Is it…"

Julian must catch my meaning because he grins softly, saying, "It's realer than anything I've ever bought in my entire fucking life."

With a vintage look to it, the regal-looking crown is more of a brass color than gold. There are eight highpoints on the full round headpiece, different jewels decorating the outside in a stunningly intricate design.

"You didn't have to get me this."

"Yeah, I did."

Half the audience chants, "Duet! Duet! Duet!" while the other half repeats, "Julez! Julez! Julez!"

Julian steals my mic from my hand, flicking it back on, and steps to the side, saying, "Welcome to The Family Julez Tour," before turning around and gesturing to me. "Lemme hear it for the motherfucking *queen!*"

The crown brings a whole other level of excitement from everyone, and I have to hold a hand up to it, keeping the bejeweled crown in place as I laugh, shaking my head at him.

"You kicking me out of here?" I call out, circling in front of him so his attention is on me and not the three guys pushing a piano on to the stage.

I've been keeping a couple secrets today.

Julian's answer of "Never" gets eaten up by the crowd growing even louder, and he finally pulls his gaze from mine, swinging it behind him.

I go over and lean into the mic in his hand suspended midair, saying, "What do you think, Julez? Wanna duet with me?"

His arm goes slack.

"They want to see you, Julian. Exactly how you are," I tell him close to his ear, covering the top of the mic by his side. "*I want you exactly how you are.*"

His cheek grazes my lips as he tries to turn his head, so I quickly tug on his hand, pulling him over to the bench in front of the piano.

"Fuck." He half-laughs, then scrubbing a hand through his own hair, he asks, "Anything in particular or you just want me to wing it?"

Only Julian could say something absurd like that and mean it. He really could wing it up here and he's not even cocky either. Just confident.

It's sexy. So fucking sexy.

I take the mic from his hold to step back. "Do you remember the song from last night?"

He gives me a flat look, like I should know better, then shakes it off, asking, "You're okay singing *that*? Here? Now?"

"It's just a song."

"Weren't you the one that warned me about this?"

"About what?"

His stare lifts to my crown before returning to mine.

"About putting up with fake shit for so long you forget what real is."

I spin around as fast as humanly possible to face an absolutely riveted audience, then swallow thickly, the crown on my head sitting a little lower than it was a moment ago.

"Since tonight's all about showing and embracing our true selves," I say into the mic, "I'd like all of you to know just how talented Julez really is."

Out of the corner of my eye, I can see Slade freaking out. He's got a phone up to his ear, and I can imagine who's on the other end. But this is our playing field. This is the one place performers get to be whoever we want to be and do whatever we want to do. The trick is to not ask for permission ahead of time. If need be, you can apologize after, but during…this is our time. As much as labels wish they had full control over this portion, the truth is they don't. After all, artists are individuals. Individuals with dreams, and desires, and emotions, and we act accordingly. If they want robots, they should hire fucking robots because humans are complex and that complexity can't be contained every minute of every day.

Julian's played his guitar on stage once before, but that was singing covers of other artists' songs. We still pay for that. Now he's about to go completely off-script with original material nobody has any rights to yet, meaning his record label isn't going to get a dime and neither is anybody else. This is truly ours.

"Now, some people might not realize how hot playing the piano is, but…" I wave a hand at Julian seated at the piano, triggering an explosion of applause. "Julez makes it look pretty damn good, right?"

Without watching his reaction, I round the piano and lift myself up onto the opposite side. We can perform the song we came up with on the spot, but we aren't reenacting any other part of last night.

"Here's a song Julez and I wrote together but haven't played anywhere else before."

Smooth as worn leather, Julian taps the same keys as he did last night, pulling me right back to the intimate moment we shared with a surge to my bloodstream.

We sing the lyrics with only a few minor changes. A word here is switched out for another more fitting term; a note there is prolonged to fit the tune better.

Everybody likes to say ignorance is bliss, but they obviously never sang on top of a piano as Julian stroked the keys because this…this is bliss. And I know why. Because like Julian implied, it's not just a song. It's real.

Soon my eyes close, and I lose myself to the song, the feeling, the acceptance blanketing my shoulders as if it's an actual, tangible thing. Lying back, I arch off the piano's surface, pouring my emotions—my *true* emotions—into my solo, and for a brief second, everything in this world feels right. Feels good. With so much bad, awful, evil out here, this kind of snippet of authenticity doesn't come around too often. Smiles are faked, laughs are unnatural, pictures are stolen and manipulated until unrecognizable. *We* are stolen and manipulated until unrecognizable.

Right now, all of that floats away, leaving my chest and stomach and conscience loose and free.

Suddenly, the instrument beneath me goes quiet, and when I open my eyes, I find Julian standing between my legs still hanging off the side. He doesn't have a mic, so hand on my crown, I move to sit back up, putting mine between us.

Last night we didn't do this part acapella but it makes sense why Julian thought to. The final verse is the blending of two identical secrets full of yearning. Yearning so strong, you'll do anything, sacrifice anything, to fulfill it, even yourself. But Julian and I sing it to each other in a way that says that kind of sacrifice isn't warranted. It's not necessary because that yearning is wholly reciprocated. We're convincing ourselves as much as the other person as we sing into my mic, and I bring my hand up to Julian's face, caressing the skin along his jawline, dipping below to the tattoo he put there just for me.

Our eyes hold like there's nothing else in this world worth looking at, and I guess there isn't. Not right now. Not when everything else falls away, leaving just the two of us. Two shut-off artists yearning for a genuine connection to someone who understands, someone who *cares*.

Just as the last word leaves our mouths, he dives forward, and I see his intention before he crushes his lips to mine.

The crowd ignites into an inferno as does my body at the feel of Julian's demanding lips again, this time much different than last night's kiss. My brain screams to put a stop to this, but my body…my body opens for him, letting his tongue sweep inside to twist with mine. Our tongues, our mouths, our bodies, our hearts, fight for that same connection, the one our eyes always find so easily, and the pieces fall into place just as quickly, reinforcing the fact that we're both in the same position. I want Julian just as much as Julian wants me. Maybe more, because while Julian's been forthcoming with his desire, I've been trying to stifle mine.

His groan over the pandemonium finally yanks me back to reality—hard.

We're still onstage. Kissing.

No, not kissing. Making out.

Christ's sake.

Getting ahold of myself, I break my mouth away from Julian's, giving him a hard look and guiding his body away from mine in one smooth motion so I can hop down, giving the frenzied crowd a wave and a smile stretched so wide my ears hurt.

Chants of "Jollette" fill the superdome, making the ball of dread return to my stomach with a swift, vicious vengeance. It never lasts for long—the reprieve from the constant worry over how the public will take you, criticize you, condemn you. Damn it.

"Look what you started," I say out the side of my mouth to Julian, and he slowly turns to face me with one hand still in the air, halfheartedly waving.

To me, he says, "It started long before this." To the crew behind us, swirling his finger above his head, he yells, "Flood it!"

The fog machines all turn on at once, flooding the stage with continuous streams of thick, white smoke.

He should've thought to smoke the stage out *before* he kissed me in front of thousands of people.

"Send for me when it clears," I tell him without so much as a glance. Even if I'm not singing, I try to avoid long exposure to smoke of any kind. It kills my throat otherwise…which he knows and is usually respectful of.

Fuck, he just had to ruin today through and through.

Julian's dragged-out steps follow me offstage, but I don't bother looking back. I only quicken mine in my escape.

He did this. He took something that was so beautiful and peaceful and significant—he *took* it—and he made it his. He wanted to end on a newsworthy note, and by God he fucking did it. That kiss is all anyone's going to be able to talk about for a week, if not longer. Not the tender, emotional, pivotal moments leading up to it. That's all that ever makes headlines anymore—scandal.

And the way he did it. Like he had a right to take that kiss. Like *I* was his to take.

Thankfully, Holter and Mary stayed back at the hotel, so my dressing room is empty when I enter it. The door never closes when I try to shut it behind me though.

Well, it *was* empty.

I don't even have to look to know who it is. He followed me all the way here. He always follows me off the stage, never giving me any time to collect myself.

"I'm not going back out there until that stage clears."

"I know. That's why I flooded it."

I spin around, searching his face for clues as to what the hell is going on with him. From the crown to the kiss, now…this. Whatever this is.

"Get out. I need to think."

His listening skills on par with mine, he sends a leg out, kicking the door shut without so much as blinking.

"Every damn time I turn my back you're running away instead of just telling me what I did wrong. I know you're mad, so just tell me."

Fine.

"How fucking dare you pull that out there," I spit. "I'm not yours to fucking—"

"Oh, you're fucking mine all right," he cuts in, making my head rear back even as he approaches. "I got your cum coursing through my body. You got mine coursing through yours."

"That single lick of precum? It dissolved before it even had a chance to hit my throat."

He keeps going, pointing to my forehead, "You got my crown on your head."

I tear it off, and bend my wrist, ready to launch it across the room, but he closes his hand over mine, gritting, "You're. *My*. Queen." The jewels pressing into my palm are just shy of painful.

"No, I'm not," I seethe before adding, "Bodee."

The air in the room freezes, and I fight a chill to stand firm because I said it and I fucking meant it.

"What did you just call me?"

"Bodee. You're exactly like him."

He visibly flinches, and his hold on my hand eases but doesn't disappear as he questions, "How so?"

"You think I can be bought."

"No, I don't," he says so low the hairs on the back of my neck lift. The crown is free of my hand and returned to the top of my head, then Julian's pressing down into my space, saying, "I bought you the crown because I knew it'd look good on you. But the crown doesn't make you my queen, Collette. Your place by my side does."

"You mean behind you?"

"I mean *beside* me."

"On the stage, right? That's why you want me to stay on for your set. So we can get *lots* of publicity," I spit, my breath feeling more like lava than air. "And you can get lots of—"

"I don't care who knows or who sees!" he roars, his touch falling away as he sends his arms out wide. "I don't care."

"I do! This is exactly why I told you I don't date celebrities."

"Why?"

"And why I told you I couldn't get involved with you."

"Why?"

Each time I reiterate something I've already told him several times over, he's quick to cut me off with "Why?" like he's not even listening, just waiting for me to let something slip.

His moment comes when he finally switches it up, asking, "Because of who?"

And I scream, "Bodee!" My chest aches, not from the amount of energy it took to get it out, but from the amount of energy it's been taking to keep it in. I never talk about Bodee, not in a positive light, and especially not in a negative manner, because either way, it always leads to more questions. Questions I refuse to answer. Questions that if I did answer would make me look weak, and I cannot afford to show weakness. Not anymore. The one time I did, it almost killed me and my unborn baby.

Julian just huffs a humorless laugh, and says, "That motherfucker."

"He made our relationship a circus. He made it a *nightmare*." An inescapable one. "Everything was coordinated. Everything is still coordinated. I'll *never* be able to get through all his hoops."

"And me kissing you out there…you feel like that was for…?"

"The same thing it always is with people like us—attention."

"That's not why I did it. It had nothing to do with who's around. It *has* nothing to do with who's around."

"Then what else was it? Because what you're describing is a luxury nobody living in the limelight has. You *have* to care about who's around you at all times." It doesn't seem to sink in for him though, so I add, "At least I have to." Julian doesn't believe he's a celebrity, but he is. He just hasn't had to answer to the mass media like I have. His life hasn't been completely rocked by scandal before. I wish I could say it's because he's lucky, but I know that's not true. I'm sure Slade and his ironclad NDAs have a hell of a lot more to do with it than luck.

If I weren't a celebrity, then it wouldn't matter as much either. The media would still be frothing at the mouth for details, but they wouldn't expect official statements from PR representatives or confirmation via a social media post consisting of a candid couple selfie accompanying a cute caption with emojis. It's not this happy accident like he's talking about.

"I couldn't hold back anymore. That's the fucking truth. I have no control when it comes to you. None. Can't you see that? Last night was the last of it. Gone. Fucking done. I want you so goddamn much. I want you out there in front of the whole world when you keep telling me I can't. I want you onstage when you're smiling at me like maybe I can. I want you in here when it's just us and you actually fucking let me have a small part of you. I want you on your bus, when your family's around and you let me have a different part of you but guard all the others. I. Want. You. Every. Fucking. Where. That's why I kissed you. That's why I still want to kiss you." His eyes drop to my mouth. "That's why I *will* fucking kiss you."

I put a hand up to stop him, but he keeps coming anyway, dropping his nose to mine, inhaling as he runs the tip over my cheek.

Next to my ear, he whispers, "I'm sorry." And just when I think he's going to say for kissing me in public, on a stage, in front of a superdome full of spectators, not to mention the entire internet once they get ahold of tonight's clips, he says, "I didn't do a good enough job."

"With?"

"Erasing all the touches that came before mine. If I did, Bodee Keys wouldn't still have this hold on you."

I'm lifted off my feet the next instant, my back slamming into the wall as Julian presses his solid erection into my center.

I manage to croak, "We can't," my nails clawing at his shoulders to get him closer despite my weak protest because I feel the same exact way, like I'm done holding back. Like I physically can't anymore.

He sinks his teeth into the side of my throat, sucking the delicate skin so hard, shivers wrack my body.

"No marks," I gasp out, remembering the hickey he left on my wrist.

His head shakes once. "No Marks. No Bodees. No one else's. Only Julian's." And the greedy hands holding my ass grip tighter as he rocks into me with an unmistakable possessiveness to match his words. "Only. Mine."

I scramble for something to stop this from actually happening, saying, "You need to get back out there."

"The smoke hasn't cleared."

"As soon as it does, you need to be there, or else you're going to start losing money."

"You still got me confused with Bodee." It's not posed as a question, but he pulls back, nodding along like he's answering it himself.

After lowering me to the floor, he goes back over to the door, and instead of turning the knob and returning to the superdome full of fans currently screaming his name, he flips the lock into place.

"We're not leaving this room 'til you learn."

"Learn…what?"

"That I'm nothing like your ex."

"We don't have time for this. Not now."

All he says is, "I'll fucking make it," reminding me of the same promise he gave Holter earlier today, that no matter how busy he might be, he'd make time for my son.

And me.

Bodee's never been able to do that. Bodee's never even tried.

The fight to stop this leaves me, just like he said…gone.

"You won't like it," I say, eyeing one of the metal chairs butted up against a circular table. The top part is exposed at least, and it does have a seat and back cushion.

"Fucking try me," is Julian's response.

"Unbuckle your pants and give me your belt," I tell him with a wave in the table's direction. "And sit in one of those."

His eyebrows lift, but he follows directions, watching me the whole time.

"You want my pants down or…"

"I'll let you know."

His right hand goes to his left hip, and with one smooth upward tug, he removes his shirt off his left shoulder, head, then right shoulder, dropping it by his feet before taking a seat.

"Collette," he says to me over his shoulder, but I ignore him, too focused on the belt and making it into handcuffs. "You better not whoop my ass over one kiss."

Both the cuffs adjusted, I hold the figure eight with a looped tail out for inspection. "We both know it wasn't just one kiss. Put your hands behind your back."

"You gonna arrest me?" he jokes, but there's an edge to his tone.

I get his wrists through each loop, then tighten them, and fasten the extra slack to the top handle of the chairback so he can't go anywhere.

"What the fuck is this shit?" Julian says more to himself than to me.

I come around to face him, asking, "Ready to play this game?"

With his jeans' zipper undone and spread wide open, I can see his hard cock jump under his boxers as he says, "I ain't fucking playin'. Do what you gotta do."

Julian has a habit of giving up his control at the first hint of it being threatened. He mistakenly believes this actually keeps him in control because he still has a say. He's about to learn what it feels like to have both his control and his say taken away.

If he wants to prove he's nothing like Bodee Keys, he's going to have to show me what he's like when he's completely out of control, both professionally and personally, because Bodee became a very dark, malicious person when his control was threatened. Julian thinks he doesn't have any control when it comes to me, but he's about to find out what no control actually feels like. And he's going to do it while being sober, so he can face his choice to not fulfill his work obligation at the same time. Before I handcuffed him to the chair he made the choice, now I'm going to make him actually look it in the face.

"Do I have your permission to touch you?" I ask because even though I'm taking away some of his say, it's not *that* kind of say I'm looking to rob him of. I'd never do that to anybody.

"I'm yours to do whatever you want to."

I'm yours…

"Do you trust me?"

"Well, you've already cut me—"

I pull my shirt over my head, and Julian blinks up at me, his eyes trailing down my chest and middle.

"Okay, what the fuck is happening? My cock thinks we're fucking, but my brain thinks we're not? And now you're shirtless which is also confusing as shit." He frowns at his arms stuck to his sides, his elbows bowing as he tests the strength of the belt around his wrists. "Are you grilling me right now? Did I do something? Because since our first kiss, I haven't kissed anyone else. I haven't touched anyone else. I haven't even *looked* at anyone else. I'm…" More confessions tumble out of him, and I have to spin around to hide a grin. He would be terrible in an interrogation.

Sitting back on his thighs, I drop my head to his shoulder, circling my hips.

"You know what men like you crave most?"

"Pussy," comes out as a ragged confession, his choppy breath on my temple.

"Power. You don't crave pussy; you crave pussy you can control."

"That…is way too complicated for me right now. Say it slower, but keep repeating the word pussy."

"See?" I kiss the side of his jaw, tracing the defined bone with my tongue. "Control. Power."

"I'm just fucking around. I'm listening. Gimme a test later and I'll ace that shit. Just, uh." He ducks his head, trying to meet mine. "Come here real quick. Lemme get a taste."

I tilt my head out of his reach, not slowing my hips once. Each rotation presses his cock into my back, and I feel him move under me, trying to meet my pace.

"Do you hear that? They're calling you to the stage." I'm sure everybody's working as fast as they can to clear the smoke, but the fans are impatient. They're positively rabid after what they just saw, and they're not quiet about it. "Your team, your fans, they're all calling for you, but you're not out there. When you're not out there, you're not just letting them down, you're letting the hundreds of people working the show down, too. When I bring up losing money, I'm not only talking about ours. It's not just *your* income you're jeopardizing, Julian."

I hear his teeth grind together, and wince from the sound. If this were happening at any other time, Julian would be turning to his trusty vices to disconnect from the reality in which we live.

This might actually be his first time facing his mistakes and those affected by them. I don't know how he's going to take it either. A lap dance can only cover so much.

Chapter 24

Collette

Ilift my hips up, slowly sliding my shorts down my thighs.

"Your fans…they really wanted to see you tonight. Some of them traveled a long way just to watch you perform on stage. Some of them memorized every one of the lyrics of every one of your songs, along with your set list from previous shows, just so they could be in the moment with you, and have that real-time, in-person connection with *you*. Some of them are crying right now at the chance to see you. Some of them are crying right now because you're not out there for them to see. Some of them will remember this night for the rest of their lives. And you can't be bothered to even go out there."

Kicking my shorts off, I settle back down between Julian's toned thighs in nothing but my panties and lace bralette.

"So get the fuck off me so I can go make their wildest dreams come true." He says it in complete monotone with a tinge of bitterness on the word dreams.

"That's not how the game works," I say, grabbing behind his neck to roll my hips down, then up, so he can both feel and see everything I'm doing.

"This ain't a game. This is fucking torture."

I sit forward, one hand on his thigh behind me, one on his knee in front of me, then sit lower, grinding my ass into his cock.

"How is it torture?"

"Because I want my fingers crammed up your pussy right now so I can feel you buck on top of my cock as I finger-fuck you, but you won't let me."

"Power," I tsk.

"No, not for power. To enjoy the hell out of it."

He strains behind me, not only testing the binds again, but also how close he can get to my back.

He's getting there.

"You're mad you can't touch me but not your fans?"

"You don't want me touching them!" he accuses with a hip-buck of his own that has me sliding backward another inch, my fingers digging into his flesh through his jeans to keep me in place—out of his reach.

"Not like that. Not sexually. I mean spiritually, with your music. With your presence."

Quietly, he says, "I don't want anyone connecting to that music."

"Why?"

"Because my music fucking blows." Under me, his body buzzes with unspent energy. "I write lyrics, good lyrics, and then my label rejects them and tells me to write different lyrics. Catchier lyrics. Lyrics that'll sell out. So, I do. I write absolute trash, trying to see how bad I can make them, and they eat it up, asking for more. More, more, more, always *fucking* more. Then they make me use producers that'll make my tracks how they want them to sound on the radio, not how I hear them in my head. And they try to put me on tours with people whose idea of a good song is a corny-ass hook on repeat for ninety seconds. Night after night, city after city, I gotta get on a stage and perform those same fucking songs to people that want a 'connection' to me through them. It's a fucking joke. I'm not even connected to my lyrics. I got nothing for them. I got nothing for anyone."

That's not true.

"What about your contract? Can't you get out of it?" He's matched with a label he had no business being matched with. Not all of them are that bad.

His tone turns almost wistful as he says, "It'd have to be the fuckup to end all fuckups."

I twist around, seeing his head drop back, staring at the ceiling as both his shoulders droop.

Is that the reason why he acts out so much? In hopes of breaking his deal?

I'm off his lap for a second, then I'm straddling him, kissing his Adam's apple, swirling my tongue around and around before moving to the opposite side of his pot of honey.

"Free one of my hands," he begs, his hips thrusting up into me. "Just one. I need to touch you. Feel how wet you are."

"I'm wet. That's all you need to know."

"No, it's not," he growls, lowering his head so fast I have to rear back to avoid his lips on mine.

We study each other through half-lidded gazes, and I tell him, "It's not your pussy."

"The fuck it's not."

Behind my back, he kicks out one of his legs, swinging it over to rest the ankle on his other thigh, and he uses the leverage to push his calf into the small of my back, shrinking the distance between our fronts.

"I ate that pussy so hard last night, I can still taste you on the back of my teeth."

His jaw dropping open, he runs his tongue over each and every one of his teeth—front and back.

"If that's all it takes, then—"

"Talk about other motherfuckers tonguing your pussy right now, I dare you. I'll rip this goddamn belt apart so fucking fast, Collette."

The calf at my back continues guiding me up his thighs until I'm sitting directly on top of his cock. My pussy clenches in anticipation, holding back what feels like a waterfall, and I start to lose my grip.

In a last-ditch effort to remain in control, I order, "Put your mouth on me."

With one last push from his calf, Julian gets me close enough to lick at my lips, once, twice, three times, the desperation shifting from him to me and back to him again until I'm not sure who wants it more now.

Our mouths dance with each other's in their own game, and I

reach down between us to free Julian's stiff, velvety cock from the hole in his boxers. His groan reverberates through me, settling in my chest as a thick purr.

My hand stroking up the top half of his cock as my pussy rubs the bottom half, I chuck his chin with mine, telling him, "I won't sleep with anyone else."

Eyes closed, Julian's parted lips graze mine as air pours out of him in spurts. "Because you're mine."

"No." I still every part of my body, willing Julian to look at me.

His eyes pop open under the cover of thunderous eyebrows.

"Because I'm mine, and I decide who I sleep with."

"Collette—"

"And I want to sleep with you." Those stormy eyebrows slowly start to withdraw their gloomy reign as they lift. "Only you, Julian." My hand and hips start moving in sync again.

"You want *me?*"

Keeping his eyes, I hook a finger into my panties and pull them to the side, then lean back with a hand on his stationary knee to roll my hips, rubbing my bare pussy on the underside of his cock. "I want you."

Cheeks twitching, he breathes, "Jesus." His eyes are no longer on mine. "You're fucking drenched."

Pushing myself up and over, I line his tip up with my entrance, then slowly glide down his shaft, my pussy stretching to accommodate each inch as I spread my legs even wider out to the sides. My teeth bite into my lips so hard I taste blood and I give in, just a little, by rolling my hips once.

"Holy fuuuuck." Julian's forehead puckers. "I'm gonna embarrass myself if you don't move. Fucking ride me—"

Instantly, I'm off his lap completely, hovering an inch above his upright, glistening cock.

"I didn't mean move like that," he snaps, his arms restless at his sides. His bent knee knocks into my ass, trying to rouse me into movement.

"You're not in control here, little lamb."

"I don't want to be in control! I want to be inside you! My fingers, my cock, my fucking tongue, I don't care what it is. I'm fucking dying not being able to touch you right now." He drops his head back, rasping,

"Jesus Christ, I never thought I'd say this, but I just want you to sit on my face already."

"Then ask."

His head rises until we're staring each other down again.

"Ask. Nicely. You want to prove you're not *him?* That you're better?" I lift an eyebrow. "Then ask. Or shut the hell up and let me do what I want like you said I could."

His eyebrow matches mine as his cock jerks below me.

"Can you *please* take my jeans down?" he asks, a smile tugging at his lips. I start to speak, but he's quick to say, "It's not for me, it's for you. *If* you mount my cock again, the zipper's gonna tear up your thighs." After a beat, he adds, "Or ass."

"You think you're getting laid?"

"I think I don't want to see you get hurt, even if you're the one doing it to yourself."

Now he's definitely getting laid.

We work together to get his pants and boxers down past his hips but leave them bunched around his ankles.

"Can you *please* free at least one of my feet?"

"No, it'll give you too much mobility," I say, pointedly glancing at his knee.

"Goddamn it." It's said with humor though, not frustration like before.

My reasoning is only partially true. Mostly it's Julian's jeans…they're really tight, and I don't have the time to deal with getting them over his shoes. Outside, they must've gotten the stage cleared because I can hear Axel on the drums now, stalling.

"Spread your legs," I tell him, and he obeys. "Wider."

His thighs separate even more, giving me an unobstructed view of his erect cock from base to tip, his balls resting heavy just below. I thought Julian was beautiful with his pants on, but this…this is a sight to behold.

"Can you *please* take your bra off?"

"Is that for my benefit, too?"

"Nah." He smirks. "That's all for me."

"Then it stays on."

His chuckle shakes his upper body. "The fuck? I can't win here."

"You're not supposed to win. You're going to lose."

"Lose what?" he bites out, a suspicion settling over his features as his arms flex just enough for me to notice out of the corner of my eye.

"Power."

His name crackles across the overhead speakers, calling for his immediate return to the stage, and I see it—the flash of panic that's usually masked by a shot or a bump by now. He covers it just as quickly though.

"People don't come to concerts just to hear songs," I say, stepping closer to tower above him, one hand reaching out to stroke his cock. "It's never been easier than it is today for listeners to stream music directly into their ears. They can hear our music anywhere, while doing anything, around anyone. They come to concerts for companionship. For connection. For hope. Music is a portal to help them find it. It doesn't fucking matter if you relate to your lyrics; they do." I point out to my side using my free hand, and his glazed eyes try to follow. "And when you shun those lyrics, or you shun the people that grasped on to them at their lowest moment, when they were searching for *anything* to make them feel better, you shun their hope, too. There are enough gatekeepers in this world, Julian. Don't be one of them."

"So I'm supposed to just suck it up basically? It doesn't matter what I want?"

My hand freezes, tightening around his base.

"Not suck it up, but you do need to stop thinking only about yourself. It's not all about you. We write the songs for ourselves, but we release them for others."

I resume the up and down movement, with a swirl along my palm at his cock's cut head.

"Not me. Mine should've never got released. I didn't write those fucking songs for myself."

"You won't be locked in with that label forever. The songs you do write for yourself, keep them. Don't throw them away. One day you'll release them for others, exactly the way you want to. But if you shut out all your fans now, nobody will be there to hear them…" My eyes land on his auxiliary cord tattoo. "…at home, or in concert."

"Yeah, I bet I'll miss out on some money," he says like he couldn't care less.

Money is not Julian's biggest motivator. I know that now. I thought it was because of the way he lives, or more accurately the way he pays for everyone around him to live. I know he still pays for all the expenses accrued on his bus even though he's hardly ever on it anymore.

Music could be his why for doing this, but I understand how it's not. At least right now. His current music doesn't even feel like his own.

Thinking he has nothing to work toward, it's easy for him to stop working, period.

And now that he's gotten accustomed to quitting, it's second nature to him. Whereas Bodee doesn't work as hard because he doesn't have to, Julian doesn't work as hard because he doesn't want to.

Neither of those should be an artist's why though. Music can't put dinner on the table, and money can't fulfill you. While neither should be underestimated, you also shouldn't depend on them as your sole reason for sharing art. You will bankrupt yourself in one way or another.

"Love at first sight," I blurt, my gaze lifting from Julian's hips thrusting up into my hand.

He stops, asking, "What?" like he's coming out of a daze.

"This very second, two strangers are falling head over heels in love with a single look. Babies will be conceived tonight, here in some dark corner, or later when they get wherever they're staying for the night. Right outside, lifelong friendships will be formed, dead-end relationships will finally get closure, healing will happen. Answers to troubling issues will be discovered under this roof. It's not because of you or me. It's because of music and the portal it creates to all the beautiful things in life that money can't touch. We're just lucky enough to get to provide that gateway to a superdome of people looking for it." I frown. "Bodee lost sight of that, or never saw it to begin with. To him, concerts are *all* about money."

"How the fuck am I supposed to perform like that for that many people over and over again?"

"You don't. It's impossible. You pick one, someone near the front that you can make eye contact with, and you perform for them like it's their life you're hoping to change that night. Everybody else in the arena, watching you on the screen, all the way up to the nosebleeds, will feel it."

"Is that why you tour so much?"

"I, uh…" My hand, wrist, and arm go fuzzy, then my head. "That's…"

Axel starts another song, and I blindly turn my face toward the door, listening to the footsteps racing past my door.

"Collette, what were *you* to Bodee?"

I return my stare to Julian, admitting, "Something he had power over. Something he could use to get even more."

Thickly, he asks, "Can I *please* kiss you now?"

"Where?"

His gaze trickles to my throat, over my breasts, and down my stomach before settling at the junction at my thighs covered by a thin strip of fabric.

"There."

I release him, and with the ball of my foot on the seat of his chair, I push off the floor, fitting both my feet between his legs. Mine pressed tightly together, I shimmy the panties down my thighs all the way to my ankles, lifting one foot at a time to drop them on the floor.

Julian's chest expands on an inhale I know is being pulled in through his nose.

My body sways forward just enough for him to stretch his neck out, but instead of kissing my pussy, he tilts his head at the last second to lay a tender kiss to my inner thigh. When he does the same to the other one, I see red streaks on the skin.

The zippers on his pants. I hadn't even noticed they made marks.

Through dense lashes, he looks up at me, and says, "Even with my hands tied behind my back, I'll still take care of you because real kings protect their queens." Never breaking eye contact, his mouth moves to my clit and closes over the nub while his dolphin bites tickle my pussy lips.

Both hands in his hair for balance, I keep Julian on my clit, guiding his mouth up and down, against me so my hips can mirror his movements.

A series of knocks at the door freezes me in place but has the opposite effect on Julian as he goes even harder, sucking my clit like a vacuum hose.

"Have you seen Julez? We need him on stage!"

With a strategic yank to his strands, Julian's forced to let go, a string of my arousal mixed with his saliva hanging in the air between my clit and his top lip.

I'm completely transfixed by the sight until he growls up at me, "Tell them to fuck off or I will."

Breathless, I shake my head and my own possessive thoughts away to say, "You need to make a choice."

"Between you or them? Easy, y—"

"Think it through, Julian. Don't just think about instant gratification. Think about everyone and everything I've been talking about."

"This is my test?" he asks.

I shrug a shoulder, telling him, "You said you'd ace it."

He glances around the room, his chest expanding and contracting. "I'll go out there…"

He did it. He actually chose what's important, and he did it for the right reasons.

I drop a foot to the floor.

"…with you. If that's okay?"

All movement stops as we regard one another.

He chose…both? But he's leaving it up to me.

"If you want, and you're ready, we can go now. Or if you wanna stay another minute…" His eyes take me in, lifting his chin for me to stand back up on the chair. "I'll finish you off first."

All restraint leaves my body, leaving behind need. Pure need. The need I've been denying for far too long.

"Two minutes!" I call out to whoever's on the other side of my door, then straddle Julian, positioning my seam above his cock before plunging right down on to his hard length until he's bottomed out inside me.

Our groans surround us like a fortress, keeping us in and everything else out.

My tiptoes touching the floor, my body stutters over his, and it's all I can do to hold still, noting every part of our bodies syncing up.

We fit. We fit completely.

Nestled deep between my walls, his cock twitches, and I moan, dropping my forehead to his.

"No condom?" he breathes as his hips surge up into mine, making my mouth fall open. "I've never gone without one."

My eyes flick up to his. "You want one?"

I always use condoms, too, but this whole thing was about being stripped raw. Not having any barriers between us felt natural. It *feels* natural.

"No." His head shakes against mine. "Fuck no. This is…fuck. So much better."

Foreheads still kissing, we both watch ourselves getting acclimated to the other.

"We're—"

"Yeah. We're fucking perfect together," he says, finishing my thought.

"I looked into it… The story of Isis and Osiris."

This time his eyes find mine.

"Isis didn't find all of Osiris's pieces. The only piece she couldn't recover was—"

"His cock, I know." Julian laughs. "Fucking sucks for him."

I laugh, too, then grab the back of his chair, and placing a heel on the small slice of seat behind him, I start riding his cock.

"She still found a way to get pregnant by him though," he says with pinched brows, and I swear I see a look resembling pain flash across his features before it disappears.

Is that why he thinks I didn't insist on using a condom? I know he's sterile and I'm on birth control.

"I'm not trying to make a baby with you," I assure him, grinding so hard our sweat squishes audibly between us. "Just fulfilling a basic urge."

Julian's body locks up under mine, so I roll my hips faster, using his solid abdomen to my advantage. Two minutes is not a lot of time, but I am already halfway there. Have probably been halfway there since The Family Julez Tour started.

Using his tight shoulders as leverage, I lift up to impale myself on him, and we watch each other as I ride him, nothing else around us breaking through our own little world until there are more knocks on the door, then Julian growls out, "Anyone opens that door is fucking dead," neither of us even breaking pace.

"Come for me, Collette," he demands.

I smirk, telling him, "Ask me to, Julian."

"*Please* come for me before we break this fucking chair."

As if to emphasize his point, the chair under us creaks.

I dig my nails into Julian's tensed traps, shortening my movements so his cock's buried to the hilt now as I roll my hips again, keeping a steady pressure on my clit.

"I thought you liked breaking things," I whisper more out of necessity than choice. "You've been trying to break my rule about this all along."

"That rule's been broken since the night you cut me and claimed me as your own."

I close my eyes from the intensity of…everything.

"You're gonna miss it," he warns though, making my eyes fly open again. No longer watching our bodies, Julian's staring right into my eyes, right into my soul, and I feel it—the moment everything falls into place, telling me exactly what I already knew but didn't want to acknowledge. It's never been about a basic urge with Julian.

My mouth falls open as an orgasm tears through me, hard and fast, my body tensing around Julian's.

"Holy fuck," he groans, jerking up into my pussy with his own orgasm.

Tremors continue to rock us both, and our mouths meet in a hungry kiss, eating each other's moans.

My heart rate still going way too fast, Julian pulls back to look into my eyes. "That's the biggest difference between me and Bodee. He wasn't your king." His hands grasp my face with gentle fingertips before moving up to straighten the crown on my head that'd slid backward. "Nothing can keep me from you because I am yours."

The bones in my body fight to stay solidified while the rest of me tries to melt at not only Julian's touch but also his words.

"How long—"

"I was free pretty much the whole time."

"So you just let me think… The power…"

Carefully, he takes my hand in his and lifts it up to his neck, placing our intertwined fingers on his tattoo, his erratic pulse beneath the colorful skin thumping as wildly as mine.

"The power's always been in your hands, Collette."

I glance between his eyes and our clasped hands, my shoulders sagging lower the deeper in thought I go.

"Come on, Poohbear. Let's go change some lives," he says, and I have to stop myself from telling him that he already did.

Chapter 25

Julian

Flipped so the back of the t-shirt is facing up, I write the words that have been running through my head all morning onto the fabric, stopping to pull the material taut every couple letters. Some up-and-coming repurposed clothing company sent the shirt over, hoping I'd wear it for my birthday bash tonight, but I thought it was missing something.

Not anymore.

If I wake to find you gone,
back I'm sinkin' to that prison of my own creation.

Creation comes out diagonal in sort of a different style from the rest—more ominous maybe?—and the marker in my hold hovers above it as I debate coloring the whole thing in and scrapping this entire idea.

It is true, but do I want everyone to know that?

Fuck it, it stays. It's in permanent marker anyway.

Kind of like how Collette's marked me—permanently. I couldn't wash that shit away if I tried. Not that I'd try. I finally got her. Got her in my hands, and not just in my head. Fuck, she's still there, but I can do something about it now.

Not right now though. After NOLA, we've spent almost every minute of the last week and a half together, until this morning when she threw my ass off her bus. It's supposed to be for the birthday gift she got me of one-on-one studio time with DJ Arique to work on any song I want, any way I want. When he's not DJing, he's also a hell of a producer, and it's actually a pretty nice gift. Very thoughtful.

I just…

I'm still trying to figure out why Collette couldn't just come with me. Is it too much to ask for her naked body to be laid out, waiting for me, with like a red bow on each nipple or something? That's the kinda gift I was hoping for. Not one *without* her.

Fuck. I'm an asshole. I really am looking forward to getting in the studio with someone not on my label's payroll; I just want Collette to be with me, too.

I glance around my bus, barely making out faces through the puffs of smoke. I doubt I'd recognize them anyway. Half these fuckers I already forgot, and the other half I wish I could forget.

You think being rich and famous is somehow gonna change everything, but it doesn't. It just changes the landscape, while everything and everyone remains exactly the same. Disappointing people are everywhere, no matter how much money you're making. They just multiply once the zeros in your bank account do, too.

Fuck that. I don't want Collette here.

I don't even want to be here.

Why couldn't Antonio drop me off? Better yet, I could've borrowed another half-mil sports car and let Collette drive me herself.

I'm not buying her excuse of needing alone time to make business calls either. This week, she's already been on several with her own producer, David Yonko, and I didn't bother her during a single one. All I did was rub her back.

And scalp.

And inner thighs.

And probably a pussy lip or two.

What-the-fuck-ever. I tried my best.

But now I'm stuck on my own bus, on the way to the studio, trying not to get my ass chewed out by some executive or another currently blowing up my phone.

Slade's been trying to fend them off by answering 'em all, but they're out for blood right now. Even from my spot at the table, I can still hear angry voices coming through the line as my agent paces the aisle, pushing randoms out of his way.

My label's always pissed at me, but me adding in the piano duet with Collette really set them off. Probably doesn't help that even after the first wrist slap they gave me for it, I haven't stopped. I just save it for the finale now so I can drag Collette backstage to fuck her brains out immediately after without making the fans wait on us again. *How's that for being professional.*

My refusal to apologize to anybody for any of it is definitely making things worse, but I don't give a fuck. Being with Collette is the only time I actually feel like myself and performing with her while singing original lyrics that I don't hate with every fiber of my being reminds me what it felt like before. Before I signed my creative license away to a money-hungry fucktrocity of a record label, before my grandma died, before I gave up on everything, even myself.

No fucking way am I apologizing for that. They can grab a spoon and eat the pile of shit they took in the middle of my career path.

The only reason why they haven't kicked my ass to the curb yet is because of the sudden increase in both album and ticket sales thanks to The Family Julez Tour trending all week.

I didn't shove my tongue down Collette's throat onstage for the pictures to go viral, I did it because I couldn't *not* kiss her anymore—Jesus fuck, I held back as long as I could—but just like she predicted, everyone latched on to the drama, the intrigue, the fucking shock factor of *The* Collette locking lips with bad-boy rapper, Julez, after not being public with *anyone* for years.

As much as I love everybody knowing I'm the only one capable of kissing *The* Collette like that, it all just feels wrong—the attention.

My marker falls to the table, and I slouch down in my seat until the back of my head hits the headrest.

If my art was actually my art, maybe I'd be getting recognition for the hard work I put into it instead of the tongue-fucking I gave the hottest popstar on the planet.

Still speaking into the phone, Slade hands me a lit joint and gives me a knowing head nod. I take it but don't put it to my lips right away. I just stare at the tip, watching the enticing white tendrils streaming out of it.

I don't rush to get high as much anymore. I still get baked, there just isn't as much of a *need* to all the time, not like there was.

"Yo, you gonna pass that shit or what?" some dude on the opposite side of the table asks, gesturing to my hand, and I frown because I don't remember him or who the fuck he's here with.

At any given time, my bus has no less than thirty people on it, which I used to be grateful for because it'd provide exactly what I need to shut everything else off. Its relief was easy to grasp, reliable to find, and instantaneous to lose myself to.

Except today, when I climbed on board again, the sight didn't give me the reassurance it usually does. After I couldn't even find a seat for myself, I almost walked right back off.

I used to thrive off this shit, constantly being surrounded by others, drowning out my own thoughts with the noise, the chaos, but now it's just stifling, suffocating. I want off. I want out.

Over on Collette's bus, it's different. It's quieter with more space to sit, to think. More room to grow.

But I can't go over there right now. I'm banished for the day. And maybe the night, I'm not sure, she didn't specify. Collette not only lets me fill her pussy now but also her bed. Well, the one above hers, which is close enough. Close enough to miss now that it's taken away from me.

Probably. It's probably been taken away from me. Hopefully I can finagle my way back in there tonight. I can't stay here.

A bottle of tequila is placed in front of me next, and just like that, everything's on the verge of being blurred to total numbness again.

I take the alcohol in my other hand, double-fisting my two oldest friends. It's ironic how the very things I'd use to make it all disappear—the people, the noise, the parties, the distraction—are now what I wish would vanish. Or maybe it's not them I want to disappear. Maybe it's just me.

Maybe it's always been me.

Collette doesn't make me feel like disappearing though. Her, her music, her bus, her son. She's like a witch, casting a spell over me with her many enchantments, except she doesn't even know it. She doesn't know anything. Not how deep she's hooked me. Not what it does to me to be exiled back to my own personal hell.

It's not her fault. How could she know? I never talk about my bus with her. I never even talk about my life with her. I want Collette and the way she makes me feel separate from the bleakness of the rest of my existence.

"Time to get this party started," Slade announces once he's finally off the phone, but I barely glance his way. Instead, I fit the joint to my lips, inhaling deeply while studying the words I just wrote.

I could show her. I could make Collette understand.

Smoke slips out between my lips, curling slowly in front of my heavy-lidded eyes, up toward the bus's ceiling.

"How much longer 'til we're there?" I ask Slade, and he shakes his head, his gelled hair not moving a centimeter.

"Are you really planning to record today?"

"I'm scheduled to," I say through the harsh smoke flowing from my mouth. Smoke doesn't affect my voice like it does Collette's. She's got a sensitive voice box or something. Doesn't stop me from making her scream my name every chance I get though. I'm practically her new vocal coach with all the exercises I've been putting her singing pipes through lately.

What the fuck am I doing here again? I should've hired a car service. Then I'd already be working on a new track, not dealing with—

"You're gonna want to cancel." Slade motions behind me, and when I turn to look over my shoulder, I have to do a double take at the two identical raven-haired beauties in string bikinis coming out of the back bedroom. "My birthday presents to you will be a lot more fun."

Presents, huh?

I give the…twins?…a more thorough once-over, and all I can think is, *how long have they been back there?* That's it. Nothing sexual registers whatso-fucking-ever, and I drop my eyes to glare at my cock hidden somewhere deep inside my jeans, not reacting in any way.

Really? Not a fucking eager jump to attention? A goddamn jolt? Nothing?

The fuck? Is he broken?

I eye the shirt stretched across the table again.

Nah. I may be broken but my cock sure the fuck isn't. His tastes, and mine, have changed, that's all. I require something different now.

"How much longer?" I repeat.

"Who cares?"

Slade beckons the girls forward, and they approach me with matching *come fuck me* smiles, and…yup, they're twins.

God.

Damn.

Twins.

Real identical fucking twins offering themselves up to me on a tarnished platter, and still, my cock's nowhere to be found. Just hiding out like a convict on the lam.

"I care," I grit, trying to avoid eye contact with the twins, trying to avoid eye contact with *everyone*. Not caring was one of my finest assets, but things have changed. I've changed.

I'm trying to fucking change.

"You won't soon. Drink up, birthday boy," Slade murmurs, gripping my shoulder while nudging the tequila in my hold.

He's serving me up everything I go for normally. I should be lapping it up. I would've been…before. Before I got a taste for *her*—who my cock's loyalty now lies with. That fucker isn't mine anymore. Just like the rest of me, he belongs to Collette, too.

Flesh and bone, mind and soul, I've been motherfucking claimed.

Now I just need to claim her back.

"Ayo, Axel?" I call out toward the front of the bus where I last saw my drummer.

His head pops up from one of the couches, saying, "Yeah?"

"Slade's got some friends he wants to introduce you to."

Axel visibly blanches, shaking his head as he settles further down into the couch. His phone's screen has his face lit up, and even from here I can see his disapproval. He's changed, too. Ever since New Orleans, he hasn't been going as hard either, in anything, especially females. I don't know for sure, but I'm thinking it might have to do with Irelynn. Dude's crushin'. Bad. I've even been letting him come over to Collette's bus, too.

Slade squeezes my shoulder a little too hard to ignore, so I shake him off me, watching his smile flicker as he jabs, "What's the matter, boss man? Can't handle two girls alone anymore? Gotta bring in Ax as reinforcement?"

I give him a long, hard stare, everybody around us falling into a strange silence, too. It's never quiet on here. Because I ensure it's not.

"The fuck are you doing?" I've been in plenty of threesomes, that's common knowledge, but the way he's saying it, it's like he's goading me, trying to entice me into another. What's in it for him if I sleep with these girls?

If it's about the money he spent, maybe he should fuck them.

"Nothing." His smile vanishes completely, and waving a hand at the twins, he says, "You should be celebrating today, not working."

"It's not work when it's with—"

"Collette?" Slade snorts loud enough to cover the growl building in my chest at hearing her name on his tongue. "You said she wasn't even going with you. Just leaving you on your own for your twenty-eighth birthday. Your people would never do that."

I'm already scoffing because who are my people? Him? The rest of these motherfuckers? I'd love to fucking know how they're mine. Because I pay for every fucking piece of food they stick in their mouths? Because they take everything from me, even my seat, even my bed, without ever even considering giving me anything in return? The people filling this bus are here to celebrate all right…every fucking minute of every fucking day, whether I'm here or not.

I didn't even think I'd make it to my twenty-eighth birthday— hoped I wouldn't—and honestly? I doubt any of these motherfuckers would've noticed if I hadn't. As long as the booze and the drugs are still here, they're good.

These aren't my people. They've never been my people. I just bought their presence so I could avoid my own.

"Don't let that piece of—"

I'm out of my seat, seizing Slade by the throat before he can make the worst mistake of his life by finishing that statement. Hell, it'll be the last mistake of his life because I'm ready to fucking end it here and now. Collette ain't a piece of anything.

"Shit, man!" somebody shouts while another person screams. Fucking dramatic-ass bullshit. I'm so tired of it. All of it.

I give Slade's windpipe a firm squeeze before releasing him and shoving him away from me.

"Lemme know when we're there." And with that, I pivot around to head to my bedroom, barking for everyone inside to get the fuck out before slamming the door shut and falling on to my bed—my wet bed.

I'm sorry, "my people" would never do *what?*

Dirty fucking fucks.

"Happy birthday, Julez!" several people yell at me as I walk up to the front door, stopping to pose for a few pictures taken by the paps stationed outside on the sidewalk. In order to get the entire club for my birthday, the owners want a certain amount of photos circulating online before I even set foot inside. Pretty fucking corny considering they're the ones that offered to host the event in the first place.

This is how I got that McLaren for a few days without paying a dime, too. Everything and everyone has a price, and public photos are the most sought-after commodity because they can produce clout the fastest, and *everybody* wants clout because clout opens more doors than talent. Artists are no longer praised for their art, not when celebrities *are* the art.

Brains are all but irrelevant, and fuck what you sound like. For real. Voice editing is the music industry's version of photo editing—it's recklessly used everywhere on everyone, and nobody's held accountable for the deception it creates.

There is no standard for truth because the truth can be ugly and ugly doesn't sell. Beauty's an all-encompassing illusion, yet if something—or someone—doesn't look good, it's—they're—basically as disposable as shit-stained underwear.

"Thanks. Have a good night," I tell everyone after standing in my usual pose of my hand shaped like a gun cradling my chin for some selfies with fans, then finally head inside. The dark hallway leading to the main area flashes from a strobe light, and I pause a moment, scrolling through my four thousand seven hundred thirty nine new messages, searching for one name in particular. I turned my phone on airplane mode as soon as I got to the studio, so it's been hours since I've talked to anyone other than DJ Arique. The last I heard from Collette was this morning when she gave me the fucking boot off her bus.

There're no texts from her though, not even a call or an email. *Does she have my email?* I should give her my email.

I should give her everything.

I freeze, my eyes hazing out at the thought—me giving Collette everything. Me marrying Collette. Even me filling her with my babies… if I could.

Could I?

My internet browser's open the next instant, my eyes touching on every part of the screen as I type, then scroll.

Vasectomy reversal. I vaguely remember hearing something about that when I went in for my vasectomy. It's real and I could actually do it. I could knock Collette up and give her more kids.

Holy shit, talk about a birthday present.

After sending out an email to the doctor that snipped me, I click on AirDrop, my chest swelling even more when Collette's name comes up.

Straightening, I pocket my phone, dragging my feet slowly as I stroll from the hall.

"Happy birthday!" hundreds of people I supposedly know shout in unison.

A socialite I know for a fact gets spray-painted in foundation from head to toe because she's covered in freckles—trust me, I've seen 'em for myself—prances through the quickly parting crowd to plant a kiss on my cheek. The corner of her lips graze the corner of mine, and I have to work to keep from frowning. Instead, I pat her back awkwardly, making sure the move's exaggerated enough for the cameras flashing around us to catch.

Friends. Friends pat backs.

I never used to think about who I was photographed with or whether or not it'd start rumors about who I'm banging. Shit, most, if not all, of them have been true. But tonight feels different. I feel different, and I don't want my name sprouting up next to another woman's anymore.

The next hour is spent shaking hands, slapping backs, and accepting bottle after bottle of the rarest liquor money can buy. I get dozens of cards full of all kinds of things, even drugs. Good drugs, too. Expensive drugs. Drugs the average person would be afraid to take, not knowing exactly what's in it, but I'd put in my body with zero hesitation. Drugs I have put in my body with zero hesitation. Since I'm not trying to do that tonight, I hand everything off to Slade, letting him put it all in the storage truck we had to rent specifically to store gifts in.

After a while, faces stained by the obvious sheen of desperation start to swim, and I have to toss back a double shot of rum just to navigate through the sea of opportunists. Never catching sight of who I really want to see though, the only person that doesn't seem to want a goddamn thing from me, I beeline to the bar for another, giving up the charade of smiling through the torture.

Elbows on the bar, I put in my order with the bartender, then start chewing on the side of my thumb, the familiar coppery tang of blood soothing my taste buds like a dose of heroine to my bloodstream. My rotten insides being pulled out by my dirty fucking mouth isn't exactly the way I thought my birthday would go, but the raw skin fits my mood spot on right now—worn thin and bleeding out with absolutely nobody the wiser.

Something with a sharp, pointed end jabs my back, and through the ceiling-high mirror behind the bottles lining the wall, I spy blonde hair half hidden just below my shoulder. She's here, and she didn't bother hiding under a wig.

Forgetting all about my thumb and feeling the first real smile of the night, I say, "Back to finish the job?"

"If I wanted you dead…"

The knife presses further into my skin, causing my eyes to close.

"…I would've done it when I had you tied up and at my mercy."

"Uh-huh." I was at Collette's mercy, maybe, but tied up? We both know those handcuffs didn't hold up the way she hoped they would.

The knife disappears, then that mouth full of straight teeth sinks into my shoulder blade. My cock reacts this time, doubling in size almost instantly, and I drop a hand behind me to find her. I palm the fuck out of her pantyless ass cheek, then bring her in flush against my back, the reminder of how hot this past week and a half's been fresh on my mind and tongue, and fingers, and cock. Never in my wildest dreams did I imagine Collette would slum it with someone like me, *especially* me. She's America's sweetheart, and I've got a box truck half-filled with drugs parked just outside. We shouldn't work together.

But we do.

I consider lighting the entire truck on fire after this party. Collette's a better high than anything inside it anyway.

Feeling out the short skirt she's wearing, I start to slide my fingers down, hoping to sneak underneath, but the moan she unleashes goes straight to my balls, and I end up fisting the material, ready to rip the fucking skirt off her body instead. Swear to fuck, I'm about to come in my pants like a horny virgin right now.

Quickly releasing her bite on me, she says, "Happy birthday, little lamb."

My eyes open, seeking hers in the mirror, but she's not looking at me. She's reading the lines I wrote on the back of my t-shirt. There's a hole burned in it somewhere back there, too, from when I dropped the joint to choke Slade, but it kinda adds to the doom and gloom vibe.

Out of the thousand thoughts that race out from her head and on to her pretty face, I can't decipher a single one.

What's she thinking? Does she understand yet?

"Julian?"

I spin to face her.

No. Don't get scared now.

I can't do this any other way. I'm all or nothing, and I've been nothing for so. Damn. Long.

"Yeah?" I finally ask when she doesn't say anything, but no answer comes. Only a smile.

A smile that hooks me all over again. Hooks me, then reels me in just like the first time I saw it.

When I dip to kiss her, she pulls out of reach, glancing around us at the dozens of phones aimed our way.

Goddamn it. Not this again. I thought out of everything, she at least understood I'm done holding back with her and I hope to God everyone in here knows it, sees it, fucking feels it. Her name's the only one I want mine next to. For-fucking-ever.

"I'll send 'em packing," I threaten, not even blinking when I say it. "Every last person here, gone with a single word." Truthfully, I wish I already had.

Collette props a hand on her leather-skirt-covered hip. Under a matching black leather jacket, she's wearing a black lace bra—it's a fucking bra—with the rest of her front naked except for a long strand necklace draped down her breastbone that branches off into multiple body chains. I want to grab a handful of the chains and drag her to me. I want to wrap both my hands around her—

"For what? A kiss? It looked like you already got one anyway." She swings her gaze over to the freckled socialite that greeted me with lips I long forgot about. I'm too busy getting lit off Collette to even notice there are other women here.

But damn. Although Collette slays in anything she wears, jealousy's by far my favorite look on her. Jealousy and whatever the fuck this outfit's called.

I thumb her pouty bottom lip, barely stopping myself from sucking it whole.

Her face morphs into something that looks a hell of a lot like disappointment when she sees my bloody thumb.

If she hadn't taken my ring, maybe I could hide it a little better.

Swallowing my nerves, I start to tell her, "Collette, I—" but she shakes free of my hand, putting space between us to ask, "How's your birthday been so far?" like I wasn't just about to bare my soul to her.

"I wasn't with you, so it wasn't worth talking about."

Her eyes search mine, and I shrug, glancing back at the bar, at the tall shot glass awaiting me.

If I drink this second double shot, maybe *I'd* be able to hide a little better.

"You didn't go, did you?"

To the studio she reserved for me.

"Of course, I went," I tell her, ignoring the rum.

Her chest damn near caves in. Was she worried I wouldn't? If it were up to Slade, I wouldn't have, which is pretty shitty now that I think about it. Is that why he was so concerned with me having that threesome? So I wouldn't be able to go?

"And? How'd it go?"

I scan over the crowd, catching the eye of DJ Arique already in the booth, a hand in the air while the other's on one of his turntables. Raised on that underground style, he combines both ways of DJing—automatic and manual—by using a mixer and two turntables with platters he can scratch on just like his idols used to.

It's impossible to describe what today meant to me. The whole experience of getting to do my art my way was insane. It reminded me of my why for creating. And Arique was fucking amazing to work with. He didn't just tell me what to do, he taught me all about the process of what *we* were doing together.

I'd already invited him to tonight's festivities three minutes after meeting him, but as soon as I found out he isn't one of those DJs who just lets a premade playlist play out on a laptop, I had to have him mix some music here, too, so I hired him. I was fully prepared to pay him. With everyone looking for at least one dance track on their albums, he's in high demand right now, but he insisted on coming tonight as a debt owed to Collette. Something about feeling bad for not being able to work with her directly. I'm not sure what that means exactly because why the fuck wouldn't he be able to work with Collette? She's an indie artist and can work with whoever she wants. Plus, she's got a shit-ton of dance tracks on her albums, and while David, her regular producer, is good, he's not as skilled in EDM the same way DJ Arique is.

Collette follows my gaze and grins, but it doesn't go near her eyes as she watches the DJ.

What did it cost her to ask him for today's private studio session? Something more valuable than money. Arique won't work with her, but he worked with me for her… How'd she swing that? And why?

Maybe for the same reason why I'm about to do this. I give Arique the signal we discussed earlier, then my voice fills every speaker in the club.

Collette notices immediately, bringing her eyes back to mine.

"This is what you did today?"

I nod, watching her closely.

"I like it," she says, then angles an ear toward the closest speaker.

The track's emotional, probably my most emotional song to date, but with an upbeat melody that has every single body in the place moving along to it.

Collette's eyes trail the club as she tunes in, but mine don't stray from her once. She takes in the words, not reacting, not judging, just listening carefully, and it gives me a slice of confidence when the most revealing part comes up.

"Baby girl, you the prim to my crude,
sitting there proper, just achin' for a rescue.
Got everyone out here thinking you is just a mood,
a passing phase,
shit, nothin' but a prude.
Wrap your arms around me like the salve to my wounds.
Forever indebted like the day Eeyore met that bear, Pooh.
He ain't never been better than in his place beside you.
Don't know how to say these feelings, they ringin' so true.
Listen to my heart, baby, and I'll tell you what you already knew.
All these nights I'm spending 'longside my muse,
Wondering how the fuck we can make it on through.
But if I wake to find you gone,
back I'm sinkin' to that prison of my own creation."

"That's from your shirt."

"It's not from my shirt, Poohbear. It's from here." I flatten my hand to my rib cage, feeling my heart trying to bust out of it.

Looking in her silvery eyes right now, all I want to do is follow through on my threat to send everyone home so it's just the two of us.

She basically stiff-arms me though when I lean forward, drawn to her in a way no lyrics could ever capture.

"And the nickname? Will you finally tell me where it came from?"

"When I met you, the cloud that'd been hanging over my head, following my every move, shifted for the first time in years. You chased it away. Just you, with your little red crop top and your sunshine hair."

I'm pulled right back to that moment, the first meeting with Collette—the one I actually remember—and with a flick of her knife, she flipped my world upside down, just like now.

"You're saying this song is about me?" she whispers, and I let out a short laugh, telling her, "They're all about you."

Hundreds of songs are sitting inside me, waiting to be let out, and every one of them was inspired by Collette. Her hair, her eyes, her throat, the feel of her hand in mine as we fall asleep. This past week hasn't just been about the sex. After each show—after Collette trusts me with her body—she trusts me with something even more important, she lets me sleep on her bus. Every night I climb into the bunk above hers, then drop my arm down below to hold her hand. I've woken up with a dead arm every morning, but I wouldn't trade it for any other feeling in the world because waking up to Collette still clutching it with hers, I've never felt more whole.

She clears her throat, and her words, "I have one last gift for you," go off in my face like a pack of C-4 because I don't want a gift *from* her. I only want her. She is my gift.

"You bought me something?" I question, venom lacing my tone despite my effort to stay calm. I don't fucking care what Collette bought me, what anyone bought me. I got enough gifts today to last me through my thirtieth birthday. I thought I made it clear that the only thing I do want, the only thing I need, is standing right in front of me, but she's tugging on my arm, making me follow after her to a stairwell leading to a lower level I didn't realize was here because I didn't bother checking.

Collette's shoulders shrug, and speaking over one of them, she says, "Kind of."

"How do you kind of buy something?"

"There was a lot of…incentive given to get this."

Incentive? The fuck?

"What does that mean?"

"It means I hope you like it."

"What did you have to give?"

"Two future gigs."

I tug on her hand, making her stop to face me.

"Here?"

"Yes, here."

Here is way too small for someone like Collette to be performing. It's a fucking club. Even without a headliner, she could sell out super-domes by herself. I don't know why she hasn't tried yet. She's always on tour with someone she probably shouldn't be…like me.

"Fuck that. I'll play with you." She doesn't need my name by hers to fill this entire club, but I still want my body by hers when she does it. I could watch her perform every night for the rest of my life and not get tired of it. "Just lemme know when and—"

Her lips cut me off, but before I can deepen the kiss, she's pulling back.

She did it. She kissed me in public.

Holy. Fucking. Shit.

"I missed you," tumbles out of me. It's only been a matter of hours of us being apart, but I don't care. Missing her doesn't even begin to cover what I'm feeling right now.

Those kissed lips lift into a small smile, hypnotizing me, and she whispers, "I missed you, too."

She descends the final few steps, revealing an entire other dance floor, except unlike the one upstairs, this one's got a giant pit of red Jell-O taking up the large space. A couple people are already sloshing around the foot-high gelatin, pushing at each other like they're trying to wrestle but can't get their footing.

"Happy birthday."

I twist my head to her, asking, "You did this for me?"

Her gaze finds mine, and I open my mouth to say something else I probably shouldn't, but somebody crashes into me from the side, causing the words to catch in my throat.

"Happy birthday, fucker," Axel says near my ear, wrapping me in a tight hug and lifting my feet clear off the floor as he bends backward. Laughing, he carries me all the way over to the pit before dropping my ass into the Jell-O—strawberry-flavored from the smell of it.

All at once, several other people jump into the red gelatinous sea, slipping and sliding and throwing handfuls of my all-time favorite food in every direction. Someone else tackles me to my back, then my hands are out, blindly yanking others to the floor as well.

After a few failed attempts, I make it to my knees, sending anyone in reach back into the thick ocean of Jell-O, only to lose my balance when they try to take me with them. It's a free-for-all in here and the smile on my face is so big it hurts. I've done a lot of crazy shit in my life, pulled a lot of stunts, wound up in even more sticky situations, but this puts all that to shame, mainly because I'm not faking anything right now. Even during my highest highs, I've had to fake a portion of my happiness. Probably because I don't ever feel like I deserve it. Any of it. Not when I'm told what to do, what to say, *who* to fucking be. The person everyone sees, the person everyone wants to see, is different from who I feel like I'm meant to be. Definitely different from who Collette sees when she looks at me, really looks at me. She thinks I deserve this. She thinks I deserve her.

Amongst all the red, I spot her sun-golden hair, and my smile grows even bigger. I don't know if I actually do deserve her, but I'm gonna try my fucking hardest to, damn it. I want to deserve her, more than I've wanted to deserve anything else in my life. With her, everything feels possible. I'm already playing instruments again. Piano and guitar aren't optional—they fucking fuel me—but I've been treating them like they are because I was following someone else's directions.

I don't feel like following shit anymore. I want to be myself, and it's finally starting to feel like I might actually be able to.

But the person who made that seem possible in the first place isn't by my side. I need her next to me. Now. Always.

I notice Slade inching his way over to Collette, and despite every molecule in my body screaming for me to steal her away from him, I hang back to see what his next move is. I've given him plenty of warnings already about Collette, so what's he gonna do when he thinks I'm not watching?

Suddenly, two sets of slim hands grip both of my shoulders, tugging me backward, and it's only when I'm flat on my back that I'm able to see who did it…the twins from the bus.

Chapter 26

Collette

"There we go," Slade mutters beside me as two beautiful girls, identical in almost every way, crawl over Julian in the Jell-O pit. The Jell-O pit I had to bribe the club owners with two free performances just to get them to agree to let me have in here tonight. The Jell-O pit I had to ban Julian from my bus all day, so I could make call after call after call, ensuring it'd be ready in time. I wanted to spend the day with him today, but an entire dance floor of Jell-O is actually incredibly difficult to pull off. It's much more labor-intensive and time-consuming than I anticipated, so after spending practically every minute together since New Orleans, I had to leave Julian to his own devices for the day in order to keep all this a surprise.

I wasn't sure how it was going to go, and I'd be lying if I said I wasn't worried all day long whether Julian would be the one to turn up tonight. Or if it'd be Julez. Or if he'd even show at all.

He did though. Julian came through with a beautiful new song, with lyrics I'll be thinking about for days to come, and he had clear eyes and even clearer intentions…until he disappeared under a pair of model look-alikes much, much younger than me. And skinnier. And sexier.

Some king of mine.

Unable to even see Julian anymore, I spin around, keeping my back to the Jell-O pit, keeping my back to him. Maybe I should just leave now. It's what I should've done from the beginning.

The problem is even with me seeing Julian coming, I still wasn't able to stop him from breaching my rules, my walls, my…

This is what I was afraid of, what I'd be afraid of every day if I was to be with Julian, actually be with him. Not only the constant worry of which version of him I'll be getting thanks to his substance abuse, but also the temptation all celebrities face on a daily basis. Dangle a carrot attractive enough in front of them and they're bound to bite.

Right now, Julian's got two.

I got him to his twenty-eighth birthday, alive and very well, so I can leave here with a clear conscience.

I can…I just can't seem to make myself.

No, I can. I will. I'm going.

I don't want to though.

But I need to.

"Back where he belongs…" Slade trails off with a smug smirk, and I freeze, cocking my head at him.

"Where he belongs?"

Slade turns my way, too. "The drinks, the drugs, the *girls*. As Bodee Keys's ex, I thought you'd be familiar with this scene."

His eyes attempt to penetrate mine, but I block them by glancing at the stairs while telling him, "I've been familiar with this scene since your mom's tit was still in your mouth, Slade. I know who belongs in it." I bring my gaze back to his. "And who doesn't."

I hear his nostrils flare more so than see them, and if I didn't know any better, I'd say I just struck a nerve…or two.

"Then why are you trying so hard to keep Julian from it?"

"Did I miss a clause in your NDA saying I couldn't sleep with your client?" And I'm not talking about the fact that we are sleeping together, I'm talking about the location where we're doing it—away from Julian's bus. I know that's what this is about, I just want to know why.

His eyes go wide as he looks around, and he practically hisses, "You seem to have forgotten all about the contract you signed."

"How do you figure? I haven't told Julian anything." I've hinted a few times, and I've come close to on more than one occasion, but I have yet to actually come clean about the NDAs Slade made me and everybody else in Julian's life sign. "As a matter of fact, I haven't told anybody anything."

"I'm supposed to believe Julian figured out what happened on top of the bus in LA by himself?"

"You don't know Julian very well, do you?" He may know Julez, but he doesn't have a clue who Julian is. If he did, he wouldn't be talking to me the way he is right now. "Julian did figure it out by himself because when he's sober—"

"Sober? Julian's not sober. I thought you said you knew this scene, sweetheart." He tsks while I try not to bristle at the term of endearment that's anything but endearing. As for the other part…I'm aware that even when Julian's around me he isn't completely sober. But he's been more sober than he usually is which is enough.

It has been enough.

It's times like today when it isn't though. Times when I don't know just how intoxicated he's going to get because that's when I lose the man I've gotten to know and…

He's currently wrestling a pair of scantily clad twins in Jell-O, I remind myself with a harsh slap of reality. I can't love someone I don't trust. I won't let myself.

Not again.

"Regardless, those NDAs aren't helping him."

Slade scoffs. "They're the only things helping him."

"That's…"

"Not true? You think you're helping him? How's that working out?" Slade gestures in Julian's direction, but I refuse to look. "You were a short-term solution, but this is where he belongs."

I flinch involuntarily. Of course this wouldn't last, whatever this thing between Julian and myself is—was?—but hearing someone else put it so plainly hurts. Physically fucking hurts. I'm just in pain overall. Why didn't Julian fight harder? Why isn't he fighting now? He told me nothing would keep him from me.

He also told me he lies.

I still stand by what I said though. The constant NDAs aren't helping Julian, maybe Julez, but not Julian.

"He needs to see the consequences his actions carry. By sweeping his bad behavior under a rug, or worse, rewarding it, you're making the good he's capable of that much less important."

"Like this past week?" he mocks.

"Yes, like this past week."

Julian hasn't just been good since our breakthrough in New Orleans, he's been fantastic. Audiences have been responding to him more, *I've* been responding to him more. He's been responsive himself. Actually, he's been amazing in every regard.

If he was that way regularly, he'd go far. Farther than even me because he doesn't have a powerful ex controlling who will work with him…and who won't. Julian was right, fourteen years later, Bodee's still got a grasp on me as well as my career.

I gifted Julian the chance to record with DJ Arique because he's a bucket list producer. Not only is Arique someone who enhances a résumé by just having his name on it, he's also a great teacher. At least he was back when I knew him, before Bodee banned him from ever working with me again. Being an expert at his craft and genuinely enjoying educating others on what he's doing, why he's doing it, and most impressively how he's doing it, I thought he'd be the perfect wealth of knowledge for Julian to tap into uninterrupted. Even if I can't access the best, I want Julian to be able to.

Shaking his head, Slade takes a swig from his beer bottle, and says, "I can't do that."

"Why not?"

He taps his head. "Long-term solution."

"Keeping Julian intoxicated and in the dark is your idea of a long-term solution?"

"Keeping him happy is."

"He wasn't happy before I got here. He's not even happy when he's loaded. He's happy when…" He's happy when he's with me. That's what he tried telling me. On his shirt and his lyrics. *If I wake to find you gone, back I'm sinkin' to that prison of my own creation.*

Slade must read my thoughts because he says, "Again, short-term solution. Take tonight for example, the moment you disappear from his direct line of vision…" His assessing examination down my body makes my lip curl. "What does he do? Returns to *his* reality, where *he* belongs. If you really knew this scene, you'd recognize *you're* the one that doesn't belong, sweetheart."

He steps into my personal space, and I strengthen my spine, not letting it slouch an inch. I will not be intimidated by slimy Slade.

Lowering his voice, he says, "Julian's about to realize the same thing Bodee did when he divorced you, cheap snatch feels the exact same as expensive snatch, but without all the hassle."

I don't know what's worse, being reduced to the hole between my legs or the ex Bodee Keys dumped.

"Oh, Julian doesn't fuck me," I bite back. "I do all the fucking. And I don't need Julian to be under the influence or for him to sign an NDA to do it. He's *happy* to let me."

"Except tonight." With a scathing smirk, his head tilts toward the Jell-O pit, and my eyes drop to the floor. "Happiness is relative, and I know better than anyone what makes Julian happy."

"If you truly wanted Julian happy, you'd find a way to get him out of his record deal."

"And lose us both our jobs?" He snorts as if it's the most preposterous thing he's ever heard of, then his expression darkens into something sinister as he says, "I won't be doing that."

As soon as I laid eyes on him, I could tell money was Slade's only motivation.

His concern isn't that I don't fit this scene, it's that I'll convince Julian to walk away from it entirely, because if he did, Julian's likely to walk away from Slade next.

I wish I could, I really do. Unfortunately, I've been down this path before, so I know how it'd end if I even tried it. I asked Bodee to fire Jack long before he sent his manager in to rape me. I hated Jack upon first meeting him, and it only got worse with each interaction. He was just like Slade except with actual pull and influence, which is one reason why my ex refused.

I wasn't dumped by Bodee, but I wasn't chosen either.

Bodee wasn't my king, and clearly, I was never his queen. If I was, there wouldn't have been any other option when I presented him with that ultimatum.

And if tonight's turn of events are any indication, I wouldn't be Julian's choice either.

But I already knew that. Julian's a celebrity and celebrities are all the same—

"Where do you think you're goin'?" Julian asks just over my shoulder, scaring the hell out of me.

I barely offer him a backward glance, murmuring, "Far from here."

During a chuckle, his arm slides around my middle, and he pulls me tight against him, the scent of strawberry overwhelming his usual spicy, sweet musk. Against my ear, he says, "You ain't goin' anywhere."

"Boss man." Slade laughs awkwardly, stepping several inches away to face us. "Finished unwrapping the presents I got you already?"

Julian's tone is biting as he tells Slade, "Your presents are on their way out."

Their way out?

"Shouldn't you be going with them?" Slade's gaze touches on mine briefly before Julian forces out an ugly laugh, drawing his attention back to him.

"Nah. I got security to do it."

"What?" both Slade and I question.

Sure enough, over on the stairwell, the girls that Julian was just in the pit with are being escorted out by two bulky security guards.

I eye Slade's profile. So, he set this all up. It wasn't Julian choosing anything, it was him being manipulated…again.

His nose in my hair, Julian singsongs, "Hope you kept the receipt," to his agent, and I finally relax into him, feeling the outline of his growing cock against my backside. He's just now getting hard which means he wasn't before, not even with two models throwing themselves at him.

I turn my face up to look over Julian's. Absolutely everything on him is red, and there's a clump of Jell-O falling from one of his ears on to his shirt.

He's adorable, in the most badass way possible. And he didn't bite the carrot that was dangled in front of him. It was a good-looking carrot, too.

"I thought…" I trail off, not wanting to even say it out loud. It's embarrassing, how much I still allow my ex-husband to hold me back.

Julian isn't Bodee, a fact he's proved multiple times already, and now me refusing to believe him isn't Bodee's fault, it's mine, and I have to stop.

I can't let Bodee control me anymore. Some of my ex's influence is out of my hands, but this isn't. *"The power's always been in your hands."* It's time I use it for my own benefit.

I brush away some of the gelatin coating his honeypot, letting my middle finger remain a little longer.

"You're in my skin," Julian rasps close to my lips.

"You mean on?"

"You're everywhere." He seals his mouth to mine, and I groan, tasting the Jell-O.

Maybe he has a point. It does taste better than baby food.

Next to us, Slade mutters something that breaks Julian's concentration as well as our kiss.

He tells Slade, "Fuck off for the night. You've done enough."

"Are you serious?"

"As a motherfucking heart attack."

"Come on. Don't be like that. It's your birthday."

"Go make sure your *presents* get out okay, then fuck. Off." The last part he growls out, and I actually have to bite on my lips to keep from smiling. Julian understands more than Slade wants him to.

One day, hopefully soon, he'll figure everything out, and there won't be a contract strong enough to prevent Slade from getting fired. All the meddling, all the maneuvering, all the masking Slade's been doing is bound to come out, especially if he's sloppy like he was tonight.

There's a moment of strained silence where Slade stares at Julian and Julian glares right back before Slade finally takes the hint and storms off, mumbling something about Julian being ungrateful. Gaslighting—a remora's last stab of defense.

"You. Me. Jell-O. Now."

Extricating myself from his hold, I spin around, keeping Julian at arm's length while telling him, "I'm not going in there."

Julian pretends to leave, then at the last second, ducks down, tossing me over his shoulder.

"Not again," I groan, reaching out a hand to cover the opening of my skirt, but just like last time, Julian's is already there, blocking my ass from view.

I'm deposited directly into the pit that's soupier than it was when we first came down here.

"Julian."

"Poohbear." He pins me with a serious look, and against all the commotion around us, it makes me laugh.

Bending down, I scoop up a handful of Jell-O, quirking an eyebrow at him.

"You won't."

I cock my arm back, launching it directly at his face, and despite his eyes being closed and covered in red, he lunges for me, catching me easily. We fall into the pit together, shaking with laughter.

I'm first to sit up, hovering above Julian to wipe his eyes clean. Before he can even get them open though, I press my lips to his, tasting the artificial strawberry on him.

"Now you're everywhere, too," I breathe between his lips, going in for more. My tongue traces the outline of Julian's sweet mouth, then I plunge inside, circling his tongue with mine. His hands find my ass, gripping tightly as he drags me over him to straddle his stomach.

Beneath his jeans I feel his cock's tip, and I slide down even lower, our centers connecting with a jolt of yearning that pulses through the rest of my body like an electrical current.

Julian breaks from the kiss suddenly, saying, "Stay the night with me."

"On your bus?"

A dark look crosses his face.

"Remember what I told you about my bus?"

"To stay away from it."

He nods slowly, a frown overtaking his face.

"Even with you?"

"Especially with me," he says, reminding me of what Antonio said about Julian never being the one on his bus. It's always Julez.

His gaze breaks from mine, narrowing on a nearby hand being held out to anyone interested. Sitting on the open palm are about seven different kinds of pills that people are basically choosing blindly from. No questions asked, no payment given, just free drugs for the taking.

"Take me somewhere."

The smirk he gives is both hopeful and wary. "Where?"

"Anywhere."

"Right now?"

"Mary and Holter are already at the hotel. If we leave now, we can be back in time to meet them for breakfast." Last I checked it was almost midnight, so it has to be close to one, if not later.

"Lunch," he counters, tucking a hand behind his head, the crush of Jell-O under it noticeable even over all the noise.

"Breakfast. I was planning on taking Holter on a bicycle tour around the city afterward."

"Lunch, and I'll buy us hoverboards instead."

"Breakfast. What will we do with hoverboards?"

"Race them around the hotel," he says with an eye roll like it's obvious. "Brunch."

"Brunch," I agree with a grin. "But I'll buy the hoverboards."

Julian chuckles. "I already did."

"You did? When?"

"After Holter complained about not having anything to do at the last hotel."

I remember. The one from a couple days ago. It didn't have a basketball court inside—it didn't even have a gym—and it was raining so hard we couldn't get outside for a walk, or a bike ride, or anything physical really. We went to an art museum instead, and Holter sulked the whole time. Now that he's getting older, he prefers to stay active, and being cooped up on a tour bus or in hotels all the time makes that difficult.

My lifestyle makes his difficult.

I sit up, studying Julian. "You bought my son a hoverboard?"

He shakes his head. "I bought three so we could all... I didn't want him to be alone."

It's not just that Julian bought Holter something, it's that he listened, he paid attention, he cared.

"How fast can we get out of here?" I ask.

Chapter 27

Collette

Aside from several strange looks at my trashed appearance, nobody says anything to me as I slip out the back and into a waiting stretch limo. Julian offered to create a scene inside so people wouldn't notice us leaving together, and thankfully, it's only a short while later when he comes stumbling out the same door I just exited.

A part of me stumbles too, watching him stagger around clumsily, and I clench the seat beneath me, wondering if he accepted any of those pills being offered downstairs.

The second the door closes though, Julian straightens, climbing into the back of the limo fully coherent again, and I breathe a sigh of relief. It's not realistic to expect Julian to be entirely sober, especially not all the time, but tonight I want him as sober as possible. After what he just told me, I just want *him*.

His thigh planted firmly against mine, he tells the driver which hotel to drive to—a different one than the one our teams are staying at—before pushing the button to roll the blackout privacy partition up.

"Pants to your ankles," I say, removing my leather jacket. The Jell-O wiped right off all my leather, but any skin exposed is red like Julian's now-stained shirt. The limo's interior is strawberry-scented as are we. It smells like lube actually.

Julian props one arm on the back of the seat, smirking, but doesn't move otherwise. "You got one more gift for me?"

I shrug, then fold my leather jacket in half to toss it on the seat perpendicular to us.

"In case that wasn't obvious, yeah. Birthday head is the best head."

When I look back at him, he's still just as relaxed. And clothed.

"Are you really turning down head right now?"

"Your pussy can suck my cock…"

"Actually, the offer was—"

"…after I'm done fucking you with my tongue."

His half-lidded gaze traces every visible inch of my body before he leans forward to grab a bottle of water off the sideboard, cracking the lid to take a long drink. Lowering his ass to the floor of the limo, he screws the lid on the bottle again, then reclines back until only his head is resting on the seat beside my thigh. Pointing at his face, he utters one of the most romantic words in history, telling me simply, "Sit."

I take in his position as well as our surroundings.

"Pull your pants down first."

"Collette, I'm not fucking around. This is the last gift I'll let you give me. I want your pussy to be my first meal for my twenty-eighth year."

I groan, my thighs already jittery. "It will be, just in a different position," I promise him, removing my thong from under my skirt and tucking it safely into my purse. You never know. Once someone sold my used, sweat-stained sports bra online after I forgot it in a hotel room. The guy that bought it would send me pictures with it in different places. Actual touristy places. The Grand Canyon? My bra's been there. The Space Needle? Check. It's insane. Irelynn blocked him on every social media platform, and eventually we had to threaten him with a restraining order when he created different accounts just to send me more travel updates.

I nod at Julian's lap. "Drop 'em."

While he's unbuttoning his jeans and pushing them down over his hips, he complains about me being a pain in his ass.

"You want me to pay special attention to your ass?"

"Don't fucking touch my ass."

My eyes roll themselves. "It's an erogenous zone."

"I'll keep that in mind," he says distractedly, already reaching out to grab at me, and making it hard to move. I manage to hold him off long enough to get my right leg stretched above his head, securing my footing on the leather seat behind it.

"What are you doin'? And why aren't you dropping your pussy on my face like I asked?"

Now I'm the one complaining about what a pain in my ass Julian is. He's so impatient. And oddly prude at times. Hasn't he ever done sixty-nine before?

Apparently not, considering he never used to eat women out.

My hands flat on the floor to frame his hips, I swing my left foot over to the other side of him so my airborne knees are framing his head.

"You gonna twerk?" he asks, his voice thick like he's under a trance.

"I…could." That wasn't my plan but, yeah, I could totally twerk like this.

With Julian's swollen cock just below my chin, I lift my head slightly, parting my mouth to let a few drops of warm saliva drip out on to the tip.

"None of that tasting shit either. I want you to swallow my fucking cock."

"I'll keep that in mind," I deadpan his words back at him.

His hands drift up the insides of my thighs hovering directly over his head, and I feel my skirt already riding up, revealing the bottom of my ass.

"Do it. Twerk," he orders.

Cold air hits my ass as my skirt is pushed out of his way, and with my knees bent and only inches off the seat, I arch my back, popping my hips so my ass cheeks jiggle up and down above his face.

"Goddamn," Julian breathes, gripping the backs of my thighs and pulling so my kneecaps hit the seat the same time his mouth latches on to my bare lips.

My head's dropped on a guttural moan, and I have to lock my elbows to keep from falling face-first on to Julian's lap.

Goddamn indeed.

Julian's making out with my pussy like he makes out with my

mouth, turning his head to suck my lips between his, and I can't even focus on one sensation because he's everywhere all at once.

Carefully, I bend one elbow, dropping it to the floor so I can suck the length of Julian's shaft into my mouth in one smooth motion. The moment his head touches the back of my throat and I swallow, a groan I can feel inside *me* tears from Julian's mouth as he shakes his head back and forth against my folds, growling like a starving animal digging into his first real catch in weeks.

Shifting the majority of my weight to my elbow, I use my other hand to stroke his base in time with my short, hungry mouthfuls since I'm limited with movement here. I'm essentially upside down, but at a forty-five-degree angle, with my ass in the air, and trying to bob on my boyfriend's cock.

Boyfriend.

Is he… Are we…

I think we pretty much are.

Julian's hands cupping my ass from above, his fingers part my crack as he dives deep, licking everything within his reach. My sensitive clit hits his chin every time he tongues my slit like a lollipop, the tiny metal balls there teasing me, and I moan around his cock, my arm nearly giving out.

Julian jerks his hips up, his mushroom head close to gagging me, but I close my fist around the base, ensuring he can't choke me completely as he thrusts off the floor and into my mouth.

I continue plunging down his pulsing cock, my mouth sucking and my fist stroking, but when Julian doubles his efforts, my rhythm grows wild, unsteady, and I stutter over him. The stimulation becomes too much, and all I know is Julian's lips and tongue and breath and hands and fingers—two of them press into my aching hole as he angles me so my clit's over his mouth, then he's sucking again, the sound of our moans and groans barely masking Julian's ravenous slurping.

He wasn't lying this time; he's making an entire meal out of me.

An orgasm builds right behind my clit, begging for just a *tiny* bit more, and when I spread my knees wider, dropping all of my weight on Julian's face, the pressure of his tongue against my bundle of nerves increases just enough that I fucking explode, my scream muffled by Julian's cock just before it slips out from between my lips.

Julian doesn't waste a second, guiding my knees down to the floor, then repositioning us so he's behind me. With one quick tug on my hips, he pushes inside me until his abdomen crashes against my naked ass.

"Oh, fuck," he says, his grip lowering to my thighs as he massages in fast, hard rhythms. His fingers dig into my skin, not painfully, just possessively, and he circles his hips behind mine, making my pussy clench around him, then the circles all but stop as he grits, "Ease. The. Fuck. Up," already out of breath from holding his own orgasm off.

But he's the one who wanted my pussy to suck his cock, wasn't he?

I smirk, and do it again, squeezing with all my might.

One of his hands disappears a second before it slaps across my ass cheek with a loud *crack* of skin against skin, and my inner walls seize up around Julian's shaft like a boxer's fist, tighter than before.

"Jesus Christ," he gasps, then reaches forward, grabbing on to the chains decorating my chest as he draws himself out of me only to immediately thrust back in. I can literally feel every single inch of him, and yet, I still want more.

I drop a hand between my thighs, ignoring my clit altogether. My fingers find the underside of his hard, veiny muscle, and I hold them there, letting the tips drift over his length as he slowly pumps it in and out of me.

"Julian," I moan, feeling so full, so complete, so incredibly turned on I don't know how much more I can take.

"What do you need?" he asks, breathless.

I answer with the only thing I can think of. "You."

The chains bite into the back of my neck, pulling my head down between my shoulders, and I watch from below as Julian's thighs contract with quick, uncontrolled movements, his fist around the chains at my chest tight and unrelenting. Waiting until he pulls almost all the way out, I contract my vaginal muscles, then he drives into me one final time, collapsing against my back as hot liquid fills me to the brim, enough to run out on to my fingers.

Just like every other time we have sex, the thought of becoming pregnant with Julian's baby glimmers like the end of a lit sparkler before I rush to extinguish it myself. Unfortunately, it just isn't possible.

I use the extra lube to swirl around my clit before feeling Julian's hand on mine, helping to coax out one more orgasm.

"Come on my cock, Collette," Julian rasps with a short, hard thrust against my backside, and I do. I come all over him, and me, and us.

My lower half convulsing, I bring our entwined hands up, licking our cum off. The flavor is a combination of sweet and tangy, with a distinct saltiness.

Julian takes me with as he sits back, and we stay connected, his cock softening inside me while I sit on his lap, catching my breath.

He's the first to break the silence, saying, "It's never been like that before."

I nod, my stare on an empty champagne flute hanging upside down on the sideboard. The tire rotations on the highway outside cause it to sway back and forth, back and forth.

"Yeah. They dull so much sensation."

"I wasn't talking about condoms."

"I wasn't either. I was talking about drugs." I let that hang in the air.

"Not all of them do," he tries to argue weakly.

"Enough of them do," I say before getting up and ending the conversation to redress.

Julian does the same, tucking himself back inside his jeans, and sitting on the seat again.

Eyes on my arm disappearing inside my jacket sleeve, I say, "About the free concerts…"

"Don't do that."

"Don't do what?"

"Don't leave me before you even leave me."

The heat in his voice has me glancing over at him.

"It was a gift. I don't want you to think you have to help pay for your own gift. I made the deal for the Jell-O pit willing to—"

"That's not what I think."

"It's not?"

"I think I want to be anywhere you are. Even if it's some jank-ass small-time bar, I'll be there."

"Julian." I tilt my head. He has to know… "After tour—"

Desperate eyes lift to mine. "*Don't*…leave me before you even leave me, Collette. If I wake to find you gone—"

"Back you're sinkin' to that prison of your own creation?" I guess, even though I don't have to.

I want this to be our normal, our life—together. I also know the chances of that happening are slim. Very slim. With drugs pulling him in one direction, and touring pulling me another, how can we meet in the middle? I'm not sure we can outside of this tour. If The Family Julez Tour is the only time we'll get to, then we should try to enjoy this while we can.

Dropping the subject, I go over and straddle him, taking his face in my hands.

"Happy birthday, Julian."

His lips stretch into a hesitant grin, then grabbing my ass to mash our fronts together, he murmurs, "Best birthday ever."

And we make out like a couple of teenagers for the rest of the ride.

Chapter 28

Collette

My eyes want to close so bad, but I fight to keep them open. If I fall asleep now, it'll be hours before I wake up again. We haven't slept a wink since we checked in, and even though we're both exhausted, neither of us are succumbing to sleep's persistent call. I don't want this to end any more than Julian does.

Seated at the round table just inside a sliding glass door overlooking a private courtyard, I snuggle deeper into the hotel's robe, grinning at Julian beside me as he fashions the middle piece of the elaborate belly chain necklace I wore last night into…something else. The rest of it's a lost cause after Julian broke a few of the thinner chains and tangled several others.

"What *are* you making?" I finally ask, drawing my knees closer to my chest as I watch him deep in concentration. My hair's still wet from a shower, and when I prop my chin on a knee, drops of water fall on to the thick white cotton.

If heaven handed out cocoons of bliss, I have no doubt this moment is what they'd be made of.

Wordlessly, Julian holds his handiwork up, saying, "A triangle," before using a butter knife to clang around in the center of it.

"Clever," I say through my spread lips.

Placing the handmade triangle on the table, Julian spears another piece of pineapple with his fork. *Our* fork technically since he's been feeding us both with it.

"I want a strawberry," I tell him with a headshake.

He teases my bottom lip with the yellow fruit, explaining, "Pineapple makes your cum taste better."

I open my mouth, biting the sweet chunk off the fork.

"I thought that was for men. Cranberry juice might be for women."

The fork bounces off the plate with a loud *clang* as Julian drops it to reach for the phone on the nearby desk.

"What are you doing?"

He ignores me, asking whoever answers, "Ayo, do you guys carry cranberry juice?" I smother a laugh, making Julian smirk even as he tries to keep his tone serious while ordering an entire bottle from room service. It's only eight in the morning and we've already ordered five different meals to graze on. I've never eaten this much in my life, and I'm so busy, so *happy*, with Julian, I don't even consider the calories I'm consuming.

"I didn't know I tasted bad," I mutter against the robe's collar once he's off the phone.

"You taste like you smell, amazing, but I take my research very seriously."

I accept the next bite, this time a grape.

"Right. And what exactly is this research?"

"I feed you, then I feed on your pussy."

I wait for him to finish, but he never does.

"And?" I ask with a roll of my eyes.

"And…that's it."

"To see which food changes the flavor of my cum?"

"Sure." Julian shrugs, winking.

I drop my head back, staring up at the ceiling with hot cheeks. "I've created a monster."

Chuckling, Julian says, "It pays to be the first."

"You said women come for you on command." A weird sound comes from his throat. Or maybe my throat. "But what about before you got famous?"

"What are you asking?"

He eyes me smugly, so I deadpan, "If you were always a shitty lay or if it was something you picked up recently."

"That's it," he says, standing up and lifting me from my chair. "I've had enough of your shit."

"Hey," I protest, gazing back at the eggs Benedict longingly.

I'm deposited on the bed with Julian falling on top of me before I can return to them though.

> "All this time I thought I was straight smashin',
> 'til my girl came along, telling me I belong in the trash bin."

I huff out a laugh and bring my arms up around his neck.

"I didn't know I was a shitty lay."

As serious as I can, I tell Julian, "You really are."

When he buries his face in my neck, tickling the skin there with tiny nips, I buck my whole body.

"Okay, fine. Fine!"

He pauses, waiting.

"You're not *that* bad."

His assault jumps to the other side of my neck, and my laughter ratchets up to decibels my vocal coach would cringe at. I try to push him off but only manage to make his own robe fall down, revealing his sinuous shoulders covered in tattoos.

Near his collarbone there's a heart with a gnarled arrow through it that I imagine has a painful story.

"Didn't you have any girlfriends?" I ask seriously, and he finally stops, pulling back to look at me.

"Are we gonna do the numbers thing? Where we confess how many people we've slept with?"

"God no." I'd rather get a root canal.

"Good." He falls on the mattress beside me, making my body bounce, then roll toward his.

"But you had girlfriends, right? And you never went down on them?"

"I told you I didn't."

I consider that, my eyes skating around the room.

Julian flips to his back, sighing. "What else you got, Poohbear?"

"What do you mean?"

"What else do you want to know?"

"Your tattoos? Do you…"

"Yes?"

"Do you get one for…"

"For?"

"Do you always get one for…you know…"

"Literally no idea. For what?"

I can tell by the smile in his voice he's enjoying this.

"Women," I say, closing my eyes.

"Women, huh?"

He hesitates, and I grimace, hating myself for asking.

"I get tattoos for a lot of things, including people, some of them women."

I crack an eye, peeking over at him, but he's the one staring at the ceiling now.

"When I feel strongly about something, I usually get it tattooed on me in some way. Even if I hate something, I'll get it inked on my skin."

"Why?"

"Because emotions are… They don't always come easy for me. Tattoos are a way to remember every one I experience even when I can't…actually…remember."

Emotions don't come easy when you flood them out with drugs and alcohol. One place Julian can't wash them off though is his skin. I wish he was capable of keeping them in his heart, too.

He could be…if he stopped the constant flooding.

"Will you tell me about them?"

"The women?"

I nudge his shoulder with mine.

"Oh, you mean the tattoos." He grins, telling me to pick out whichever one I want.

Scanning him over, I choose the letters on his knuckles. They spell the word "MAMAS" on one hand, then "BOY" on the other.

He blows out a breath I feel bang around inside my own chest.

"Your mom. You've never told me about her."

"She was…" He thinks for a minute, then says, "You know as a kid everybody thinks their parents are idols, especially their moms? So full of life, so beautiful, so perfect. Right?"

Remembering my mom, I don't move a muscle. I thought the same thing about her, about both my parents. When I went with Bodee—when they handed me over to him—I still thought that. That they were doing it for me, to help me and my future. But it wasn't for me or my future. It was for theirs. They gave me away for their own benefit just like Bodee did.

"I thought that about my mom, too, I guess, except I started noticing the cracks, the imperfections, way earlier than most people do. Not at thirty, or twenty, or—"

"Sixteen," I add quietly, admitting, "I wish my parents' sheen would've worn off then."

"So you wouldn't have met Bodee?"

I think back over everything I've been through. Thanks to my ex-husband, this journey's had one too many dead ends, more wrong turns than I can count, an entire mountain range of scandal, but I can't actually find any regret in going through any of it. Would I be who I am today without it? Would I still have Holter? Would my fans be connecting to the songs written from the heartache all those obstacles caused?

Would I be in this hotel room with Julian right now?

"How old were you when it happened?" I ask him instead of answering. Just like Julian can't regret getting his record deal because of where it led him, I can't regret meeting Bodee because of where it led me. Necessary evils are just that—necessary.

"Probably around six. Kindergarten."

"Six years old?" My heart aches for six-year-old Julian. "What happened?"

"Alcohol."

"And drugs?"

"I didn't used to think so, but now…now that I, uh… Now it seems pretty likely. But I don't know where the fuck she had the money for any of it. We were dirt poor. Mold in the corners of every room you walked into, a hole in the floor in front of the fridge, broken locks on the doors, no hot water, lights we kept off because if they even did turn on, they'd flicker. Recently, I've been noticing *all* the cracks, and the more I look, the more I see…me."

"My family wasn't anything close to what could be called wealthy, but we weren't dirt poor either," I tell him. "My parents worked odds-and-ends type jobs, only when they felt like it though. They were dreamers, the kind that thought love ruled all, and nine-to-fives were just distractions from what was really important. They always managed to make our home life seem comfortable enough that I didn't really think about how we afforded things. Like, every Sunday morning, they'd make crepes together, and watching them giggle like high schoolers in love, I used to feel so happy, so loved, and I'd sit there dreaming about having the same thing one day." I shake away the fantasy from trying to take over yet again all these years later, and continue with my original point. "Now, looking back, I can see the cracks, too. Even still, I wouldn't consider our situation dire enough…"

I take a deep breath, exhaling until my lungs deflate completely.

"I wouldn't consider our situation dire enough for my parents to sell me off to Bodee."

"They really did that? They sold you to that motherfucker?"

"Essentially." I nod. "And I don't see myself in those cracks. I see the exact opposite route I've chosen to take of making the constant, stable drive for work my life's mission. They avoided work for love, but I've avoided love for work. The only time I tried to make the two go hand in hand, the results were catastrophic, and I was…"

"What?"

"I was given away anyway."

"You mean up? You were given up by Bodee?"

"Yes." *No.*

Julian hums to himself, then says, "I killed her." And before I can even muster a single response, he adds, "My mom. My grandma, too. I killed them both."

"What do you—"

"Even before I was six, my mom drank. It just didn't seem like a problem. Or maybe I was too young to understand that it was. My dad left her when I was a baby, so it was just us. I didn't know anything else. I didn't know anyone else, not even other adults. No babysitters, nothing. She was my whole world. So, when I started going to school, and I learned things like days of the week, then would come home and she wouldn't even know what day it was because she was so drunk, I just thought maybe she needed some help. Help for little shit though, shit I thought everyone needed sometimes, you know? Like getting her water and medicine when she had a headache, putting the popsicles in the freezer because she'd always put them in the fridge, putting a towel over the spot on the couch she pissed when she couldn't make it to the bathroom, putting her to bed in the mornings because she stayed up all night drinking. I didn't know that she needed help help—big help. I didn't fucking know any better. I thought I was doing what was best for her."

"You were just a child, Julian."

"Then I got older, and I started catching on that maybe that's not how all adults were, at least not the teachers at my school. I wasn't allowed to go over to my friends' houses and I never really felt like asking anyone to come over to mine."

"Because you still had to help your mom so much?"

"Had to." He nods. "It was still…automatic. Like it was normal. There were things I just did every day. Before school, I put water and crackers out next to her, making sure she was on her side so she could find them easier and so she wouldn't choke on her puke. After school, I'd check our apartment for puddles of puke, or piss, in case she got up while I was gone. She confused my closet for the bathroom a lot."

"No," I groan, already knowing where this is heading. Julian didn't kill his mom just like he didn't kill his grandmother. He only feels responsible for their deaths.

"Fifth grade, this motherfucker showed up. Was just there when I got home from school one day and never left. With another mouth sucking down enough liquor to float a New York City nightclub, money was… We didn't have any. We never had much before he showed up, and we had even less after he showed up. We lived in section eight housing, and we ate thanks to welfare. The only way I ate besides the free meals at school was by using my mom's food stamp card, but Barney—"

"Barney? That's a terrible name."

"Terrible name for a terrible guy."

"I hate him."

"Me, too," he says like he's in agony at the thought of this guy. "Barney would trade people for anything. Nothing was off-limits for him to trade.

He'd buy someone food using my mom's card, then trade cash for it, a lot less than he'd spent on the fucking food to begin with. I got pissed, and I got more pissed every fucking day I went home to a place with more beer in the fridge than there was food in the cupboards."

Tears fall from my eyes, streaking down my temples. That's not how children should be treated. That's not how anyone should be treated. Neglected. Forgotten.

"What'd you do?"

"I tried not to be home as much. As soon as I'd wake up in the mornings, I'd leave, and just sit at the bus stop hours before I needed to. I was fucking starving all the time, and the only place I could get anything even close to a full meal was at school, so I counted down the seconds until I'd walk through those doors."

"For breakfast and lunch only?"

He nods. "Yeah. No dinners. I went…" He blows out a breath. "Fuck, there was a time there that I don't even know how long I went without eating an actual dinner."

Now I understand why it's so important to him that I eat. He knows what living with a growling, empty stomach does to a person after a prolonged period. I never thought about it that way. I was only ever concerned about the image of the outside of my body, not what I was doing to the inside of it. The truth is I can imagine plain as day how Julian felt all those years ago. I feel that way most days, except I can eat. I can eat whatever I want, whenever I want because I have the means to do so. He didn't. And I'm choosing not to so I can *look* good, so I can keep up with impossible industry standards I know aren't healthy or realistic in any way.

I make a promise to be better about eating regularly, if not for myself, then for that hungry little boy who couldn't make the same vow.

"I'd still check on my mom though. It *was* our normal. I'd make sure she was okay before leaving, every day. And she was. She always fucking was."

Louder, he says, "Being at the bus that early, I waited with the older kids. First the high schoolers, then the middle schoolers. There were these teen guys… They would get there earlier than the rest of the high schoolers, and they would battle each other. Every morning, like clockwork, they would show up, and jump right into whatever lyrics they'd just finished working on. Or they'd come up with them on the spot. They'd hold competitions where they'd pick a random topic and they all had to freestyle something about it. They were using words that sounded like lyrics but felt like confessions, confessions that could've come straight from my own life about my own shit, so I tried it when I was by myself, saying some of the things I was feeling. Doing it in the form of a song made the truth seem less fucked up than it actually was. It was the only thing that made my anger go away. It felt natural, like I was born to do it. So, I didn't stop. I couldn't. I rapped all the time. Every fucking minute of every fucking day, I had lyrics running through my head, giving me something else to focus on."

I nod along, all too familiar with the feeling myself. Songwriting is therapeutic in the best and worst of ways. All art is really, but singing the actual words of your pain…there's no hiding your meaning. A painting can be interpreted a thousand different ways but only the painter knows the truth. A songwriter slices open their veins and bleeds the truth into their lyrics.

"Did you ever rap with them?"

"Eventually I worked up the courage to try. There was a lot of shit-talking in the beginning because I was so much younger than them, but after a while, they got it. They understood that I needed it just like they did. I wasn't trying to fit in; I'd actually found where I fit. All of us started going earlier then. It was like an unspoken thing, where we all just leaned on each other and the words of our shared problems."

He grows quiet for a long time, but I don't rush him. When he speaks again, it's strained.

"And it was on one of those mornings when my mom died."

"No, Julian." I sit up, leaning over him, my tears falling from my face down on to Julian's robe. "It wasn't your fault. You weren't responsible for your mom's life or death. You were a child just trying to survive any way you could. Don't you see? You needed music just as much as you needed food."

"I needed music while my mom needed me. I chose rapping, and it killed her."

I shake my head, drops of water flinging in all directions.

"I chose rapping, and it killed my grandma. Two weeks after I signed my record deal, she died, too."

As much as Julian loves rapping, he also resents it. His disdain toward being labelled "just a rapper" makes more sense, especially given that he doesn't even get to use the lyrics he wants. The lyrics about his real life, about his hardships, those are the words that'd resonate deeply with audiences just like those teen boys' did for Julian during one of the hardest times of his life. Music changes lives, but it can also save lives, and I believe it saved Julian's. Unfortunately, the same can't be said for his mother. Or grandmother. One thing I do know for certain is music isn't responsible for killing either of them. And neither is Julian.

I cradle his own wet face in my palms, telling him, "Their deaths are not because of you, or your rapping, or your music. You found a way to express yourself. That's it. It didn't kill anyone. *You* didn't kill anyone."

"My mom's drinking—"

"Was her choice. It had nothing to do with you. Isn't that what you told me when I thought you were drinking to hurt me?"

His entire face winces.

"It felt like a punishment," he rasps.

"I know." It doesn't matter what Julian told me, how much he ensured me that his drinking isn't aimed at me, it does still feel like a personal slight when he does it, just like last night when I saw him ordering a shot at the bar. I immediately took offense, and I can see why he felt that way as a child…and possibly still feels that way as a man.

Julian wipes the tears on my cheeks using the knuckles marked with the MAMAS BOY letters. "I'm not just taking after her," he whispers quietly. "I think I *am* her."

"You're not her." I kiss him, the salty tears caught between our lips. "You're protective. And you're generous. You're kind and thoughtful. You go without, so no one else around you has to. You're loyal even though you try to act like you don't want to be. You're honest when it counts. You're both funny and fun, one of the most fun people I've ever had the pleasure of being around. You steal all the attention from every room you walk into with that charming smile of yours. Even on your worst days, you're fucking magnetic. I find myself wanting to run after you anytime you walk away, absolutely terrified I won't get another chance to see you again, because if I didn't, I'd feel cheated for the rest of my life." The confession sounds foreign to my own ears. I haven't said anything like this out loud to anyone. I never even felt like this with anyone to want to, not even Bodee and I was with Bodee for years.

Making sure I don't blink, I tell him again, "You're more. To me. To everybody."

I'm pulled to him in a kiss so fast, I don't even get my lips open in time before his tongue slips right past, licking inside like flames chasing a line of accelerant. Those tattooed knuckles press into my cheeks and guide me exactly how he needs me to get closer.

A knock at the door is the only thing that breaks us apart as Julian turns his head to the side to yell, "Leave it at the door!" before finishing much softer, "I'll get it later," looking up at me again.

"We don't have much time, little lamb. Brunchtime is approaching."

"I would've had you back for breakfast, you know that, right?"

I lick his chin, over his piercings, up his lips to the tip of his nose, then admit, "I would've stayed for lunch."

"I gotta work on my negotiation skills."

"And your interrogation skills. You folded like a lawn chair."

Grinning, he shakes his head. "Pick another tat."

"The broken wing."

"For my grandma. She was an angel. She took me in after my mom died. We lived seventeen minutes away from each other but we'd never even met before, then all of a sudden this kid with a chip on his shoulder showed up on her doorstep. I spent the summer before middle school pissed off at everyone and everything, including her. I wouldn't talk to her or anyone else, but I wrote lyrics…everywhere."

"Of course," I say, propping my chin on his chest.

"Of course," he repeats. "That's what eventually opened the conversation, then bonded us. Music."

"Because she was a music teacher?"

"Yeah. When school started again, mine got out earlier than hers, so I'd take the bus over to sit in on her last class of the day. Then after, she'd teach me one-on-one. I was still really angry, like fucking *angry*. And she showed me how to channel my anger into multiple outlets. Instruments, singing, songwriting. The more, the better. I couldn't get enough. Music, in any form, was the only thing that helped me not feel so angry all the fucking time."

Although anger is technically a primary emotion, in this case it was definitely a secondary emotion, born from another, or most likely multiple others. Julian's anger stemmed from not only sadness at losing the only person his life revolved around, but probably shame, too. Shame for what he thinks he did to lose his mother, shame because she made him feel insignificant with her actions. And being so young, the seed of shame planted, took root, then proceeded to grow from there. And so the anger grew too, right alongside his other emotions to safeguard Julian externally while he grappled with them all internally.

Channeling that anger into his art only to then have it judged, dictated, and ultimately taken away from him later in life, brought the emotions he'd been protecting so fiercely to the forefront in an overwhelming comedown he wasn't able to face, so he turned to another outlet…the one that was originally to blame—alcohol. Alcohol led to drugs, and eventually, he lost control of all of it, his grasp on not only his emotions, but on himself as well. Julian still thinks he's insignificant because nothing's ever chopped down that shame tree flourishing deep inside him.

"Julian?"

"Yeah?"

"I love…" I swallow loudly. "…watching you perform." I could say it, what I was going to, that I love *him*. I've tried not to, but it happened anyway. I'm scared that love will take over me like it did my parents though, so it's better, it's safer, if I just keep it to myself. This tour will be over in less than a month and then it won't even matter anymore.

He eyes me for a full minute before saying, "I love…watching you perform, too."

Does he feel the same way? Could he say he loves me, too? And mean it?

Less than a month.

"Tell me about the bullseye," I say quickly, referencing the top of his spinal cord where there's a bullseye with solid black circular bands.

"I've been stabbed in the back so many times, I thought I'd make the target easier to find." He shrugs.

"You *want* people to stab you in the back?" My words come out ragged with regret. I stabbed him in the back, not metaphorically like he's talking about, but literally. Technically it was just a nick, but the thought that I might be considered one of the people he's referring to makes me nauseous.

"It's inevitable. A given. A guarantee. There are more coming, always. I just want the ones that are readying their knives to stop fucking around and hit the mark already."

"You want to die." I don't ask it, I state it, and Julian doesn't bother denying it.

Instead, he says, "Mm. I don't…" He pauses, thinking about it. "I don't think I've done a lot of good in this life. I don't think I deserve… I know I don't deserve it."

"Deserve what?"

"Any of it. Everything I've been given. Starting at my birth and everything that's followed."

I won't admit to loving Julian in the traditional way, but I can show him how much he means to me in other ways, in ways I know he'll understand.

I brush his neck tattoo and murmur,

"A face conjured by dreams."

My lips fit over his.

"A body destined to keep me awake."

Julian's breathing picks up as he stares into my eyes.

"Making me rethink it all, every last touch that came before.
With his hands sneaking in my chest and voice speaking to my head,
Afraid he's got me wound 'round his finger so tight,
Now I'm addicted to the man hidden outside the light."

"Me?" he asks.

"The man cloaked in shadows, king of the underworld, my very own Osiris." I nod and press a kiss to his lips. His match mine immediately, the intensity spiking faster than my heart rate. I pull back before we lose ourselves completely, telling him, "Good doesn't have a time limit or an expiration date. You can start doing good at any time. And you do deserve the life you were given. You just haven't made it your own yet."

"Is your life your own?"

"It's as close as I'll probably ever get it," I say more wistfully than anything. I don't think I can ever truly consider my life *mine*. There's just too much hanging over my head.

"What about your tattoo?"

"Which one?"

"The one on your finger."

"I may stay quiet, but my music can never be silenced." I bring my right hand up to put my index finger to my lips in a shushing motion, so the music note tattooed on the side of the top knuckle is on display for him.

"What are you quiet on? What is it you're not saying about Bodee?"

"I'm not—"

"I just fucking told you everything, Collette. Laid all my shit out for you. Don't bullshit me. Not again. I know you hate him. I know he did something to make you hate him. Tell me what it is."

"On the outside, Bodee and I were compatible. We made sense. On the inside, we were very different people."

"We're very different people."

I consider that statement before agreeing, "On the outside, we are."

"And on the inside?"

"On the inside…" On the inside, I want to believe we're the same people after the same things, but I don't know for sure because Julian doesn't know for sure. He's still finding himself. He never even determined if he wanted children before robbing himself of the chance by getting a vasectomy.

I only know who he's not the same as, and that's Bodee Keys.

"You know those people with stamp collections?" I say instead. "They usually dedicate an entire room in their house to organize, admire, memorize their extensive collection."

"Are you being serious right now? I don't know anyone who'd do that, no. That's fucking…I don't know. Am I the stamp collector in this setup?"

I roll off Julian to lie beside him. "No, Bodee is. Bodee collects secrets like that. He accumulates them like any other enthusiast, even where there aren't any to be found. Except unlike most stamp fanatics, Bodee does use his collectibles…for blackmail."

"Did he use blackmail on you?"

"He tried."

My chest feels like the ribs have been airlifted out of my body, and I search the ceiling for any sign of where they went.

"How?"

Where Julian uses his anger to protect his raw vulnerability, I use redirection, avoidance, or even flat-out lies when necessary. Being politically correct isn't very effective with Julian because he can smell the lie—my lie—a mile away. He has this knack for sensing what I'm not saying.

But I know what happened back then and that's enough. I've never wanted or needed anyone else to know for it to be real. I didn't need anyone to believe me for what happened that night to ring true. I *know* what Bodee did. I know what he was willing to do, to have done to me. He proved it by standing outside that room while doing nothing to help me.

Choked silence fills the room until I scratch out the words, "The common currency from pretty young popstars is the popstars themselves." That's a belief far too many people in this industry actually buy into, then double down on. "To people like Bodee, everyone has a price, and if a price is too high, he'll tweak the market himself until it's not. He creates certain…scenarios to devalue the goods while also adding to his collection." Bile burns the back of my throat.

Julian bolts upright. "The fuck does that mean? What'd he fucking do?"

I shake my head, trying to dislodge the lump in my throat. If my words earlier felt alien, these are as unfamiliar as if I were attempting to speak a different language for the first time. I haven't told *anybody* about what really ended my marriage to Bodee. I've chosen to carry this burden alone for almost fourteen years, and now that I'm finally considering sharing, I notice it's not my ribs missing. It's the weight from a vile secret being shifted around, loosened for removal.

But just like my true feelings for Julian, I can't reveal this either. Not entirely.

I can…but I won't.

"Collette." Julian's heavy breathing echoes off the walls.

"He set me up. Bodee put me in a compromising situation that he thought would bring me to heel while also giving him leverage over me. He just didn't count on me getting myself out it. I did though. I got out, and I've never looked back." That's all I'm going to say about it.

"That's not enough. You need to tell me—"

"No. Not now. Not today."

Julian's at a point where he feels he can share his dark past with me, which I'm grateful for, but I'm not there, and I don't know if I ever will be.

"We don't have a lot of time left," I tell him, referring to more than just today. "I don't want to waste it talking about Bodee."

"You never wanna talk about Bodee."

I put my index finger in front of my lips again, and give him a sad smirk behind it, saying, "I stay quiet by choice."

"Why?"

"To protect Holter. I love and respect my son enough not to trash his father in front of his face or anyone else's. Even if I didn't, even if I decided to tell the truth about Bodee, it wouldn't matter. I told you, nobody goes after Bodee Keys and lives to tell the tale."

Hoisting himself on top of me, he gazes down at me, and says, "You did."

And just like last time, I confess the ugliest truth of all, saying, "No, I didn't."

Pulling his head to mine, I try to forget all about the monster who doesn't even need to hide under my bed to haunt every facet of my life.

Chapter 29

Julian

I tug on the end of Collette's ponytail as she tries to get by me, making her stop and gasp.

"You better not mess up my hair."

"Poohbear, look around," I tell her, my arms out wide. "We're at the beach." Why the fuck is she even wearing extensions anyway? She looks fucking incredible with the long blonde ponytail to her ass, but I wanna swim in the warm salt water with her body against mine as we jump the waves. You know, couple shit. The way it stands now, I can't even get her to go within three feet of the shoreline, and I've been fucking trying.

Instead, we're playing touch football with Holter and Bare…who's now sitting down, stuffing his face.

"Ayo! What the hell, man?" I yell at my bodyguard, his bald head looking redder by the second from this brutal Texas heat.

He's not the only one either. Swear to God, I can see the sun's rays raking across all our skin right now. SPF 100 ain't doing shit for us out here.

"Break time," Bare mumbles around a mouthful of hoagie.

The fuck.

Collette hands off the ball to Holter, then beams at me. "A break sounds good to me. I'm thinking nachos."

Nachos, huh? Not only has this woman had an appetite on her lately, but I haven't even seen any packets of baby food.

"Break from what?" I ask her because what am I gonna do? Not give her shit? I don't think so. She's way too fun when she's feisty. "You barely ran."

"That's a lie." We stare each other down, neither of us willing to blink. I didn't stutter. She took two, three steps max. But then she says, "We both know I've been running through your mind all day," making a smile pull my lips apart.

"Stealing pickup lines is a punishable offense," I tell her. I'm pretty sure I've used that line before, at least once. What can I say? It's a good one.

She only blows me a kiss, trudging away from my sorry ass just sitting here, watching her go.

That view though…

"Heads up!"

I automatically shoot my arms out in front of me, catching the football Holter just launched my way like a fucking torpedo.

Damn, this kid's got an arm.

"Are you sure you don't wanna play football instead of basketball?" I ask Holter, twirling the ball while still trying to keep an eye on his mom's ass swaying in her sheer wrap-thing.

"Football?" he questions, and I shift my focus to him, seeing his head tilt like the idea's never occurred to him.

"Yeah, football. You'd make a hell of a quarterback."

Holter's basketball game's got nothing on this. Before Collette and Bare decided to join in, he and I were tossing the football back and forth between us for at least an hour, and his smile didn't dim once—a smile he never had any of the times we've shot hoops together. Even right now he's got a megawatt cheeser fucking shining as bright as the sun in the goddamn sky. He thinks he should like basketball, but I know he doesn't.

"And…how many hotels have football fields?" he asks, catching my pass easily at the same time his question pummels into me like a linebacker. Some hotels, the upscale ones with more amenities than their silver-spoon-chewing guests know what to do with, have basketball courts. But football fields? The answer is none. He knows it and I know it.

"You don't think your mom would figure out a way for you to play?" The woman would level mountains for her boy.

"I think it would give my mom one more thing to hate herself for."

Holter's a good kid. He shrinks himself and his wants for his mom's sake. Most kids wouldn't. Hell, most adults wouldn't.

"She doesn't hate herself," I tell him through a chuckle. I'd know if Collette hated herself.

Wouldn't I?

Holter pauses, his throwing arm cocked up near his head. "You haven't heard her cry herself to sleep at night yet."

The ball spirals toward me, and I consider moving in front of it and letting it nail me in the fucking face. It'd hurt less than hearing what Holter just said. *Cry herself to sleep?*

"When does she do that? On the bus?" My bunk's directly above hers, and I've never heard her crying.

"Maybe. I'm not always there, but I've only heard it when she's home."

"Because she misses being on tour?"

He gives me a strange look, one that feels like pity for being such a fucking dumbass. Which I am. It was a stupid question. Collette wouldn't cry over missing tour life; she'd cry over missing her boy. Collette hates how much time is taken from Holter when she's touring without him, and she's always trying to make it up to him, but not with material items like most rich assholes would resort to. She actually interacts with him, goes out of her way to. She doesn't just love Holter, she legit likes him, too, which I didn't know was a thing before—parents liking their kids and genuinely wanting to be around them.

My mom sure the fuck didn't seem to enjoy my company unless I was wiping puke from her hair. And my dad…dude didn't stick around long enough to find out.

But if Collette's crying while she's at home with Holter, how could she miss him? Maybe that's not why she's crying.

What *is* she crying about?

I glance over at the beach bar where Collette's placing her order. The hotel's got a stretch of private beach, and they reserved the end of it just for us for a little more privacy. I spy enough motherfuckers sporting telephoto lenses sprinkled in with the other hotel guests to know we're not actually flying under the radar though. They're getting their shots regardless. Same as the dozens of regular guests sprawled out on their blankets, pretending to talk on their phones that are all coincidentally aimed our way. Most of them are somewhat pulling it off, but a few forgot to turn off their flashes, giving them away every time their phone lights up.

Fucking scavengers. As of my birthday a couple weeks ago, Collette and I aren't hiding our relationship—or whatever it's called—anymore, but the public still wants any juicy detail they can get from us. We haven't exactly put a label on us, but there is an us which is all I give a shit about, along with the fact that I can touch and kiss her whenever the fuck I want now. I mean, I try to do Holter a solid by not slipping his mom the tongue in front of him, but otherwise it's fucking on. No more pretending, no more holding back. Physically.

Everything else…we're both still holding back. I shared my past life with Collette but haven't been completely open with her about my present life. Even though I'm pretty sure she has a good idea what happens on my bus, I still keep who I am with her separate from the person I become over there.

She's still holding back on me, too. Like what I *think* she was about to say to me the morning after my birthday. I *think* it was the same thing I was about to say to her but chickened out on. I want to tell Collette I love her. I will tell her. I just…want a little more time with her before I fuck it up. *If* I fuck it up.

I did every other time. That's why I don't let myself love anyone anymore.

But I didn't just fall for Collette. I fucking dove. So, now I gotta do everything I can to make sure I don't fuck it up, starting with figuring out what really went down with Bodee. And why Collette cries herself to sleep at night when she's home. I don't know if the two are related, but I don't know that they're not. I do know she hasn't had a real relationship with anyone since Bodee. I know she admitted to putting work over love because of her parents' all-consuming relationship, but also secretly wishes she had what they had, or at least a healthier version of it. Even I found myself wanting a love like Collette's parents when I heard her talking about them. Not the selling-their-daughter-off part because fuck that. More so the crepe part, the traditions-that-make-a-house-feel-like-a-home part—I want that. I want it all.

But still not the giving-anyone-away part. I let too many people in my life slip through my fingers already and I'm not doing that shit again.

Maybe that's why Collette cries…because she wants the same thing.

"How about we let your mom sleep in tomorrow and you and I can check out the gym first thing in the morning," I tell Holter. That can be a tradition, between me and him. We can work out together. His throws are almost knocking my ass over and he don't even have real biceps yet. If his little twig arms can do that, kid's gonna be a fucking machine after putting on some muscle.

Holter doesn't even try hiding his suspicion, asking, "You work out?"

I snort like it hasn't been months since I even looked at a weight.

It's like riding a bike.

Probably.

Guess I'm finding out tomorrow morning.

"Don't make me have to show you up in front of all these girls," I say with a knowing grin. I see the way he's been eyeing all the teenage girls out here on vacation with their parents. One of them already tossed a Frisbee over with her number written on it. Holter blushed, kinda like he's doing now, before tossing it back to her with an apology. He's still talking to that girl he took out to dinner in Cali. At least that's who I assume he's texting every minute of every hour of every day.

Holy shit, people with money are different, even their kids. With their smartphones, and unlimited plans, and their reliable fucking networks, they want—and get—twenty-four-hour access to whoever they're interested in. They don't have the attention span to wait for nights and weekends to make calls, or God forbid, deal with spotty reception. They have no idea what it's like to pine after something or someone. None. That's why all the new songs are shit, and everyone is gobbling up old-school stuff again. Back then, going without was a regular part of life, and it made for great fucking music.

A screaming crowd coming down the boardwalk snags my eye, and I glance at Bare, who's already out of his seat, trying to determine whose direction he should go in—Collette's or Holter's. I don't even know what to tell him either. Are they coming this way?

Another dumb question. Of course, they're coming this way. But why are they screaming? And…not running? Usually the screaming goes hand in hand with ankle-breaking sprints, but this mob is moving at a snail's pace.

Whatever's happening, I just need to make sure both Holter and Collette are covered.

I turn the opposite way and launch the ball into the air in a high arc.

"What was that?" Holter laughs. "Sun get in your eyes?"

"Must've," I mutter while he offers to get it just like I knew he would.

To Bare, I gesture at Collette, walking backward to make sure I keep myself between Holter and the boardwalk clusterfuck.

Collette looks up from her spot at the bar, and at first nothing on her changes, then ever so slightly her spine stiffens as she pulls her shoulders back, almost like she's preparing for a fight. And now I wish I would've went for her and put Bare on Holter because if she's fightin', I'm fightin'. Simple as that.

Who's she fighting though? She doesn't even have a blade on her, only because there was nowhere to put one in the bikini she's wearing.

Bare posts himself next to her, saying something in her ear, but she shakes her head before throwing a cautious look over her shoulder. But her eyes never touch me. No, they're all for her boy.

Holter jogs up to me, asking, "What's my dad doing here?"

Finally, a good question 'cause what *is* Bodee doing here?

Low and fucking behold, Bodee Keys steps through the crowd and heads straight for Collette, planting a kiss on each of her cheeks with zero surprise of finding her there whatsoever.

Bare tries to linger near her but ends up getting roped in to helping several other security guards enforce some kind of crowd control so the celeb pair doesn't get trampled.

"He didn't tell you he was coming?" I ask Holter, and out of the corner of my eye I see him shake his head.

"No. He didn't."

After a minute of us watching the shitshow under the gazebo, he buries one of his feet under a pile of sand, mumbling, "He doesn't tell me anything."

I shift on my feet, kinda wanting to hug Holter right now. I don't, but only because I don't really know how that shit works. Would he appreciate it? Return it? Shove me off him and call the cops?

Instead, I cross my arms over my chest, feeling too many emotions battling bare-knuckle inside it at once. Normally, I'd be at *least* three margaritas in by now, and most likely passed out facedown in the sand, getting the mother of all sunburns. This is…a lot to take in and process. I'm not good at processing either, not even my own shit, and this is someone else's. I just know I don't want Holter to feel what he's gotta be feeling right now. I don't want him to feel what I felt. He deserves better. Better than Bodee.

"Maybe he's here for another overnight with you," I say even though it's a long shot. Holter's dad is a toolbox. An empty toolbox. The kind that sits in the corner of a pristine garage, looking spotless for years on end, but ain't got a damn thing going on inside. Bodee gave up Collette, then spends practically zero time with his own son.

Fuck him. Fuck him double.

"Doubt it," Holter says beside me, not even bothering to go greet his dad. Not that he should have to. That's on Bodee. Again.

"Why's that?" I ask carefully. It's not really a secret that Bodee's an absent dad—we're all clued in on that shit by now—but Holter's tone… it's not like he's feeling sorry for himself. It's like he's stating a fact. He *knows* Bodee's not here for an overnight with him.

The small restaurant gets cleared out for Bodee and Collette, then Bare and Bodee's security detail hold everybody off, so the two of them can talk privately.

Must be fucking nice. All I got was the tip of the beach, but this motherfucker gets the entire beach plus anything on it he wants.

Not Collette. He can't have Collette.

Holter blows out a breath, so I finally look over at him.

Or Holter. Bodee can't have Holter either. *Can he?*

I don't want him to.

"I can only go with my dad when this guy that works for him takes a vacation, and since Irelynn is the one that books them for him, we would've known ahead of time."

That's what Collette asked last time. *"Is Jack enjoying his vacation?"* It felt like it was code talk at the time, but I guess they really were talking about the guy's vacation. But…why?

"Who's the guy?" And why would Irelynn book his vacay? A name as big as Bodee's gotta have at least one of his own personal assistants, if not more.

"His manager."

Collette makes Bodee's manager go on vacation before Bodee's even allowed to see his son. And Collette's assistant is the one that sets it all up…*for* him?

There's gotta be a reason. A big one.

"What's his name?" I ask, already trying to place a face, but it's hard because I don't remember any manager being there the time Bodee and I exchanged blows. I don't remember much of anything from that night except the satisfying crunch of his cheek against my knuckles.

"John Davies, but my mom calls him Jack for some reason."

None of this makes any sense.

"What'd he do?" Better yet, why the fuck does Bodee still keep John-Jack on his payroll if Collette won't even let the guy around her kid? She lets me around Holter and I'm a grade-A degenerate.

Holter frowns. "I'm not sure. Something before I was born, I think. My mom said he's like Slade, but you know? Without all the NDAs."

I can't be sure if an earthquake happens or it's just the ground beneath my feet that shakes, but reality seems to shift all at once, and I almost sway sideways, completely disorientated.

What in the fresh hellpit does that mean?

I try to focus on each word Holter just said, but the only thing I get out is…

"NDAs?"

"Isn't that what they're called? Those contracts Slade forces everybody to sign? I didn't have to sign one though. My mom fought him when he tried making me because I'm underage, and well, she didn't want you anywhere near me…at first. You know until…" Holter trails off, dropping his gaze to the ground, the ground that I swear hasn't stopped moving but nobody else seems to notice.

Collette didn't want me near Holter because I am a grade-A degenerate.

Or was.

Am.

Trying not to be.

Sometimes.

I wish I didn't have to try at all. I wish I would've been enough for Collette and Holter from the very beginning. I wish…a lot of things.

"He makes everybody sign one, huh?"

Holter doesn't lift his eyes, only nods.

"Even your mom?"

"I know she had to before she could go on tour. That's how she got us our own bus."

The fuck? I *gave* Collette that bus.

Or at least I thought I did. That's what Slade made me believe anyway.

That's what I let myself believe.

It's so easy to be blinded by your own delusions when you're a big fish in a little pond. Small eyes looking for small dreams with even smaller outcomes.

But then you're shown the ocean, and someone like Bodee Keys, who's actually big, comes along to prove you're really just…nothing. A nobody. *A never-was.*

He half-laughs, saying, "My mom's really good at negotiations." And I almost laugh, too. Or I would if I thought my chest could handle it.

So instead, I nod, lost in thought. Lost in general. I need to figure out what the fuck's going on, and not just today but what's *been* going on. Here I thought I had all these people around me, having my back, having some shred of discretion, but no. I got nothing. For years, my biggest fuckups have largely stayed under the radar, and yeah, I always wondered why, but I never got stuck on it. I figured it was because the people I was surrounding myself with were cool, discreet, loyal.

Nah. They were contractually obligated to keep quiet.

The worst part is Slade's been doing all this behind my back, without me even knowing. Without me even realizing.

And now I'm finding out Collette—*The* Collette—joined my circus of contract-bound freaks under those same circumstances. Why didn't she ever say anything about it? Why didn't anyone?

NDAs are a regular part of this business—I've even had to sign a few myself—but I never knew they were a regular part of *my* business.

What does that say about me? What does that say about what I'm capable of?

Mass destruction, that's what. I'm a walking, rapping disaster.

But that, I already knew.

It's no wonder Collette didn't want anything to do with me.

At first.

Like Holter pointed out though, that was *only* at first. Now we're practically inseparable, so there must be something redeemable about me.

Maybe I'm not the degenerate I used to be?

Maybe people can change.

And maybe, just maybe, I already have.

If I hadn't, I'd be heading to the bar for an entirely different reason. I'm going to the bar, but I'm going for Collette.

She's shaking her head, laughing at something her ex just said, not in a humorous way, but in a sneer, and I'd like to take whatever he just said to her and shove it up his ass, because if Collette's sneering at it, I would, too.

"Let's go see if your dad wants my autograph," I half-joke, already walking. I'll give him my signature, if only so I can be by Collette's side right now. Not in front of her, not behind her; right fucking next to her.

Holter follows, but slow as shit. He drags his feet in the sand the entire way, making me think he might be the only person that wants to see his dad less than I do right now.

"Come on. We just gotta see what he wants," I tell him before praying to whoever's willing to listen that whatever Bodee wants aren't the same things I want, because if they are, there aren't enough NDAs in the world to keep me from doing something stupid.

Chapter 30

Collette

"How'd you do it?" Bodee repeats for what might be the third time since he showed up unannounced to corner me at this beach bar, demanding I explain how I got The Mousais gig. The one that has not been made public yet.

"How'd you know?" I also ask for the third time.

"You forget I have friends everywhere."

Of course I didn't forget, I just didn't know he'd made one so high up.

I've never been nominated for an award, let alone asked to perform at one of the shows, but recently, The Mousai Awards reached out, wanting me to perform. I suspect it has to do with the attention The Family Julez Tour's been receiving ever since Julian and I added our duet with the piano, but I can't be positive. I'd like to believe it's because I've earned it fair and square. I've busted my ass putting in the work, continually fighting against the never-ending current called Bodee.

That's probably why he's here now, pissed off that I somehow made it past.

"I earned it," I tell my ex smugly, just to rub salt in the wound.

Regardless of the real reasoning, it's a huge honor to perform at The Mousais. They're the highest-ranking televised music award show we have in the US. I haven't shared the news with anybody outside my team because it's not a done deal yet as negotiations are still very much in progress. If it were just me, contracts would've been signed already, but I want Julian up there with me, and the academy is…hesitant. Julian has a reputation. He doesn't always show up, and even when he does, sometimes he's under the influence. He curses like crazy, in real life but also in his songs, and he's got tattoos that'd need to be covered in order to appear on a platform of that size. And so, I'm fighting. I'm fighting for his career as well as mine. I've already seen what an amazing musician Julian is, now I want the world to see, too.

As soon as I get the green light, I want to be able to tell Julian myself first. I know he'll be just as excited as I am…assuming I can get The Mousais to accept.

This little hiccup with Bodee might hinder that, but he hasn't brought Julian's name into the mix yet, so maybe he doesn't know.

I plan to keep it that way.

He's been interfering in my career all along; I'm not going to let him derail Julian's, too.

"You can't."

"I will," I reply, fully aware my voice has no chance of reaching anyone's ears thanks to Bodee's minions keeping everybody out of earshot, even the bartender and servers.

"You're going to step down."

Taking a sip of my spicy mango Michelada, I smirk, telling him, "I won't." I was right. He is mad. I'm actually getting ahead, I'm actually getting somewhere, and Bodee didn't cause it, nor can he stop it. For once, I'm completely out from under his—

He places a folder on top of the bar.

"What's this?"

"Open it."

Slowly, I flick the top over, immediately regretting it.

Pictures, dozens of them, stare up at me from inside the folder accusingly. Some are of me and Julian outside the strip club that first week of tour when we were at each other's throats for reasons neither of us were willing to articulate at the time. Some are from inside the club, during lap dance I received. Some are of me being manhandled on top of the bus the night of the rainout. Bottom line is they cast me in a provocative light.

Obviously, Bodee's been keeping track of me—no, spying on me—but for how long? And to what extent?

"You *will* step down," Bodee says, raising the hairs on the back of my neck.

I've always been extremely careful to keep a low profile where my sex life is concerned. Unfortunately, Julian doesn't even know the concept of low profile. He's loud, obnoxious, colorful, crazy, fun, and The Family Julez Tour has emulated that to perfection.

"How'd you get these?" I ask, pointing at the lap dance photos. Whoever took them had to have been inside the club that night after Julian paid the bouncers at the front. It was a hefty stack of cash he handed them, too.

"I have friends *everywhere*, blondie."

"Can they really be considered friends when you coerce them into compliancy?"

He steals the glass right out of my hand, and takes a swig before shrugging a shoulder, saying, "Those make the best kind of friends."

So he's threatening to leak the photos if I don't turn down The Mousais. Besides the fact that none of them show me technically doing anything overtly sexual, mostly hinting at it, the truth remains, I do like sex. I'm not going to be embarrassed or apologize for it. One of the men in the photos, I'm with now, and Julian wouldn't be upset at all if these ended up in the tabloids. Some of them are already public anyway.

"Well, as unpleasant as seeing your face at such a close proximity was, I must excuse myself to go do…literally anything else." I close the folder, then slide it over in front of him. "If you want to leak these, leak them, but I'm not stepping down from The Mousais. I'm not scared of a few slightly scandalous pictures, Bodee. I've dealt with, and came back from, far worse. I was married to you after all."

I'd leak the pictures myself before I let Bodee control me or where my career goes again. At least my demise would be at my own hands for once.

Over the top of my glass, he says, "You know, you've changed since you've been away. Much more…spirited."

Away? He makes it sound like I went on a spa retreat for the last fourteen years.

I take my Michelada back and place it on the bar top a little too aggressively. I'm not touching my lips where his were, and he doesn't deserve my drink. He doesn't deserve anything from me, including my time.

"If by spirited, you mean I'm a lot harder to break, then yes, I've changed," I say, pushing away from the bar.

"Finally, a challenge worth taking," he says so calmly, too calmly, before brandishing another folder from behind his back and balancing it on top of my discarded cocktail glass. "You always were a little too sure of yourself."

I eye the folder, dread filling my gut. What does he have? What did he do?

"Is that why you've made it your life's work to constantly bring me down? I do *nothing* to you."

Bodee slides forward, too close for my own comfort, and I have to fight my body's natural reaction to him for the cameras that are still aimed directly at us. We may not be in earshot, but we are in full view like this.

"Wrong," he grits between his teeth, his anger getting the better of him as his brown, almost black hair shakes. "You do nothing *for* me, Collette. You're a gnat that served her purpose long ago. If you weren't the mother of my child, I would've squashed you the second you walked out my door."

I can't hold back my scoff. Oh, that's where he draws the line? But having his child's mother raped, that was okay?

"The only reason you're able to continue to buzz around the globe, performing your pathetic music, is because I allow you to. But I can end it. I can put a stop to the pathetic tours with pathetic 'musicians' you've managed to procure from the pile of no-names I've left for you to dig through."

It's no wonder I tour nonstop. It's an obsession in itself chasing after, then landing someone who'll actually dare to work with me. Any act big enough to draw Bodee's attention is out, leaving me with mostly up-and-comers to choose from. I can't walk away from touring, it's all I fucking have.

"Now," he says, collecting himself with a tug on his shirt's collar. "Open the folder."

I shake my head. "Fuck you and fuck your orders."

A commotion behind Bodee has my eyes scanning the crowd, but I can't see Julian and Holter anymore, only hear them as Holter calls out, "Mom?" making my heart rate spike. He's so close to this. He's too close to this.

Julian's tearing someone a new asshole about not letting him by while Bare's voice booms the same sentiment, and I can tell they're both facing off against Bodee's security team. Bare was merely a pawn in all this. We're all pawns.

Bodee shrugs like he's unaffected, but it's so forced I see right through it. Why is it so hard for him to accept I'm succeeding? Why does it even matter anymore?

"Don't open it, and we'll let Holter see what's inside."

I smack the folder off the glass, causing it to fall open. All I see, all I need to see, is Julian holding a rolled up hundred-dollar bill to his nose, and judging by the blue tips in his hair, it was taken during this tour. Every person within Julian's orbit has signed an ironclad NDA for this exact reason, so pictures like this don't make the gossip circuits.

I don't bother asking how Bodee got these because he'd give the same vague answer. I only stare at the face of the man who I wish was by my side right now.

When faced with a crisis, the initial response is typically to fight or flight, but that doesn't necessarily mean they're the only reactions. Sometimes the best thing to do is nothing. Sometimes you just have to hunker down and weather the storm, if there even is one at all. Julian snorting coke can't be all that surprising to anybody that's ever listened to his songs, and it's certainly not career ending. Musicians all around the world drink and get high. Musicians and drugs—they're pretty synonymous, not as much as they were in the eighties, but still prevalent enough not to get condemned for.

What Bodee is threatening me with is not the smoking gun he thinks it is, and if I'm not worried about it, then I know Julian wouldn't be either. He has a hierarchy for who his own bodyguard is supposed to save first in dangerous situations, and me and my son are at the top. If it came down to him facing public scrutiny or a performance that could change my career, he'd never, ever put his own interest first.

If Julian were here himself, he'd tell Bodee to go fuck himself. Since he's not, I do it by telling Bodee, "Leak them. Leak them all." I was planning on Julian and I securing The Mousais together, but if we lose them, then we'll lose them together, too.

When I sidestep my ex-husband, he mirrors me, putting himself in my way.

"All? But you haven't even seen them all."

Stretching his arm past my middle, he sifts through the photos until one of me is revealed, then it takes everything to keep my chin from dropping to my chest.

Head up, smile on, and don't show weakness.

He keeps moving photos around, making sure they're all visible, halting to let me absorb each and every one.

Do. Not. Apologize.

"Knifeplay, blondie? John helped you unlock a kink, I see."

I instinctively flinch from the reminder of what I had to do to escape that room, that house, that life. *Bodee.* What I had to do to escape Bodee.

Except I didn't. Not really. If I had escaped him, I wouldn't be falling apart from the inside out on a Texas beach while hundreds of onlookers watch on.

"Where did you? How?" Whoever took the pictures he's got high resolution copies of would've had to… There's no fucking way.

He hasn't just been spying on me, he's been stalking my every waking move.

"How isn't important. Why is."

"Then why? Why are you doing this? Any of this?" My hands fly wildly around the gazebo restaurant like even they don't want to be near Bodee.

His scowl's so reprimanding I want to slap it off. He had to know there was a risk I'd cause a scene. I've stayed quiet for this long, but everybody has their breaking point. I feel mine quickly approaching.

"Why... Why do you think you're qualified to perform at The Mousais?"

"Because I—"

"You're ungrateful. Any success you've found, or will ever find, is *my* doing. Not yours. I found you, I styled you, I trained you. I taught you everything you know. You don't get to perform at The Mousais unless I say you do. Unless my name's accredited."

So that's why he's upset. Because I earned something on my own merit. Even if it was with Julian's help, it still wasn't with Bodee's.

"You groomed me from my sixteenth birthday until the day I walked out," I say, voicing the thoughts I've had for years but have never uttered out loud. "The things you 'did for me,' you did for your own gain, not mine. The only thing you taught me was how not to be because I fucking loathe everything you are and everything you stand for. And I am grateful. You were a curse, Bodee Keys, and I'm grateful I survived you."

"Step down from The Mousais or I won't just ruin both you and your druggie boyfriend's reputations beyond repair. I'll pull the plug on this tour, as well as the next one, and the next one, and the next one, until the only fans that'll even remember your names, are worm food. You think you survived me, Collette?" His chuckle is terrifying, the kind that haunts nightmares. "I haven't even begun. I've been taking it easy on you. I've been playing with you for my own personal amusement. You're like a dog chasing its tail around and around and around because you're not talented enough to try anything else."

"I'm talented enough to get The Mousais." The second the words leave my mouth, red stains Bodee's face, and I rush to knock over a wineglass with my elbow. The crash of glass is loud enough to do exactly what I wanted—distract Bodee so I can snatch the paring knife the bartender left behind on his cutting board while also capturing our audience's *full* attention. Now if he tries to get physical with me, I have two weapons—witnesses and a knife. Bodee fears one more than the other...only because he hasn't felt the tip of my knife yet.

"Mom!" Holter shouts again, but I don't make the mistake of removing my eyes from Bodee.

"Don't you think it'll seem a bit suspicious?" I ask him. "Us having a tense conversation just before all those photos get leaked?"

Nodding jerkily, he says in a practiced, professional tone, "She's always had a sex addiction. Even her family tried to warn me, but I *loved* her. I thought I could help Collette. On our wedding night, when I caught her trying to seduce my longtime, trustworthy manager, it became clear I couldn't, and as much as it broke my heart, I had to file for an immediate annulment."

"What?" That's not even close to true. Not one word.

"I've never come forward with the truth because she's the mother of my son. I thought after he was born, she'd put all that behind her, turned over a new leaf, but she fooled me. She fooled all of us. I was made aware of the photos…" He pretends to gulp. "…from an anonymous source, and I thought I'd offer Collette my support once again. I rushed to her aid, but she wasn't interested in seeking help. She became insolent. You can watch the videos yourself and see how violent she became when faced with the truth."

"What are you doing?"

He drops the tone, reverting back to his normal self.

"Warming up. Nobody cares where news comes from anymore, only how big a splash it'll make. But should fingers start pointing my way, I've already got my story prepared along with photographic evidence, eyewitnesses, security footage from my house, the list goes on. What do you have?"

What do I have? I have my truth, but nothing to back it up. None that I could actually rely on. Any witnesses I found could be turned by Bodee. Any proof is long gone. All that remains intact from that night is…

"Jack's face."

"We perfected the cover-up story for that ages ago. Collette…step down."

I whip my head back and forth, stuck in this mental institution Bodee insists on keeping me in. "No."

"Why can't you do as you're instructed? Why do you *always* have to make everything so hard on yourself?"

"Because I'm not a fucking dog, Bodee. I don't belong to you."

"Everything about you belongs to me," he spits, then pauses. "Including that abortion John failed to complete."

A wave of nausea so strong bowls into me, almost knocking me over. Was that his main objective in siccing Jack on me? To try to terminate my pregnancy?

"So I'll be taking him with me today." He pulls his phone out of his pocket, eyes fixed on the screen as he unlocks it.

"What do you mean you're taking *him*? Holter? You're not taking Holter. That was never discussed."

"You can retrieve him in two weeks."

Two weeks. The Mousais. As soon as Bodee steps on to the red carpet with Holter, people will be raving about Bodee Keys as a single father which will lead to talk about our relationship being the jumping point for my career. He'll get the credit he thinks he deserves.

"No. I'll let you walk into The Mousais with Holter by yourself, but you don't get to take him today. We made an agreement. You agreed."

If he tries to take Holter with Jack around…

"You *agreed*," I repeat, feeling myself losing my grip. He's never taken things to this level, not with Holter.

From the beginning, the same rules have been in place. In order for Bodee to have access to Holter, his manager had to be out of the picture. Jack had to be *gone* before Holter could even leave my supervision. And Mary had to accompany Holter to ensure he was properly cared for since Bodee is Bodee. Becoming a father didn't change who he is fundamentally, and I'll never trust him to be a decent human being, especially not at the risk of my child.

Bodee proved early on he was only interested in looking like a good father, not actually being one, so he's only taken Holter on a handful of overnights in the past thirteen years, and only for one or two nights at a time. Nothing close to two weeks.

During any of the times Bodee did choose to flex his father muscles, even the shorter, hour-long visits, I've paid a pretty penny for the elaborate vacations Jack went on. Me. No one else. And we're talking remote locations accessible only by boat or helicopter or seaplane, with exotic meals served around the clock.

Not only have I paid mentally, physically, emotionally, for what Bodee and Jack did, I've paid financially. I've *paid* to keep my son safe.

Still, he wants more.

"Are you really doing this because I got The Mousais without your help?" I say, trying to verbalize how insane this is.

He barely spares me a glance, still focused on his phone. "Are you conceding?"

"I'm not giving up anything. Not The Mousais, and certainly not Holter. You can go fuck your—"

"I could always take both from you," he murmurs to himself like he's seriously considering it.

Both? What does that mean?

He turns his phone around to show me a draft of an unsent email, and I balk. "What is this?"

"Tell me. Who's it made out to?"

"I don't know—"

"That is Honorable Anne Matheson." Bodee's thumb scrolls down, revealing digital versions of the photos still sitting on the bar. The ones of me and Julian by the river that day. The ones I have no idea how the hell he got ahold of in the first place.

"She's a judge?" I choke out, wishing my voice didn't carry the tears I'm desperately trying to hold back.

"Family court judge. Another friend of mine. A *good* friend, very reliable." Motioning over my head, he calls out, "Let my son through. I want to tell him the happy news."

"No. No, no, no." One-handed, I scramble to get all the photos sorted, then hidden back in the folder.

"Two weeks or I take him permanently."

I stop to stare at my ex.

"Why? We both know you don't even want Holter full-time." It hurts to say but it's true. Bodee would've tried it the second I gave birth, or any other time during his son's thirteen-year life, but he hasn't. He truly only cares about himself.

"And we both know what I'll do to keep you from getting what you do want…"

He doesn't have to finish his statement. One way or another, Bodee will always find a way to win. My reputation being questioned and beaten and dragged through the mud, I can handle. My son being taken away from me, I can't. Which he knows and was holding on to as his trump card.

I loosen the paring knife I'd been keeping in my palm, then angle it directly under Bodee's bottom right rib—the side out of everyone's view.

Keeping my voice for him alone, I tell him, "Irelynn will handle everything to ensure Jack's out of the country by tonight. You'll take Mary with you today and she's to be by Holter's side the entire two weeks. At any time, if I hear, see, or even think Jack's within thirty feet of Holter, I will finish what I started, then I'll do the same to you." My eyes trace Bodee's baby-smooth cheeks, the same place I sliced Jack's wide open all those years ago, leaving behind a scar from one ear to the other.

"Mom, what's going on?" Holter asks as he makes it past the guards.

"Smile and nod if you understand," I whisper to Bodee. I'm not backing down. I refuse to. He can threaten and bully all he wants, but I know the one thing he won't risk is a public downfall, and with all these people watching our every move right now, this could become very ugly, very quickly for Bodee. I'll make sure of it.

With a smile designed for fame, he nods, and we grin into each other's faces all while I discreetly press the tip up into his rib cage.

Satisfied from his sharp intake of breath, I tuck the knife away again.

Just before our son reaches us and our façades can fall back into place completely, and with enough underlying menace to make my skin cold, Bodee says, "Break a leg."

I gnash out between my teeth, "If you weren't already dead to me, I'd kill you myself." The only thing I need to break is this curse. I haven't survived it at all. I've just been fooling myself.

Bodee reiterates that point by whispering, "Dumb bitch, true legends never die."

Chapter 31

Collette

"What were they of?" Julian asks, and I tear my gaze away from my phone's screen, briefly looking down at the worn, sandy boards we're walking over. One hour until the wheels on Bodee's private plane lift from the tarmac its currently parked on, eagerly awaiting Bodee and Holter and Mary. Thank God Mary was nearby and able to get here quickly. Now Irelynn and I just have to get Jack's trip squared away.

"You and I, outside the strip club," I say, returning my attention to the travel itinerary Irelynn sent over for review.

Approve. Approve. Approve. I don't care what I have to pay, just get that asshole out of the country. If only it was a one-way…

"We weren't doing anything wrong out there."

"Inside, too."

"What do you mean? He's got pictures from *inside* the club? How'd he fucking swing that?"

"How'd he swing getting any of the photos in his possession?" My voice is unrecognizable, void of any emotion whatsoever.

"What else does he have?"

The toe of my sandal catches on a loose board, but Julian shoots a hand out, catching me by my elbow.

"Fuck, would you stop? What else does he have on you?"

"It's not just me."

Julian's quiet for a while, then asks slowly, "What was I doing?"

My eyes meet his. *Do I really need to say it?*

He winces, it's brief but it's there, before he chuckles, saying, "Shit. We can go get your boy back right now if that's the case."

"Julian…"

"Collette. You think I give a fuck if people know I do drugs? Let that motherfucker leak everything he has on me. Holter will be back with us in no time."

"He has more."

"Of?"

I glance at my phone again, reading Irelynn's short reply that the ticket's been purchased and the car's on its way to pick up Jack.

I drop my hands by my sides, exhaling. "Me. Us. He's got everything."

The forced optimism on Julian's face is quickly replaced with something much darker, making him look scarier than Bodee ever did.

"What. Does. That. Mean?"

"Where should I start?" I bark out a laugh, my insides splintering in a way I've only ever felt once before. "He's got everything, Julian. From the first day of tour until now. He's even got us that day by the river."

"But…it was just my back, right? I was blocking—"

"You're not listening. He's got *everything*. The photos were taken from across the river, so they show, in great fucking detail, everything you were doing to me."

"That's impossible," he spits.

"Is it? Take a look around." I gesture at the paparazzi still scuttling around like crabs in the sand. Today's gonna be a big payday for them. They got a lot of material. "Look at the size of the lenses they have here today, and that's when they're close enough for us to actually see them."

Paps will go to any lengths to get the perfect shot, it's literally their job. The more salacious the better. That's how photos of celebs on yachts are caught without the stars ever realizing they're under surveillance. The photogs don't just go puttering up next to a million-dollar mansion on water in a fishing boat they rented for the day and announce themselves. Their lenses have lenses.

"So he, Bodee, has pictures right now of you with your skirt up?" he questions, his fists clenching and unclenching by his sides, and I can tell he's working to control his temper in front of those same lenses still aimed at us as we make our way to the hotel.

Bodee knew exactly what he was doing catching me out here with my guard down, and with as many bodyguards as he brought along to make it even more of a display, he couldn't have planned it any more perfectly.

He even accounted for my defiance. He didn't like it, but he was ready for it nonetheless with not only a plan B, but also a plan C *and* a plan D. When Bodee Keys comes for you, he comes prepared. There's nothing half-assed about his takedowns.

He was right, he has been taking it easy on me.

"And he threatened to leak those?"

"Yes, but he's not going to now." I frown. "Or he is, but he's holding off while he has Holter. I don't know actually, he didn't say. But he has hard copies, digital copies, and who knows what else, so he could do whatever he wants with them, whenever he wants."

"Why didn't you fight for them? Why didn't you try to get them back?"

"Because I don't care!" I whisper-shout. "I have bigger things to worry about right now than pictures of my pussy making the rounds." As stressful as it is knowing Bodee could still leak those photos at any given moment, it's nothing compared to the worry I feel for my family. I won't be able to relax until I have confirmation Jack's in the sky, heading in the opposite direction as Holter and Mary.

We resume walking in strangled silence before Julian bursts, "So what? Fuck it. We're together now. I'm not ashamed of anything we've done together. It fucking sucks people might see you like that, but if that's what's keeping you from getting Holter back, I say call his bluff and see if he actually does it."

If I thought I could cry right now without falling apart completely, I would. This is how Julian and I are the same inside.

"I already did that," I tell him quietly.

"Then why'd he still take Holter?"

"Because Bodee's not threatening to only go to the press. He's threatening to share the photos to the court system, to a judge he's got a connection to, so he can take full custody of Holter."

"Jesus Christ. They're not *that* bad. Enough to take your kid from you?"

"Maybe alone, no. But me using a knife to cut your shirt off immediately after gives it a different angle Bodee could work into anything he wants." Oh God, his concocted story of my "sex addiction." It wasn't just that his brain had actually thought something like that up, it's how practiced it already was. He could, and would, sell the lie of me being a knife-wielding sex-fiend as easily as he sells albums. "All the photos he has might be harmless by themselves but combined…they won't look good if presented together."

"Why now? Holter's thirteen years old. Why didn't he fight for custody before now? It doesn't make any sense."

"I don't know," I say quickly, contemplating if I should just tell him about The Mousais. I didn't want to until I knew for sure it was a done deal. I wanted it to be a surprise, not something I break to him while blackmail's hanging over my head.

"The pictures…something doesn't add up about them. We would've heard *something* about them already. Someone should've posted them by now."

"It wasn't regular paps," I agree. "He paid someone to follow me."

"Why the fuck would he do that?"

"Same reason Bodee does everything, to get what he wants."

"What does he want from you?"

I can only shrug, avoiding his penetrating gaze.

"This whole time, ever since you guys broke up, you've never been with anyone else, right? Not publicly?"

"It's not like that. He doesn't want me back." He wants me ruined, destitute, no legs left to stand on. He wants to be able to prove what happens when you turn your back on Bodee Keys. Bodee Keys can make you, or Bodee Keys can break you, and if he's not getting credit for one, he'll most certainly find a way to get it for the other.

"Guaranteed this isn't the first time he's had you followed."

"It wouldn't be difficult. Everywhere I go people are photographing me anyway." As if to prove my point, a bachelorette party at a volleyball court drawn in the sand screams my name, waving overeager hands above their veil-covered heads. The ones not waving have their phones pointed directly at me, and I wave back automatically. It's robotic, but it's enough for them to go back to their game without requesting anything more of me.

Small miracles.

Eyes taking in the beach full of people like the person responsible for spying on me will magically present themselves, Julian says, "You should've told him to fuck off."

Under different circumstances, I'd smile—I knew that's what his reaction would be—but I can't even muster the strength. I can feel myself waning.

"Believe me, I tried. Once he brought up Holter, that was the end of the conversation basically. I couldn't do anything."

He turns to me, saying, "I know. Just like Bodee knows. Your boy's your kryptonite, the one thing that can take you out and make you agree to whatever conditions he drops at your feet. Whatever he wants, he's playing to win, but…he won't take you to court."

"How can you be sure? Bodee's unhinged."

"He's unhinged, but he's not stupid." His hand fits in mine, and he brings both up between us, singling out my tattooed finger. "If he took you to court, you wouldn't stay quiet about whatever it is he did to you."

I don't tell Julian that I can't. Bodee's already thought of that. My silence didn't give me leverage; it didn't garner my hands power. All it did was buy Bodee and Jack enough time to make their story bulletproof.

"Let's go to the airport, tell Bodee to go fuck himself. We'll grab Holter and bring him back here with us," Julian says, shrugging. "If Bodee still wants to play games after that and leak photos, we'll sue him. Slade's got lawyers on speed dial for this kind of shit." His jaw grinds side to side and his eyes take on a sharpness I couldn't decipher even at my best, which clearly, I'm not at right now.

"Your lawyers aren't big enough to go up against Bodee."

"You mean *I'm* not big enough to go against Bodee." There's a bite to his tone now, almost like he's mad at me instead of my ex. I haven't done anything but try to protect my family, which was starting to feel like Julian was a part of.

"None of us are big enough to go against Bodee. He will win, but even if there was a small chance he wouldn't, he'd do everything in his power to make damn sure I lose." He's been winning this whole fucking time. Watching my entire life through a well-placed telescope, he's essentially spent the last fourteen years soaking me in kerosene while waiting patiently for the most opportune moment to light the match. This isn't just a takedown, it's an assassination.

"Hold on. Wait. We gotta do somethin.'" Julian reaches for me, his own hand shaking as I back up.

I dodge him though, telling him, "I need some time alone."

"It doesn't help. It never does."

"How would you know? You're always surrounded by people."

Julian straightens to his full height, his form so much taller than mine, and sticks a hand in his pocket.

Bare's behind us, far enough away not to listen in…I thought anyway because his eyes flash at his boss, taking in his shift in body language.

"The ways we choose to cope, right?"

"You don't cope. You run."

He waves a hand at me. "What are you doing right now?"

"What I should've done from the very beginning, getting away. Far from here."

"You don't mean… Collette?"

"Whether it's now or later, it's bound to happen, isn't it? A tour-mance only lasts as long as the tour does." I don't know why I say it, just that it feels equal parts empowering and weak—empowering because I just hurt someone, weak because it hurt me worse.

<blockquote>
"Here I thought you were fixing me up,
stitching me up,
shoulda known all along you'd be the one zipping me up."
</blockquote>

As he speaks, he mimics the movements like he's zipping up a body bag around himself, and it's painful to watch, even more painful than what I just said.

I bite my tongue until I taste copper.

A streak of anger wanders on to his face as his hand turns into a finger pointed directly at me. "Stop trying to fucking leave me before you even leave me."

I close the distance between us, saying in his face, "I'm already gone, Julian. A part of me, the best, most important part, just left with the man who controls every aspect of my life. You want to know why I can't be your queen? Because I'm not even my own." Then spinning on my heel, I speed-walk up the rest of the boardwalk, plastering a fake smile on a face that doesn't even feel real anymore. None of this does.

Except it must be because no nightmare's ever made me this afraid.

I bypass the hotel, unsure where I'm going or what I'm doing.

I consider flying straight to Tennessee to call Bodee's bluff like Julian suggested. But what if he's wrong? What if Bodee's not bluffing at all? Could I survive Holter being taken from me?

No. There's not a doubt in my mind I wouldn't.

Can I survive two weeks without him?

Yes. I probably wouldn't if Mary wasn't with him.

For my peace of mind, I hope Bodee leaves Holter and Mary the hell alone once they reach his massive estate, but for Holter's sake, I hope his father actually takes the time to get to know him. Bodee called him a failed abortion.

I cover my mouth, swallowing down the vomit making its way up my throat as my body starts convulsing in fear, in shame, in white-hot anger.

I let Bodee take Holter. I *let* him walk away with my son, my child, my reason for breathing.

I should've passed on The Mousais.

But if I quit now and give in to Bodee's demands, that doesn't guarantee it'd stop him from making more in the future. It doesn't really matter what I do, he'd find something else, anything else. Just like I told Julian, whether it's now or later, some things are just that inevitable. Bodee Keys won't stop until he's ruined me and everything I've worked for.

It doesn't really matter what I do.

I've tried my best for years to do the right thing, say the right thing, *be* the right fucking thing, and one quick email could rip everything I hold dear right out of my hands.

Powerless hands.

Perhaps I've been powerless all along, and it was pure arrogance to think otherwise, but nothing could've prepared me for this. This is one of the rare times in my life that I feel powerless, yes, but so much more. More so than the night I faced off against Jack, more so than the night on top of Julian's bus, more so than when my parents handed me over to the devil incarnate himself.

More because now I don't just feel powerless, I *am* powerless.

If I'm not really in control, what's the point in pretending I am?

What's the point of any of this?

Nothing I do matters.

Chapter 32

Julian

Where the fuck is she? And why couldn't I come?

After almost getting into it with three of Bodee's meatheads, all I wanted was to be there for Collette. And keep Holter safe, even from Bodee. And beat Bodee's ass…again. But now, here I am, alone in my hotel room, looking like a dumbfuck who couldn't pull off even one of those things.

It might not be so bad if there was something to drink around here.

I completely fucked myself by calling ahead and asking the hotel to remove all the alcohol from my suite. That's what I get for assuming I could do it. For assuming I could just…not drink. I thought I'd give it a try for Collette.

But I am a dumbfuck, a sober dumbfuck which is honestly worse because a drunk dumbfuck at least has an excuse.

I need a drink just from Collette throwing the term tour-mance in my face. Is that really what she thinks this is? If so, I'm an even bigger dumbfuck than I thought for not letting that shit be known sooner. I don't know exactly what we are, but tour-mance…no. We're not a fucking tour-mance.

We can't be. Whatever's happening between us feels so much

stronger, so much deeper, than the tour-mances I've seen. Those are like friends with benefits. This ain't that.

I'll tell her that myself when I see her.

Where is she? She turned off her phone, so I know she's gotta be upset still. Upset with who though?

Bodee obviously.

Fucker.

But why was she upset with me at the end there? I wasn't the one running or hiding. I was ready to own up for everything I did in the photos. It's a new concept for sure—me being responsible—but I was down to take a crack at it. I'm not used to facing my past mistakes. It's like looking in the mirror after spending a long day in the sun. Your eyes struggle to adjust to the hazy light at first, but when they do, who you see looking back at you is practically unrecognizable. I don't re-hash my fuckups because I don't want to. I don't like how they make me seem, how they make me feel. And usually, I don't have to.

It wasn't until today that I figured out why I haven't had to. Slade's been covering my tracks all along the way with a thick coat of legal jargon, so I didn't need to take responsibility for any of the shit I've done, or the damage I've caused.

Now that I do finally have a reason for facing myself—my past self *and* my present self—in the mirror, I wish I wasn't doing it alone. But I am. Alone. Alone and unsure. *What the fuck do I do?*

What the fuck *can* I do? Every idea I had Collette shot down.

I'd do anything to make Collette's pain disappear. I'd do anything just to have her, period. Even when shit is falling apart at the seams, she takes the edge off the harsh bite of reality I prefer to avoid at all costs. It *hurts* feeling this much, especially after going so long not feeling at all. I don't know how people do it every day.

I just wish Collette was here.

Pining. I'm motherfucking pining. Perfect songwriting mentality. Writing a song won't get us out of this though.

I don't know what will, but I know it ain't sitting in this hotel room by myself pining.

The next instant, I'm already down the hall and in the elevator, staring at the framed poster of the onsite gym I was just telling Holter about. I wish he was here, too. He's not even my kid and I feel like a piece of my body's missing not having him around. The pain I'm feeling…Collette's must be a thousand times worse right now.

Out of all the snapshots Bodee was able to get his hands on, I know that motherfucker's seen plenty of good ones, too. The ones where Collette wakes up early after performing late into the night just so she can take Holter around whatever city we're in, showing him how different the world works outside the snow globe of privilege his mom's career has afforded them so far. She works hard at her job, but goddamn, she works even harder at being a good mom.

I pull up the album on my phone that's full of pictures I've taken of Collette and Holter, landing on one of my favorites. One day, between sound check and showtime, I found them both snuggled up together on this tiny-ass couch in her dressing room. They were passed out, but Collette stirred when I opened the door, instinctively pulling Holter closer to kiss his temple. It was one of those moments that you know is special and not everyone gets to experience, so I took a picture so I could always remember it. I actually thought about getting it tattooed on the back of my leg but haven't yet since that might be weird. For Holter. Not for me. I'd love to have that kid close to me forever.

Later, when Bruce, our tour manager, found me still watching them, telling me he needed Collette for hair and makeup, it took everything in me to wake the two up because if it were up to me, choosing between work and family, I'd choose family—even one that isn't mine. That's why it was easy for me to tell Collette to call Bodee's bluff. I'd sink my entire career for either of them, but it's not just mine on the line. It's hers. And her boy. Not just her boy…Holter's her whole world.

I see why she didn't risk it…now. On the beach I was hopped up on adrenaline, not thinking everything through.

It's probably why Collette was pissed at me. I'm not much of a plan-of-attack type of person. I'm the guy that starts swinging through the fog before it even has a chance to clear. If I hit something, fucking great. If I get hit, so be it; at least I didn't go out like a punk. But the shit that went down today? I gotta be smarter. Bodee Keys didn't get where he *is* today by swinging blindly, and he's not gonna get taken out by someone doing it either.

My hands shake with need. Need for a fix. Need for a fight. I start flipping through more photos to keep them busy during the ride down to the lobby. It'd be so fucking easy to line up either one right now, man.

But Collette doesn't need me like that and neither does Holter. Their needs outrank mine.

Before this tour, I'd only take selfies when fans asked me to with them, but since I started spending time with Collette and her boy, I've probably taken hundreds—with Collette, with Holter, with them both. After pausing on a few of those, I go to some others. The first pic is Holter trying to copy Collette's backup dancers during practice. Another one's of Collette reading a book out loud for everyone on the bus, changing her voice for the different characters so we'd all laugh. Then there's Collette applying mascara to the top of Bare's head to look like hair when we had shit else to do on a rainy day.

My thumb hovers over one I don't remember taking, and I expand it, realizing it's because I didn't take it. *Did Collette?* It's of me and Holter, and we're smiling at each other as we prepare to run down the street in front of one of those speed trap machines cops leave on the side of the road. It was on a quiet road with zero traffic, so we thought we'd see who was faster. I remember handing my phone off to Collette before lining up next to Holter like we were about to race. I didn't know she took a picture of us.

Fuck am I glad she did.

I swipe, finding pictures of both of our individual speeds on the electronic reader board, further proving my point that Holter should play football. Collette's kid fucking smoked me that day.

Too bad shit like this doesn't make headlines. This is the shit that should matter. The *only* shit that should matter.

It's all that matters to me.

I'm sneaking between the elevator doors before they're even fully open, charging through the lobby, not giving a shit about the people calling my name. I just want my woman already, and I know exactly how to find her.

"She in there?" I ask Bare standing by my bus's door, grateful I sent him after her. Not for blackmail like Bodee would've done, but to make sure she was safe. To make sure she didn't do anything stupid…like walk on my bus by herself.

When Bare first told me where Collette was, I didn't believe him. I warned her so many times not to come here.

But the look on Bare's face confirms it, and now I'm pissed the fuck off, my gratitude gone in a flash. Bare should be inside, keeping eyes on her.

Actually no, fuck that. He should be carting her ass off. My bus is a sinkhole for morality. I should know. I specifically designed it to be that way.

"I tried," is all he says as I pass him, and I can tell he's tired. There's so much I could say right now, so much rage waiting to be unleashed, so much fear looking for an outlet to hide behind, but all I care about is getting to Collette. She came here without me, willingly. That tells me everything I need to know. It's bad. So fucking bad.

Hauling my ass up the stairs, I feel like I'm a kid all over again, the sheen of what I thought was great falling away to reveal something fucking ugly, insidious. What once gave me comfort, now doesn't. Seeing my bus through eyes that aren't for me and my use, but for someone else's, changes everything.

I spot her right away, and that same feeling I experienced at our first performance, when she was by herself amongst a stadium of rabid fans, fills my chest, making it tight. Collette's standing—a good sign— watching a girl beside her play a harmonica using only her nostrils, but her eyes keep blinking long and slow as she tries to focus—not a good sign. Jesus fucking Christ, Imma start swingin'.

No. I can't. Collette needs me to have a level head.

Axel stands, saying, "Finally." But I don't even bother acknowledging him as I make my way down the aisle, that same urgency as before demanding I go even faster. I definitely don't have the headspace to deal with anyone else right now. Irelynn didn't call me. Bare didn't call me. Axel didn't call me.

Why didn't they call me?

Someone hands Collette a shot, and she goes to toss it back without even asking what it is or who poured it. I used to do the same thing, nightly. Okay, daily. Every day I'd drink whatever was put in front of me, and even now, looking at the bottles littering every available surface, the itch to do just that is strong. But seeing Collette do it? Panic so intense it nearly buckles my knees floods my body as I pick up my pace, getting to her in time to take the glass right from her hand. I drink the shot instead, leveling my eyes on hers as I do, daring her, just fucking *daring* her to fight me on it.

She doesn't, which tells me what I already knew: Bare's not the only one who's tired. We all are. Today siphoned the life out of all of us. I hadn't even realized until today what Holter brought to the tour. He brought life…to everybody. I thought having a kid around would be a major buzzkill, a drawback I didn't feel like putting up with, but he wasn't.

If anything, Bodee's the fucking buzzkill, coming in here and taking away the only good, innocent thing this tour had going for it.

And now I'm about to steal the next best thing and hoard her all to myself. If I can't, I'm not sure there will be anything keeping me from drifting down my ever-trustworthy sinkhole of destruction.

Leaning casually against the counter directly across from her, I rasp, "Welcome to my kingdom," hoping she can't hear the fear in my words. Hoping nobody does. What if I hadn't shown up? What would've happened?

Collette keeps eye contact, tipping one side of her mouth up, and I almost fold, falling at her feet. I don't do scared, but this woman's got me fucking shook.

I keep up the act though, playing along when she greets me with, "The King of the Underworld."

Without flinching, I greet her back, saying, "The Queen of Lost Souls." Whether Collette wants to admit it or not, she's got mine in the palm of her hand, and I'm as lost as they come. I'm the runaway train that everybody's been turning a blind eye to.

Everybody, but Collette.

"I thought I was supposed to be *your* queen?" she slurs with an eye roll as she blindly grabs a bottle from the assortment behind her.

The most pristine disaster I've ever seen and it's at my own hands. Bodee might've been the one holding the photos, but I alone hold the starring role in every single one of them. I ran Collette off the tracks myself. That's why no one called me. Why would they? What could I possibly do to help *The* Collette? I'm not fit to help anybody, not even myself.

Guilt burns the back of my throat, and my eyes fall to the liquor in her hold. I lick my bottom lip, brushing my dolphin bite piercings with the tip of my flattened tongue.

"*You're trying to hurt me!*" she'd screamed when I was drinking away my own emotions, just like I want to do now. Just like she's doing now.

I lift my gaze to hers.

Punishment. That's exactly what this feels like—watching the person you love not only suffering but pretending like they're not by seeking relief in the bottom of a glass. Fuck is it familiar, yet somehow hurts even worse than when my mom did it.

Collette raises her eyebrows in her own dare, and since I've been itching for a fight, I shoot to the other side of the bus, pulling the bottle from her grasp.

"And I thought queens were supposed to be stronger than kings," I say as I bring the liquor up to her mouth.

She takes the hint, parting her lips to accept a quick pour, but before she can close them to swallow, I crush my mouth to hers, sucking the liquid into mine instead.

I can hurt myself by drinking too much all day long. She can't. Not when I'm around. I'd rather swallow her pain whole before she can even get a sip. Whatever it takes to spare her suffering because *that* I can't stomach.

Keeping her close, I table the bottle.

"I'm *sick* of being strong," she whispers, her eyes fluttering. "I want to fall." Through her lashes, she glances back up at me, and says, "Fall with me."

My head's already shaking as I say, "Way ahead of you."

Then I remember something else Collette said to me. *"You're not in a position to catch me, Julian."*

I wasn't then. I'm not now either, but I'm not about to let that stop me from trying.

"How about I catch you instead?" I offer, trailing my hands down to hers.

We stare at each other, the two of us caught in our own world, then I pull her after me, not waiting for an answer because there really isn't one. This isn't Collette, and I have no intention of letting it become Collette. I've inserted myself into her life but haven't even considered letting her into mine. And I never fucking will.

"What will we do?" she asks once we're outside.

"First, we gotta sober you up."

After that? No clue, but my freestyle game got me this far.

Chapter 33

Collette

I groan, the bright lights standing out against the dark of night practically burning my eyes. Technically everything's burning my eyes right now. I just want to close them for the night already. For the week. No, for the next *two* weeks. Then I can wake up, have Holter back, and forget any of this ever happened.

But even I know that's not possible. If it weren't for Julian showing up, I could've maybe forgotten about today. At least for a little while. That's all I wanted. To forget. To not feel all of *this*. My body aches from the blows Bodee delivered, and he didn't even have to touch me to land them with perfect precision.

"Pancakes?" I ask, but Julian shakes his head, fighting a smirk that makes me change my mind about wanting to sleep. I want to kiss him. One kiss…that never, ever ends.

"Not pancakes," he says out of the side of his mouth as he guides me through the swinging door. "We're here for crepes."

My eyes fly to his as he checks his watch.

"Crepes?"

"Aw, fuck it. By the time we get 'em, it'll be after midnight," he says almost to himself. Then to me, he grins, saying, "Sunday morning crepes."

Everything gets blurry, even the waitress that jams a couple of menus against Julian's chest, telling us to sit wherever we want.

"How'd you find this place?" I ask as he leads me to a corner booth.

I think it's in the corner. I can barely see right now. It's really bright in here and my eyes are swimming.

"GPS," he says, laughing.

"But you knew they'd have crepes?"

"I ate here last year." He pauses. "I wrote here last year. Maybe I ate, too, I don't know. I just remember seeing people around me ordering crepes and thought it'd make good hangover food."

"I'm not hungover."

His voice comes out stern, more stern than I've ever heard, as he scolds, "Not yet, but you will be if you don't soak up some of the alcohol you just dumped in your system."

"I'm gonna pass out," I tell him plainly, just so we're clear.

He only looks over the menu, saying, "You're gonna eat some motherfucking crepes first."

I get lost in him, his eyes moving so fast it's hard to keep up.

"Why were you writing here?"

His eyes cease all movement. "You saw my bus." Four words that feel like four thousand.

I saw. Before my eyes turned against me, I saw.

"Is it always like that?"

He nods, resuming his perusal of the menu. "Sometimes worse."

"Worse?"

"Sometimes I can't even find a place to sit."

That's right. Or sleep. I remember that one morning he had an indentation on his forehead from falling asleep at a table.

"Why not just…kick everyone off?"

Julian stops reading again, this time to look at me and ask, "Then what would I do?"

I relax against the cushioned booth, barely resisting the urge to snuggle myself and rest. I'm so fucking tired.

"Write, for starters."

He shakes his head, returning his attention to the menu. "It'd be quiet."

"And when it's quiet the questions come. 'Why'd they do it? What'd you do to deserve it? Could you have done anything to stop it?'"

Leaning forward, Julian cranks his head over his shoulder. "Where's our server?"

"'Was it even your fault?'"

"Jesus. It might be Monday morning by the time we get someone to take our order."

"'What if—'"

"Collette," Julian snaps, and I close my mouth. "Fuck. Yes, okay? I don't like rehashing the worst parts of my life and the noise helps. It helps…just, it helps."

"Only for so long though."

"How do you know?"

The waitress appears, apparently not giving a single shit who we are, and Julian gives her our orders. I secretly love that he orders for me. Not because I like someone talking for me, but because I like that he knows me well enough to guess what I'd order myself. He gets the orange ricotta crepe for himself and the ham with pepper jack for me—exactly what I would've chosen if I could make out the options.

The waitress leaves with an eye roll I feel down to my marrow. She *really* doesn't care.

I envy her.

"Because the questions used to come for me, too," I confess quietly. "In the beginning."

"Questions about what?" he asks innocently, making me instantly suspicious. There's not an innocent bone in Julian's body and I know his body well.

I eye the tabletop, tapping the tines of a fork against the scratched surface. *Tap, tap, tap.* I could do it. I could tell him. The alcohol didn't make me forget, but it did give me a false sense of freedom.

It's not like he'll believe me. It's not like anyone will ever believe me. Not with Bodee's diabolical plan to disprove my word.

So, I say it, the sentence I've never said aloud, to anyone, ever. "Bodee's manager tried to rape me."

After a minute, Julian asks, "John Davies?"

My gaze flies to his, finding a terrifying beauty there. If he could spit fire, I have no doubt he'd be doing it right now. The world would be in embers in seconds because not only does he believe me, he's also *mad*.

"I call him Jack, but yeah. You know him?"

"If I did, I wouldn't still be sitting here after you just told me that."

"How did—"

"Holter told me."

My eyes widen, but he rushes to add, "Sort of. He just said his dad's manager had to go out of town before he could visit Bodee. I figured something was up with the guy."

I'm back to staring at the fork, wishing that I could do it—be free. From Bodee, from everyone's expectations…even my own. I'd say whatever I want. Eat whatever I want. *Do* whatever I want.

I'd carve my initials into the side of the table like countless others have done without considering the consequences. Or I'd stand up and dance badly because my body should be just that…mine. Or I'd scream until my voice gave out.

I don't do any of those things, because I'm a hypocrite. I preach about being authentic meanwhile I let Bodee dictate my life just as much as Julian lets his record label dictate his. The only difference is I don't complain about it like he does. I don't do *anything* about it.

"When was this?" Julian asks, his voice balancing on the edge of that anger he's well acquainted with.

"Our wedding night. There was…a lot of buildup and strain on our relationship leading up to the wedding. Things were not good for a while and were only getting worse. Then we found out I was pregnant, and Bodee announced our engagement without ever proposing, so I felt stuck between—"

"Who all knew you were fucking pregnant? John Davies?"

"All of Bodee's camp knew. Bodee…" I don't know if I should say it. I don't know how to without needing a shower immediately afterward. "I think Bodee's plan wasn't just to obtain blackmail leverage over me, but to also…" I don't want to say it. I need to though. I need to break my silence. I need to make it real to someone other than just myself, then I'll be able to see just how bad it really was. Our eyes collide as I force the vile words out of my mouth, telling Julian, "I think Bodee wanted Jack to cause me to miscarry."

"You're saying Bodee knew what John was going to do…before the attempt was made?"

I nod, bringing my legs up from under the table to hug my shaking knees.

"He set it up."

I confess everything to Julian, purging my soul of every last remnant of Bodee's transgressions. Without Bodee's secrets weighing me down, I don't feel dirty like I expected. I feel lighter almost, maybe even a touch freer. I explain how I got away that night, realizing it's not just Bodee's secrets I've been holding on to, but my own as well.

When I finish, I expect Julian to run out of the restaurant in search of my ex. Instead, he reaches across the table, gripping my hand gently before helping me climb over the top to sit next to him.

Once I'm tucked against his side, Julian apologizes. He apologizes for not knowing sooner, for not being able to do anything then or now.

"There's nothing you could've done. This is…my mess."

"Why do you call him Jack?"

"You've never seen him?"

He shakes his head. "Why?"

"Because you'd know. I carved his face up like a jack-o-lantern."

"Shit. Is that why you carry a knife now?"

"Yeah," I say, watching as the waitress reappears, dropping off our plates before disappearing back into the kitchen area just as quickly.

Eyes on his crepe, Julian asks, "Was there ever a situation where you thought you'd need to use it on Slade?"

"Slade?"

He rotates his head to look at me. "You said Jack's like Slade without all the NDAs… Why? What'd Slade do to you?"

"Did I say that?" I hurry to shove a giant piece of the too-hot crepe in my drunken mouth. Who did I say that to? Certainly not Julian. I'm forbidden from saying anything about those to him.

"That's what your boy told me."

I know for a fact I didn't say that directly to Holter. Most likely he overheard me saying it to Irelynn because even though Irelynn doesn't know what Jack did, she knows enough to understand what him being like Slade means. Holter's the only person that didn't have to sign an

NDA, so I shouldn't be surprised he's the one who spilled the beans about them. Before I even met Slade, I went to war with him about it and almost didn't agree to tour with Julian at all. Holter's been a part of this life longer than Slade. My son's never spilled any behind-the-scenes tea…until now.

I avoid Julian's questioning stare, taking another bite of melty cheese while trying to ignore the way air rushes into my lungs as I gasp for oxygen. Just thinking about Holter hurts. It's only been a matter of hours and I already miss him like a bird misses the sky.

"Are you angry?"

He shrugs, finally breaking his laser focus to get his own bite scooped on to his fork. "About John? Fuck yeah. About Bodee? Abso-fuckin'-lutely. About Slade? Depends on what he did to deserve being compared to a rapist."

"I did threaten him with my knife once when he grabbed my arm, but that was when we first met, and you and I weren't…" I motion between us. "Luckily, that was enough. I never came close to actually using it on him. But the reason why I dislike Slade has less to do with me and more to do with you."

"Why?"

I widen my eyes, telling him, "You already said it yourself."

"Oh. You mean the NDAs being kept from me?"

My head kind of wobbles from side to side, making me dizzier than I already was. The NDAs are part of it. Mostly it's because Slade doesn't have Julian's best interests at heart, only what'll put money in his pocket and keep money in his pocket. I doubt Julian's own pockets even factor into it.

"Why didn't you ever say anything?" The question comes out like an accusation but flimsier. He really doesn't understand, but he's hurt and wants someone to blame.

Wrong person.

I consider my options, which admittedly aren't great. I could remain silent like I've done so far and allow Julian to continue to be taken advantage of by his own agent-slash-manager…and who knows who else. Or I could blow this shit wide open and tell Julian the truth—all of the truth. It's obvious he's unhappy about the fact there even are

NDAs in place. I doubt he'd like the entire reason behind them being a secret. It's not my business and *I'm* upset about it.

The sloshier part of my brain shrugs, and says, *I'm already being threatened with one court case. What's another?*

"I didn't say anything because I signed a contract agreeing not to. The NDAs Slade makes everyone sign aren't just to prevent your business from getting out. They're to keep you in the dark, too."

"In the dark? About what? And why? What's the fucking purpose?"

"Because when you're sober and something goes wrong, you're way more sensitive than you think, and you tend to overreact," I say bluntly, getting the hang of brutal honesty quite quickly.

"But the NDAs—"

"The NDAs are a secondary precaution. For the most part, you take care of the sobriety bit for them. And when you don't…"

"Slade tries to do it for me," Julian guesses correctly. Or maybe just states.

Nodding, I confirm, "Julez is a cash cow that Slade and your record label have every intention of working into the ground." I also sum up everything Slade said to me at Julian's birthday party. It takes a lot more effort thanks to the earlier shots, but eating helps and I feel better once I'm done. The room has finally stopped spinning, too.

Julian, however, is glaring at his plate like he'd like to throw it.

Caged animals will only behave for so long before they remember they are in fact animals capable of wreaking absolute havoc.

"Are you mad at me?" I ask through a wince awaiting his answer. With my head clearing up, I'm remembering more. The things I said to him on the beach. The look on his face when he found me on his bus.

Julian snaps out of his reverie, glancing over at me. After giving me a thorough once-over, he says, "Nah. Not you, Poohbear. Basically everybody but you."

I laugh a sad, sympathetic sound, then apologize right back, for everything, even the stuff I'm not responsible for. I'm so sorry for what he's been put through, what we've both been put through. We're both survivors attempting to navigate swell after swell without the help of, or the detriment of, anyone else. Surviving by ourselves is the only way we know how but sharing our struggles with each other has helped lighten the load. At least for me. Just having Julian know, and believe me, gives me courage, gives me strength.

"Do you really think this is just a tour-mance?"

The desperation in both his voice and his eyes put a knot in my stomach because nothing I say will be able to ease it for him. I'm dealing with the same exact feeling. What is this? What are we?

"I don't know, Julian. I don't know." As much as I hope it's not just a tour-mance, I don't see how it can be more. My next tour is already lined up after this one. I won't have this kind of time or energy to give him, to give us. That's just me. He hasn't even shared what his plans are.

"So, what now?"

He pulls out his phone, telling me vaguely, "I got a couple things in mind."

While he's busy texting, I take out my credit card, but without looking away from his phone, Julian snatches it one-handed and pockets the card in his own pants before removing a wad of cash to place on the table.

"My treat," is all he says, still focused on his phone. A few moments later, he's helping me out of the booth, asking, "Feeling better?"

"Yeah, actually. You?"

He smirks, saying, "Almost."

Standing just down the street from the hotel the rest of my team's staying in, I take in the two buses towering before us.

What are we doing here?

Julian's bus is still teeming with partiers, but thankfully he's not leading us over to it. Instead, we're just hanging out next to the black Escalade Julian hired to drive us around…waiting? For something? Julian won't say.

The door to his bus opens, and three guys practically stumble down the stairs before rushing over to get selfies with Julian. With a tight jaw and hard eyes, he poses like he usually does, then nods them away from us, settling into a casual stance of leaning against the SUV beside me.

"Why a gun?" I ask him when we're alone again.

"Why a gun what?"

"Why do you pose with your fingers in a gun?"

"'Cause I was told to, fuck if I know why. You got something against guns?" he teases. "You got at least one knife stashed in every outfit you wear."

"Knives are easier for me to justify. Guns ruin people on both ends, while knives only ruin one."

His head turns toward mine, so I add, "Or at least I tried to ruin one." A hideous scar did nothing to hinder Jack's life.

"He'll get his," Julian promises, but I shake my head, thinking, *no, he won't*.

Angling his body to face me, Julian says, "I've been thinking."

I mirror him, asking, "About?"

"About those photos Bodee has."

"What about them?"

"We could say we were just acting for a music video."

I raise my eyebrows at him. "Won't everyone figure out that's a lie when we don't actually produce one?"

"We could. We will."

"For what song?"

Julian shrugs his free shoulder. "I'll write one."

"When?"

"Now. Right now. Then we can start shooting as soon as I can get enough people out of bed to help film it."

That's…not how it works, which he knows because he's got a dozen or so music videos under his belt already.

"You can't fix everything."

Julian stares at me, his jaw flexing before he says, "Watch me."

It's honorable that he's trying, I do realize and appreciate that, but it's also unrealistic. Julian can't even fix his own problems. Mine are just that—mine. I got myself into all this. I'm going to have to get myself out of it, too.

I change the subject by gesturing to the buses and ask, "So what are we doing here?" While Julian's is lit up like a beacon of debauchery, the inside of mine is pitch black.

Or it was pitch black until a light inside just flicked on. The windows are one-way glass, so from out here we can't see who's inside, only that someone obviously is.

"Umm…" I side-eye Julian, and he frowns. "Does that have to do with you?"

"No. Who'd be in there? Antonio?"

"I'm not sure." Deep inside my purse, my phone pings with a notification, so I shove a hand in to search for it.

Another black SUV, a Suburban though, pulls up behind the Escalade, the headlights nearly blinding us.

"Ayo, kill the lights!" Julian barks, pushing off the Escalade with a hand shading his eyes.

The driver doesn't listen, only reverses and pulls away after the man in the passenger side gets out.

The same time my fingers close around my phone, I hear Slade ask, "Did you get my messages? I've been blowing you up."

Julian's expressionless face only shakes. "I turned my phone off after I texted you to meet me here."

Is that why we're here? For Slade? Is he going to confront him about what I told him?

The crepe in my stomach threatens to make a reappearance, but I swallow profusely while trying to unlock my phone. First, to check for any new texts from Holter or Mary, then to read the email Irelynn just forwarded me.

"The Mousais," Slade says.

I look up from my phone, finishing, "We got it."

"What?" Julian asks, glancing between us.

"The offer just came through," Slade says. "They fucking want you to perform."

"On the main stage or one of the parties?"

"On the main stage, during the main show, last act of the night. We're closing it out," I answer with a grin.

Ignoring his agent, he asks me, "You did this?" It's all I can do to nod as my feet move on their own accord, leading me right into his open arms.

I did do it. Not only did I get them to agree to my terms of performing with Julian, but I was able to surprise him with the news.

It wasn't all for nothing. Something I did actually matters.

Our mouths meet in blazing intensity, our mutual excitement transferring from one to the other and back.

"Can you believe it? The fucking Mousais," Slade interrupts, gripping Julian's shoulder and shaking it, effectively cutting the kiss short.

Keeping me in the crook of one of his arms, Julian grimaces like he can't stand Slade's touch, and asks him, "Did you accept yet?"

"No, I was waiting to talk to you about it."

"Do it. Accept."

"Right now?"

"Right now." Julian motions at Slade's phone. "And text Axel to get out here, too. I gotta tell him something."

"You didn't even look at the contract," I tell Julian, and he looks me in the eye, asking, "I'm playing with you, right?"

I give him a slow nod.

"Then that's all I need. I'm in."

With Slade staring at his screen, his eyebrows hike up to his slicked-back hairline, but he doesn't comment, just does what Julian told him to. When he's finished, he drops his phone by his side, saying, "Done."

"Good."

"Axel should be out any minute. What'd you want to talk to me about?"

Julian manages to pull me even closer, brushing a tender kiss on my forehead. It's so tender, I tense up, expecting the worst—like a goodbye—but then he replies to Slade, telling him, "You're fired."

It was a goodbye all right, just not to me.

Julian's firing Slade?

Slade rears back, his gaze bouncing between us. "What?"

Axel chooses that moment to appear…from my bus.

"The fuck were you doing on there?" Julian stops to ask him.

The drummer's face splits into a grin as he points a thumb over his shoulder. "I was helping Irelynn…"

That's it. That's all he says.

Julian and I look at each other, and I try my hardest not to laugh. I'm sure he was "helping" my assistant. These Family Julez boys, they are something else.

"What's up?" Axel asks, and Julian nods at Slade.

"Just firing this motherfucker."

Axel freezes in his tracks to do a golf clap, saying, "'Bout damn time, brother. 'Bout damn time."

"Boss man, what the fuck?"

"You heard me. You're fired. Get your ass on that bus, pack up your shit, and fucking go."

Julian fired Slade. Just like that. Someone that's been with him for two years, and knows his schedule, his life, his needs, his everything, he just…fired.

I can't tear my eyes off the scene. It's like watching the northern lights. You know they're real, but you've never seen them for yourself, so when you actually get to, my God, they're fucking glorious. Except in this instance, seeing Slade getting what he deserves is a hundred times more gratifying. If I do get sued by him, this moment right here will make it all worth it, so I make sure to hang off every detail.

To Axel, he says, "Make sure he takes out the rest of the trash when he leaves."

Axel sobers, his voice nearing disbelief. "You want a deep clean? How deep?"

"Fucking deep. I don't wanna see anyone that's been using me or my name when I come back."

"Oh, shit. That's gonna be…" He looks behind him. "Everybody."

"Clear 'em out," is Julian's last order on the matter.

"What?" Slade repeats before getting ahold of himself to pin a glare on me. "Is this about something she—"

"*She* has nothing to do with it," Julian spits, tucking me behind his back to get in Slade's face. "*She* was always supposed to stay out your fucking mouth, but you don't listen."

My jaw begins to lower on its own accord, so I prop it up with a fist.

"You don't know what you're doing."

"Maybe, but I know what the fuck I'm not doing and that's sticking with your ass. I better not see you anywhere near me or Collette again. We're done."

"What about The Mousais? We got—"

Julian gestures between them. "*We didn't get shit.*" Glancing over his shoulder at me, he says, "*We got The Mousais.*"

I step out from behind Julian's cover, standing beside him, and narrow my eyes at Slade. If he even tries to take credit for that, I have receipts just waiting to prove him wrong.

Slade attempts to send me one last glare, but Julian growls out a warning of, "Try me, motherfucker," that has Slade's gaze sinking very quickly.

Axel follows him on to the bus, announcing the party's officially over, then the night air fills with loud, angry protests.

"You know he's stealing something on his way out."

Julian turns to open the Escalade's back door for me, saying, "He can take whatever he wants. I got everything I need right here."

My gaze scours over him, waiting for him to say something else. Something to signify he's joking maybe. But nothing comes.

"Where are we going?"

"To get some new ink."

Julian gets tattoos when he feels strong emotions. What's he feeling right now? Good? Bad? Both?

Stepping up to him so we're toe to toe, I touch my lips to his, gauging how he'll react, and almost instantly, I'm hauled against Julian's front as he deepens the kiss.

He tears his lips from mine, and with a creased forehead, he says, "It's not a tour-mance. Not for me."

A feeling I've never felt before but have always coveted fills my body, starting at my battered heart and rapidly spreading to the rest of me. My fingertips and toes tingle with it until it feels like my body is levitating. It's just an illusion though because I'm not floating at all. I'm falling.

On top of all the other confessions I've given tonight, I give Julian another one by saying, "Me neither."

Chapter 34

Collette

Just over the loud buzzing, I hear Julian ask, "Can I see it yet?"

His impatience never ends.

I shake my head, then stop when the tattoo artist, Finley, pauses to squint at me, the noise halting along with the pain. It's been a while since I've gotten a tattoo, and I forgot how much they hurt. They're kind of like childbirth in that all you remember is the result, not the hours of agony leading up to it.

"No, not until it's done or else it won't be a surprise," I tell Julian. On the way over, I decided to get a tattoo, too. Julian insisted I go first but won't stop trying to catch a peek from the doorway he's been stationed under since Finley started.

"Now stop making me move before you get me in trouble."

Finley speaks up, saying, "Won't be no trouble, miss, but your gems might come out less precious than you'd like."

"Gems?" Julian echoes, and I drop my head back on the tattoo chair, squeezing my eyes shut.

What part of "surprise" do these men not understand?

"Don't tell me you're getting a string of pearls in the palm of your hand," Julian jokes.

The tattoo artist answers him, saying, "Nope. On her wrist."

"Christ's sake. Do you mind?" I mock-scold them both, smothering a grin as my body continues to hum with something that has nothing to do with the alcohol my system's still burning off the last remnants of.

Aside from those two little shots he took in front of me on his bus, Julian's been sober the whole night, but everything about his body language screams the same thing as mine—he's intoxicated, too.

We're drunk on each other right now.

"Sorry, miss," Finley mumbles, his concentration briefly flicking from my wrist to my face.

Julian had to wake him up just to tattoo us at three o'clock in the morning—eight hours before his shop even opens—and while he's been polite and accommodating beyond belief, he has yet to grasp the concept of keeping mine a secret.

"But since Mr. Julez is paying—"

"He's not paying. I am."

"With what?" Julian asks, wielding the credit card he confiscated from me back at the diner.

"I'll get that back one way or another."

I glare at the plastic card before he tucks it back into his pocket, saying, "Don't threaten me with a good time."

"Did you decide what you're getting yet?" I ask, and he simply nods, smirking.

"And…what are you getting?"

He parrots back, "It won't be a surprise," making me groan.

With Julian, it could be anything. On the car ride here, he was talking about getting a radar machine, the automatic kind that tells drivers the speed they're going, and the only explanation he gave for it was that it means something to him.

Finley finally finishes, wiping the smear of ink and blood away with a vicious excuse of a paper towel before inspecting his work. I hold my breath, hoping there're no issues that need fixing because my wrist is on fire. I just paid—Julian just paid—to have a needle prick the thin, tender skin probably thousands of times, if not more. It doesn't help that I got the tattoo directly over the veins, tendons, and arteries there either.

After getting the okay, I hide the irritated skin from Julian on my way to the bathroom, and when I return, he's the one on the chair, his shirt balled up under his head as he reclines lazily.

Mine was easy to keep hidden thanks to Finley's body largely shielding it from view, but Julian's torso is completely exposed.

"Do you want me to wait out there?" I ask, pointing out of the private back room we've been in the last couple hours.

With his lids at half-mast, Julian shakes his head so quickly I almost miss it.

"You want me in here?"

"I want you with me." His rough whisper tickles my spine even from where I'm standing, then one handed, he helps me on to the table to straddle his thighs just above his knees.

Thankfully, the tattoo artist pretends not to notice as he prepares everything.

Julian pulls out the marker he always keeps in his pocket, asking me, "Would you?"

"Would I…what?" I counter, arching an eyebrow at him.

"Would you give me your autograph?"

I start to laugh only to stop when he doesn't so much as crack a smile. "Really? Right now?"

Nodding, he places the marker in my upturned palm. His eyes never stray from mine, and the longer I look into them, the more weight they hold. All of this feels heavy, even me, like my center of gravity just shifted, anchoring me to something other than Earth.

"I guess." I blink. "On what?"

Beside us, Finley pauses what he's doing to stand from his chair, mumbling something about needing to use the restroom.

Julian's colorful hand goes to his chest, drawing my attention away from the abandoned tattoo gun, and he points one long finger at his sternum.

"Julian?" My eyes search his.

"You got your name on your back because you're the only one that's ever had it." His knees bend, sending me forward, and my newly tattooed arm that's been crossed over my front reaches out near his head to catch my weight. "And since you're the only one that's ever had my heart, I want your name on it, too."

My eyes drop to his lips, then to his chest.

"That's not just your heart." The heart lies slightly to the left. I should know, mine's beating against my ribs like a rowdy prisoner desperate to escape from its cell.

"You don't have just my heart." His voice lowers. "I'm so fucking in love with you, Collette."

A million reasons why this is bad spin in my head, trying to find purchase, but I swat them all away to bite the marker's cap between my teeth, pulling it off, then I sign his chest just like I'd sign anything else put in front of me, even crossing the double T's with an exaggerated swipe.

Not once do Julian's eyes move from my face, and when I'm done, I recap the marker, tossing it aside.

I lift my forearm, twisting it to reveal the fresh ink.

"Gems… They look good," he says thoughtfully.

I smirk.

Starting at my wrist where my pulse point is located and extending up the long axis of my arm toward the crook of my elbow, brilliantly colored jewels appear to be spilling out from my radial artery. Finley did an amazing job making it seem realistic with what looks like skin peeled back in certain places.

"They're jewels because this tour changed everything for me," I whisper as my voice cracks, unable to keep my emotions in check. "Head over heels, inside out, I'm so fucking in love with you, too, Julian."

He cups the back of my head, dragging me to him, and our lips lock together like they alone are responsible for sealing our fate. Fleeting kisses don't compare to everlasting ink, but somehow in this moment, that's exactly how it feels.

"Is it safe for me to come back in now?" Finley asks from somewhere outside the door, and chuckling, I try to sit back.

Julian doesn't let me go though, calling out, "You got any cameras in here?"

"No, sir. We offer this room specifically to clients tattooing the more delicate areas for added comfort and privacy away from others, but none of our tables are filmed. The only cameras we have onsite are in the waiting room and outside the front entrance for security purposes."

"Perfect. Give us ten minutes and you can double your fee."

"He's kidding," I say, attempting to wiggle back down Julian's thighs, but his hold on me tightens as he thrusts his growing erection against my center.

"The fuck I am," he says to me, then to Finley, "Ten minutes."

Not needing any other incentive, Finley tells us he'll be outside, taking a smoke break…for ten minutes, then closes the door.

This is crazy. We can't have sex in a tattoo parlor after everything that just happened with Bodee.

I search around the small room. No chance of someone sneaking photos for my ex. No cameras. No blinking lights. No windows. The only mirror is the one above us, so I know it's not a two-way.

We can…but—

The tip of Julian's hard cock straining beneath his jeans hits my clit. We can.

"Ten minutes? You think that's enough?" I tease, biting my bottom lip to stifle a moan. We have to keep this quiet. And quick.

"Are you kidding me? I almost jizzed in my pants watching you sign my chest just now. Stand up."

"On here?"

"On here."

He lifts me up, quickly tugging my pants over my ass and down my legs, then his pants are taken care of next.

"Vegas. Tonight. Let's go."

Tonight? I guess it's technically morning, but still…Vegas? Now?

"There's only one reason people go to Vegas for a night," I say, smirking down at him.

"Keep your feet flat and sit on my cock."

Gripping my thighs, then ass, he helps lower me into a frog position, lining up his rigid cock under my throbbing pussy.

I understand why Julian couldn't wait. I don't want to wait another second to have us joined either. It's like a sickness, but stronger.

Healthier though? Jury's still out.

I've never actually had a romantic relationship that was healthy to know for sure.

Maybe I'm the jury and I alone can decide what I want and don't want. But that's just it, I've been so focused on avoiding what I don't want, I've ignored figuring out what I do want.

I sink down on to his rock-hard length, groaning from the different angle.

This. Today. I want it.

I want Julian.

With his hands clamping my sides, he guides my body up and down his upright cock.

"Oh God," I breathe, dropping my head back to gaze up into the mirror on the ceiling.

Julian lifts his eyes, meeting mine, and together, we watch our bodies move in sync as I ride him slowly. Suddenly overcome with so much emotion, so much love, it takes everything in me not to close my eyes and cry.

"Would you ever? Get married in Vegas?"

The top of my throat exposed to the mirror above us, I study myself swallowing thickly, then Julian. Would I?

If I do get married again, the location doesn't really matter to me as I just want it to be a small, intimate affair without magazines present, or mandatory cell phone collections because we don't trust the attendees not to leak our special day for a quick buck. I want to look like me, with my own hair, and a dress I choose myself instead of getting one from a company for product placement. My first wedding started off a sham. I'm not making the same mistake for my next one.

Julian drives his hips up, the tip of his cock hitting the right place deep inside me at exactly the right angle, causing my lips to tremble around a silent scream. He repeats the move, making me forget where we are entirely, and this scream comes out audible. More than audible. Inescapable.

Finley who?

"You're on my skin, I'm under yours. Today, tomorrow. Vegas, a church. It doesn't matter when or where, mark my words, Collette, you will be my wife."

"Is this a—"

Julian doesn't let up as he continues pistoning into me from below, robbing my ability to finish my sentence.

"A proposal?" He laughs, sitting forward. Wrapping his arms under my armpits, his hands come up to grip the top of my shoulders, pulling me down as he thrusts upward, and he says, "It's a fucking promise."

Everything goes black as my orgasm detonates, unfurling inside me at warp speed, and I barely make out Julian's groan as he comes, his release warm and heady.

While I'm carefully dismounting his cock by shifting my knees to the table one at a time, a dollop of his cum falls out of me on to his lower abdomen. Using two fingers, Julian scoops it up, and with an arm around my back, he draws me into his chest, making my torso arch toward him. The fingers with the cum tease my folds before he pushes both digits between them, then without further prompting, my body starts rocking into his palm. His semi-erect cock is slick against my ass crack, bookending me with hot, wet, continuous stimulation.

"I love you," spills out of him again and again as our noses bump into each other from the deliberately slow motion, then he switches it up, saying, "I'm getting it reversed."

"What…" I pant as his fingers curve, massaging my clit from the inside.

"My vasectomy. I'm getting it reversed after the tour. Imma fill you with all the babies you want."

"Julian," I warn, the familiar inferno ramping up inside me just waiting to explode.

He increases the pressure, whispering, "Imma give you everything you want," against my parted lips, and my entire lower half seizes up, my pussy muscles clamping around his fingers like a vise as I come on his hand.

After a long, searing kiss, Julian rasps, "My queen." Then he helps get us cleaned up and dressed again.

By the time Finley returns, we're in a similar position to the one he left us in with me sitting on top of Julian, our hands restless as we smile into each other's eyes. Our bodies are marked now—forever—and they're done being denied connection.

This tour didn't just change me; Julian did.

His love did.

Chapter 35

Julian

"You seen Collette anywhere?" I ask a passing roadie carrying a tote box, but he just shakes his head.

I stop to look back at where I just came from, scanning the faces now filling the hallway.

Where'd she go?

Shit's been crazy around here lately. When we're not onstage, we're prepping for The Mousais, and when we're not prepping for The Mousais, we're talking about them. We've had meetings around the clock because every tiny detail has to be discussed and agreed on before being discussed and agreed on again. There's no room for fuckups on live TV, at least not on The Mousais' watch. Collette and I have had to deal with photo shoots, video shoots, interviews, rehearsals…all while still traveling and performing our regular sets for The Family Julez Tour. I just got done recording the piano melody of the song we're performing on The Mousais since I won't be playing it live. They don't want us to just do what we've been doing, they want us to do something else entirely. So unfortunately, me and Collette making out on the piano's out.

We've barely had any time to ourselves which is why I'm looking for her now, to squeeze in a few minutes together before tonight's final concert.

As insane as all this has been, I wouldn't want to do it with anyone else.

I finish off my Jell-O, tossing the cup into a trash can as I head toward the dressing rooms, in case she's already in hair and makeup. Instead of barging right in though, I end up hesitating outside the closed door. What if she's talking to Holter? They FaceTime every day, sometimes twice a day, and as much as I wish I could hop on and catch up with him, too, I try to give Collette all uninterrupted time with him as possible. He is her son, even if…I mean, I wish…

I miss him, too.

I lift my hand to knock only to freeze when I hear her voice— I'd recognize it anywhere—except it's not coming from her dressing room. It's coming from…

A quick glance in both directions of the hall, then I'm following her voice like a sailor would a siren's.

The locker room?

I'm leaning against the wall just outside the locker room, listening to her fucking belt Lady Gaga's part in "Shallow" while trying to keep my shit together. Even after all this time, performing with her night after night, her voice still slays me dead.

Some things are unavoidable, like hurricanes in August and peas tasting like shit. Me loving Collette with everything I got falls under the same inevitable category. It was always gonna happen, it just took a while for me to wrap my head around completely. The only other women I've ever loved, died, and I didn't want to risk that. I still don't. But there's a reason why we met, and I'm pretty fucking sure that reason's fate. We're destined to be together.

Fuck. It's still crazy to believe. I'm in love with *The* Collette and she's in love with me. Now *that* I'll admit might've had more to do with luck than fate, considering she's way outta my league.

Her voice trembles, so I push my body off the wall, joining in with Bradley Cooper's part of the shared post-chorus. My voice isn't as croaky as his, but I pull it off as I enter the locker room, dueting with my queen.

Collette's lying on the floor of the large shower space, her back arched off the tiles as she sings for her motherfucking life. Her open eyes catch on mine as soon as I round the corner, and I see they're fucking full of built-up emotion.

What are you doing, Poohbear?

She hits every goddamn note of the bridge and chorus, then we finish it out together with a repeat of the post-chorus.

I fall to my knees beside her, dropping my forehead to her stomach, inhaling her sweet peony scent until my lungs ache. She never lights the candle on her bus, just keeps the lid off, so she always smells like it.

Her hands find my throat, automatically feeling for my pulse.

"What's on your mind?" I muffle against her shirt.

"This."

I rotate my head to the side.

This. Why'd she say it like that? Like what we have—what we are—can be summed up in one word.

"If this was just a tour-mance, I'd have Bruce keep adding dates for the rest of my life so I can stay on tour with you forever."

Her stomach heaves under my ear with a small laugh. "He asked me about staying on for more stops."

I lift my head, looking her in the eye.

"What'd you say?"

She sucks in a breath, and in that one inhalation, I hear what she's been doing a damn good job of hiding—guilt. Fuck. I'm not gonna like this.

"I can't. I already committed to touring with someone else after The Mousais."

Where does that leave us? Does that even leave an us? Or are we really just "this"?

"So what about—"

"I don't know how any of this is supposed to work, Julian. It's going to be a lot of effort and patience on both our ends, and I just… I don't know."

"We'll make it work." We have to. I refuse to accept anything less. Anything less than being with Collette isn't worth having. I already tried it for the first twenty-seven years of my life, I'm not about to go any more without her. Fuck that shit.

She sighs, and I can tell she's thought about it, probably been over it many times in her own head already. Why hasn't she said anything to me then?

"You can't promise that. You can't promise—"

I sit back on my haunches, telling her for what feels like the hundredth time, "Watch me. Tell me you're in, and I'll do whatever it takes, Collette."

"Julian."

"Whatever. It. Takes."

She watches me for a bit, then asks, "What about your…habits?"

Habits? I don't crave alcohol or drugs or anything other than Collette anymore.

I don't crave them as often.

I don't crave them as strongly.

I crave them, but it's…it's hard to explain. It's the edges. They're too sharp sometimes and I need them dulled, just a little, not much.

If I hadn't smoked that J on my way over here, I wouldn't be able to handle this conversation the way I am now. This shit is…

What exactly is this?

"Once the tour ends, it'll be better," I lie, knowing damn well the last time I came off tour, that slingshot out of the spotlight hurt like a motherfucker. To go from too-bright fame to basic anonymity, it's the quickest, strongest, *sharpest* whiplash there is. A comedown—like Collette described. Now that I know what to expect, it probably won't even be as bad this time. I'll just be missing my woman on top of it.

And Holter.

"*I'll* be better," I tell her, praying I'm not lying.

Collette's expression softens, and I swear I see a flash of pity.

"I don't need you to be better, little lamb. I just need you to be you."

"I am. I am me," I tell her, leaning over her pliant body, craving her touch as much as I'm craving another joint. "This is me."

"Now." She runs her fingertip down my nose, over my lips, lifting my chin. "Now you're perfect."

I can't help it, I bend my elbows and steal a kiss. In no reality that's ever existed am I perfect, but fuck if Collette doesn't make me feel like I could be.

I'll do it. I'll stay sober. I was sober before…before I wasn't. It can't be that hard to go back to being sober. If I tried, I'd know that; but that's the problem, I've never fucking tried. I never had a reason to. Now, I have multiple.

"Collette, after tonight's show, let's go to Vegas—"

"No." Her hand falls away, revealing that badass jewel tat she got. "Don't ask that of me right now. Don't ask me to marry you because you're scared of losing me. Ask me to marry you when there's no chance you ever could."

Is she saying there's a chance now? I could *lose* her?

My eyes sting, so I harden my face, hoping it chases away the wetness I feel forming. *Fuck you, tears.* I'm not crying.

Then, for good measure, I call my good ol' friend anger out for an assist.

I'm expected to walk, breathe, *live* a straight fucking line, meanwhile Collette gets to run off, doing whatever tour she wants with whoever the fuck she wants.

"Whose tour is it?"

Her eyes move from mine to the ceiling above us.

"A new girl group. They're big in Belgium and hoping to get some traction in other countries, too, starting with the US."

"Belgium?" I shake my head. "You're just as addicted as I am."

"To what?"

"To touring! Fuck. Isn't it fucking obvious? You agreed to go on tour with me. With *me.*" Thank fuck she did, but it's still a dead giveaway that she don't know what's good for her. "By now you should be choosing your own schedule, headlining your own fucking show, not dropping everything to ride other artists' coattails wherever they tell you to."

"You have no idea what you're talking about." She pushes on my shoulders, sliding out from under me to stand and look down at me—looking down at me 'cause she is the one with the fucking coattails.

She just ignores them to chase her own high of touring as much as possible.

"What about Holter?"

"What about him?" Her hackles rise, warning me away from the subject, but nah, I don't listen for shit either, so I push it, asking, "Is he going with you this time? Are you gonna make him miss out on the chance to play basketball? Or are you leaving him with Mary to open for some unknown girl band America's never even heard of?"

I'm not the only addict here. I'm just the only one willing to admit it.

Pain makes its way across Collette's face so plainly, my body rocks forward, and I wish I could take it back. Anger's so deceiving. It never helps me in the ways I need, only in the ways I think I want.

"Holter is none of your business."

I jolt to my feet, meeting her eyes to admit, "I love Holter, too, Collette." I knew I did, but was struggling to accept it because my love…it kills.

You can't fight destiny, just like I can't knock fate.
If love were a choice, I swear I'd pick hate.

I tried to, I swear. Hate didn't take for either of them though, and now I love them both, more than I've ever loved anyone.

"You do?" she asks, her spine softening a fraction.

"Yeah. I'd do anything for either of you." Didn't I prove that when Bodee appeared out of nowhere, involving Holter in his random flex of power?

Nothing about it seemed random at the time though.

Was it random?

I study Collette's suddenly blank expression.

"The Mousais are what set Bodee off, huh? He found out somehow?"

The sudden subject change doesn't even faze her. Almost like she's been anticipating this. No, not almost. She has been expecting this.

Goddamn it. She's still hiding things from me.

"He knew I was in talks to perform, yes. He demanded I turn it down."

"Why?"

"Why is he always trying to stop my success? Because he doesn't have a hand in it anymore."

I remember what DJ Arique said about not being able to work with Collette directly.

"He's still got a hand in it," I mutter to myself, but Collette hears it and nods.

Bodee's been determining who Collette can and can't work with her entire career to keep her right where he wants her—just successful enough for him to be credited for his discovery of her, but not enough to surpass him or his influence.

But…that doesn't mean Collette hasn't been able to find her own success. She has. Even before The Mousais, she's gotten other big gigs just by herself, and he never reacted like this. It still doesn't make sense why he went so hard now.

"Did he know your talks included me being up there with you?" It can't be a coincidence that only hours before we got confirmation I'd be performing with Collette—a feat Collette alone is responsible for pulling off—Bodee showed up trying to nix the whole thing.

"He didn't mention your name, but he has an inside source, so I don't know what all information he was privy to. It's possible."

That's it. That's the missing piece to this whole puzzle. Bodee found out I'd be performing alongside Collette, and he didn't just want recognition for his ex-wife's accomplishment, he wanted *all* the recognition. With Collette and I not only singing together but also being together, he wouldn't have gotten it. He'd still be mentioned for sure, but not necessarily accredited. To get that, he'd need to remind everyone of Collette's origin story, and what could do that better than the child they made while they were together?

"He's still got a hand on *you*," I say painfully, because that hand wouldn't have had the means to pull any of this bullshit if I hadn't put Collette in potentially scandalous situations to begin with.

Collette doesn't bother denying it, only saying, "And until Holter turns eighteen, he'll continue to."

Even if she's right and Bodee did decide to leave her alone then, that's over four years off. For four more years, she's just gonna keep touring her ass off with anyone who'll have her, missing out on everything she wants, everything Holter wants, everything I'm offering her?

And she's just gonna *let* Bodee keep that level of control over her and her career?

"Why didn't you agree? You could've. It wasn't a done deal yet. So, why didn't you walk away when Bodee told you to?" Her ex threw everything he had at her, and she still didn't cave.

"Because I wanted you to be able to experience what's been kept from me."

"You didn't have to. That's not your job."

She laughs a bitter sort of laugh, and I already know I'm not gonna like what's next.

"Isn't it though? That's why I was hired for The Family Julez Tour…to improve your image."

Called it. I don't just not like what she said, I fucking hate it.

"Which they got right. It worked. You're performing at The fucking Mousais. It doesn't get any better than that, Julian. Your label will have no choice but to listen to your ideas now."

I was half-joking about extending this tour. I want to stay on tour with Collette, but I don't want to stay on *this* tour with her. This tour is controlled by the record label I've been trying to get out from under for the past two years. No matter what I've fucking done, how far I've taken things, I can't get them to drop me.

I shake my head, telling her, "You weren't hired for that. I requested you."

"You never considered why they agreed?"

I don't answer. I can't. I'd do something like cry, but it wouldn't be a sad cry, it'd be an angry cry. I'm that fucking pissed off right now.

"You label wants you, and they've proven they'll do anything to keep you."

Shit, if that's true, then I'm as fucked as Collette is with Bodee. Neither of us will ever be free.

"Let's just get through tonight, so we can focus on The Mousais," she soothes, her tone along with her body language transforming before my eyes. Her lips even spread into a smile for the first time since I entered the locker room, but it's forced, fake. Placating. She's placating me just like all the others used to do.

I recognize it for what it is now. I know the reason behind it, too—to keep the ticking time bomb from blowing everything up.

"Yeah. The Mousais," I make myself say, grabbing her hands to kiss her middle finger, the one she used on me that first day, then the pointer finger with the music note tattooed on it.

Her silence started as a choice, but it's turning into a death sentence.

I've killed every person I've loved. This time, the only person I'm killing…

Is myself.

Chapter 36

Collette

Julian and I walk the red carpet at The Mousai Awards side by side, stopping every couple steps for the long row of press, posing the same way we did in our now infamous billboard shots—with my hand over his crotch and my back to the cameras while I gaze into Julian's eyes. Sticking with the jewel-tone aesthetic from The Family Julez Tour, I'm wearing a floor-length backless emerald gown that has high-reaching slits up both thighs, and long sleeves. I did ask the designer to cut one of the sleeves though to display my new tattoo, so technically it only has one long sleeve. On top of waves of midnight-blue hair falling down my chest sits a crown, the one Julian gave me.

Meanwhile, Julian's in a well-fitted white tux with matching emerald-green lapels, pocket square, and lining, and he left the shirt that came with it off entirely so his tattoo of my signature is also showing from under his unbuttoned jacket. His tips are freshly dyed a deep blue, too, making us look like rock-and-roll royalty.

Unfortunately, it doesn't feel that way.

Or maybe everybody walking these things feels like a fraud. It's hard to say because I only know what's happening inside my own head, and right now, it's a wreck.

Every time Julian and I pause to get photographed, our eyes lock on each other's like they normally would, but something's off. Even half tuned in, I can feel it. Holter hasn't arrived yet, and just like whenever I'm on tour without my son, I'm counting down the minutes until I see him in person again. Bodee always makes an entrance, and this place will swell up like a tidal wave when he does, so I've been paying close attention to the spikes in energy around us while still trying to sell this happy, put-together image to the press and surrounding crowds.

The Family Julez Tour wrapped three nights ago, then we took the red-eye here immediately after. Since the moment we landed in LA, it's been one thing after another. In between back-to-back rehearsals, it's been dress fittings and promo shoots, both requiring full hair, makeup, and nails each and every time. The barrage of colors, fabrics, mic checks, and blinding flashes have left little time for me and Julian to follow up on our conversation regarding our relationship.

The first time either of us even got a break that matched up with the other's was when we climbed into the limo to come here. The ride over was the longest stretch of silence we've had in the past two weeks, but there was nothing relaxing about it. It was tense and unnerving, and I hated it. Julian's usually loud, boisterous, and wild. Tonight, he's distracted. And it feels like he's been distracted ever since our last private conversation together.

Eventually, we come to the end of the carpet, meeting up with Irelynn along with Julian's newly hired assistant, Tomás, who are both already waiting for us. We step off to the side, and our stylists immediately rush over to poke, and smooth, and fluff, and tuck while Axel finishes up his walk along the step-and-repeat behind us. As soon as he joins us, his hand brushes the back of Irelynn's, causing her to blush a deep crimson color that rivals the carpet we just traipsed across.

Neither of them has admitted to being together, and I have to wonder if it's because what they have is an actual tour-mance.

I peek at Julian, but his focus is still elsewhere. At least I know he's sober right now.

I'm almost positive he's sober.

Obviously, logistics is my biggest concern for our relationship, but Julian's sobriety is a *close* second. Maybe even tied for first truthfully.

I have a child, an impressionable teen that I'm trying to raise into a good man. The only father figure he's had, the only father figure I've been able to give him, is not who I want my son to take after. Getting involved with Bodee was an unfortunate mistake, but one I can't take back. All I can do now is make sure I don't do it again. Mistakes are lessons disguised as hardships, and as hard as mine was to make, I'd like to think I've learned from it.

Since we've been together, really together, Julian's been amazing, not just to me, but also to Holter and the rest of my team that feels like family. He's really cleaned up his act. He fired Slade, and he got rid of all the remoras.

The question running on a continuous loop through my head now is, will it last? Because I remember the person Julian was before we were together, and every time things didn't go his way, he disappeared under a cloud of marijuana smoke or into the bottom of a bottle. Or more accurately, both. He's pretty liberal with his substance intake.

It won't just be different once he's not on tour anymore, it'll be worse. During tour, we were in our own little solar system where we were wrapped up solely in each other, letting our love warm us thoroughly, but after tonight, the galaxy's about to open up, showing us how cold the bite of reality actually is.

Parenthood, relationships, they don't always go according to plan, and that's exactly what he'd be signing up for with me. In one fell swoop, he'd get it all—a girlfriend and her kid. A family essentially. I'm not expecting him to be Holter's dad, but he would be an important part of my son's life, and with that comes a certain amount of responsibility. Responsibility Julian knows nothing about. Responsibility he's only glimpsed in small doses so far.

As a songwriter, Julian's really good with words, and he's almost got me convinced he could do it. He says he does want kids with me, that as long as his vasectomy reversal works, he'll keep me pregnant until I decide I'm done having babies, and yet, that prospect still scares me as much as it excites me, maybe more.

I tour. It's what I know, it's what I do. I have no plans to stop, or even slow down anytime soon.

I want to.

Julian makes me want to even more.

But I'm not sure I can. I don't know *how* to not be on the road constantly.

Just like I don't know how to stop loving, wanting, and needing Julian.

"Julez! Collette! Give us a smooch!" a photog shouts at us.

Julian's smile doesn't reach his eyes as he gives me a peck just long enough for the cameras to capture. When he starts to pull away, I bite down on his bottom lip, forcing him to meet my gaze head-on.

What's going on with him? Is he having reservations, too? Or are they just mine reflecting back at me?

All the attention suddenly surges in the other direction, toward a commotion on the other side of the carpet, and I don't have to look to know that Bodee Keys just arrived.

Julian's top lip lowers on to mine the same time his hands cup my ass, pressing us so tightly together oxygen couldn't sneak between us, then he's kissing me roughly to the point that I let out an involuntary moan. Neither of us closes our eyes, the otherwise silent exchange filled with more feeling than I thought possible in such a public setting.

Releasing me all at once, he rushes out, "I love you, Collette. I love you. No matter what happens tonight, just remember that I love you and I'll always fucking love you."

"I love you, too, but what's going to—"

His focus shifts over his shoulder, so I follow his line of vision to see Bodee disembark his limo followed by Holter. Holter spots me immediately, then pulls a face like he's unhappy in his black and white tuxedo. Tears pool at the corners of my eyes at the sight though. It's not his first time in a tux as I've brought him to many award shows as my guest before, but he's become such an incredibly mature young man, all without me being around to witness the transition in its entirety.

Beside Holter, Bodee oozes a flawlessness only obscene wealth can buy. All the reservations in the world couldn't have prepared me for what Bodee ended up putting me through. Drugs weren't his addiction. Power was. Not power among the people in his life, power *over* the people in his life. The closer you were to him, the tighter the hold on your collar he wanted to have.

Julian's right, Bodee does still have a hold on mine.

Bodee believes I'm his dog. Julian believes I'm his queen. I simultaneously feel like both and neither. While my crown is physical, my collar leashed to Bodee is only psychological, and yet neither one feels like it belongs. The weight each carries is heavy. One's holding me back while the other…is currently refusing to meet my eyes after a profound declaration of love.

What just happened? Better yet, what's about to happen? I can feel the unease in Julian as he stares at Bodee.

"Julian?" I ask, pulling his face to mine. "What's going to happen tonight?"

A mask, one I've never seen him wear before, falls over his face, and he forces the saddest grin to ever exist as he says, "I'm getting you the keys to the kingdom." Then he's pulling me after him, on to the red carpet again, not even letting me process what keys to the kingdom could possibly stand for. Did he buy us a house? And why does it look like he's gunning for Bodee?

Is he taking us over to him? To fight him? What's going on right now?

"Hey, Julian…" I say, glancing at my ex as he pretends not to notice our advance. "We'll just see them inside." This is literally what Bodee wanted, to garner copious amounts of praise and adoration by simply walking the red carpet with Holter…by himself. If I rob him of that by crashing his grand appearance, I don't know how he'll retaliate.

And if Julian throws a punch…

He can't throw a punch. Not here. Not now. Julian got lucky during their previous fight. If it was in a setting as public as this…like I told Julian, nobody goes after Bodee Keys and lives to tell the tale.

The very reason why Bodee let me, he's now threatening to take away if I don't give him this moment.

The invisible collar around my throat tightens, making it hard to breathe. What if Bodee sends that email?

Julian stops to murmur near my ear, "He wants everyone talking about him, right? *This* will get everyone talking."

Without waiting for a response, he walks us right up to Holter, not Bodee.

At least that's something.

"Hey, man. You get taller since you've been gone?" he asks with the first genuine smile he's managed in days before enveloping my son in a hug, and while my collar eases slightly, the crown's weight on my head increases.

I'm torn between two lives, two worlds—who I've been and who I want to be, who I've been with and who I want to be with.

The heat of Bodee's stare on the side of my face burns as if the sun itself was bearing down on me, so I can tell every time it moves from Holter and Julian to me, and back again.

"Bodee," I greet with a fake smile, leaning in for an even faker hug from him. "How was the flight here? Everything went well, I hope."

The amount of cameras aimed at us doubles as more photographers sprint over, wanting to capture the moment, and we hold each other at arm's length like two best friends reuniting at long last while ignoring the screamed, desperate pleas for each of us—any of us—to look directly into a lens—any lens.

With his eyebrows raised, he bows his head just so to make his lips less readable. "Just a bit of unexpected turbulence."

Julian and Holter separate, then I'm wrapped in a bear hug as well from my teen son who just might've grown taller since I last saw him.

"Hey, you."

His body relaxes against mine as he breathes, "Hey, Mom."

My eyes fill with tears all over again, and the words "I'm sorry" sneak out like a whisper in the night—pointless yet monumental. While they probably mean nothing to him, they mean everything to me because I am sorry. I'm as sorry now as I am any other time I'm away from him for long stretches of time. I'm also sorry he has a father I don't trust to be alone with him. Most of all, I'm sorry I can't figure out a way to fix any of it.

We're just pulling apart when Bodee brushes past me, saying quietly, "You will be," before summoning someone official looking over to him to whisper something in the woman's ear.

"Let's all get some pictures together," Julian suggests with a cunning smirk toward Bodee.

My ex doesn't bat an eye, saying, "Great idea," his arms out wide in invitation because make no mistake, this is his world. He's only allowing us to visit it.

Together, we awkwardly shift into a pose comprised of all four of us, but I don't bother with a smile as I stare ahead, letting my eyes unfocus to the tumult around me and on me and in me. Is this what a dog chasing its own tail feels like?

Maybe Bodee was the one that had it right all along.

Chapter 37

Julian

"There must be a mistake," Collette tells the usher even though the paper on the seat clearly reads "Bodee Keys." Collette and I were here last night until eleven o'clock practicing, and these same seats were for Collette, Holter, and me. Now though, they're labeled for Collette, Holter, and Bodee.

Apparently, the three of them will be sitting together in the front row while I'm...

I mentally count the rows to where my name's now posted.

Twelve. Twelve rows back.

I'm performing on the main stage tonight, and they decided to seat me twelve rows back—otherwise known as the fucking nosebleeds of these types of award shows—at the last minute.

That motherfucker.

Bodee comes up, asking like he didn't have a hand in this, "Is something wrong, Collette?"

"We're just waiting for Julian's seat—"

"Julez?" Bodee cuts her off while giving me a look that shows me he forgot I beat his ass once before. "Need help finding the way *back* to your seat?"

Back.

See, I had to search around to know where my seat was, but Bodee walked up already knowing.

This is his payback for my little stunt outside. That's fine, good even. I want him rattled, just not near Collette and Holter, especially if I'm not around.

He already got a little too close to Collette when greeting her. I don't care if it was for the cameras, Bodee shouldn't be allowed to touch her ever again. Or any woman. If he encourages rape of others, there's no way he's honorable enough not to do it himself, too. Dude don't have honor; he's got a death wish, and I can't wait to fucking fulfill it.

I eye his jawline, then temple. Only two hits and I'd end this cockroach disguised as a country star. I wanna throw down with him right now so fucking bad, but I can't. That's anger trying to take over, and I gotta be smart about this.

How am I supposed to keep Collette and Holter safe from twelve rows away though?

"I'm not sitting without you," Collette says to me before checking around my newly assigned seat, looking for someone to trade spots with.

She ain't sitting in the nosebleeds though, not because of me, and sure as fuck not because of Bodee Keys. His reign over her ends tonight.

"You won't." I give her a soft peck, then sit in the seat reserved for her. With a smirk, I tell her, "Your throne awaits," gesturing to my lap.

"Thirty seconds," blasts through the auditorium's speakers. "Clear the front, please. Thirty seconds."

"Mr. Julez, if you'll please follow me."

Neither of us acknowledge the usher as I help get Collette comfortable on the tops of my thighs without the slits in her dress flashing anybody what's underneath.

"Twenty seconds. Clear the front. Twenty seconds."

All settled, Collette glances at the awkward, obviously-not-paid-enough-for-this-shit usher, daring him to argue first, then Bodee.

My smile reappears, growing wider. Damn. Glad to see her with some of that spark again. Ever since Bodee blindsided her at the beach, she hasn't been completely herself, at least not the version I've seen all tour.

"Thanks, man. We're all set here," I tell the usher, and he finally moves to leave, plucking the folded twenty from my fingers as he goes.

Holter drops into the seat next to us, and chuckles. "You guys are crazy. The people behind you can't even see the show."

Collette mumbles, "Which one?"

On the other side of Holter, Bodee's talking with another country singer, and he lets out an obnoxious-as-all-fuck laugh that's so fake it should come with a warning label from the FDA.

"Ten seconds!"

Even busy memorizing the feel of Collette's back pressed to my chest and her ass split over my cock, I still notice the way everyone around us is breaking their necks to gawk at our untraditional position. Everyone I catch, I nod at, watching their eyes fall over me suspiciously before moving to Collette seated on top of me. I don't know what the fuck their problems are honestly. The worst of my tats are covered by my sleeves, and I'm not even being graphic despite the smell of my girlfriend's pussy reaction to my cock being so close is tempting the absolute *fuck* out of me right now.

Whatever. They better get a good look while they can 'cause after this, I ain't coming back. I won't be allowed.

A shot of something that feels like adrenaline but sadder runs through my veins.

I ignore the way it makes my muscles ache, and taking a deep breath, I try to focus on Collette and Holter's hands clasped together on top of my wrist, hoping it'll warm me straight through and burn off whatever the hell's invading my body.

The program begins with the host's long-winded introduction, then a follow-up performance from a punk rock band, but all I can think about is how bad I want to rotate my arm and hold on to both Holter and Collette—forever.

More of that feeling fills my limbs, curling my fingers around the armrests until my knuckles turn white and my veins bulge.

I can't back out. This is the only way to free both of us, all of us, including Holter. His dad's a loser. A fucking criminal. More so than me even.

Most of the drugs I do are legal.

According to Collette, Bodee's fucked over at least half the people in here. He should be getting the same heat I am right now, but because I appear dangerous, I'm the one attracting all the attention.

Right? That's why they're looking at us?

At the next commercial break, I zero in on all the stares aimed in our direction, watching them after they move from me to Collette… to Bodee. The thing is, they don't just stay as curious stares once they reach him though. They morph into disgusted sneers.

If they all hate him so much, why don't they do anything about it? Because he's got judges in his back pocket? Because he's got the kind of pull to change the seating chart at the biggest award show in music history at the last fucking second?

Yeah to both. A big fucking yeah.

Everybody has something they're afraid of losing, and Bodee's sick enough to capitalize on those fears for his own personal gain.

Like Collette. She has the power to destroy Bodee, but she refuses to pull the trigger. In her mind, guns ruin people on both ends, and she's got too much to lose to even try.

But I don't. After we leave here, Collette will take off for her next tour, Holter will return home with Mary, and I'll have exactly what I started out with—nothing.

The cameras start rolling again, and the host announces the next presenters, then two A-list movie stars who dabble in musicals cross the stage to introduce the nominees for the Best Country Album, and to nobody's surprise, Bodee's ugly face appears as one of the nominees. I swear he's grandfathered into that shit or something. I can't remember a year he hasn't been nominated.

Now if he's gonna win or not…I don't know. His latest album was pure shit, but he does have someone around here by the balls, so maybe.

I still hope he loses. I'll legit cheer.

"And the award goes to…" one says before both presenters yell into the mic, "Bodee Keys!"

The devil works hard, but Bodee Keys works harder.

Bodee lumbers to his feet, acting all stunned and shit, then he pulls Holter up into a dramatic hug. After stretching that out for ten seconds too long, he hesitates in front of us, staring down at Collette. She tenses on my lap, or I tense under her, I don't know, but if he reaches for her right now, I'll kill him because while Bodee Keys might work harder than the devil, I love harder than anyone. That's why it's so goddamn lethal.

The cameraman that'd been kneeling in front of Bodee to get his reaction rotates his camera our way, so now he's picking up the exchange between the infamous exes.

Collette manages to say, "Congratulations, Bodee," without adding, "for buying another award for yourself, you dirty piece of shit," because she's a true professional.

Since I'm not though, I straight up meanmug the bastard on his way past.

The cameraman remains where he is, and at first, I assume it's to get Holter's expression during his dad's fake-ass acceptance speech, but instead, Collette's face appears on both the giant screens hanging above the stage.

What the fuck?

Her smile wobbles when she catches sight of herself onscreen until I nudge her out of view by pretending to rearrange my legs under hers.

They cut to Bodee at the podium, and he thanks the crowd, holding a hand to his heart like he's touched.

"Thank you. Thank you." He waits for the applause to die down. "I'm always honored to receive recognition for all of my accomplishments. Just as I'm honored to have helped so many others achieve their own."

His eyes land on Collette, and again, her face comes up on the screens for everyone to see. *This sick fuck.*

Collette turns her gaze on Holter, trying to play it off like that's what Bodee's referring to, but it's obvious as shit what he means. He helped Collette get here.

"When you're as blessed as I am, it's important to pay it forward. I'm happy to announce one of those kindnesses *finally* came to fruition tonight as Collette, who got her start as my opener after I hand selected her, prepares to perform here, onstage, for the first time ever."

The crowd goes crazy, as they should. It is a fucking achievement, no matter how Collette got her start.

With the cameraman trained on Collette's profile, I wait for the screens to switch from Bodee to her before quietly telling Holter, "Might wanna look away." I grip Collette's jaw and bring her lips to mine. My tongue massages hers as I wrap my other arm around her middle, holding her tight, and she responds beautifully, opening up for me just like she always does. I don't have to look to know our kiss is being broadcast to the live audience as well as the viewers at home, so I close my eyes and enjoy it.

If Bodee wants to take anything from Collette—the son she alone birthed and raised or the credit for the career she built and maintained herself—he can come down here and try, because I already got a bullet with his name on it, and unlike everyone else in this room, I ain't gun-shy.

Echoes of Bodee's throat clearing into the microphone do nothing to cover the snickers, whistles, claps, or catcalls, and I'd bet my right nut he wasn't banking on that happening.

I finish the kiss with Collette, only pulling back an inch to breathe her in while Bodee wraps up his self-centered speech.

"Don't leave me before you even leave me," she says, and I open my eyes, finding hers drowning in tears, the show on another commercial break.

"I'm already gone, Collette." Because *she's* the best, most important part of me, and she's already made her plans…not one of them involving me.

Out of the corner of my eye, I see her hand lift, but I'm quick to catch it with mine, not letting her touch my throat.

"We were always on borrowed time, remember?" I tell her. "Isis couldn't keep Osiris with her for long."

The thirty-second warning sounds just as Bodee breezes by us, and Collette turns, her eyes tracking his every step.

She says, "I've already been to hell once. I'll come find you."

I'm a liar, I lie my ass off, and normally, I do it without a lot of consideration about what it does to the people I'm lying to, but after hearing Collette lie to me…I might have to stop that shit. Lying fucking hurts. It causes other feelings to crop up, like hope, and that's just cruel. Even if she tried to come find me after this, I wouldn't let her.

I watch Bodee shake hands with the people closest to his seat, and tell Collette, "Let's just focus on the performance."

With more bitterness than the first time she said it, she responds with, "Which one?"

We don't talk again after that, not even when categories for pop and rap come and go without either of our albums mentioned—which we knew but it still doesn't feel good to see—until eventually a producer finds us, letting us know it's time to head backstage to change outfits and get ready for our performance. But as soon as we stand to say goodbye to Holter, Collette's body tenses, her gaze locked on something over his head.

"Come with us," leaves her mouth in a rush.

Holter frowns. "On the stage?"

"Backstage. I won't be able to see you."

He takes in our surroundings. "I'm literally in the front row, Mom."

"He's fine, blondie. Leave him."

Even with his hands weaved in front of his mouth, I can see Bodee's face get this smug expression on it. What kind of fuckery did he pull now?

On the short list of things Collette's actually afraid of, Bodee's at the top followed closely by his right-hand man. Luckily, John Davies is supposed to be out of the country until tomorrow.

Throwing around a quick glance just in case, I search the sea of tuxes for anyone with a nasty scar, but all these douchebags sporting sky-high hair plugs look alike. No visible scars as far as the eye can see. Too much makeup hiding the imperfections.

I don't know why Collette's freaking out and I don't need to. This is better anyway because my original plan involved Bare being nearby, but he's currently seated by the back doors with the rest of the bodyguards. It's a good idea, keeping all the beef next to the entrances...until you realize the evil's already inside.

"Come on, man," I say to Holter, sticking a hand out to him. "Your mom's right. We need you up there with us. You're our good luck charm."

He looks from my hand to my face, asking, "Are you guys gonna make out again?"

"It's yinz. Are *yinz* gonna make out again."

We both laugh as I pull him to his feet, then I offer for him and his mom to go ahead of me so I can keep an eye out. If John is in here, I hope the motherfucker's got a seat close by because if what I'm about to do doesn't kill him, I'll do it myself.

It's pitch black except for my lighter's flame as I hold it to the tip of the blunt between my lips causing weak murmurs from the audience below to break up the silence. Inhaling, I pocket the lighter, then remove my black suit jacket, dropping it by my feet. I roll the sleeves of my black dress shirt up, one arm at a time, all the way to my elbows, before undoing the top three buttons at my chest. This isn't how we rehearsed it, but if I'm doing this, I'm doing it my way.

I remove the blunt from my lips to ash that shit on the floor, blowing out a huge cloud of smoke over my head.

Behind me, Collette's breathing increases as she tries to build up her frame before the apparatus strapped to her yeets her body diagonally at thirty miles an hour.

I hear my cue and perch down directly on top of my floor marker, picking up my mic while twisting the lit tip of my blunt into the hardwood until it dies out.

"What are you doing?" Collette hisses, but the next words I say are into the mic as I freestyle in front of millions of people…live.

Luckily, production agreed to let me switch up the intro, spitting a rap acapella before the song actually starts. All I had to do was give them the lyrics beforehand so they could make sure they weren't explicit or offensive in any way.

Collette has no idea.

And honestly, neither do I, because the lyrics I gave them aren't the ones I'm using. They were only a decoy to get approval.

I'm making this shit up on the spot.

The spotlight aimed at me and only me flicks on after my first line, and I keep going, bobbing as the energy churns inside me, looking for its way out. I'm not used to staying still while rapping—I like to fucking rock—but this is different. This one's full of emotion, too, just not the crazy, jump-around-the-stage, smashing-shit kind. It's everything I'm thinking, everything I'm feeling. As I think the words, I say the words, and soon I'm rapping so fast, bobbing so fast, my shadow beneath me practically vibrates.

On the last line, I feel a huge shift, like all my energy finally found its escape, and I fall forward, landing on my knees, my head hanging low.

Fuck.

The light cuts off, and through my gasping, I hear Collette hiccup.

Before I miss my next mark, I shove to my feet, taking the choreographed three steps back to find Collette in the dark.

"Julian." Her whisper grips my heart, squeezing.

Did she like it? Hate it? Did she understand it? It was the first goodbye I've been able to give. Because of my music, the women I love usually get ripped away before I can give one. Since I'm the one doing the killing this time, I wanted to make sure my music was the goodbye. Before Collette, it was the only thing keeping me alive, so I guess it's my goodbye to them both.

Music's vital to me, but performing it isn't. Not the way I've been forced to anyway, because that's not for me, that's for others, and the moment my label took away any choice I had over its distribution, it no longer felt like a gift at all. It felt like it was being sold for cheap entertainment, like *I* was being sold for cheap entertainment—like a whale being kept in an animal theme park. A pool is not a substitute for the ocean. It's a prison with a shiny surface to hide the forced isolation.

Tonight, I'm finally breaking out.

We get in position just as the spotlight comes on to shine on us both, then she sings while we stare into each other's eyes. Hers are red with tears stuck to her extra-long lashes, while mine are closed up tight, hiding my next surprise.

The rigging jerks her from my loose hold, up and behind me to the other side of the stage, and I pivot, facing the crowd to sing alone while members of the stage crew hustle in the darkness to pull Collette down and secure her foot under one of the footholds sticking out of the hardwood flooring. Even knowing what's coming, my body blindly senses Collette's every move, wanting to go to her, wanting to call this whole thing off.

But I can't.

The stage goes dark, and another three steps back with three additional to the left, then I'm with her again, pretending to hold her. I can't actually hold her for this to work and I can't be the one to catch her either. *Not that I ever could.* I have to let her be free.

I have to let her be free.

Our spotlight flashes on, and we sing our verse together, except Collette's foot accidentally slips out from under the foothold keeping her grounded before planned, and she goes flying out of my "hold" early.

Automatically, I reach out because my body does still call to hers, but just as quickly, Collette pulls her hand clear of mine, hitting her notes perfectly despite the sudden, unexpected pressure on her diaphragm. Always the performer. Always on point. She was made for this life.

She can recover from anything, while I swallow handfuls of pills hoping I won't.

That's why it has to be me. I knew that. I know that.

Collette gets moved to her next spot okay, and going even more off-script, I walk right for her, bringing the spotlight with me.

The crew members are supposed to unhook the carabiners from the harness around her middle so we can finish the song standing together, but I get there before they can, forcing them to scatter away from the light. Leaving the carabiners attached, I wrap my free arm around Collette for real this time, my palm flat against her tight white bodysuit as I press her body to mine.

Other than her eyes going wide, there's nothing else she can do, so she sings and I sing and we sing until the very last note of the final verse, then I pull her free of the foothold, and with one last searing gaze into her silver-green eyes, I take her mic, and let go, sending her airborne.

"No!"

Her natural blonde hair blowing out around her shocked face, Collette disappears from sight, and I face the audience as they sit frozen, trying to decide if that was part of the choreography or if something went wrong.

"Bodee Keys sleeps with underage girls, and his manager, John Davies, is a rapist." My deep voice booms, putting an end to any shy, awkward applause. "Together, they coordinated a rape on a woman who was not only sleeping, but also pregnant." I have to pause for the gasps of outrage. "They avoid going to jail because when Bodee Keys isn't setting up sexual assaults, he's blackmailing and paying people off to get what he wants. Members of the academy of this show, judges, people *everywhere* are in Bodee's back pocket, giving him the freedom to do whatever he wants to whoever he wants without—"

My mic shuts off, my spotlight goes black, and I'm pretty sure they cut the feed because I can hear a shit-ton of production members storm the stage, ranting.

Under the cover of darkness somebody screams, "He swindled fifteen thousand dollars from me for a fake business venture!"

A woman calls out, "He roofied my friend!"

About a dozen or so other female voices speak up, saying, "Mine, too!"

Damn. He's even worse than I thought.

Someone in the crowd chants, "Arrest Bodee Keys!" and it spreads like wildfire, the entire auditorium repeating it over and over again.

Some of the overhead lights slowly start to grow brighter, so I spin around to face where Collette went, knowing she can see me. I make a gun with my hand one last time, putting it up to my temple instead of under my chin, then I pull the fucking trigger.

On the outside, me and Collette are different. On the inside though, we're the exact same. We're both junkies, searching for the next high that'll hopefully mute the pain. Whether it's for a night, a week, a lifetime, we both crave that escape so bad, we put it above all else, even when we know we shouldn't. Hers is touring, mine is the kind of mental oblivion only drugs and alcohol can provide. And since neither of us is willing to give up that escape completely, the cause of the pain will continue to haunt us. To rule us.

But I just took out both our ghosts—my career as well as Bodee's, so now she alone holds the keys to the kingdom, and she's free to run it however the fuck she wants.

Collette never needed a king to prosper, I only cleared the way for her to.

Chapter 38

Collette

He didn't. He couldn't.
He could. He did.
Why did he?

There's no way Bodee's going to let Julian get away with this, and there's even less of a chance his record label will either. He…

He did it knowing that. His actions leading up to this moment prove it, including him putting a figurative gun up to his head afterward. Julian just committed career suicide.

"It'd have to be the fuckup to end all fuckups," he'd said when I asked if there was a way for him to get out of his record deal.

Did it have to be *this* fuckup? Those were not his secrets to tell. And in front of Holter no less.

I can't believe Julian did this. And sending me six feet in the air beforehand? I never would've let him go after Bodee.

God, if what those women said is true though… If Bodee is drugging women…

I know Bodee orchestrated a sexual assault against me, but I have no way of knowing if he's done the act himself. Him drugging women… whether it's for Jack or himself, it doesn't really matter. Julian's right, Bodee should be in jail.

And I should've gone after Bodee myself a long time ago to ensure he was.

"Julez!"

Oh no.

The stage is mostly cloaked in shadows still, but one spot in particular is lit up well enough for me to make out Bodee tackle Julian from the side. The two men immediately fall to the floor, wrestling and throwing brutal punches at one another.

Bodee just attacked Julian—publicly. Not just publicly, but onstage at The Mousais. What is he thinking?

He's not thinking. Bodee Keys is not thinking right now, which means he's sloppy, more likely to make mistakes.

"Mom! What's happening?" Holter yells, running over.

"Pull on my foot," I tell him. The people responsible for helping me down during the performance are currently trying to break up Julian and Bodee's fight, leaving me stranded while being pulled in two different directions.

Oh, the fucking irony.

"Is what Julian said true? Or what the others said? Did Dad do—"

"Holter, just help me get out of this, okay? One thing at a time." I can't confirm the other allegations revealed against Bodee tonight, but I can't dismiss them either. As far as what Bodee did to me, now is not the place or time for a discussion I never even planned on having with my son.

With Holter's help, my toes finally skim the floor, and together we manage to get one carabiner unhooked. As more bodies fill the stage, someone bumps into Holter's shoulder, causing him to release his hold on me, and without my foot wedged under anything, I'm hoisted back up into the air, only one carabiner supporting my weight this time. Without the counteracting pull from having both straps attached, I'm now eight feet off the floor, dangling by one side of my hip.

Shit.

I survey the stage's perimeter, searching for a ladder or anything tall enough for me to reach.

"I heard you were into knifeplay these days, but restraints, too?" I hear below me, and freeze. *Oh God, no.* He can't be. I thought I saw a glimpse of him earlier, but he couldn't. He just couldn't.

Except he is. Jack is standing directly beneath me, staring up at me as his gaze touches on my chest, then the rest of my torso, taking in the harness with a creepy leer that makes my skin crawl.

"Collette, you've really taken your addiction to a whole new level. Why don't you come on down, so we can get you the help you so clearly need."

My "sex addiction." That's the story he and Bodee are going to stick with and try to run into the ground along with my career.

Which is the furthest thing from my mind right now.

The beads of sweat building at my hairline aren't for me or my career, they're for Holter because Jack's standing right next to my son, a place I've fought my ass off to make sure he'd never end up. Now that my worst nightmare's come true, I'm tied up and helpless. I'm as useless now as I've ever been, otherwise, I would've done something before now to prevent this from happening.

"Holter, find Bare."

"But, Mom."

"Do it. Go."

"What about you? What about Julian?"

It doesn't escape my notice that neither of my son's top concerns are his own father. Unfortunately, it doesn't escape Jack's either.

"Hey, Holter. I apologize we're only just now meeting. Your dad speaks very highly of you, and he'd want me to see to it that you're taken care of when he can't do it himself." Jack puts his hand out to shake Holter's, and I suck in my already labored breath.

"Don't touch him," I warn.

Holter eyes Jack's hand, asking, "Who are you?"

"I work for your father," is all he says since his name and title were just exposed to the world.

Bending backward, I tug the white legging free of my calf-high, skintight boot to reach inside. My fingers graze the tactical pen knife I stuffed in there earlier, then I carefully slide it out, trying not to drop it. It's sleek like a pen—because it is an actual pen, too—and fits in tight spaces I wouldn't be able to store a regular knife. Since I've never had to use it, I'm not even sure if it's strong enough to accomplish what I'm thinking. Immediately, I uncap it to start sawing at the strap anyway, not once considering it's the only thing currently keeping me from free-falling sideways eight feet down.

"Holter, go find Bare."

Holter ignores me, asking, "You're John Davies, aren't you?" before crossing his arms over his chest and looking Jack in the eyes. "What'd you do to my mom?"

"Your father and I have only ever tried to help your mom. She's a tortured soul in need of—"

Holter steps closer to Jack, trying to make himself look twice as big. "What'd you do to her?"

Regardless how fast I saw back and forth, the blade cuts through only one or two fibers at a time, getting me absolutely nowhere, and the noise picks up as the stage becomes more congested, some people working to separate the fight, some scrambling to figure out how to get me down safely. Several people with headsets call up for me to stay where I am until they can lower me down themselves, but I'm not doing that.

The chaos drowns out Jack's words to Holter, but my son's voice floats up to me clear as a whistle. "Then how'd you get that scar?"

Again, Jack's response is muted.

"You fell?" Holter questions, glancing up at me. I can see the wheels in his head turning, and he scoffs, telling Jack, "The only thing you fell on was my mom's knife. You did something to her."

The second Jack's hand touches my son's shoulder, I lose all sense of propriety. I'm literally hanging by a thread over Hollywood elite, and honestly, I couldn't care less. All I care about is getting Holter away from Jack.

And so, I use the name I vowed to never let leave my lips again because of how disgusting it feels and tastes and sounds, shouting, "John Davies, you rapist pig bastard! Get your fucking hand off my son!"

I catch the strap above me flat in my palm, then pull with all my might, lifting myself up enough to unhook the remaining carabiner. Holding my weight one-handed, I flick my other wrist out quickly, throwing the sleek cylinder-shaped knife like a dagger. On its swift descent, the sharpest side slices Jack's knuckle, the one still on my child's shoulder, and he hisses, watching as the tip stabs into the stage.

In the next breath, I'm falling to the floor, too. My left ankle makes an awful snap of a sound, but I don't feel a break. I'm running on adrenaline and the need to protect my child…I don't feel anything.

Glaring at me while I retrieve my knife, Jack taunts, "You missed."

With my free hand, I swipe at Holter, shoving him behind me.

I tell Jack's scarred face, "I don't miss," which Holter confirms, saying, "She doesn't miss."

"That was a warning. Don't touch my son again."

"Or what?" His bottomless pits of pupils shift all around us.

He's baiting me because even though the cameras broadcasting The Mousais are off, every other type of camera is still in full use right now, aimed at the debacle this stage has become. Anything I say right now can and will be held against me, so I better make sure my words are digging someone else's grave, instead of my own.

I've chosen to stay silent about my time with Bodee for so long, and now that I'm faced with my past, I don't know where to start. There's *so* much inside me waiting to get out. I'm scared if I let out even the smallest amount, it'll all come crashing down like a fifty-foot wave carrying a fifteen-second swell. I can't let that happen right now. I have to choose carefully not only what I say, but how I say it.

Julian crawls over Bodee, kicking him off as he stands, and with his black shirt now in tatters, he pushes through the crowd, asking, "This the guy?" blood spraying out from between his lips.

Without waiting for an answer, Julian throws a punch across the bridge of Jack's nose, going down on top of him as Bodee's manager crumples to the floor.

"You're fucking dead."

Julian obviously doesn't share the same reservations about choosing his words wisely…now. He certainly did earlier.

Christ's sake, did he put any thought into what would happen after he called out Bodee Keys on national television? Like logistically? How did he see it going?

Security swarms the stage, screams ring out like hymns in church, and amidst all the pandemonium, Bodee manages to appear like the devil he is, snarling, "John!"

My ex takes a step toward the fighting men, but I block him, jiggling the pen knife between my fingers, and warn him with one simple word, "Don't."

Bare jogs up, parting bodies like an ocean liner cuts through waves, so I tell him to take Holter back to the hotel.

"Mom? I can't…"

"Collette…" Bare starts too, eyeing his boss cutting an elbow across Jack's face.

"Julian gave you the order himself," I tell Bare, and if Julian could talk right now, he'd give it again.

Bare knows I'm right. Holter's the priority. To me *and* to Julian. Sadly, not to Bodee. A fact he continues to prove every chance he gets.

Holter, being every bit my child, refuses to budge, using that same technique as before to make himself appear bigger, stronger, older.

"I'll meet you at the hotel," I say, because while he may be bigger and stronger, he's not older. He doesn't need to see this. He's already seen more than I ever wanted him to.

"What about Julian?"

"He'll…" I swallow. I don't know. Others are working to pull Jack and Julian apart now, but the sound of body blows is unmistakable. Julian doesn't want Jack to be able to walk away from this unscathed.

And I don't either. I don't want Jack or Bodee to walk away unscathed. The sad truth is they probably will though, and *that* I really can't have Holter witnessing because I don't want him to think that's how life does work or should work.

"He'll be okay," I say, not really knowing if he will.

Bare finally gets Holter to move, but after only a few steps, he turns toward Bodee, saying, "Dad?"

Bodee lifts his chin, a myriad of scratches marring his usually perfect skin.

"It was Mom, wasn't it? What Julian said earlier."

Every cell in my body comes to a standstill, allowing my heart to plummet from my chest to…I don't even know where it is now. Gone? Maybe. It feels like it.

"Son, I've only ever tried to help your mom. She's a tortured soul—"

"Did your publicist write the same script for both you and Jack?" I ask. "Because that's the exact same wording he used."

"I hate you," Holter says, and my eyes fly to his. Luckily, he's staring at Bodee.

Not luckily. I'm glad his hatred isn't for me, but I never wanted Holter to hate his father; I wanted him to *have* a father.

Bodee never did try filling the role though, not for his sake or Holter's. Two police officers drag Julian up to his feet, each one holding an arm behind his back.

"Bare, take him. I'll get Julian." And I will, even if I have to go to hell to do it.

Julian's had my back, now it's time I have his. Together, we *can* take on Bodee and Jack, but he didn't finish the job. Not yet. He only opened Pandora's box with his public accusations. He didn't rip the lid clear off with proof. I may not even have proof.

But I know who does and he hasn't been thinking straight since he arrived.

So, after Bare and Holter leave, I choose to see this through myself by keeping my attention locked on Bodee, prepared to poke my ex's over-inflated ego until it pops like a balloon.

"How are you going to recover from this one? Your peers hate you, your son hates you, I hate you, and if they don't already, the public will hate you, too."

"Collette," he chides, his sneer full of real blood and fake bravado. "Perception can always be altered. Hate comes and goes as easily as love."

Does it? At times hate may feel just as strong as love, but in actuality, it isn't nearly as powerful. Hate can't heal, or lift, or promise, or persevere. Hate is like a chokehold—you can fight it, or you can succumb to it, but the choice is always yours to make. Love is like poison—you don't get a choice at all, only an antidote steeped in time and distance after you've already been infected. Where hate can disappear at a moment's notice, it can take years for the potency of love to lessen.

Bodee mistakes the two because he's never known true love, not even for himself.

"Besides, none of this will stick." He waves a hand at what sounds like Julian being carted off by the officers, cursing as he goes. "Your boyfriend's a drug addict and you're a whore. Nothing you two say can touch me."

"Is that so?" I ask with a chuckle, showing him how wholly unconvinced I am.

"Yes. It is," he bites out.

"Back when we were together, you used to be quite the force. You could get anyone to do anything you wanted with the snap of your fingers alone. Then, you started losing your touch, and it took more effort from you."

The edges of his lips quiver, but he tries to hide it, saying, "You're lying through the teeth I paid for."

He didn't pay for my teeth. He bought me clear aligners to straighten them…when I was sixteen years old, just a growing teenage girl.

Shaking my head in mock-disappointment, I ignore his jab, and shrug. "Now, it's almost sad the lengths you have to go through to get people to do your bidding. Your name, your legacy, your influence, they're not what they used to be. I performed here tonight and there wasn't a damn thing you could do about it."

"Couldn't? I couldn't do anything about it?" His voice is harsh and icy like January in the Northeast. "You haven't seen what I'm capable of yet."

I lift my chin to take a step in his direction, my ankle screaming from the weight shift. *Perhaps Bodee got his wish and I broke my leg after all.*

"What are you capable of? Really? Oppressing my career? Maybe back when you still had some balls on you, but certainly not now." I eye him up and down. "I just played The Mousais—a gig I earned myself. Nothing *you* say can touch *me*. I'm untouchable." And because I know men like him hate, absolutely hate, being laughed at, I laugh. I laugh so hard and so loud, it borders on maniacal, but it does the trick.

Bodee roars, "*I'm* untouchable, you stupid cunt!" He grabs one of my arms while simultaneously silencing me and the rest of the amphitheater.

If a pin dropped in here, it'd trigger an earthquake; it's that quiet. Save for Bodee's voice of course. The vein in his forehead bulging, he yells in my face, "You got The Mousais the same way you got me, by spreading your goddamn legs! Julez didn't make you, I did! And just like the last time you forgot that, I'm going to enjoy reminding you!"

"By ordering John Davies to rape me again?"

Ordering Jack to do that the first time wasn't to punish me or make me more agreeable like I used to believe. It was to break my spirit, to break *me*, by either the act itself or the subsequent miscarriage they were hoping to elicit. But even if it had, even if they'd succeeded with their plan, it wouldn't have lasted forever. A woman is who and what she wants, whenever she feels like it, and eventually I would've found myself again.

Like now.

After years of living in fear of Bodee, I can finally feel the collar binding me to him molting away from my throat.

Bodee lowers his voice, bragging, "I wouldn't have to order it. After weeding through the thousands of photos I've collected of you over the years, he'd do it voluntarily. *After* I took my turn with you."

A collective gasp finally penetrates Bodee's belligerent stupor, and he blinks, glancing around like he's just been startled awake from a bad dream.

I seize my moment to lean in close, telling him, "Legends may not die but villains do. You'll be lucky if there's anything left for the worms to feast off your corpse when I'm done with you. Rest uneasy, Bodee, I'm coming for you." Then I rip my arm out of his hold, standing entirely on my own as I stare unflinchingly in his cold, calculating eyes to let him see I will no longer be cowed by him.

I run my gaze over Jack next, sitting with his head between his knees, and tell him, "Enjoy your freedom because you're going to prison." Maybe not tonight or tomorrow, but I'll see to it myself Jack ends up behind bars. "I hear a pretty face is a hot commodity in there… Looks like you're screwed."

To both, I say, "See you in the courtroom. I'll be the one up on the stand, testifying against you."

I will not be cowed by *any* man.

From the sound of it, I probably won't be the only woman pressing charges against Bodee or Jack, but if it comes to that, I'm ready to battle them alone. Self-preservation might've passed as an excuse for not going after Bodee Keys before, but not anymore. Not after discovering there could possibly be more victims.

Bodee's reign of terror in this business and in my life is over.

Chapter 39

Collette

"Axel found him," Irelynn says, looking up from her phone.

"Where?"

Julian bailed himself out of jail before I could, so we've been holed up in my hotel suite, staring at our phones, searching for him ever since. His own phone's going straight to voicemail, and nobody's seen him, not even Bare.

She looks back down, shaking her head. "I don't think—"

"Just tell me. I need to know."

She blows out a breath. "He's in a hotel room."

I sit with that for a minute, wondering how much I do need to know. Considering I'm Julian's girlfriend, I need to know all of it.

Bracing myself, I ask, "By himself?"

"Axel said it's a party. *His* party." His…Julian's. He's back to his old ways, ran straight to them with open arms and an open wallet, I'm guessing.

It's not even all that surprising. Julian hates being alone. He hops from one distraction to the next, never stopping long enough to figure out what it is he really wants. What he needs.

He needs someone to care about him, truly care *about* him. Not *for* him. That's enabling, and he's been enabled long enough.

"Will you stay here with Holter and Mary until I get back?" I ask her, standing slowly. Mary went to bed a couple hours ago, and Holter fell asleep on the couch, watching a movie. We had a long talk when I finally made it out of The Mousai madness. He didn't ask as many questions as I thought he would, maybe because…he already knows. In his heart, he knows what kind of person Bodee is. The publicity father-son meetups undoubtedly clued him in, along with just being his usual observant self while around his father. He wasn't shocked that Bodee and I don't actually get along, but he was hurt I hid my true feelings, among other things.

I let a lot of people down with the choices I made regarding Bodee Keys, including myself. *I'm* disappointed in me, and it's going to take some time to forgive myself for all the damage my silence caused.

"Of course, but…" Irelynn follows me to the door, frowning at my obvious limp. "What about your ankle? Should you even be walking on it?"

"I…don't know." The amount of effort it takes just to hobble around worries me. The excruciating pain shooting up my calf with every step I take worries me. I have to be able to stand, to dance, to *perform*. "We'll make some calls when I get back," I tell her. I didn't want to seek medical treatment until Julian was free. Him being out of harm's way means more than my ankle. He means more to me than that, period.

Yet another thing I stayed silent on but shouldn't have.

Staring at the ajar door, I pause, inhaling until my lungs hurt worse than my ankle, then I push through smoke as thick as wool to enter the hotel suite.

Carefully leaning against the nearest wall for support, I cross my arms over my chest, purposely avoiding inspection of the needles on the table next to me.

Instead, I focus on Julian. He's lounging wide-legged on a loveseat in the middle of the sitting room, a pair of women beside him as a third stands between his legs pouring a long stream of tequila into his mouth.

"Celebrating?" I say loud enough to get his attention.

Almost immediately, he wrenches his face away, causing the dark amber liquid to spill down his cheek, over the many cuts he accumulated from earlier, but he doesn't so much as flinch.

"The fuck are you doing here?"

"I came to collect you," I answer honestly, and he laughs, trailing off as a lit blunt's handed to him. His bottom lip is swollen and both eyes have dark circles turning into deep bruises already. All I want is to go over and kiss him. Kiss away his pain. Kiss away tonight.

And maybe kick him because what is he doing? What the hell is this?

Head low, Axel strolls over to me, saying, "Hey, Collette," softly. Apologetically.

I give him a grateful nod, telling him, "Hey," along with, "Thank you," since he is the one that found Julian.

Julez. He found Julez.

"Ayo, don't—"

"Shut up!" Axel yells at Julian like an older brother losing his patience with his younger sibling even though I know Axel's younger by a couple years. "Shut the fuck up. I'm just talking to her, okay? If it really bothers you that much, get off your fucking ass and do something about it."

Julian remains where he is but continues to glare at Axel as he tokes off the blunt.

Facing me again, Axel runs a hand through his hair, saying, "Fuck." He points at the foot currently resting on top of my other to ask, "How's the ankle?"

"Sprained." Or worse.

Probably worse.

"No way?"

I shrug. "I don't know. Maybe."

"You should go to the hospital."

"Hospitals have real doctors," I murmur, shaking my head.

"And you only see fake ones?"

"I see ones that'll okay me for tour."

Axel frowns.

"What's wrong with your ankle?" Julian snaps.

"Didn't you see the fucking videos?" Axel spits right back. The videos of what transpired on stage, including Bodee's outburst in my face, are circulating online at this very moment, have been for hours now, and they're only gaining momentum.

Just me being seen here could threaten my credibility, but I can't walk away from Julian. I never could.

"Why would I need to see the videos when I was fucking there, fighting off—"

"She landed from twelve feet off the fucking ground right next to you, and you didn't even notice. You didn't even care."

"Fuck you. You don't know what the fuck you're talking about."

"Fuck you. You're an idiot. You're the one that put her up in the rafters, then fucking left her hanging there."

I don't bother correcting Axel on how high up I was. I'm too busy trying to figure out…all of this. Julian doesn't want Axel talking to me, but he's acting like he himself doesn't want to talk to me. He didn't come back to our shared suite after his release, and he didn't expect to see me here, at a hotel across town from the one we booked, either. Did he think I would break up with him for what he did onstage?

Or was that him breaking up with me?

During the ceremony, he acted like…

He acted like he was getting ready to say goodbye.

"Don't leave me before you even leave me."

"I'm already gone, Collette."

Then his spontaneous rap that sounded like a fast-paced serenade but felt like a goodbye…

He did say goodbye.

Every rib contracts, making my chest *ache*.

I knew this was coming, didn't I?

Naturally, I had my doubts around the longevity of our relationship, which led me to consider the very real possibility that it wouldn't make the long haul. As much as I hate to admit it, a breakup seemed probable…at some point.

I never could've imagined it'd feel like this though. Like a piece of me, a different piece than the one Holter holds, is being ripped away just as ruthlessly as when Bodee showed up, whisking Holter out from under my nose.

Did he really break up with me without even technically breaking up with me? One rap and we're done?

Julian pretends to gasp, pulling my gaze to his. "If your ankle's jacked up, how will you run away to go on your precious little tour now? Maybe you won't be able to tour at all, finally making you a true has-been."

"So, we're right back to where we started, huh, little lamb? The has-been squaring off against the never-was?"

One of his eyebrows tries to lift, but it's caked in dried blood. "If the crown fits…"

"It fits," I tell him, not even sure what either of those statements mean, just that he's pissing me off the longer I have to sit here and watch him make a fucking mockery out of our relationship. The relationship *he* pushed for. The relationship *he* broke my walls down to get to. The relationship *he* made public before I was ready. The relationship *he* promised would lead to me being his wife and carrying his children one day.

The relationship that changed my life.

Goddamn him.

With a hard expression, he trails his middle finger up the back of one of the women's thighs, and I don't even hesitate to grab my knife out—my real knife—and flick the blade open. "I warned you, Julian. One finger. Remove it or I'll remove something on you that'll make you more like Osiris than you ever thought possible." I punctuate my words with a smirk so nasty I'm not sure I even look like myself. I definitely don't feel like myself.

All I know is I didn't agree to a breakup, and as my man, Julian's already been made well aware that I don't fucking share.

Julian's nostrils flare, but his hand drops to his lap, probably to guard his cock now that I've threatened to cut it off, then he scoffs, "'Cause you have a say."

"Absolutely, I do. You're *my* boyfriend. You're *my*—"

Julian lunges forward off the back of the loveseat. "I'm a crack in your armor!"

Arms out wide, my ankle threatens to give out as I ask, "What armor? The one that just got stripped from me in front of millions of people?"

"All right, party's over. Everybody out," Axel speaks up, gesturing at the door. "These two need some privacy."

"For what?" Julian leans back, the picture of blissed-out ignorance once again.

It's an act though. It's all an act. He's not as trashed as I thought, and he's not as clueless as he's pretending to be.

Julian knows exactly what he's doing.

Axel waves between me and Julian, saying, "To work *that* out."

"This? This is nothing." Julian shakes his head, glancing around at the bodies leaving as if he's considering joining them.

Far from here, right?

How far we've come just to end up exactly where we started.

"What?" I choke out, swearing I must be the one that's high because…what did he say? *Nothing?* "What did you just say?"

His glassy gaze hits mine. "You heard me."

"Say it again."

"This. Is. Nothing."

"You bastard."

Julian pretends not to hear me, and I lick my dry lips before telling everyone to hurry their asses up while tucking my knife away. Like cattle that need herding every now and then, they eventually manage to make it out.

When the door closes on the final guest, I say, "After everything you put me through tonight, you're going to sit there and say this is nothing? That we're nothing?"

"We are."

"Since when? When *exactly* did you decide to end us?" Was it actually tonight? Or was it before?

He shrugs. "Right around the time you did."

"Which was?"

"You tell me, Poohbear." Usually he uses the nickname in a sweet, endearing way, but right now he's wielding it with a derogatory edge, like a dull knife that's still capable of permanent damage. "How *exactly* were we gonna work?"

"Because I'm going on another tour?"

"Because you'll always be on another tour!"

"And you'll always be wasted!" I scream back, my chest hurting so bad I think it might actually burst.

"Exactly." His head falls to hang limply at his chest. "I'm a crack in your armor. I thought only Holter held that honor, but…" Two of his fingers lift half-crooked. "I do, too."

"What are you talking about? What fucking armor? I told you, there's nothing left. Tonight—"

"Nobody knew who I was talking about. I was careful not to use your name."

Christ. That was the only thing he was careful about.

"You really haven't been online at all, have you? It's everywhere."

He meets my eyes through long lashes. "What is?"

"Bodee's confession!"

Julian's quiet for a minute, and I can see his brain working to sift through the sewage he's been dumping in it the last few hours to make what he did feel justified, to make what he's doing feel justified.

"Bodee didn't say shit."

All I can handle is a headshake.

He frowns, still sifting. "Did he?"

My head feels detached from the rest of my body at this point, it's moving so fast.

"What the fuck did he say? To who?"

"Who do you think? To me! What you started, Julian… You opened a can of worms, then walked away before dealing with the mess."

"Walked away? Collette, I was dragged away in handcuffs. I was arrested!"

"For your own actions! The ones you chose to do alone, without telling me."

"I had to! It was the only fucking way!"

"Way for what?"

"For you to be free!"

I startle from the intensity in his tone and expression.

"Free of Bodee? Or free of you?"

His swallow echoes throughout the room.

"Both."

"You don't get to make that choice for me," I say, my voice breaking, my resolve right along with it.

Watching me, Julian's eyes fill with tears, and one slips out, rolling down his cheek before he turns to look away.

Julian looks away. He looks away. After all that, he just looks away.

"Someone needed to. I'm a liability. Bodee and I both were."

"A liability? Julian, I love you."

"You know what happens to the people who love me. I drain them until they die."

The thorny devil lizard. Julian not only believes he sucks other people's love dry, he thinks he kills them in the process.

"So…what? Is that what tonight was about? Is that why you're…" I don't want to say it. I don't want to put a voice to it and make it real. "Is that why you're breaking up with me?"

With zero reluctance whatsoever, he says, "Yes."

I feel myself falling backward, my equilibrium thrown off, so I steady myself by grabbing on to the back of the closest chair.

"Goddamn you. Goddamn you! You promised! You promised me you wouldn't hurt me anymore!" My voice strange to my own ears, I glance around, surprised to find it didn't come from someone else. Everything about me is unrecognizable right now.

When Julian gives no reaction, I scream, "This is hurting me! You're hurting me! You promised—"

He stands so suddenly he sways, too. "I lied! A life with me would be nothing but hurt."

"You don't know that. You're not even giving us a chance to see."

"I can't. I…can't. Everyone that loves me, everyone *I* love, dies, and I'd rather there be a world where you exist without me, than one without you in it at all. I can't fucking risk it. I'll never fucking risk it. Not you. Not your boy. Not. You. Collette."

"Do you know what that's called? Sacrifice. The kind that sets deep love apart from regular love. You taught me that. But if you love me, truly, deeply love me, the kind that has the power to soak a person from head to toe before they even realize it's raining, there wouldn't be any other choice. Come back to me, Julian. Come back to me and stay."

For a moment, I think I've gotten through to him, I've brought Julian back, but then in a blink, he's Julez again, pointing at me and saying, "You almost had me going there. Where was all this 'no other choice' talk when I was asking you to go to Vegas with me?"

Stepping around the chair, I sit on the edge and gaze up at him. "I won't marry you until I know I'm marrying *you*."

He holds his arms out to his sides. "I'm me. I've been me, but that wasn't enough to bring *you* back, to make *you* stay. I wasn't enough."

"This isn't you. When you're like this, you're angry. You're mean. You're bitter. You hurt people. You hurt me."

"*I* hurt!" He falls backward on to the loveseat again, repeating, "I *hurt*. Every day I'm broken down, smashed to fucking pieces. People everywhere think they know. Think they have a fucking clue about me and what I've been through. About my life, my art. I put out a song, one song, any fucking song, and it's not just the song that gets ripped apart, it's *me*."

"I know," I whisper. He's not the only one. It happens every single day. Like a firing squad of relentless insults, they never stop coming.

"I don't go online anymore because I can't. Every fucking time I do, I see entire threads saying it's a good thing my mom is dead so she can't see how bad my music is. Threads I'm tagged in! How am I supposed to ignore that? How is that okay?"

"It's not okay, Julian. I'm sorry you have to see that. I'm sorry. It's not okay."

This life takes a toll on all of us. A harsh toll that people like to explain away because of how much money we make. It doesn't even matter how much we actually make, it's assumed we make more, much more, so we should be able to handle the criticism that comes with it. Criticism is one thing. Bullying, verbal assault, and death threats are another, and nobody's immune to those. Sticks and stones may break bones but words—even typed ones—burrow. They burrow until they're so deep nothing can fish them out completely, not even money. Especially not money. Money can't keep you company. Money can't buy you warmth, love, acceptance.

Money is temporary, but the effects from incessant psychological abuse can, and do, last forever.

Just this morning I saw a post with an unflattering photo of me with a caption about how Julian's munchies must be rubbing off on me. The only thing I had to eat for the rest of the day was a single pouch of baby food. Even knowing I had to prepare for one of the biggest performances of my career, I just kept imagining people staring at my stomach, and so, I didn't eat. I didn't fucking eat. After doing so well, and finally feeling like I had a handle on it, one photo is all it took for me to slide right back into old habits.

It shouldn't affect us, yet it does. We're human, too, and flawed ones at that.

"Everyone has a fucking opinion. Except me. I gotta keep quiet about everything, just keep my head down and put out more songs I hate for them to shit all over, then smile for their fucking pictures, wondering why the fuck they even want one." He scoffs, picking up a random bottle, bringing it to his lips. "This is the only thing I have a say over. The only thing I get to myself that no one can take from me."

"I'm not trying to take anything from you. I'm only trying to keep you."

"The Family Julez Tour is over, Collette. Go home." After taking a long drink, he adds, "Or go to your next tour. Just go."

"If you don't stop, you'll end up exactly like your mom." I hate saying it, but I need to. Nobody else will.

Julian's on the same path his mom was except he has access to more, better, harder stuff than she ever did.

He also has access to something else his mother didn't have—rehab.

"You need help."

"So do you."

A puff of disbelief leaves my lips drier than before. "Excuse me?"

"What about your addiction?"

"It's not—"

"Could you give up touring?"

I seal my lips together, not sure how to answer him. Not sure I can answer him. Could I?

"You're worse than I am because you're still bullshitting yourself into believing you're not an addict. First step in recovery, Poohbear... admitting you have a problem."

Is my constant touring a problem? Yes. Deep down I know it is. There are so many things over the years I've missed out on because of touring. So many milestones I'll never get back.

So many gigs I put first.

But is it an actual addiction?

I just thought I was doing what I had to. Bodee tried to bury my name, so I fought to keep it alive. Days turned into months, and months turned into years, then before I knew it, over a decade had passed and here I am, still fighting like I was in the beginning. When will I be able to stop?

Or I guess the better question is, when will I allow myself to?

"You can't, can you? It's why you cry yourself to sleep when you're home, because you know as much as you want to stop touring and give Holter a stable home life, you *can't*."

A searing flush races through my body, making me feel feverish. How does he know I do that? He's never even been to my home.

Did Holter tell him? If so, does that mean Holter knows I cry at night?

Of course, he does. He's observant and I'm a bad mom.

Am I a bad mom? I'm not a great mom. Not nearly as good as I wish I could be. Not nearly as good as I could be.

I've only ever tried to protect Holter, but maybe I went about it in the wrong ways.

One of the many topics Holter and I discussed earlier was my work schedule. He tried to use my ankle as an excuse for me to get out of touring for a while, and even seeing the hope on his face, I outright downplayed my injury to him. To my own son, who was thrilled by the prospect of having me home with him a while longer.

I chose touring over him, and it wasn't the first time. I almost chose touring over Julian, too.

I did choose touring over Julian. I knew he didn't want me to go on another tour right away and I was willing to do it anyway.

First step is admitting it. I do. I have an addiction.

My twisted, hollow stomach cramps with more than just day-long hunger pains.

I have more than one addiction.

"I don't know what you want from me. You're breaking up with me, but you want me to stop touring. Do you truly not want us to be together? What the fuck do you want, Julian? Tell me."

"I want you to get everything you want."

"I want you."

"You want me…but. You want me…but sober. You want me…but on your terms."

"I want *you*. But—"

"See?" He thrusts a hand out at me. "You want me, but."

"I want you, Julian. You. Not the person drugs and alcohol make you."

"Drugs and alcohol are me just like touring is you. We can't change who we are."

We stare at each other for a long time, tears streaming from my eyes as his remain red, puffy, and unreadable. Julian looks like a warzone full of emotional carnage, and I feel like I just walked through one. I'm wounded. Shattered.

I want to collapse in on myself and forget today ever happened. Forget any of this ever happened. But I can't. Addiction is a lifelong struggle, one we'll both have to battle on a regular basis. It doesn't just go away over night because you wish it would. Usually, you need something to force your hand, a wake-up call, a fork in the road; whatever it is, something *has* to give in order for change—real change—to occur. I hate that it's us.

Even with our breakup serving as the catalyst though, it can't be the reason.

"We can't change who we are…for other people. If you're only doing something for someone else, and not yourself, then you're guaranteed to fail. You gotta want it," I say, quoting what he told Holter that day on the court.

In order for either of us to overcome our addictions, I cannot be his salvation, and Julian cannot be mine.

I shake my head, watching as Julian's throat bobs with…something I can't place, then I pull out my phone, typing and sending a series of texts. Texts for me, texts for Julian. Texts for our future, should we both choose to have one together.

I'll follow up with emails later, but right now I need to at least get the ball rolling. I can't walk away otherwise.

When I look at Julian again, his thumb's up to his mouth, and he's gnawing at the skin he chews on when he's feeling nervous, when he's feeling unsure, when he's feeling, period.

He's scared I'll go because then he'll be alone, but he's even more scared I'll stay because all he's ever been is alone. Julian's not only conditioned to expect trauma, he welcomes it…on what he believes are his terms.

That's what all of this was about—self-sabotage. Yes, he ruined his own career with tonight's actions, but that was not his main purpose. Neither was calling out Bodee. Those were only by-products of his main goal, which was to take control of a situation he no longer felt in control of. He thought I was going to break up with him, and maybe, eventually, I might've—I don't *know*, neither of us do for sure—but instead of fighting, instead of trying at all, he broke up with me first. He gave up. He gave up control, he gave on me, he gave up on us, he gave up on himself. He did exactly what I feared he'd do when faced with a real-life relationship with real-life ups and downs and disappointments, he *chose* to return to his safe place. The place no one can hurt him any more than he's already hurting himself.

"Whenever you choose, now, tomorrow, next week, next month, you'll have the pick of any rehab facility in the country. All paid. I'll help you any way I can, but you have to decide to help yourself…for yourself. I can't save you, Julian. I tried, but you weren't ready. You weren't willing."

Even so, it still feels like I'm the one failing him. I wanted to be the one person to stand by his side, his queen in not only his rise but also if ever he were to fall, and I'm not going to be. Hopefully just for a little while.

Pushing to my feet, I approach the loveseat, keeping Julian's eyes as I bend down to one knee, then the other in front of him, the bones in my ankle clicking noisily.

"Collette…"

As soon as he notices my hand coming at him, his body tenses up, so I slow my advance, showing him my intention as I reach for his throat. My middle finger locks on to its usual spot, right on the lip of

Julian's tattoo, immediately sensing his pulse beneath the thin skin, then we're both motionless.

"I promise to keep reaching for you, little lamb, if you promise to give me something to reach for."

"Collette. It's… I'm…" Tears streaming down his face, he leans away from my touch before leaning back into it. He's still conflicted, and being pulled in opposite directions, just like I was.

"I love you so much," I tell him.

"Don't." The tears turn into hot rivers, splitting over my fingertips to run down his neck in wavy rapids, soaking his neckline.

"I love you, Julian."

Holding back any response at all, his body convulses on a poorly contained sob.

The sight's too much to take, so I shut my eyes, picturing him the way I want to remember him.

All these years I thought falling in love was the hard part, but I should've been worried about the falling-out part because making myself walk away from Julian without knowing if I'll get to see him again, is the hardest thing I've ever had to do.

Love is a salve, not a staunch. It can only soothe wounds for so long until you're bleeding out and need an actual remedy. Both Julian and I are hemorrhaging right now from letting ourselves go untreated for so long, and in order to effectively stop the blood loss, we have to learn how to love ourselves first.

"If you don't come back to me, I swear I'll come find you myself. Please, please don't make me have to. Come back to me," I beg him, then I get up and leave, taking the needles by the door with me.

Chapter 40

Collette

I'm staring at the painting on the wall when Tanya, my new assistant, walks into my suite, asking, "All good?"

"Not quite." I hold a pair of ruby earrings out to her with shaky hands, and ask, "Could you please help me put these in?"

The last seven months have been…trying, to say the least. In all the seats I've been filling lately—from my psychiatrist's to my ED therapist's to my lawyer's to the courthouse's—none have been on a tour bus. I can't say I've quit touring for good, but I've quit touring for today, and that's all I can do, is take things one day at a time. Just like overcoming my eating disorder, I can't get ahead of myself, I can't take my eye off my main priority of becoming and staying healthy, or I'll risk losing focus altogether.

After I walked out of Julian's hotel room, I made major changes in my life. Changes I'd been wanting to make for others but couldn't quite commit to. Once I chose to implement those same changes for myself though, it wasn't hard to commit anymore. Which isn't to say anything about this new journey has been easy; quite the opposite. I've been torn apart and put back together again in therapy, in the media, in court. I've faced challenges everywhere I look, none more so than the mirror because *I'm* my biggest task now, not my image, not my name, not even my sales or ranking in the charts. My mental health and my physical health—those are what I check on every day and have to work hard to maintain with love and patience and kindness and forgiveness. So much forgiveness. Even more during weeks like this past one.

All week I've been in a courtroom, facing off against Bodee. The fact that I haven't had to do it alone makes things harder for me personally because I do carry a lot of guilt, but easier in that there really is strength in numbers. Strength and solidarity. So far twenty-one other parties have come forward with accusations against Bodee Keys, ranging from coercion and sexual assault to fraud and extortion. Sadly, I know that's not all. There are probably many more victims choosing to stay silent, too scared to blow the whistle, just like I used to be. Not anymore. Now I use the voice I've spent over half my life improving against my ex, and I won't stop until some form of justice is delivered.

John Davies—I finally came to terms with using his real name, only because it makes him more of a mortal and less of the undefeatable monster I'd created in my head—already had his reckoning at his own trial last month when he was sentenced to fifteen years in prison. It was obvious Bodee thought he'd be able to pin everything on John, because he stabbed his manager in the back so quick, it made my knifework look childish. And if it weren't for Bodee's now-viral confession at The Mousais, it might've actually worked because unfortunately, a woman's word isn't always enough. Usually, it's only after a man corroborates her story that it's even considered plausible. Luckily, I got that when several A-list male celebrities with squeaky-clean reputations backed me after Bodee tried to backtrack the statements he made that night. One of those voices being DJ Arique's.

In an effort to redirect the heat aimed at him, Bodee did end up leaking the photos of me and Julian. I sent cease and desists to every outlet that shared the pictures for illegally distributing explicit images taken without permission along with defamation of character, and they were taken down within a matter of days. Copies are still circulating the internet, but there's nothing I can do about that without exhausting a ridiculous amount of resources. Resources I've needed elsewhere, like securing full custody of Holter as well as our new home.

We moved off David's estate and rented a small house of our own, one that wasn't a driveway away from the kind of family life I couldn't give Holter but always wished I had. We miss having our friends so close, but it's for the best. Holter and I have found our own new normal, and I don't cry at night as much, at least not about that.

"There," Tanya says after fastening the last earring, stepping back to inspect her work. "How do you feel?"

"Sweaty."

We chuckle, and I grab a handful of tissues, stuffing them under my armpits. Thankfully, I'm wearing a black strapless jumpsuit, so at least there's no risk of pitstains.

"David should be landing his helicopter on the roof any minute."

I nod absently. "Okay. Good." His wife, Kim-ly, has been here since seven o'clock this morning, and I'm sure she's already waiting up there for her husband, more than ready to ride home in the chopper after working herself to the bone making sure everything for tonight's charity event is set up exactly the way she planned it. I helped out where I could, when I could, but Kim-ly is the one who really spearheaded this whole affair. As a silent partner, David was hands-off in the party-planning department from the beginning, with the exception of entertainment. David insisted on booking the artist himself. Or band. Or magician. I don't even know because he also insisted on keeping that part of this evening a surprise. Hopefully someone tells me before I have to announce the act since I'm the sole host of tonight's gala. I trust him though.

Someone knocks on the door, so Tanya excuses herself to answer it.

"Is she ready?" I hear Kim-ly ask.

I smile, standing from the chair to toss the damp tissues in the wastebasket. My ankle healed up nicely, thanks to me taking enough time off to actually let it. It wasn't broken after all, but I think Bodee's curse over me is.

I meet my friend in the doorway, freezing when I see her. "Date night?" I ask, pointing at her flowy, mint-green, halter-top gown.

With her hands clasped in front of her as she practically bounces in her spot, she nods the biggest grin, her cheeks disturbing her shiny, blue-black hair.

"You look stunning," I tell her. "You'll have to tell me all about it tomorrow."

"Ride up in the elevator with me? David has something for you. A last-minute donation item for the auction."

"Sure." We have a project manager for stuff like that, but it's been a while since I've actually seen my producer in the flesh. We haven't recorded anything new for months, which is about how long it's been since Holter and I were last over there for dinner. Almost all of our meetings for the gala were held virtually, too. You'd think we moved out of state, not a few neighborhoods over.

After grabbing my clutch, I follow her out, and during our wait for the elevator, she fills me in on the catering issue she got resolved a mere hour ago.

"Thank you so much," I tell her once we're moving inside the elevator. "We couldn't have done this without you."

"It was my pleasure. I hope David likes it."

"David's coming down?" I ask, tilting my head her way. "Why are we meeting him on the roof then?"

"I imagine so he can walk in with two beautiful women on his arms."

"He's staying?" This is complete news to me. Typically, David avoids these types of events, and I wasn't notified he'd be making an exception for this one.

"Of course. He wouldn't miss this for the world," she says, her eyes on the rising red numbers.

"Should make for an interesting date night," I say.

"Indeed."

Before I look away, I notice her lips stretch even wider.

"Did you two get a sitter for the night?"

"Yes." *Maybe they got a room here.* "You?"

"Holter tried fighting me on it because he thinks he's too old for a babysitter..."

"Tai, too." Kim-ly laughs.

"...but with all the craziness from the trial and everything..." I trail off, taking a huge breath. "Mary's staying the night with him." It was nice having her around today before I left the two alone. Mary has become a sort of mother figure to both me and Holter, so not having her nearby these last several months has taken some getting used to. I'm not sure

I fully have though. She's the only maternal influence I've had since I was sixteen and I genuinely enjoyed having her around.

"Wise choice. We caught Tai sneaking a girl out of the theater room last weekend."

My eyes go wide. "I didn't even consider girls. I'm not used to being…around."

She turns toward me, her smile finally dropping. "How are you liking it? Being home?"

"I'm liking it," I answer simply to a question that's anything but simple.

"Have you heard from him?" she hedges, and without even saying his name, I know who she's talking about.

I shake my head, scared what'll happen if I try to answer that.

Five days after I walked away from Julian, I was notified he'd checked himself into rehab. I was hopeful. Elated really. He did it. He chose to quit.

Almost immediately, Irelynn came to me and gave her two weeks' notice. She was off to follow Axel around the world. Apparently, what they had wasn't a tour-mance, and Axel had a name to make drumming for other artists besides Julez.

Before those two weeks were even up, it was all over the news that Julian left rehab early. He'd chosen again.

I reached out to Tomás, to suggest different programs—maybe another one would be a better fit—but both he and Julian blocked me. Bare was already working for another celebrity, so he wasn't any help either.

Other than a post from Julian himself where he informed fans he was taking an indefinite hiatus, I haven't seen or heard anything about him since. Not in the news. Not from Irelynn. Not from anyone. Every night I stare at my phone, wishing it'd light up with his name as much as I wish it wouldn't. I miss him so bad it hurts. But it hurts more imagining the damage he's causing himself by not getting the help he needs.

I promised Julian I'd find him if he didn't come back to me…but how much longer am I supposed to wait? I refuse to believe it's over between us for good, but the more time that goes by without hearing from him, the more faith I lose.

We arrive at the highest floor of the hotel, and with the staff's help,

Kim-ly and I find the roof's access just in time to greet David, then we're all back in the elevator, going down this time.

"Your hair's a mess." Kim-ly laughs, helping her husband fix the damage from the wind. "You can't look like this for your first time on a stage."

I turn to gape at my friends, asking David, "You're going onstage?"

"Do you mind sharing some of the spotlight tonight, Collette?" David asks with a grin while his wife licks her palm to run over his strands.

"David, after the last seven months, I will happily hand you *all* the spotlight." I've had enough to last seventeen lifetimes. "I'm just… shocked. Why didn't you tell me beforehand? This is huge."

"Blame her," he says, jerking a thumb at his wife, and she laughs, smacking his hand before grabbing it to hold.

It's difficult to look at the couple as they gaze so tenderly at one another and not feel it, the tug I always get whenever I'm reminded what being loved by Julian felt like. It's that piece of me he took with him, I know it. God, how I wish he'd bring it back already. Bring him back. I just want Julian.

"Oh," I say, shaking myself. "Where's the item for auction?"

"Uh." David glances at his wife, and she shrugs. "How about a helicopter ride around LA?"

"With you?" I can't hide the skepticism in my voice. David's not that kind of pilot. He doesn't do tours, only flies himself and his family around when needed.

"Sure."

Both my friends avoid eye contact with me for the rest of the ride down, then the elevator doors are opening to the lobby, ending the strange silence.

David extends his elbows out to me and Kim-ly, so we each take one, exiting together.

The three of us stroll through the ballroom, stopping to make introductions along the way, until it's time to make opening announcements, then we drop Kim-ly off at a table.

Fearless, David beelines toward the staircase leading to the stage, and I have to pull him to a stop.

"What?" he asks, clueless to this side of the business.

I smile, telling him, "Usually we go around from behind, through the backstage." I point at the stage. "That way the curtains can open to us."

Trapping my arm between his elbow and ribs, he leads me up the staircase anyway, saying, "This way's quicker."

I can't help but laugh, shaking my head on our way to the center of the stage. His first time in the spotlight and he's already shaking things up.

We greet the room, introducing ourselves as well as the charity we started together. It's my first time being onstage with someone other than Julian since The Mousais, and to be honest, I don't really like it. It feels clunky and unnatural. I've been onstage with many, many other performers, but never formed a connection with any of them like I did with Julian. We became in sync with each other in a way most bands that have been performing together for years can't even achieve. We weren't just together, we were one.

The longer I stand up here, beside David, the more uncomfortable I get, and I wonder if I would've even been able to pull off another tour without Julian. He told me before that he only wanted to tour with me, and now I finally understand what he meant. It doesn't feel right without him. I don't feel right without him.

"Next up, how about an original song by Collette?" David says after we run out of awards and certificates to give.

"Me?" I question into my mic while my other hand hides inside one of my pockets at my hip, fidgeting, because I didn't know I was singing.

I drop my mic by my side, murmuring between unmoving lips, "I thought you took care of the entertainment."

"I did."

I tilt my head at him, frowning. "But—"

Behind the curtains, someone starts drumming.

I shoot a look down below, finding Tanya with her phone up like she's recording. Next to her is Kim-ly, who's crying.

"Thanks, David, I got it from here."

My heart stops at the voice. Fucking stops.

It's his voice. *His* voice. Here. Now.

The curtains open to reveal Axel at the drums, keeping a steady beat, and Julian sitting on a stool, cradling a guitar while speaking into the microphone.

Our eyes find each other's instantly, like magnets slamming together in an explosion.

Every person in the room rises, clapping. It's been months since Julian's even been seen in public, let alone put out any new music, and it's clear I'm not the only one affected by the sight of him.

"Thank you. Now, if it's all right with Collette, Imma go ahead and do one of the songs she wrote." His lips form a smirk. "With a spin to it, of course."

I run my gaze over him, taking him in, but my eyes betray me by filling with water. The parts I do manage to make out before my vision blurs look good though. Really, really good. Julian's put on some weight and his eyes are clear. He's got an ear-to-ear smile that radiates that charm of his I've always admired. He looks happy, healthy.

"What do you say, Poohbear?"

My smile matches his, and I nod.

Julian's fingers start strumming, and he croons into the mic, the whole time keeping my eye like we're the only people in the room. The only people in the world.

Hearing him sing the song I wrote for Holter, the one I sang at the children's hospital, brings even more tears to my eyes, so I quickly wipe at them. How does he remember all the lyrics? I sang it once and we never talked about it again.

This song, it's about the all-consuming love you have for someone else, someone you've never met, but the second they enter your life, you feel like you've waited forever to know them. There's no link between you and this other person, then suddenly there is and it's strong. So strong not even death could break it. I felt it the moment I laid eyes on my son.

Is that what Julian's trying to tell me by singing this particular song? That he feels that way about me?

Please don't let this be a tease. I can't walk away from him again. My heart couldn't handle it.

I couldn't handle it.

Slowly, Julian stands from the stool, approaching me like the fish being reeled in by the fisherman—powerless.

My lips twitch with uncertainty. What do I do? Keep smiling? Or sing along because I wrote this song and have the lyrics memorized like the back of my hand?

I drop my eyes to his fingers, his wicked, skilled fingers. With the audience just as absorbed, Julian doesn't need a microphone, so he leaves it behind, singing loud enough for everybody to still hear him as he continues playing.

Suddenly, the guitar is swung around to his back, then he drops to his knees in front of me, breaking into a rap that definitely wasn't in the original.

"Buttoned up tight, with that pop of straitlaced.
Always strugglin' to come undone,
even when its written 'cross your face."

I laugh through the tears because I'm pretty sure I've put the strait-laced image to bed now.

With a crisp punk rock sound carrying a raspy R&B undertone that he can transition smoothly into a rap, Julian's a polymath of musicality, making him so damn hypnotizing to watch.

He continues rapping about how I was brought in to save his image but I ended up saving his life instead, then the last line he says to me and only me, as he gets to his feet, his forehead an inch from mine.

"You and I both know this shit ain't ever gonna fade."

I open, then close my mouth, nervous what might come out. Nothing I feel for Julian faded in our time apart. Nothing. Not even my worry.

What if he's not actually healthy? It's not fair to get my hopes up, or his.

Looking between my eyes, he speaks first, saying, "I'm back, and Imma make good on all my promises."

That tug I've been feeling, it disappears, and in its place is that missing piece, making me feel whole again. I can see why Isis went through the trouble to collect the pieces of her husband's body, and how she used her grief over him to become more powerful. She needed Osiris with her because they were one.

"You're back?"

He nods and presses his forehead to mine. "I'm back…to stay."

"Can we talk? After? I have—"

"Go ahead," David says, taking the mic out of my slick hand. "Let me take the spotlight off of you for a while."

"Thank you, David," I tell him. "For everything."

Julian bumps his fist with David's, then takes my hand in his, pulling me behind the closing curtain to follow him backstage.

Axel gives a proud smile as we pass, saluting us, and beside him, Irelynn's grazing a cymbal with one hand sporting a near-blinding diamond ring on it while waving enthusiastically at me with the other.

She was in on this surprise, too? Neither of them breathed a single word to me.

They didn't tell me they were engaged either. Or…married?

Did they get married already?

One thing at a time…

"Since when are you and David friends?" I ask to Julian's back, loving the way it shakes. I miss his laughs. I miss him.

"Since he bailed me out of jail and let me crash at his pad for the last four months."

I tug on his hand, making him swing around to face me.

"What happened?" I didn't know he went to jail. After he left rehab, it was like he fell off the face of the planet. There's been no news about him.

"Just…hold on. That's not what I wanted to lead with."

"What did you want to lead with?"

"Us."

I eye him. "Is there an us anymore?"

"Come on."

He shows the way to a room on the first floor, my stomach twisting into a pretzel as he swipes the keycard to let us inside. The last time we spoke was in a hotel room.

"There'll always be an us, Poohbear." He lifts his t-shirt up, the t-shirt I gave him when we were still on tour together. It has my side profile on it and I've got my lips around a lollipop. Nothing says popstar like sucking on a lollipop.

Pointing at my autograph tattooed on his chest, he says, "You have my heart, remember?"

I pull his shirt down, leaving my fingertips hooked into the waistband of his jeans.

"And the rest of you?"

"You already know every fucking inch of me belongs to you."

"I meant *you*. How are *you*?"

"I'm clean. Been clean for four months, two days, thirteen hours, and like…" He checks his diamond-encrusted watch. "…fifty-seven minutes."

"Is that true?"

He shrugs, grinning. "I don't know. People always seem to remember that shit down to the second, don't they?"

We both laugh and it feels good. Freeing.

"No, but for real. I've been clean and sober for four months."

"That's amazing. Congratulations." My arms beg to hug him, to wrap him up and never let go, but it still feels too soon. He looks and sounds like my Julian, but different. Better.

"What happened?" I ask again.

"I just… I wanted to be sober for you, but I didn't have you, so I just kept going back."

"Julian."

"I know, it wasn't the right reason. You were right. But hear me out. I was locked in that addict mentality. Any reason I had for getting sober was a reason for using, too. You not being with me made me want to try, but you not being with me made me want to give in just as bad. It's easier to give in, Collette. It's so fucking easy. So I did. Over and over again until I landed my ass in jail."

"How'd David find you?"

"I found him. I knew, or I thought, you were still living there, so I called him. To see how you were doing, how Holter was doing. I was, uh, I was kinda hoping you were there, at his house, eating one of those family dinners yinz would always talk about, and I'd get to hear your voice maybe. You know, in the background." His eyes grow red and watery.

"You used your one phone call to ask about me?"

"Yeah." Stepping closer, his breathing deepens, changing the atmosphere. "There's nothing else worth talking about."

"Julian," I warn with a twist of my head to keep my mouth from going straight to his. "What changed?"

"Me. Finally. After hearing about you skipping out on tour, and finding your own place with Holter, I hung up with David and something just clicked. I spent that night in jail, realizing where I'd end up if I didn't stop. The next morning David surprised the fuck outta me by bailing my ass out, then he took me to his place and I saw where I could end up if I did stop."

"He has a pretty good setup," I agree. One I coveted every time I saw it.

"I'm done touring. I'm done making songs I hate. I want to make music my way, on my schedule, like David."

"But David's a producer." He travels for work occasionally, but he doesn't *have* to. Artists will travel to him just to work with him, and labels will foot the bill because he's worth it.

Julian stares at me.

"Is that what you want? To be a producer?"

"I want to make all kinds of music. I always have."

A smile splits my face until my cheeks hurt. "You'd be good at it."

"And I want a home…" His eyes darken. "…where I'm with my family every night."

"You'd be good at that, too." He's good at anything he tries.

"Shit," he hisses. "I fucked that up. I want a home where I'm with *our* family every night."

"Our family…"

"I told you Imma fill you with babies."

"But—"

"Since you weren't living in his guesthouse anymore, David let me stay there while I figured my shit out. It gave me a safe place, away from everyone, to focus on drying out first, then I started going a little crazy with nothing to do, so David taught me about song structure and making beats. Once I proved to myself I could stay sober and I had something to keep me busy, I decided it'd be a good spot for recovering, too.

I rescheduled the appointment I blew off after The Family Julez Tour wrapped, and I got the reversal."

His vasectomy.

"Did it work?"

"Wanna find out?"

We hold each other's eyes, neither of us sure what the correct move here is. Do we? Don't we? We both want to, but…

Does that mean we should?

"Tell me about you," he says, sitting on the bed and patting the space next to him.

Instead of sitting down on a hotel bed, only inches away from Julian, the sexiest man I've ever met, I lean back against the wall, sticking my hands in my pockets, then I talk to him. I tell him all about the last seven months. The good, the bad, the ugly, the beautiful.

"No more baby food?"

"No more baby food."

"No more of that tasting bullshit?"

Remembering what he said that one time in the limo, I quirk an eyebrow at him, making him chuckle.

"No. I eat regularly now."

He grows serious to question, "No more touring?"

I give my head a soft shake. "Nothing planned."

"Where's Holter? I thought he'd be here with you."

"With the trial still going on, we've both been lying low. This is my first time doing an event since The Mousais actually."

"Bodee's getting the shit kicked out of him. The press are eating him alive."

"Yeah." I glance at my toes in my strappy high heels. "All this time I thought I'd catch more flies with honey than vinegar, but it turns out, semen is the most effective."

His chuckle is so dark it makes me smile. "So, fuck him?"

"Fuck him."

"Damn, I love you. I'm sorry I started all that, then left you to deal with it by yourself. I'm sorry I haven't been by your side to help you through it. I'm here now though and I ain't goin' anywhere."

"I love you, too, Julian. And I've missed you…a lot. But what

happens now? Don't you have to stay clean for a year or something before you can be in a relationship?"

"Since when do I follow the rules?"

"I'm serious. I don't want to risk your sobriety if you're not ready."

"I don't know if there will ever be a time that my sobriety isn't at
risk, Collette."

I tuck my chin to my chest, understanding that statement whole-
heartedly. Fighting addiction is not a one-time battle, it's a series of daily
battles leading up to a war that never really comes to fruition.

"But…"

My gaze lifts to him while my head stays lowered.

"Being without you, it's hell. Drugs, alcohol, partying, they took me
away from you. Mentally, emotionally, and then physically. I'm fucking
done wasting a single second being without you. You were never an option to me, and I'm sorry I treated you like one. You're it for me. Always,
forever, and long fucking after." He pins me with open sincerity, love,
and hope. So much hope. "If you're down?"

I push off the wall, stepping between his knees, then with a handful
of his blond hair—now free of blue tips—I tilt his head back, and lick
from his chin up to his nose. Over his groan, I say, "I'm down."

My feet are lifted off the floor as Julian stands, taking me with him,
then he spins us around and deposits me where he was just sitting.

"As the first and only woman to ever bring me to both my knees,
it's only right that you bring me to one." Dropping to his knee, he holds
up a small box, opening it to reveal a ring with a five-carat antique sap-
phire surrounded by dazzling diamonds. After a deep breath, he asks,
"Will you be my wife?"

With my middle finger on his pulse, I feel his heartbeat as if it were
my own, then I close the space between us, kissing him for the first time
in seven months and tasting pure magic.

"Of course I'll marry you," I tell him after breaking for air. "But I
prefer you on both knees."

"I know you do, Poohbear." His other knee hits the floor, and with
a smirk only the king of the underworld could pull off, he says, "I got
no problem worshipping my queen."

Epilogue

Julian
Two and a half years later

I toss my keys on the counter, switching Lyric from my left arm to my right.

"Ayo."

Holter freezes at the bottom of the stairs, his mouth guard hanging from his mouth while his face remains glued to his fucking phone.

"We leave in twenty minutes, so no…whatever the hell you do in there."

He finally looks up at me with a snarled lip he picked up this past summer at football camp. "I'm just getting a shower."

I roll my eyes. "Yeah, okay. And I'm the Virgin Mary." Propping Lyric in the crook of my elbow, I even slap my hands together, glancing skyward for effect.

Holter groans and stomps the rest of his way up the stairs. That kid jerks it in there, I don't care what he says. I was sixteen years old too once. That's basically all I did.

To pictures of his mom, but nobody appreciates when I say that.

"Twenty minutes!" I shout because fuck if I don't gotta repeat everything three times for him to listen. I know I was a total shit when

I was a teen, but damn, at least Holter's got cool parents. *At least he's got parents, period.*

"Why do I have to go again?" he pokes his head over the banister to ask because he also believes he needs to repeat everything three times, and apparently the first two conversations about this exact topic earlier didn't take.

"Lyric." I stand his sister up on the kitchen island, holding her hands tight. "Do you wanna see Mommy sing?"

"Yeff!"

"I can't hear you."

"Yeff!" she screams with a bounce in her knees that obviously helps project her little voice even further than if she hadn't. *Obviously.*

"Sister wants to go and you know what that means," I say to Holter, grinning as innocently as the actual Virgin Mary.

Now he's the one rolling his eyes, mumbling, "Brother has to go, too."

"Damn right." I lift Lyric up by her armpits. "Besides, it's not every day you get to see your mom perform onstage for thousands of fans."

"It literally is though."

"Your brother's attitude stinks," I tell Lyric, and she plugs her nose, blanching like she can actually smell it. She's the fucking best. I had no idea kids were this fun. Holter used to be, too, until his balls dropped and he stopped caring about anything other than girls, football, or the car his mom and I bought him for his sweet sixteen.

Sweet, my ass. Holter took off without a backward glance the second those keys touched his palm, sending Collette into a crying fit for three days straight.

Truthfully, he actually is a good kid. He gets good grades, he's the starting quarterback for his new high school, and he's on track to get a full ride to basically any college in the country that has a football team. Kid never even gave me any shit for slipping into dad-mode back when I married Collette either, probably because he was just happy to finally have one.

I always said Bodee Keys was a fucking bum. *I really hope he's hating his time in the clink. He's only got a few more decades left.*

"And it's not every day. Only Friday nights, Saturday nights, and

Sunday afternoons after Sunday morning crepes!" I yell up at Holter, chuckling when he shakes his head.

Tonight was the homecoming game and Holter didn't make court, so he's pissy. His ex-girlfriend did though along with one of his good buddies. *Hollywood drama's got nothing on high school drama.*

I smile thinking about the video I got of it all. I'll show it to Collette later, making sure to add my own commentary to the teenage reality show we clearly live in. I never miss a game and I record them all, whether Collette makes it or not. She tries to catch as many as her schedule allows, but it's harder for her because she gets mobbed by fans wanting photos and autographs. You'd think after living here for the last couple years, the locals would be used to us by now.

Turns out there's more to Vegas than just shotgun weddings because not long after ours, Collette landed a residency here, and we've been living the desert life ever since. Her show on the strip only gets bigger and better each year she's signed on, even through two pregnancies. It's true what they say, what happens in Vegas, does stay in Vegas. At least we did.

Mary comes down the stairs, cradling what I assume is my swaddled newborn son but could easily pass as a bundle of blankets, and scolds Holter for leaving the water running.

"Hey," I say before Holter can disappear in the bathroom.

"What?"

"What'd Morrison say when you guys shook hands after the game?" Jake Morrison is the quarterback for Holter's school's biggest rival, and he and Holter don't get along for shit. Naturally, I hate him and his dad. I'll probably have to put him in a chokehold or something. The dad, not the kid. Unless he's eighteen already…

Nah, just the dad. Holter can handle his own.

"The usual."

"'Tell your mom thanks for last night'?"

"Yep."

Motherfucker.

"You oughta kick his ass next time yinz play them."

"Bad language," Mary tsks.

I jerk my head back like I do every other time she says this shit, telling her, "But, Mary, bad language is the only language I know."

"You write beautiful songs and those are the only words you know?"

"You think my songs are beautiful?" That might be the nicest thing she's ever said to me.

"Then you'd have to kick every guy on my team's ass because they all say stuff about Mom," Holter says, getting us back on track with what matters most—my wife. Who *loves* my dirty mouth, by the way.

"Think your coach would let me come down to the field next game?" I ask him, and he gives me an unamused look like I wouldn't actually.

I give him one back that says, *Um, yes, the fuck I would.*

Did he forget the last time I was invited to The Mousais? The scene I caused? Shit, nobody else has.

Fine, he knows I wouldn't post up on a bunch of teens, but I would beat up their dads at the very least, which he also knows to be true because I've already done it. A couple times. Okay, a few. I've got a short fuse when it comes to people fucking with my family.

Ending our stare-off, I tell him, "Eighteen minutes now, smartass."

He laughs, walking away.

"He finished the whole bottle," Mary says, switching Cannon up to her shoulder to burp him.

"He did?" I ask, impressed. He's picky with bottles. The boy only likes certain nipples and nothing compares to his mother's. He's already got taste for quality.

I put Lyric down, telling her to go find her headphones, then take Cannon off Mary. Heading out to my studio, I hold him against my chest with one hand while rubbing his back with my other. This stay-at-home-dad gig is like juggling a book of matches, a lit cigarette, and a can of gasoline, but I wouldn't trade this shit for the world. There've been days when I've had all three kids in my studio with me, and I still managed to record fucking bangers.

Music is something I *want* to share with my kids. It runs in their veins as much as it does mine, so of course Imma make this a family affair. Holter's got a good ear when I can snag his attention long enough, and Lyric belts like her mom even though she has a very limited vocabulary still. Cannon…Cannon's an infant. He eats, shits, and sleeps, then sleeps some more. But maybe when he's a little older, I'll teach him how to play the triangle in his great-grandma's memory. She'd love that.

I listen to my messages while getting one big burp along with a handful of gas-smiles out of Cannon that I like to pretend I provoked with just my voice alone, then I return to the main house. Artists from all over come to my home studio to record their songs. I pull crazy hours, but they're hours that I get to choose. So I can go out there and work from two in the morning until six when Holter's getting ready for school, come in to see him off, then head right back out 'til Collette and the little ones wake up, no problem.

During the week, Collette's here kicking ass as a full-time mom, then on the weekends, she's back to raising the bar as America's favorite popstar. She doesn't tour at all anymore, and I don't think she ever will. Neither of us will. We got too much to stay home for.

Mary hands me Cannon's diaper bag with his headphones sticking out the top. We moved Mary out to Vegas once Lyric was born, and she helps out any time we need her, which is mostly on the weekends, nothing like the hours she was pulling with Holter. She actually has her own life now, with a boyfriend and everything.

Lyric dances into the kitchen already wearing her headphones and almost busts her face on the handle of a drawer during an intense-as-shit spin.

Jesus Christ. *And I used to think mosh pits were dangerous.*

"Holter! You better be ready!"

"Can Andy come with us?" he asks, jogging around the corner, a towel around the back of his neck.

"Andy, your fullback?"

"Yeah."

"No."

"Why not?"

"Because motherfucker's crushin' on my wife."

"Language."

"She's wearing headphones, Mary. She can't hear me. Right, Lyric?"

Lyric gives me a thumbs-up with a smile I know she learned from her mom.

Holter and I look at each other, then laugh.

"Get your sister," I tell him, letting Mary know what time we'll be home.

Cannon's passed out in my arms, and Lyric's replaced the towel, sitting on her big brother's shoulders. We're standing backstage, waiting for Collette as she wraps up her third and final act. I've seen this show dozens of times, but it still feels like the first time, every time. I never get tired of watching her perform.

Finished, she runs over to us, and since I already know what she's gonna ask, I hold out Cannon to her, but she doesn't grab him like she usually does. She kisses his forehead, then asks Holter to put Lyric down to hold him for a minute.

Before he can, one of her dancers passes by and offers to take Cannon instead. She's been with Collette for as long as Holter's been alive. I think she's his godmother actually. Uncle Axel and Aunt Irelynn are Lyric's, and David and Kim-ly are Cannon's. Technically David could be all of ours since he's helped us out so much, especially me. He played a huge role in helping me make the transition into the producing world.

Flashing me that smile that made me fall in love with her, Collette grabs my middle finger with hers, linking our matching tattoos up. Hers is a Q for queen and mine's a K for king. The tattoo artist tried selling us on getting them on our ring fingers, since we're married, but our middle fingers hold more significance to us. I mean, shit, hers brought me back to life. That's pretty fucking significant.

"Sing with me."

She does this sometimes. She knows I could go the rest of my life without setting foot on another stage, but she also knows I'll never turn down performing with her.

Also, I give her everything she asks for. And most things she doesn't.

"Which song are we doing, Poohbear?" I ask, letting her lead me out to the stage.

The audience erupts into applause, so I smile, throwing up a wave to everyone.

"For tonight's encore, I'd like to introduce you all to rapper, singer, songwriter, producer, and the hitmaker responsible for my latest number one selling album…my husband, Julez!"

Another thing I never get tired of—being her husband.

"Just start and I'll follow," she says over the cheers, handing me another mic.

"You want me to come up with something right now?"

"Don't tell me you finally ran out of inspiration," she teases close to my ear, and I grab her hips, watching her own pulse in her throat pick up speed.

"You *are* my inspiration."

She laughs, bending backward until her hands touch the floor, then she does a backflip out of my arms. At thirty-seven, she could do cartwheels around her competition that's half her age. Or backflips. Or anything she sets her mind to 'cause she's that good.

Before she can even stand to her full height, I'm already spittin' into the mic about a woman who's as strong as graphene—a super-material that's apparently the strongest in the world.

That same woman smiles across the stage at me, singing a piece about a man so hot he could melt graphene.

I don't know anything about its melting point, but I mouth, "Who?" at her anyway, pretending to be jealous.

She laughs again, pointing at me, then we meet in the middle of the stage, our voices coming together seamlessly.

Nothing about life is easy, not my addiction I have to work to beat every single day, not raising a family when I've never even been in one, not counting my kids' baby food each night to make sure my wife hasn't relapsed, not running a successful business when all I've ever done is fail.

Except this.

Loving Collette is as easy as breathing for me, but it did take a lot of sacrifice on both our parts to make it here, with her looking at me the same way I look at her—like I'm staring at my soulmate.

Having her by my side, loving me back just as thoroughly as I love her? Hell, that'll go down as one of my life's greatest achievements.

And the high I never have to come down from.

Check out my website amarieauthor.com for playlists, inspiration boards, and up-to-date news.

Also by

A. MARIE

Creekwood Series
Detour
Changing Lanes (Julez and Collette play a cameo in!)
Blind Spot

Standalones
Let The Light Shine Through

Acknowledgements

Thanks to the girl working at Staples who caught a peak of the rough draft of this story when I had it printed there and told me I should be proud of myself. You have no idea how much I needed that right then. Like…no idea.

Thank you, reader. For reading, for supporting dreams, for your words of encouragement to authors you love, for the reviews of books you enjoyed. It all means so much, to so many, even if it doesn't seem like it.

Thanks to my family for putting up with me being utterly consumed with this story and these characters from page one. This was my longest book yet and I know it took a lot of my time. Thanks for being patient and allowing me that time. Thanks for talking me out of quitting countless times. Your support is everything to me.

Thank you to my beta and creative liaison, Shanna. Your support and help never ceases, and I'm so damn appreciative.

Murphy Rae, this was your best book cover yet. Five covers with you later and I'm still so blown away by your talent. Thank you so, so much!

Brandi Z., thank you for all your help and speed and patience on this one. I know it was much longer than either of us were expecting but you came through! Thank you, thank you.

Judy, thank you for your ever-reliable help and support. I can't tell you how much finding you has improved my mental health through what is such a stressful time.

Stacey, just like the rest of my books, thanks for making the inside of this one look so good.